THE
SACRED
CIPHER

#1

TERRY
BRENNAN

Kregel
Publications

The Sacred Cipher: A Novel

© 2009 by Terry Brennan

Published by Kregel Publications, a division of Kregel, Inc., P.O. Box 2607, Grand Rapids, MI 49501.

Cover image created by Terry Brennan.

Published in association with the literary agency of WordServe Literary Group, Ltd., 10152 S. Knoll Circle, Highlands Ranch, CO 80130. www.wordserveliterary.com.

ISBN 978-0-8254-2426-7

Printed in the United States of America

11 12 13 / 5 4

To my wife, Andrea,
and to my children,
Michael, Patrick, Meghan, & Matthew
Only love is eternal

ACKNOWLEDGMENTS

First, I must thank God for the gift of writing. As Joan Baez has said, the gift is from God. My job is only maintenance and delivery.

There would be nothing on paper without my wife, Andrea. Not only does she keep me focused on the important, sane, and healthy, but she also willingly sacrificed a year of Saturdays so this dream could have life. Without her, I am but a shell.

To Andrea, again, and Meghan who were my first readers and shared only excitement.

To Marlene Bagnull, whose selfless dedication to other writers is legend. The dream was born and nurtured at her writers' conferences in Philadelphia and Colorado.

To Wanda Dyson, who believed in me when all I had was an idea, and who gave so much, so freely, to make the idea a reality.

To all those along the way:

Angela Hunt and Nancy Rue—faithful teachers and encouragers;

Kathy Vance—who blessed me with volumes of information about the archaeology and history of Jerusalem, along with a firsthand view of the current politics and social conflicts in Israel. I pray you will soon return to the land of your dreams;

Rachelle Gardner—agent, friend, and truth-teller;

All the great folks at Kregel Publications—Miranda Gardner and Steve Barclift, who were my early champions and extended so much grace when the project was endangered; Dawn Anderson, editor extraordinaire, sweet and gentle with a rookie author, who invested so much to make this book so much better; Cat Hoort, thanks for the cover and your infectious enthusiasm;

Fred, Steve, and Mike—my spiritual brothers, so quick to laugh at me, and themselves, who kept me grounded and gave me hope;

Bobby Watts and William Jin—how blessed is a man with true friends.

PROLOGUE

1889 · ALEXANDRIA, EGYPT

Only three types of buyers entered the Attarine—the foolish, the fraudulent, and the forewarned. The foolish, who acted on whim instead of wisdom and expected to fleece an ignorant Egyptian native; the fraudulent, expert in identifying well-crafted forgeries, anxious to pass them on for great profit; and the forewarned, who searched for treasure but were wise enough to employ someone who knew the ways, and the merchants, of the seductive but evil-ridden Attarine.

Spurgeon knew the risk. But treasures awaited in the twisting, narrow stone streets snaking away from the Attarine Mosque.

He had Mohammed, he had a gun, he had money—and he had God.

Peering down the darkened alley, Spurgeon worried that, perhaps, he didn't have enough.

Mohammed entered the alley and disappeared from view. The alley was gray-on-gray, denied sunlight by overhanging, second-floor balconies adorning almost every building, their shuttered windows barely an arm's length from each other. Joining with the dark was a riot of refuse; crazed, cadaver-like dogs; and powerfully pungent, unknown odors.

The Attarine District was home to the greatest concentration of antiquities dealers in Alexandria, both the illicit and the honorable. A person could buy almost any historical artifact along the ancient streets of the Attarine. Some were even genuine. And Charles Haddon Spurgeon was on a treasure hunt.

He held his breath; he held his heart; and he stepped into the dark.

At the first fork, Mohammed Isfahan was waiting. Spurgeon's heart slowed its pounding pace. Mohammed confidently led the way, weaving in and out of the shoppers and the strollers who clogged the tight byways. It was early morning, before the sun began to scorch the stones, and Spurgeon was grateful for the moderate breeze off the Mediterranean. At his size, the heat sapped his strength and soaked his shirt within minutes. Though the morning was warm, Spurgeon hoped to get back into his hotel, under a fan in a shaded corner of the dining room, long before the withering heat began blowing from the Sahara. On one of his regular trips to the Middle East, Spurgeon was trolling for ancient biblical texts and Mohammed, recommended by the hotel's concierge, promised he knew where to look.

Now fifty-six, he was England's best-known preacher, and he grudgingly accepted the considerable influence and power he had earned as pastor of London's famed New Park Street Church for the last thirty years. Spurgeon was the first to admit preaching was his passion.

But Spurgeon was also the first to admit that books were his weakness. He typically devoured six books per week and had written many of his own. Now, scuttling through the twilight of the dusty alley, Spurgeon sought to slake that hunger in the shops of the Attarine.

Rounding a curve in the street, Mohammed paused alongside a curtain-covered doorway, pulled aside the curtain, and motioned for Spurgeon to enter. Inside the shop, not only was the atmosphere cooler, but it also carried the rich scent of old leather, soft and smooth like musty butter. Mohammed bowed reverentially as the proprietor emerged from the rear of the shop. He was a small man of an indeterminate age. What defined him were hawklike, ebony eyes overflowing with wisdom, discerning of character, and surrounded by a brilliant white kaffiyeh. Mohammed spoke rapidly in Arabic, bowed again, and then stepped back as the proprietor approached Spurgeon.

"*Salaam aleikum*," he said, bowing his head toward Spurgeon, who was startled when the man continued in perfectly cadenced English, "and peace be with you, my friend. It is an honor for my humble shop to welcome such a famous man under its roof. May I be permitted to share with you some tea and some of our little treasures?"

Wondering about the origin of the shopkeeper's English, Spurgeon responded with a bow of his own. "*Salaam aleikum*, my brother. You honor me by using my language in your shop. But I must ask, how have you any knowledge of me?"

"Ah, the name of Spurgeon has found its way down many streets. I am Ibrahim El-Safti, and I am at your service. My friend Mohammed tells me you are interested in texts that refer to the stories of your Nazarene prophet, is that correct?"

"I would be honored to review any such texts as may be in your possession," said Spurgeon. He took the chair and the tea that were offered by El-Safti and waited quietly as the shopkeeper sought and retrieved three books. While Spurgeon studied the books, one in Aramaic, one in Greek, and the last in an unknown language, Mohammed and the shopkeeper retired through the doorway, stepping outside the curtain.

Spurgeon slipped into a scholar's zone, focusing intently on the words before him. But the breeze turned, pushing aside the curtain in the door and carrying the words of Mohammed and El-Safti into the shop and up to Spurgeon's ear— one well trained in Arabic, among many other languages.

"What of the scroll?" Spurgeon heard Mohammed ask.

"Do not speak of that scroll in front of this infidel," El-Safti countered, his voice stronger and more virile than it had been earlier. "You know what our tradition holds; this scroll would be of great benefit to the infidels, both the Jews and the Christians. We are to hold it in trust and keep it out of their hands at all costs."

"You speak like an imam," Mohammed said. "No one knows what is on that scroll; no one has been able to translate its meaning. How do we know what it contains?"

Spurgeon forgot the books in his lap. He heard a more interesting story floating on the breeze.

"If it can't be read, is there any difference in whose hands it rests? I believe the English preacher would pay handsomely for the privilege of owning something he doesn't understand. Ibrahim," said Mohammed, "look at me. It could pay for your daughter's wedding."

"Do not tempt me, Mohammed," El-Safti said. "That scroll has remained here for two generations, and no one has ever requested to see it. Quiet, now, and let us see what may interest the Englishman."

Spurgeon attempted to return his attention to the books, but his eyes were pulled back to the men as they entered through the curtain. El-Safti reverted to his perfectly subservient composure as he stepped before Spurgeon. The only thing out of place was an amulet—a Coptic cross with a lightning bolt flashing through on the diagonal—that slipped from the neck of his robe as he came through the doorway.

"Do these books meet with your interest?" El-Safti asked.

Spurgeon rose from the chair and handed the books back to El-Safti. "I am disappointed to tell you, my friend, that you may have been swindled. The book in Aramaic is a fraud, and a poor one at that. The Greek, I have two copies in my library. And the third is in a language I have not seen before, but does not appear to be Semitic. Tell me, do you not possess anything more authentic?"

A moment's silence passed through the shop. El-Safti's pitch-black eyes flickered with offense.

"My humble apologies," El-Safti said. "Your reputation as a scholar is well earned, Dr. Spurgeon. But perhaps I do have something that you would find interesting. It is very old, but of indeterminate age." El-Safti walked to the back of the shop. "It is an infidel's mezuzah, nicely etched, wrapped in a very colorful piece of Moroccan silk."

Disappointed in the books, Spurgeon's interest increased at the mention of silk. His niece's birthday would be upon him when he returned to England. Perhaps there was a prize here, after all.

El-Safti slipped into a small closet at the rear corner of the shop and could be heard snapping the hasp on a lock and moving a chain. Silence, then a stream of Arabic epithets, as El-Safti recoiled from the closet.

"Forgive me," he said, his wild eyes looking first at Spurgeon and then at Mohammed. "It is gone. The scroll, it is gone."

First fear, then unbelief, fought for dominance in El-Safti's weathered face. His hands trembled as he wrung them together.

"Allah has punished me for my greed," El-Safti said, slipping back into Arabic. "Mohammed, remove this infidel. And hurry back. We must think. We must find the scroll. We must find it before it is lost forever."

—⁓⁓—

Three days later, Spurgeon wandered through the Alexandrian bazaar, his work for the trip complete and his passage for London booked on a ship leaving the next morning. But his mind kept drifting back to El-Safti and the nearly hysterical look on his face when he discovered this mysterious scroll had disappeared.

What could have caused the man such fear? he wondered, his hand exploring vibrant textiles and metal trinkets as he strolled through the bazaar. It appeared he was willing to sell. Even if it had been stolen or lost, why react so severely when he was about to sell it anyway?

He was about to turn a corner and walk away from the bazaar, when a soft voice coming from a shaded corner of a building caught his attention.

"Effendi, Dr. Spurgeon, please, may I have a moment of your time?"

As Spurgeon turned to the sound of his name, an elderly man in well-worn, but once-fine, clothes stepped out of the shadows, bowing deeply from the waist.

"Please forgive this unwarranted intrusion, but I knew of no other way."

"How do you know who I am?" Spurgeon asked, taking no step toward the man, who looked more like a beggar than a prince.

"You have walked these streets many times, Dr. Spurgeon, searching for treasures in books and letters. What has been more memorable for my people, why you are well known and highly regarded, are the many kindnesses you have done for our children, so many who have been healed by the doctors you sent. It is why many in this city watch out for your safety."

Spurgeon's curiosity spiked. "So, what can I do for you?"

"More than likely, it's what I can do for you," said the old man. "A few days ago, you were in the Attarine. There was some discussion about a scroll. Allah be praised, I believe I may be able to help you."

The old man, whose face was deeply wrinkled and the color of old leather, pulled from within his kaftan a brightly designed piece of silk. Spurgeon took a step toward the elderly Arab, then another, joining him in the half-light of the building's shadows in spite of a gnawing unease.

"I had the good fortune of being in the Attarine at the same time you were in the shop of one El-Safti," said the old man. "I think you were quite fortunate that the document El-Safti sought was no longer in his possession. I think, had you purchased this document, you never would have left the Attarine with it in your possession."

"So you stole it?"

"Effendi," the old man demurred. "I am only the recipient of Allah's provision and a defender of your highly esteemed person. If, however, you have no interest in this trinket, perhaps I should take it elsewhere?" As the man began to return the silk-draped object back into the depths of his kaftan, Spurgeon quickly stepped even closer and laid his hand on the man's arm.

"Please, my friend," Spurgeon said, looking into the old man's peaceful eyes. "It would not be appropriate to send you away without at least examining the gift you bring me."

"Many thanks," said the old man. He bowed his head but never took his eyes from the Englishman. "Here, please join me by this table so that I may display to you this treasure."

Overcoming his reluctance, Spurgeon stepped to the small table that stood in the shadows of the building. The old man opened the silk cover, a purse of some sort, withdrew an engraved metal tube, and laid it on the table. Moving closer to the table, Spurgeon began running his fingers over the silk purse, fascinated by its color and the strangeness of its designs, symbols of long, swooping lines dancing across a bloodred sea.

"Ah, yes, it is a beautiful purse, is it not?" the old man said. "But I believe you may be even more intrigued by what is inside." With that, the old man took hold of the handle on the side of the cylinder and, turning the metal shaft that extended through its center, began extracting a rather plain, parchment scroll. What was on the scroll, however, was far from plain.

Spurgeon leaned over the table, adjusting his spectacles for a better look. The parchment itself, probably sheepskin, was remarkably well preserved, indicating a majority of its life had been spent in a dry climate, not here in Alexandria where humidity would have destroyed it. On the surface of the parchment were written twenty-one columns of symbols arranged in seven groupings—three vertical rows of symbols in each of the groupings. It was an odd construction. Spurgeon, however, was more intrigued by the symbols themselves, a series of simple, yet stylistic, characters. "What is it?" he asked.

The old man shrugged.

"I don't know what language that is," said Spurgeon "I don't know if I've ever seen anything like it. Tell me, what do you think it means?"

"Forgive me, Effendi, but I do not have a great deal of time," the old man said, turning to face Spurgeon. "I have a desire to dispose of this treasure. Perhaps you would be willing to take it off my hands for, say, three thousand piastres?"

Spurgeon ran his fingers over the cylinder and entered into the obligatory negotiations.

By the time each had argued, cajoled, and conceded, Spurgeon purchased the purse and the metal tube for fewer than fifteen hundred piastres, only a few English pounds. Spurgeon was quite satisfied with himself. He had just purchased a fine gift, the beautiful silk purse, for his niece's birthday. Wrapping the tube tightly back into the silk purse, Spurgeon covered it with a discarded section of burlap and tucked it under his arm. Turning to leave, he was startled by two things: first, that the old man had already disappeared into the bazaar and, second, the lurking presence of Mohammed Isfahan, pressed into a darkened doorway across the street.

Spurgeon's walk back to his hotel was much more brisk than usual, in spite of the heat.

≈≈≈

1891 · LONDON, ENGLAND

With a speed that belied his bulk, his umbrella lying on the ground, Spurgeon regained his feet and began running downhill, looking for lights and praying for help. He turned twice, skidding on the stones but not breaking his pace, until he came to much-needed rest in the darkened alcove of the apothecary shop on Weston Street.

Spurgeon loathed his dread. He mocked himself: where was his faith? Yet hidden from the light, he drank in the night air in the deep draughts of a desperate man and tried to free his mind to make a clear decision. Every shadow became a warrant for his destruction. He held the package loosely, tucked into the large pocket of his woolen overcoat, afraid that if he grasped it too tightly, his anxiety might transmit some signal to those who were in pursuit. Yet he dared not let it go.

The tide waited for no man and for no ship. If Spurgeon intended to reach the Thames on time—and the cutter sent from the trans-Atlantic steamer *Kronos*—he had to find a way out of this doorway. He was more convinced than ever that he had to get this package, his precious scroll, on that ship.

Lord, you are in control, he silently prayed. *So why am I so frightened for my life?*

Spurgeon pressed himself deeply into the doorway, seeking the darkness. He held his breath to quiet his gasping, but still his heart hammered in his chest. His eyes, wide with alarm, darted from corner to shadow to alley to street. He strained to extend his ears further into the night. All this he did while holding himself rigidly still.

A movement, a sound, and his life could end in an instant.

At any other time, the streets of London would have held a great hope, a feeling of fulfillment, of calling, of destiny. These were his streets and his people, and he had moved through them and walked over them for so long they had almost become a part of him, except for tonight. The streets were the same. The city was the same. The fear was new.

Rain slanting hard behind the wind drove the sane and the sensible indoors. From the shelter of the darkened shop's doorway, Spurgeon willed himself to silence. The street was empty except where the rainwater sluiced along the gutter in the middle of the cobblestones. But Spurgeon no longer trusted emptiness. He scanned every dark space for some sign of movement.

Curse the pies and the pastries and Mrs. Dowell's cooking. Once a symbol of growing affluence and influence, Spurgeon's girth now slowed his legs when he needed speed and sapped his endurance as he ran for his life.

Twenty minutes earlier, Spurgeon had stepped out of his parsonage in Newington, Southwark, and into the driving rain. It was a walk he had taken scores of times before, in good weather and foul. It was a simple task, after all. Walk down to the Thames, where the cutter would dock. Meet his old friend Captain Paradis. Exchange a package and some good wishes. And be off again for the warmth of the fire waiting in his study. A simple task.

Spurgeon walked quickly down Great Dover Street, toward Weston Street and the Thames, trying not to look over his shoulder. His umbrella helped deflect much of the downpour but also restricted his vision. As he turned into Black Horse Court, by habit, his gaze swiveled to the rear. For weeks, his anxiety had been fed by a foreboding that he was being watched, followed. With the rain pounding on his umbrella, he failed to hear the fast-approaching hoofbeats on the cobblestones. The horse missed him, but the front wheel of the livery wagon caught his shoulder as it flashed past, driving him back to the wall and down to the sidewalk. Spurgeon may have thought it an accident except for the arrow that thudded into the wall next to his head, and the second that clipped his coat as he twisted to look at the first.

He had fled for his life, leaving both his umbrella and his dignity on Black Horse Court. Now, here he was, not far from his church and his world—cold, wet, hiding in the dark, terrified of some unknown, but very real, threat.

Spurgeon often wondered if the scroll he held in his pocket would lead others to pursue its path, bringing them to him. Now he had his answer.

Soaked to the skin, remaining in the dark, Spurgeon twisted his head to the left and tried to look up the street. A shadow moved on the right in a garden, and another on the left in the lee of a stable. But what Spurgeon focused on was the shape coming around the corner and toward his hiding place. *Please God,* Spurgeon mouthed in silent prayer. The shape slowed and stopped halfway down the street. Spurgeon waited. The door opened and closed, and the shape slowly moved forward. Spurgeon waited. Only as the hansom came abreast of his hiding place did Spurgeon toss himself out of hiding, arm raised. "Cabbie!" Startled, the hansom driver reined up. Spurgeon was already scrambling through the door and into the cab. "Shad Thames, the docks at Curfew Street—quickly, please—we must get there before the tide."

A snap of the whip just as Spurgeon spun his head. The cab rocked forward, so he would never be certain. But snatching a look out the rear window as the cab began to move, Spurgeon caught a momentary glimpse of what appeared to be two men clothed in kaftans and kaffiyeh, running in the shadows of the buildings on either side of the street. Two arrows thumped into the back wall of the cab, their pointed barbs his only companions as the cabbie raced to the river.

⌁⌁⌁

1891 · NEW YORK CITY

"Your wife's strudel is always the highlight of each crossing."

"Thank you, Captain Paradis. As soon as she heard you at the door, she went to the kitchen to prepare one in your honor. But we will both have to wait until after dinner, I'm afraid. Here, sit," said Louis Klopsch. "What have you brought from Charles this time?"

Captain Timothy Paradis reached into the canvas boat bag that was propped against his chair, the one with *Kronos* stitched on its side. "I'm not sure, Dr. Klopsch, but this one is certainly not a book." Paradis lifted a bundle from the bag and cautiously unwrapped it.

Making sure debris fell into the boat bag and not onto Mrs. Klopsch's clean floor, Paradis shook off remnants of sawdust and held aloft an ornately designed, red silk purse. From the purse, he withdrew a metal tube about the size of a collapsed telescope, with designs etched on its surface.

"Reverend Spurgeon said I was to deliver it to you, and you alone," said Paradis, passing the tube into Klopsch's hands. "And I was to do it personally. Reverend Spurgeon was quite emphatic on that point, I must say."

Dr. Louis Klopsch's friendship with the famous London preacher Charles Haddon Spurgeon extended well beyond the two years since Klopsch had purchased a unique newspaper owned by Spurgeon, *The Christian Herald and Signs of Our Times.* Klopsch continued publishing the newspaper, and it had grown into a place of prominence among New York City's faithful.

Klopsch hefted the metal tube in his hands. "I mentioned to him once that I had an interest in ancient documents," he said to Paradis. "Now, I have no more room to store the gifts he, and his colleagues, have sent me from around the world. I have a closet there, in the hallway, which is full of books from Dr. Spurgeon. Believe me, I'm grateful. But . . ." Klopsch shrugged his shoulders. "And this . . . what could this be? It is very . . ."

Gerta Klopsch stood silently in the doorway, a towel in her hands, a smile on her full face, and the smell of cabbage swirling in her wake. "It is lovely," said Gerta. "But I think it must wait. Louis . . . Captain . . . dinner is ready."

After two weeks eating in the galley of the *Kronos,* Paradis was up and out of his chair in a lick.

"Well, we'll just put this away for now," said Klopsch. He returned the tube to the silk purse, which he fastened shut. Entering the hallway to the dining room, Klopsch stopped, turned a key in the lock, and opened the door to a closet.

"Upon my word," said Paradis, "I never dreamed you had so many . . . you are right, sir. There is no more room."

Klopsch pulled the silk purse tight around the metal tube and wedged it into a small space in the corner of a bottom shelf. "When next you see Charles, please tell him what you witnessed here tonight." Klopsch closed the door, turned the key, and escorted Paradis down the hall. "Please, tell him no more . . . no more books."

⌁⌁⌁

The *Kronos* was moving on the tide, sliding smoothly out of New York harbor, when Captain Timothy Paradis caught the smell of apples on the air and was reminded of Gerta Klopsch's apple strudel, the last piece of which sat on a bench to his left, wrapped in brown paper. It was then he remembered the letter.

The letter from Spurgeon to Klopsch that was inside the purse. The letter he had forgotten to tell the doctor about.

⌁⌁⌁

1896 · NEW YORK CITY

"Louis? Do men from the mission know our address?"

Dr. Louis Klopsch lowered his newspaper and considered his wife's question. "No, Gerta. Why do you ask?"

Gerta Klopsch took a step into the sitting room, her twisting hands tangled in the embroidered apron that tried valiantly to cover her ample proportions. "Today, two men came. Strange men . . . foreign . . . they look like sailors. They come to the gate in back. I surprised them when I went out with wash clothes. They asked for you by name. Who should know we live here?"

Klopsch laid the paper in his lap, the last gasps of a brittle winter sun barely piercing the windows of their home, a small, two-story Federal-style house in Lower Manhattan. He didn't like the sounds of this. He and Gerta made their home far enough away from the Bowery Mission—on Ryder's Alley, a thin, L-shaped lane between Fulton and Gold streets—that none should stumble into their yard by mistake. In the two years since he had purchased the facility, a rescue mission for the homeless and derelict along New York's infamous Bowery, this was the first time that anything like this had occurred.

"These men, what was their purpose?" he asked. "Did you inquire why they sought me?"

"No, Louis . . . forgive me. They ask for you. I say you are not here. And they leave. Quickly. I can ask them nothing more."

Klopsch rose, placed the newspaper neatly on his chair, and crossed the room to his wife. He rescued her hands from the wrinkled apron and held them softly in his own. "All is well, Gerta." He placed a finger under her chin, tilting her face toward his. "There is nothing to fear. I will discover more about these men, of that I am certain."

—∽∼∾∼—

Klopsch was confused, unsure about the sound that woke him that night, until he heard it a second time. Breaking glass.

He slipped out of bed—fortunately Gerta was a sound sleeper—and pulled his pants under his nightshirt. Suspenders hanging at his sides, Klopsch moved silently to the top of the stairs and listened to the night. He felt a chill draft rising from the floor below, brother to the one rising up his spine. A crackling sound . . . two thumps . . . and Klopsch edged swiftly down the stairs, his body leaning back against the wall.

Klopsch heard a muffled crack to his left as he cleared the final step. Standing in the foyer, he hesitated for just a moment—should he grab his heavy-handled walking stick or try to light the gas lamp? In that brief moment, a dark shape backed out from the closet to his left and into the hall. The shape appeared to be carrying bundles in his arms.

"Stop!" Klopsch grabbed the stick in his right hand and raised it over his head. Feet ran into the darkness, the back door burst open, and two shadows fled into the yard before Klopsch could move an inch.

———

Gerta, her hand to her mouth, stared at the pile of discarded books in the hallway, the glass scattered on the floor of the sitting room, as Klopsch came back from securing the back door.

"Louis, what is this?" she whispered. "Your desk." She waved a hand at the mangled papers and broken bindings pulled from overflowing bookshelves. She turned to glance at the broken door to the closet. "Your books. Why should someone do this?"

"Bandits . . . robbers, I suppose. Perhaps they were searching for money."

Klopsch walked over to the closet door. The wood was shattered, the broken lock lying on the floor. He picked up one of the old, leather books from where it had been thrown into the hallway.

"They were searching, yes . . . but not money," said Gerta. "Perhaps those men from today come back."

It was an old book. Written in Latin. He stroked the leather binding, straightened the gilded edges where they were gouged. "Why would anyone want to steal these books?"

Klopsch picked the books up from the floor and, one by one, returned them to the shelves in the closet. He was no fool. Neither was Gerta. Danger lived here.

"Perhaps in your new office, you should a safe put." Gerta's brow furrowed at the closet with the shattered door, the one that held so many of Spurgeon's treasures. "A big safe."

PART ONE

CIPHER'S CALL

1

THE PRESENT · NEW YORK CITY

Tom Bohannon looked at the gap between the ladder and the scaffold. It wasn't that far. Tim Maybry, the construction manager, had just done it, stepped off the ladder with a spring, landing on the wooden plank while grabbing the metal scaffold frame with both hands. It wasn't that far. But once he stepped off the ladder, there was no going back. It was either land on the wooden plank or land on the hard, ceramic tile floor thirty feet below.

Bohannon, slightly overweight, but still fit in his late fifties, stood on the ladder and knew two things. He wasn't going to get on the scaffold without getting off the ladder. And if he wanted to see what was on the other side, what had so excited his construction manager, he needed to get on the scaffold. Eyes fixed on the wooden plank, he stepped into space. A flashing moment of panic, and he was there, grabbing the metal scaffold, pulling in a deep breath. Looking to the left, he saw Tim waiting, smiling. "Okay," Bohannon said with a shrug. "Okay, I'll be right there."

Keeping his eyes straight ahead, Bohannon inched his way along the plank on the scaffolding and ducked into a very snug space behind the organ pipes. Maybry was in front of him, leading the way through the tight, dark crawl space between the pipes and the wall. Maybry disappeared to the right. Reaching the same spot, Bohannon peeked into a short, narrow crevice. He followed Maybry, shimmying through a hole that had been punched in the wall.

Bohannon hit the floor with a thud. He didn't care. His eyes had already been scanning the room, flashing back and forth, astounded at what he was seeing, a secret room hidden behind the organ pipes in the chapel of the Bowery Mission.

―――〰〰―――

The room was tucked in behind the organ pipes, hard against the connecting wall of what had been a casket maker's factory a hundred years ago, suspended, high up in the vaulted ceiling, at the very rear of the Bowery Mission's chapel. Coated with decades of dust, Tom Bohannon, executive director of the mission, saw that the room was furnished in antiques: a large, oak desk against the wall facing the organ pipes, with a matching chair; on the side, a row of six, four-drawer oak filing cabinets; and against the far wall, a large, antique safe that occupied the entire wall. The room was small, the ceiling less than six feet off the floor. Bohannon had to stoop to maneuver his way around the small space. Within moments, he and Maybry were covered in soot and dust.

"We found it by accident, this morning," Maybry said as Bohannon crossed to the rank of filing cabinets and began opening the drawers. "One of the workers dropped his hammer, and it must have fallen through a crack and into the room. When he went behind the organ pipes and couldn't find it, he realized there must be something behind this wall. You know these guys. You've got to watch them all the time."

"Is Henry Chang running this job?" Bohannon asked as he rifled through the file folders in another drawer.

"Not on this job," Maybry said, wiping his hand through the dust on the desk. "I've got a crew of guys from the Middle East—Lebanese they said, but hey, who knows these days. They must need the work because their bid came in under the Chinese. Anyway, my foreman came up as the guy was digging a hole in the wall, and here we are."

Bohannon started working on the second cabinet, flipping through the files, his back to Maybry. "How could anybody ever get in here?" Bohannon asked as he opened another drawer.

"This room is part of the original building, before they purchased the casket maker's building behind," said Maybry. "Before the organ bellows was removed, there must have been a way to get up here to clean the bellows. It looks like the door was over here in the corner. For some reason, it was covered over, and the room was forgotten. Hard to believe, with all this nice furniture."

"Hard to believe; that's an understatement," said Bohannon as he began rifling through the files faster and faster. Behind him, he heard Maybry move toward him.

"Do you know what this place is?" asked Bohannon, turning to face Maybry with a pack of file folders in his hand. "It's the office of Dr. Louis Klopsch, the first president of the Bowery Mission. These files, these cabinets, appear to be filled with Klopsch's records, the ledgers of the mission, and copies of all his correspondence."

Maybry, a trusted compatriot who had worked with Bohannon and the mission on several other projects, walked over to one of the cabinets and began searching through the drawers himself. "You mean this stuff has been hidden up here all these years?"

"It could get even more interesting, now," Bohannon said, pulling a file folder out of one of the drawers. "I think this is the combination for the safe."

Both men turned to face the other side of the room, where the immense, antique steel safe dominated. The decorative touches at the corners had muted over time. The safe had to be more than eight feet wide and five feet high, barely under the low ceiling, and a good three feet deep. It had double doors on the front that, when opened, would give access to the entire safe. In the center of each door was a raised, decorative design, blooming, steel geraniums, red paint still dully visible in the crevices of the flower's petals.

"If he kept his ledgers and records in these file cabinets," said Maybry, turning to look at the oak cabinets, "I wonder what he could have kept in a safe that large."

Bohannon drew a sheet of paper out of the file folder and stepped up to the steel door, his uncertainty and anticipation growing. It took a moment, but he realized that the dial for the combination lock had to be sitting under the large, floral-design ornament on the front of the door. Pressing here, pushing there, Bohannon finally located the spring switch, and the floral design swung away. He spun in the combination, heard the bolt drop, and pulled hard on the twin doors.

Bohannon moved more than the doors did. "Here, grab one side."

With Maybry tugging on one side and Bohannon on the other, the doors creaked, squeaked, and barely moved. Then, like opening a vacuum-sealed can, they swung apart with a *whoosh.*

Bohannon stepped from behind the door and stood in front of the safe. His mouth dropped, his eyes popped, and his breath stopped—and not from the accumulated dust.

The safe was filled, packed to the edges, with what looked to be dozens of museum-quality books, scrolls, manuscripts, and pamphlets. There was more gold gilt in that safe than one would find at a convention of military despots. *Without question,* thought Bohannon, *whatever the specifics of the contents, this collection could prove to be priceless.*

"What are you going to do now?" Maybry asked. There was no answer from Bohannon.

—⁓⁓—

Nondescript shadows in the night, the four men descended the gangplank. Few lights shone at this end of the vast dock on Staten Island. And at 3:30 in the morning, few people were moving in any part of the facility.

With the silent sweep of a serpent, the four men melted into the darkness separating staggering stacks of cargo containers. They paused at an unobserved junction.

"You know your targets. You have your directions." Sayeed Farouk once again inspected the three men before him. He could find no detail that would raise an alarm. All of them were dressed in the colorless work clothes of veteran seamen. Though all of them were hardened in body and devoted in ideology, none of them projected the frenzy of a zealot. They looked foreign, but not frightening.

"Remember why we are here." Farouk looked each of his brethren in the eyes. "We are here to restore the honor of the Prophet's Guard. Now that the mullah has discovered this connection between the infidel Spurgeon and this mission, we have been offered this great opportunity to serve—perhaps to serve unto death and become a revered martyr."

Farouk reached under his shirt at the neck and withdrew an amulet, a Coptic cross with a lightning bolt slashing through on the diagonal, and watched as the other three echoed his movement. Each man held his amulet firmly, next to his heart. "May Allah be praised!"

Slipping the amulets back under their shirts, the four men exchanged glances, then peeled away in four separate directions.

Thirty minutes later, stepping off the Staten Island Ferry at the awe-inspiring tip of Manhattan Island, Farouk casually wandered into Battery Park. He found an unoccupied park bench, well into the shadows, stretched out his body on the bench, rested his head on his seabag, and went to sleep. It was still dark when the policeman lightly struck the sole of his shoe with a nightstick.

"Come on, you can't sleep here. You've got to move along."

Wearily, Sayeed rose to a sitting position. "Officer, then, could you tell me how to get to the Bowery Mission?"

2

Joe Rodriguez was a down-to-earth guy. Lean, strapping, muscular, his 6-4 frame and intense brown eyes combined with a relentless stride and boundless energy. Raised in the South Bronx, the son of Puerto Rican natives, his "New York attitude" sometimes added an alarming edge to his already imposing figure.

Stepping across the void and onto the scaffolding at the rear of the Bowery Mission's chapel, Rodriguez brought something much more important to his friend and fellow Yankees fan than his size, his attitude, or that he was Tom's brother-in-law. Joe Rodriguez was also curator of the periodicals room in the massive, main research facility of New York's public library system—the Humanities and Social Sciences Library—a historic, Beaux-Arts land-mark building on Fifth Avenue that was often incorrectly referred to as the "main branch." Rodriguez was both a computer wizard and one of the most highly respected apologists of library science in the country. He had worked his entire career for the New York Public Library System, the last fifteen years in the historic marble halls of the research mecca on beautiful Bryant Park, and had authored two acclaimed books explaining how to unlock the astounding research and information resources of the world's libraries.

Rodriguez rapidly realized he would need all of that skill and experience if he was going to help his brother-in-law create a catalog of the volumes now before his eyes.

"I never expected this," Rodriguez said, bending at the waist under the low ceiling. He stood close to the safe, intently inspecting what he could see of the books, scrolls, and other documents stacked throughout the interior. "Tom . . . this . . . is amazing."

"That's why I was so anxious to get you down here." Bohannon stepped toward Rodriguez and leaned his hand on the door of the massive safe. "I don't know what to make of this. But I need to have some solid information to give to our board."

Rodriguez looked at his brother-in-law and realized he had never seen Tom so animated, or so nervous. Joe Rodriguez found a kindred spirit in Tom. Tom and his sister, Deirdre, were raised in a Catholic family. But when their parents became "born-again Christians," it was Deirdre who was much more active in living her faith than her older brother. Tom was sort of lost in limbo. Joe could relate to that. He was a lapsed Catholic and the object of Deirdre's constant prayers.

Rodriguez recognized that there was some of the kid, some of the investigator, some of the taskmaster present today as Bohannon eagerly watched him caress the volumes in the safe. Tom's excitement meter was topping out. "Let's get going, eh?" he said to Joe. "Let's find out what we have here."

"Tom, I'm sorry to disappoint you," said Rodriguez. He stepped away from the safe, inched across the room, and rested himself against the old wooden desk, giving his neck a break. "But I can't examine these books here. This place is filthy, and the contents of that safe could be worth—who knows what? We should get some of the airtight bins we have at the library and transport the entire contents of the safe back to the archival-recovery room at HSS."

Bohannon stared at him blankly.

"Humanities and Social Sciences . . . the library on Bryant Park?" said Rodriguez.

The old plaster, broken through to create a rough door, smelled like decaying chalk. Rodriguez could feel the grit in his teeth. His throat was desperate for water. No more desperate than the look on Tom's face.

"You can't do that Joe . . . not yet." Bohannon stood at the safe, his left hand resting on the top of the door. "I need to know what's in here first. We—"

"We, nothing," interrupted Joe. "C'mon, Tom, look around. The best thing we can do for these books and documents is to get them out of here. Get them in an environment that's a lot less threatening than this dusty attic. What's the matter with you?"

Tom crossed the room and leaned on the desk next to his brother-in-law. His eyes were on the safe.

"Joe, I know these books can't stay here," he said. "But I need to know . . . at least have some information about . . . what we've found before we move anything. I report to a board of directors. There's a 'need-to-know' factor involved here. I have a responsibility to tell them, but I don't even know what we've discovered. Look, let's get the stuff out of the safe. Make a list of what we've found, some assessment of what it's worth, and then I'll know what I'm talking about. After that, we can move the books to a safer place. Whaddaya say?"

The back of Rodriguez's neck, where his spine met his shoulder blades, tightened into a knot. He looked around at the tight space, the dust of ages, and he shuddered. But he also had a boss to whom he reported.

"Okay . . . but this is how it's going down," emphasized Rodriguez. "First, we clean this place—with the safe doors sealed. We get some of the airtight bins from the library. We'll catalog all this stuff, but"—he raised an index finger to punctuate his point—"anything I find that is precious or dangerously fragile goes in a bin and returns to the library with me, immediately. Is that a deal?"

———∿∿∿———

Over the next two days, Rodriguez orchestrated a meticulous process designed to preserve and protect the books while creating a catalog of the safe's contents. Their first challenge was to clean the office, removing as much of the dust as possible, and then to create within the office as many clean surfaces as possible on which to place the documents. Rodriguez set up his laptop and connected to WIFI, not only for record keeping, but also to help investigate and identify the contents through Libweb, the Worldwide Internet Library Network. They also secured the room with a solid door.

Then began the painstaking process of gently removing each item from the safe and minutely investigating it—first the cover and the edges, then the contents of the book, hoping to uncover its origin and pedigree.

Between the two of them, Rodriguez and Bohannon began closing in on some answers. The majority of the documents in the safe had been sent to Klopsch by his colleague, the nineteenth-century English preacher Charles Spurgeon, who had accumulated them during his many regular trips to the Middle East, or by those associated with Spurgeon whom Spurgeon had asked to forward biblical documents to Klopsch.

After the safe was emptied, Rodriguez inspected its various small drawers and cubbies. There were three small, inlaid drawers built upon the center shelf of the safe. The two smaller drawers were closed and locked, and they had yet to find a key among the contents of the safe or the office.

Opening the middle drawer, Rodriguez discovered a bundle wrapped up in a delicately designed silk covering—a purse that was fastened shut. As he opened the purse, a sheet of paper fell out and into the drawer. Rodriguez placed the purse on a shelf, picked up the paper, and began to read. "Hey, Tom . . . listen to this . . ."

> *Dear Louis,*
>
> *I am enclosing a document of the utmost importance and sensitivity. Within it are written certain assertions, which, if true and verified, will dramatically alter our understanding of the past, our perception of the present, and our hope of the future—a future that may breathe of the same atmosphere you and I now draw into our lungs. It is also one of the most dangerous documents in existence. A document that I am convinced some men would commit murder to possess and other men would commit murder to destroy.*
>
> *I convey it to you and place it into your sacred trust with a prayer to the Almighty for your safety and a hope that you may discover how to unlock the veracity or illegitimacy of the document and its claims, while at the same time avoiding any undue risk to your personal well-being and the well-being of that anointed endeavor you have undertaken along the Bouerie in New York.*
>
> *You may place your absolute trust and confidence in Dr. Schwartzman of Trinity, a true friend of Christ and an able ally for your vital pursuit. Wire me with any revelations. May our Lord and Saviour hold you in His most faithful hands.*
>
> *Charles*

Perspiring from the cramped quarters in the small office, Rodriguez's damp skin rippled with an icy apprehension as he watched Bohannon walk over to the shelf and pick up the silk purse. "What could this little package contain that would have Spurgeon fearing for his safety and the safety of his friend?" Bohannon asked. He turned it over in his hand, unfastened the clasp, reached inside, and withdrew a metal cylinder, about the girth of a midsized telescope. "Joe, what do you think this thing is?"

Reaching out his gloved hands, Rodriguez took the cylinder, gently placed it on the space he was using as a workbench, and pulled a lamp closer for more light. A round, engraved metal container, about four inches in diameter and about eight inches long, it had a thinner, metal rod running through the center. The rod had been turned on a lathe, producing knurls and nubs for decoration on both of its ends.

"This is a mezuzah," said Rodriguez, "a scroll container. The most common type of mezuzah is the small container most Jewish families affix to the frame of their front door. You take a small piece of paper, write on it a segment of the law—the Torah—and insert it into the mezuzah. A religious person will touch the mezuzah and kiss his finger every time he leaves or enters his home.

"They can be made of many materials, but metal is one of the longest lasting and most common. This one looks like bronze. It's not the most beautiful or ornate case I've ever seen, but it sure looks old. See," he said, pointing to the side of the case, "the metal has begun to pit. What started out with a luminous shine is now streaked with age. And there are signs of hairline stress fractures along the surface."

Gently turning the case over, Rodriguez scanned its surface. "You know, a religious mezuzah is never meant to be removed, never allowed to be discarded, because it contains the words of God." He continued his examination while he contemplated what he knew about these scroll holders. On one side of the metal tube, tightly secured to the side of the container, was a thin, three-sided, metal appendage about the size of a pencil but in the shape of a "U," with the open side against the cylinder. After some inspection, Rodriguez figured this metal addition was a handle of some type, but it appeared to be sealed to the side of the cylinder, apparently with wax.

"In order to get rid of a mezuzah, it has to be buried," he said, gently inspecting all of the container's pieces. "Many synagogues around the world have repositories where mezuzahs and scrolls are kept until there is a quantity large enough for an official burial. But some are never emptied. One was discovered in Cairo with scrolls written in the hand of Maimonides. Besides being used for religious purposes, a mezuzah was often a protection for important documents."

Gently twitching the metal rod that ran through the middle of the cylinder, Rodriguez detected a tightening and slacking of something inside, a movement that also produced the slightest movement in the metal handle. "Hmm . . . there is something in here."

Bohannon came closer, hovering over the table where his brother-in-law was so carefully working.

"There is definitely something inside," Rodriguez said, "most likely a parchment that's attached to the rod and released by pulling on the handle. But there appears to be only one way to get it open and get a look at the parchment inside. We've got to try and unroll it, using the handle." He looked down to the metal case on the bench. "There's just no guarantee what will happen. The parchment could break. Once we break that wax seal, the parchment will be exposed to air and humidity again and could begin to deteriorate."

Bohannon looked him squarely in the eye. "It's a risk, right?"

"Yeah," said Rodriguez, nodding his head, "but Spurgeon must have risked opening it up. And it survived well enough for him to send it to Klopsch."

"It looks like a number of people have gone to extraordinary lengths to ensure the safekeeping of this mezuzah. If there is a scroll inside, they obviously wanted somebody to read it," said Bohannon. "Seems to me it would be a crime not to take the risk. Go ahead. Let's see what's inside."

With the metal case still resting on the workbench, Rodriguez took a small, sharp knife and cut into the wax seal. Then he grasped the metal rod in his left hand and turned it slowly until he felt pressure from inside. Like a thief trying to crack the combination of a safe, Rodriguez, his eyes closed, tried to sense the willingness of the parchment to move. As his left hand made minute moves to turn the metal shaft, his right hand slowly drew away the handle, pulling out the parchment. It was surprisingly easy.

"There is very little drag. The parchment inside is turning freely," Rodriguez said, his eyes still closed. "I don't feel any breaking or tearing." Well before he had reached arm's length, Rodriguez abruptly stopped.

"I think that's it. There was a slight pull up on the handle," Rodriguez said, opening his eyes.

"What is it?" Bohannon asked. "I've never seen anything like it."

The Spurgeon parchment lay on the table in front of them, stretched out between the engraved metal mezuzah and the small metal handle that had been on its side. Rodriguez stared intently at the handwritten characters on the surface of the scroll.

The parchment was about five inches wide and just short of two feet long. It was covered with twenty-one columns of symbols arranged in seven groupings—three vertical rows of symbols in each of the groupings.

"These symbols are unique," Rodriguez puzzled. "I expected it to be in a language I didn't understand. But this—I don't even know what these characters are. They're not Asian, they're not Hebrew, and they're not Cyrillic. It doesn't look anything like Greek. And it certainly doesn't look Roman. I've got to tell you: I don't know what I'm looking at."

"That makes two of us," said Bohannon, twisting his head to get a look from another angle.

Rodriguez got up from his chair, turned his back on the table, and looked out through the rough opening the workers had pounded into the wall. The door was open for ventilation, and two of the Middle Eastern workers, no doubt curious, were watching them from the doorway. Rodriguez made a mental note. *We need to install a much more secure lock on this door right away. And I need to get this stuff out of here.* Turning back into the room, Rodriguez leaned against the huge, old safe that had harbored the scroll and other antiquities. His head hanging down between his folded arms, Rodriguez forced his mind to focus.

Suddenly, he turned back toward Bohannon and the table.

"Tom, just from a preliminary review, the books and documents we've found in this safe are rare and valuable. Which means Spurgeon and his friends only sent things to Klopsch that they knew were important or hard to find. Association gives this scroll a high level of importance. Factor in two other things we know. One, it's been treated lovingly and carefully for a lot more than a hundred years, and it was provided its own special compartment in this safe. Two, in his own hand, Spurgeon described it as 'of the utmost importance and sensitivity.' What else did he write?" Rodriguez stepped over to the desk where Spurgeon's letter had been inserted into a quart-size ziplock bag. "'It is also one of the most dangerous documents in existence. A document that I am convinced some men would commit murder to possess, and other men would commit murder to destroy.'"

"Maybe that's why Klopsch needed such a big safe," offered Bohannon.

Rodriguez rubbed his chin, his head slowly nodding up and down. "Tom, I don't have any idea what may be in this document. But everything in me is saying it's a precious piece of history. And if we allow ourselves to get involved with it . . . well . . . I don't know where it's going to take us."

Silence wrestled with dust to fill the space.

"You found this thing, and it belongs to the mission," Rodriguez said softly. "I don't know what you were planning to do with it. But from a librarian's point of view, this is fascinating. With your permission and with your help, I'd like to find out what this scroll is and what it means."

"It's probably going to take a lot of your time," said Bohannon.

"That's okay," said Rodriguez. "I'll put in as much time as it takes. Until your sister tells me I've got to stop."

———~~~~———

"At this point, they don't know what they are looking at or what they should do with it. But they are searching."

A hand slipped out of the darkness and reached for one of the hoses coming from the hookah in the middle of the table, pulling it back into the blackness where he sat.

"The tall one has great strength," said Hamid, leaning into the table, his voice low. "He prowls like a lion. He will be formidable . . . if they discover the scroll's story."

Music, flutes, drums, cymbals at a frantic pace pounded the room, making it difficult for them to hear even themselves. Smoke filled the small bar, a lethal fog that cloaked their meeting and lay on their skin like a dry sweat. Yet their caution was at its highest level. They were in the belly of the Great Satan. Even whispered words carried great risk.

"Have they spoken to anyone else?" The voice from the darkness was clear in spite of the music.

"No." Ishmael pulled long on the mouthpiece, holding the smoke before exhaling a thick, blue vapor. "They are still in the room. It is now tightly locked, a heavy wooden door. The deskmen patrol regularly."

"They will move, soon." Sayeed Farouk emerged from the darkness, his red-rimmed eyes boring a hole through the haze. "They need more knowledge. Perhaps, if we eliminate the head, the body will wither before it grows more parts. I will stay close to him. Monitor his every move. Come to know his habits. Hamid, stay with the tall one. Ishmael, lease the truck. Bring it to the garage. We should wait no longer."

3

Few palaces could rival the stately grandeur of the Humanities and Social Sciences Library nestled on the east side of Bryant Park in New York City. Tom Bohannon had been inside the massive building a few times in the past while doing research. But on this Monday morning in mid-April, faithfully trailing his long-striding brother-in-law through the marble halls, past the many guard posts, and deep into the private and off-limits rooms of this national landmark, Bohannon was in overloaded awe of the incredible facility.

With seventy-five miles of bookshelves in the building itself and another fourteen miles of stacks extending underground, it was one of the greatest institutions for scholarly investigation in the world. Its collection of fifty million books, manuscripts, maps, prints, and literary and artistic treasures grew by ten thousand items a week and was visited by ten million people a year. Walking through its halls, his footsteps echoing back to him, Bohannon was surrounded by some of the greatest works of some of the greatest minds in history: the first Gutenberg Bible brought to the New World, Thomas Jefferson's handwritten copy of the Declaration of Independence, Shakespeare's First Folio, a manuscript of George Washington's Farewell Address, the diaries of Virginia Woolf . . .

As a former journalist, Bohannon was awed by such a vast collection of information. As a book collector, he was a little covetous. As Joe Rodriguez's sidekick, he was scuttling to keep pace as Rodriguez raced through corridors, ducked inside obscure doors, and darted down spiral staircases.

Rodriguez cut to his left and stepped into a brightly lit office. "Listen, Sammy, I need your help."

Swinging away from his computer to face the two men was a muscular, compact, Mediterranean-looking man with a dense shock of jet black hair and thick, black-rimmed glasses. "Sammy, this is my brother-in-law, Tom. Tom, this is Sammy Rizzo, the best mind in this whole mausoleum."

Sammy Rizzo hopped off his chair, and Bohannon scrambled to cover his surprise. Rizzo was short, the top of his head barely reaching to Bohannon's belt buckle. Rizzo came toward Bohannon, a sly grin on his face, offering a small, pudgy hand.

"Hi, Tom, glad to meet you," said Sammy, a smile spreading under his hooked nose. "Yeah, I'm a dwarf. But hey, get over it. I have. So, Joe, what can I do for you?" Sammy turned away from the speechless Bohannon.

"Sammy, first, I've got to tell you that this is for me, not for the library," said Rodriguez.

"Well, let's sit down. This might be a lengthy conversation." Rizzo motioned for Joe and Tom to sit at a small, round, meeting table just off the center of the room.

Rizzo's office was small but exquisitely customized. In the corner farthest from the door was a horseshoe-shaped desk that reminded Bohannon of the "slot" desks designed for editors at a newspaper. But instead of having a news editor inside the curve of the horseshoe and other deskmen arranged around the outside, Rizzo's desk was shallow enough for him to access the entire surface. One flat-screen computer sat at the apex of the horseshoe, where Rizzo had been sitting when they entered, and another flat-screen computer was located on the left wing of the horseshoe. The surface of the right wing was elevated from the rear, like a drafting table, with two huge lamps overhanging it. Across from the desk, flanking the door, was a floor-to-ceiling window that let in much of the light and helped this subterranean room feel less claustrophobic.

Bohannon settled into a chair. Everything was designed to Rizzo's scale, though his desktop and the meeting table were set at an average height.

Rizzo grabbed the chair from his desk and rolled it toward them. He pushed a lever, and the chair body dropped, allowing him to easily climb aboard. Pushing another lever, Sammy popped up to eye level. "Okay, so it's not library business. Thank God. I need something interesting to keep me from going completely nuts."

Rodriguez looked sideways to Bohannon, who gave him a resigned nod of his head. "Sammy . . ." Rodriguez hesitated, trying to shape into words what he needed to say. "I've known you a long time . . ."

"Wait a minute," Sammy interjected, his voice a threat. "I'm Gracie's god-father. And remember, I'm the one who keeps Deirdre company all summer while you camp out at Yankee Stadium. So if you're gonna tell me you've got another woman, I don't want to hear another word. If you're here to borrow money, it's got to be less than six figures. Or if Bohannon here is in the CIA and you're recruiting me to infiltrate Al Qaeda in Pakistan, I'll think about it."

Rizzo glared menacingly first at Rodriguez, then at Bohannon.

Despite himself, Bohannon burst out laughing, only to be immediately joined by both Rizzo and Rodriguez.

"Sammy, you are nuts," Rodriguez said.

"Okay, come on, whatcha got for me?" Sammy asked, rubbing together his knobbled hands.

Sobering up, Rodriguez looked at his old friend. "Tom and I have found something that I don't understand, something we're trying to figure out. But, Sammy, there're a few things I've got to tell you before we get started. One is, we're not going to tell you everything. Forgive me. I trust you with my life; you know that. But I need you to trust me. You don't want to know it all. So, if you push too far, I'm just gonna shut down."

Rizzo nodded his head in agreement, even more intrigued.

"Second, I've brought you only a portion of what we found. It's a small portion, a rough copy that I made myself. But I hope it's enough for you to help us get started. And lastly, I need you to promise, seriously, that you won't breathe a word of this to anyone, especially not anyone here at the library."

Sammy Rizzo, head cocked to one side, contemplated the request, but only for a heartbeat. "You've got my word."

"Okay," said Joe.

Rodriguez reached into the inside pocket of his sport coat and pulled out the paper on which he had painstakingly copied a small portion of the scroll's text. He unfolded it and turned it around so Sammy could take a look. "Have you ever seen anything like this?" Rodriguez continued to hold the paper while Rizzo scanned it intensely, leaning in from his chair.

"Hmm . . . let's put it over here on the table," Sammy said. He swiveled his chair toward the elevated section of the desk and snapped on one of the large, hooded lamps.

Rodriguez spread the paper on the table, pinning down its edges.

"Been a long time," Sammy said, slowly grazing his fingers over the symbols written on the paper. "Been a long time."

Rizzo dropped off his chair, toward a low set of shelves. Sorting through a stack of binders, Sammy pulled one clear. He grabbed his chair and rolled it in front of the computer screen. Bohannon noticed the specially rigged keyboard and mouse combination that swung out to meet the chair. Rizzo's fingers flew over the keyboard, darting in and out of Web sites, opening and closing pages.

"If this is what I believe it is, it is very rare," he said without looking over his shoulder. "Makes me wonder where you got it. And what—Wait, here it is. Joe, take a look at this."

Sammy pushed himself away from the computer terminal so Bohannon and Rodriguez could move closer and get a better look at the screen.

Before their eyes were several characters in what looked like an ancient script. "Here, let me print it out," said Rizzo. Grabbing the sheet of paper as it emerged from the printer, Rizzo kicked a shelf at the side of his computer table and propelled his chair toward the drafting table, Rodriguez guiding it the final few feet. "Here, Joe, you scan it," Rizzo said, handing the sheet of paper to Rodriguez. As Bohannon watched from behind, Rodriguez slowly moved the paper with the printed characters above and beside the columns of characters they had brought with them. The two sets of symbols had clear similarities— sweeping curves and extended, pointed tails.

"There . . . there," said Joe excitedly. "That's a match, right? That's a match, Sammy?"

Rodriguez made room for Rizzo to roll closer to the two pieces of paper. Rizzo traced the lines and curves of one symbol with the tip of his forefinger while transmitting that touch through his eyes to the symbol on the other page. Several times, he repeated the process, a ritual of recognition that didn't seem to fully satisfy the diminutive scholar. "It's close—it's real close, but there's something else going on here. It's not an exact match, and it should be.

"But there's one good thing," Rizzo said, spinning around toward them. "I know what it is. And I know where it came from."

4

Sammy Rizzo plugged in an electric kettle that rested on top of a small filing cabinet. "I've only got tea, so that's what you get." Rizzo made a fast intercom connection to someone elsewhere in the library, while he directed Bohannon and Rodriguez to take seats around a small, meeting table in the corner of his office.

"I'll give you guys a short history lesson while we're waiting for that water to boil," said Rizzo, as he joined them at the table. "First, how did this sheet of paper come about? I mean, you don't have to tell me your secrets, no offense, but how did you two come to be in possession of whatever it is that you copied these symbols from? Come on, Joe, this is not your line of business."

Rodriguez looked at Rizzo with a scowl on his face. He knew Rizzo would help them regardless, with or without more information. But he also felt his colleague deserved some kind of explanation.

"Sam," Rodriguez said solemnly, leaning across the table to emphasize his words, "obviously, we've discovered something we think may be significant. Tom has unexpectedly found a number of antiquities. Among them was a document that contained this writing. We couldn't even identify the language, let alone decipher what it meant. So we came to you for help, hoping you might be able to identify what we're looking at."

Rizzo rocked back and forth in his chair. He took off his glasses and began to rapidly clean the lenses with the bottom of his bowling league shirt. "As long as this isn't a forgery or a joke of some kind, then I can tell you that these symbols come from a very old document, perhaps two thousand years old. The document is likely parchment rolled up as a scroll and very well preserved. Parchment is made of animal skin, most likely sheepskin. If it was kept in a moist or humid environment or in one with dramatic climate changes, the skin would have shrunk and expanded hundreds of times, destroying it and anything written on it. Parchment in the desert, however, seems to last forever. We have scrolls from twenty-five hundred years ago that are still legible and in good shape because they were kept in a desert area with little humidity.

"How's that so far?" Rizzo said, a twinkle in his eye as he perched the glasses on the crest of his nose. "A regular Sherlock Holmes, eh?"

"I knew you were the right guy," said Rodriguez. "You are pretty much right on the money. The letters, the ink, is faded a bit, and some of the letters may have separated or cracked. But the scroll itself is in pretty good shape. So what else have you been able to figure out?"

"I've figured out that I'd like to see this scroll for myself," he said bluntly.

Rodriguez and Bohannon looked at each other with questioning glances. How far did they want to take this with Rizzo?

"Sam, if I were you, I'd want to see this scroll, too. I understand that," said Rodriguez. "And I know you could help us try and figure this thing out. But one of the reasons we're being as careful as we are is that in the package with this scroll was a letter, a letter warning about the danger of this document, that people would kill for it. Whether that's still true today, who knows? I mean it sounds like a cheap adventure novel, but it's possible this could get dangerous. I just want you to understand what you may be getting into. Tom and I, we're just curious enough, and just crazy enough, to want to find out. So what do you think it is?"

Sammy Rizzo's eyes sparkled. "It's not what I think it is; it's what I know it is."

——◠◠◠——

The whistling kettle broke into Sammy's thoughts.

"Hey, Tom, would you mind getting that?" Sammy nodded at the filing cabinet. "There should be some sugar up there, too."

Rizzo wrestled with conflicting emotions. Part of him felt the elation of a prospector with a shiny nugget in his hand. Another part of him was heavy with the knowledge that the nugget was fool's gold. He waited while Bohannon busied himself with the mugs, then pressed on, aware that his information would soon crush the excitement in the room.

"I'm sure you've both heard of the Rosetta Stone. We all learned about it in school," he began. "But do you know why the Rosetta Stone was such an important find?"

"Sure," said Rodriguez as they stirred and blew on their steaming mugs. "It gave us the ability to understand Egyptian hieroglyphics."

"That's right," said Sammy, "but it wasn't that simple. From the time the Greeks discovered the first hieroglyphic writing in Egypt about three hundred years before Christ, deciphering those hieroglyphic images had been an impossibility. Plenty of theories were offered, but none of the theories held up under scrutiny. Hieroglyphs were an unknown and lost language, and historians despaired of ever understanding their meaning.

"The Rosetta Stone is an ancient stele, or stone tablet, inscribed with the same message in three languages . . . two Egyptian languages and classical Greek. The stone was created in 196 B.C. It's a decree from Ptolemy V, the fifth ruler of the Greek's Ptolemaic Dynasty that ruled Egypt for over three hundred years. The decree repealed certain taxes and instructed that statues should be erected in temples. Making decrees and carving the decrees on stones was common for the Ptolemys," said Rizzo, as he warmed to the task. "They would make several copies and then display the stones in key locations all over Egypt in order to maintain support for the dynasty. As Greeks, it was critical to the Ptolemaic rulers that all people could understand the decrees. So the stones were inscribed in several languages to be read, not only by the local people, but also by visiting priests and government officials."

A soft knock on the door was followed by a young, African American man who walked in and silently handed Rizzo a small, soft-cover booklet and a manila folder fairly thick with documents.

"Thank you, Kevin," Rizzo said, looking up. "I appreciate your getting this to me quickly. I owe you one."

The young man nodded his head, turned, and left as silently as he had entered. Rizzo was back into his story before the young man had reached the hallway.

"After Napoleon's 1798 campaign conquered Egypt, the French founded the Institut d'Égypte in Cairo, bringing many scientists and archaeologists to the region. But the stone wasn't discovered by scientists. It was discovered by a guy who was digging a ditch." Rizzo picked up the small booklet, opened it, and, referring to the book now and again, continued with his history lesson. "A French army engineer discovered the stone in July of 1799 while he was guiding construction workers at Fort Julien near the Egyptian port city of Rosetta. Recognizing the uniqueness of his discovery, the engineer called his general, who dispatched the stone to the Institut d'Égypte, where it arrived the next month. The French then announced its discovery.

"Once Napoleon returned to France, leaving behind his soldiers and a couple hundred French scientists and scholars, it was like the stone was a war magnet. Both the British and the Ottoman Turks attacked Egypt. The French soldiers valiantly resisted for two years, but the British ultimately captured Cairo. French troops and scholars, with the stone, fled to Alexandria in hopes of escaping to France, but the British blockaded the port and soon captured Alexandria. That's when the real fun began.

"If the military battles were fierce, the scholarly ones were even more intense.

"The French refused to hand over the archaeological and scientific discoveries they had made in Egypt. The British general—Hutchinson, I believe—was anxious to send home more booty for the newly completed British Museum, so he continued the blockade, refusing to allow food, water, or supplies through to the French. In response, the French declared they would burn all they had found, rather than surrender it to the English, at the same time hiding as many of the objects as they could.

"Imagine," said Rizzo, his gaze swinging back and forth between the two rapt listeners, "if the French had followed through with their threat. Imagine all of the history, all of the knowledge that would have been lost forever. But the British had a solution.

"While a couple of the British scientists were bargaining with the French, telling them they could take home some biology specimens, English soldiers secretly infiltrated the French quarter, broke into the institute, and carried off the loot." Rizzo flipped a page in the folder and scanned the contents. "Colonel Tomkyns Hilgrove Turner, who escorted the stone to Britain, personally seized the stone from General de Menou and carried it away on a gun carriage.

"Wow, this stuff would make a great movie, wouldn't it?" Rizzo said with a big grin.

"You see, even at that early stage, even though nobody had the foggiest clue what was inscribed on the stone, scholars and scientists were convinced that the keys to deciphering hieroglyphs were on the stone because one of the languages was Greek. Since we understood the Greek, we would probably be able to figure out the other languages. But it wasn't that easy.

"More than twenty years passed, and no one—not the scholars at the British Museum, not the French, who had made plaster casts of the stone before it was swiped by the Brits, and not any other linguist—had any success making the connection between the Greek translation and the other two Egyptian languages on the stone."

Rizzo took a deep breath, drained the remainder of his tea, closed his eyes, and stretched back in his chair, sharpening the edge of the silence.

"It was a physicist—a physicist!—who finally figured out the key. The guy's name was Thomas Young, and he had a revolutionary insight. Young discovered that some of the hieroglyphs on the Rosetta Stone wrote the sounds, not the letters, of the royal name, Ptolemy. From there, a French scholar named Champollion realized that all hieroglyphs recorded the sounds of the Egyptian language, not the letters, and his discovery laid the foundation of our knowledge of ancient Egyptian language and culture. He unlocked the stone."

Without a twitch, Rodriguez and Bohannon waited. And waited some more.

"So . . . ?" Bohannon finally said impatiently. "So . . . what does all that have to do with our characters? Those aren't hieroglyphs."

"No, they're not," Rizzo said softly. "In fact, those symbols are even more unknown, even more difficult to understand than hieroglyphs. Those symbols are the third language on the Rosetta Stone," he said, a note of triumph in his voice. "Those symbols are Demotic."

"Demonic?" Bohannon squeaked.

"No, not *demonic*," Rizzo chided, bringing a blush to Bohannon's cheeks. "*Demotic*. It's an ancient type of writing that was used in Egypt for a thousand years, up until about the third century. It was used primarily for business and literary purposes.

"You know something," he said, pulling on his earlobe, "it's been over two hundred years since that stone was found. Two hundred years during which the best minds in the world have pored over every swoop and swirl on its face. And even with the Greek and the hieroglyph to work from, only half of the letters of the Demotic language have been deciphered. Of the fifteen symbols that have been identified, linguists have only been able to figure out the meaning for eleven. The University of Chicago has spent years trying to complete a Demotic dictionary and has done a great job, without a significant amount of success in clearly understanding the entire language. Duke University has many examples of Demotic, mostly from the wrappings of mummies, and hasn't made much headway. The Louvre in Paris has an extensive collection of Demotic language samples, and it's still a mystery to them."

Bohannon whispered loudly in Rodriguez's direction. "Perhaps the Louvre should apply the DaVinci Code to this Demotic. Maybe that would solve the puzzle."

"You guys are a riot," sneered Rizzo. "I'm just trying to help you out here. You want to go read Dan Brown, go ahead. He's not going to help you a bit."

"Oh, come on Sammy, lighten up," said Rodriguez. "You've got to admit, that was a pretty good line."

"Yeah, but you're not going to be laughing when you realize you may never figure out what this scroll actually says." Rizzo pushed on the arms of his chair to gain more height, leaning into the desk to pierce Rodriguez with his gaze. "The problem is that Demotic has defied every attempt at translation for hundreds of years. It's impossible. Don't you realize it yet? You are never going to be able to translate this. You will never know what it says."

Rizzo dropped back into his chair and watched as hope drained from Rodriguez's face.

"Sammy, is it really that bleak?" he asked.

"Look, guys, I wish I could help you here. This is one of the most fascinating things I've seen in years. But there are some daunting, inherent problems that anyone will face if they try to decipher Demotic. The first thing you need to understand is that Demotic was originally a spoken language, not a written language. As the language became more commonly spoken, it began to be translated into symbols for written communication. But from all of the different specimens of Demotic that have been discovered, one of the few consistencies is that the language changes with the circumstances." Rizzo stopped for a breath and looked at his guests. "The language changes depending on who was writing it, their handwriting, what they were writing. Different types of texts—letters; economic and legal documents; administrative documents; religious, literary, and scientific texts—were all written in differing versions of the language. And it changed from location to location, especially around Cairo. Those differences have stumped scholars for centuries."

"Well, then, how did you know what this was when you looked at it?" Rodriguez asked.

"I know what it is," said Rizzo, looking up, "but I don't know what it means. Demotic was unique to its time, even in its construction. Its letters are much more flowing and joined, similar to each other—another reason it is difficult to translate. Where something like Akkadian is all triangles and lines in differing formations and quantities, a pattern you can follow, Demotic is beautiful but unpredictable. Look."

Rizzo whipped around and typed into his computer. Soon, he was on the Web site of the Oriental Institute at the University of Chicago and had pulled up the introduction to the Demotic Dictionary Project.

"Look, look at this letter *Q*. It looks like a side view of a kid's sled or a toboggan—with a desktop attached to the top of the curve. There are 105 pages of definitions for this letter and its combinations. It takes 8.6 megabytes of memory . . . just on this one symbol. Not a word, a symbol! The first five meanings are 'length; high ground; a plant; work; high.' Here, here's another one that will truly drive you nuts. This letter, *F*—it sort of looks like a wavy 'x'—it can mean 'hair, viper, lift, steal, and fly.' How does that make any sense? And those are just the first five meanings. The Demotic Project in Chicago started with the easiest letters. Once they translated the easier symbols, they moved on to the more complicated. One letter, *C*, has 164 pages of definitions. They expect those that are left to decipher will have a lot more meanings than the ones they have already done.

"This language may have represented the spoken idiom of the time, how a Southerner sounds if he visits New York. You know it's the same language, but it is hard to understand. Over time, the written form of Demotic diverged more and more from the spoken form, giving Demotic texts an artificial character."

Rizzo swept his arm in the direction of the drafting table. "Gentlemen, the document you copied those symbols from could be more than two thousand years old." He paused for effect. "A remarkable find. But its meaning? Its meaning is a secret, protected by a lock that has no key."

A long, deep sigh escaped from Bohannon, who rubbed his forehead with the palm of his hand. Rodriguez had his hands clasped at his chin, fingers entwined, eyes on the floor.

"It looks to me like we're all running down different paths but coming to the same conclusion," said Rizzo. "Where in the world do we go from here?"

Two heads nodded in assent.

"Well, I know one place we're going. C'mon," said Sammy, whipping his chair behind his desk again and shutting down his computer. "C'mon, let me buy you a beer. We've got a lot to talk about."

5

Bohannon's mind was reeling that week, trying to remain balanced between his responsibilities at the Bowery Mission and the remarkable discoveries connected with the mysterious scroll. Even though it was deep into Friday evening, Bohannon felt obligated to return to the mission and finish his final tasks for the week. As he walked up Madison Avenue and turned right on 32nd Street, he was oblivious to the soft April night, the exotic bird store on his right, and the constant stream of people in and out of Artisanal, the popular restaurant and cheese shop.

Bohannon swiped his MetroCard in the turnstile entrance, turned left on the subway platform, and then instinctively walked to the far end of the platform where he'd be in the best position to disembark right at his exit. He dodged an obvious tourist, head buried in a foldout map, and squeezed himself into one of the typically packed rush-hour trains—the 6 Downtown. Bohannon held firmly to the stainless steel pole in the middle of the train, completely encased in other bodies without making eye contact. In a city of more than eight million people, eye contact could often be misinterpreted. And who needed that hassle? Waiting patiently for his Spring Street stop, Bohannon was pounded into by a body from behind, driving him into the pole. At the same time, he felt two hands slip under his arms from behind, lightly groping for something.

"Hey!" Bohannon shouted, alarming those around him and spinning quickly to confront his assailant. Facing a middle-aged man with Middle Eastern features, Bohannon went on the offensive. "What do you think you're doing? Keep your hands off me," he said menacingly. "What are you trying to steal?"

Bohannon was agitated, angry, and feeling superior. That ended.

"Are you accusing me?" the man said through a thick accent. "Are you accusing me?" he said again, his voice rising to a shout. "You call me thief? You call me thief! Who are you to call me thief, you persecutor? You white Americans, ever since the planes you are convinced that all Arabs are murderers and thieves. *I am no thief!*" he screamed, his diatribe continuing without letup. The commotion was so disturbing, there was now space around Bohannon and this man as the other riders pressed farther and farther away from the threat. "Prove it. Prove it. You want to call the police? Come, let us call the police. I will call them myself," he screamed.

The train doors opened, Spring Street. Bohannon made sure his wallet was still in place, then pushed past the man, disgust in his eyes and relief in his gut, happy to get out of the train along with a score of others. "*I am no thief!*" followed Bohannon through the turnstile exit.

God help me, he thought as he ascended the steps to Spring Street. *That was crazy. What a madman. You never know what you're going to find on the train.* He stood at the corner of Spring and Lafayette, waiting for the light to change, running his hand through the thick, copper-colored hair at the nape of his neck.

Lafayette was a busy, four-lane street, a major feeder route for taxi cabs heading uptown for the more lucrative fares around Lincoln Center or the Theater District, as well as for delivery trucks and commercial vehicles. Bohannon's mind was spinning with images from the confrontation on the train, wondering what the man had been after.

He had no consciousness of a truck picking up speed on Lafayette Street, a truck that veered to the far left and began bearing down on the crowd waiting at the corner of Spring Street. His mind focused inward, he didn't register his fellow pedestrians fleeing, not until the last possible moment. The headlights, too close, were caught in the side of his eye, massive motion closing fast. Bohannon recklessly threw his body forward and to the left, stepped on a box at the curb, vaulted over a green postal storage box, and rolled over the trunk of a parked car, falling into the street. As he scrambled for his life, he heard screams cut short and the sickening, crashing, smashing of metal-against-metal as the truck exploded into the newspaper and magazine store on the corner, crushing some bodies beyond recognition, impaling others with flying shards of broken plate glass.

Bohannon's mind struggled, unable to focus either on the disaster facing him or whether he was still in danger from oncoming traffic. Using the fender of the car he had rolled over, Bohannon pulled himself to his feet, knowing for sure he had seriously sprained his weakened left ankle again—too much volleyball in college. He edged behind the car and looked at what, a few moments ago, had been a place he had passed thousands of times and just took for granted. Now, the missile of a truck was halfway into the store, its right front wheel up in the air, still spinning, as the truck was perilously tipped to the left. Already, people from every direction were responding. Two firemen from the Ladder 23 Station House a few hundred feet up Lafayette Street were already crawling through the ragged metal that was once the store's facade, first-aid bags over their shoulders, another half dozen of their mates not far behind.

Dazed, uncertain of what hurt, wondering how he had physically managed to launch himself over this postal box, Bohannon turned to see pedestrians swarming around the truck's cab, trying to extricate the driver . . . or were they trying to kill him? Uncertain of why, but certain of the necessity, Bohannon shakily made his way around the remains of the truck to the driver's side and pushed close as civilian rescuers drew the limp, bloodied body of the driver out of the cab. Beginning to succumb to the loss of adrenalin, Bohannon felt foggy, but his mind did register that the dead driver was of Middle Eastern heritage. And there was something else. What was it? Bohannon's half-working mind focused on the unique amulet hanging around the man's throat, a Coptic cross with a lightning bolt slashing through it on the diagonal.

Funny, Bohannon's brain transmitted. *Where have I seen that before?*

"Sir, are you okay?"

Bohannon focused on the present. In front of him stood a fire lieutenant, a young man with a concerned look on his face. "Sir, do you hear me?" Bohannon's mind retreated. *The amulet, where have I seen it?*

"Sir . . . sir, can you respond to me?"

Not that long ago.

"Medic!" the fire lieutenant shouted.

The volume clicked with Bohannon. *The train . . . the man . . . that man . . . he had an amulet on, too. Yeah, . . . same cross . . . same lightning bolt. Strange. Two men, same necklace, a few minutes.*

"Sir, we're going to give you something to make you comfortable until the ambulance can take you to the hospital. Sir? Sir . . . are you with me, sir?"

What're the chances? Bohannon began to drift off. *Two guys . . . some club . . .*

Red lights were flashing in all directions, paramedics, police officers, and firefighters running back and forth. The critical, the bleeders went first, those with a chance for survival. Then the walking wounded, many glassy-eyed and disoriented clutching broken or crushed limbs, their hands gently resting on a heavily bandaged head. In their midst was Bohannon, bruised, scraped, limping on a rapidly swelling ankle, full of questions without answers. The body bags came last. For them, there was no hurry.

6

Bohannon lay down in his bed, hoping that he would be asleep as soon as his head hit the pillow. His body still bore the bruises and wounds of his near-death experience with the runaway truck ten days ago, but his schedule had given him little time to recover from the accident or process much of anything. So he lay awake again, his mind betraying his body as it raced over the events since the scroll had been discovered.

The days since his accident had been a numbing blur. Monday through Friday, he tackled his usual responsibilities for the Bowery Mission, overseeing the operation of its four ministry sites, pursuing several strategic options while keeping a steady hand on the organization's administrative functions. Determined not to shortchange the mission with his time, Bohannon kept to his normal schedule, in the office by 9:00 AM, out of the office somewhere around 7:00 or 7:30 PM.

But that wasn't the end of his day.

Leaving the office, Bohannon would then jump on the Uptown 6 at 33rd Street and travel just one stop, to Grand Central Station at 42nd Street. Up the escalator and out the doors into Pershing Square, he crisscrossed the streets depending on the "walk" signs and quickly made his way over to Fifth Avenue and the staff entrance to the Humanities Library. Joe had supplied him with an "all access" pass that was valid twenty-four hours a day, and even though by now Bohannon knew all of the guards who manned the staff entrance, he was closely scrutinized each time he entered the library, and nearly body-searched each time he left. But leaving didn't come for several hours.

Bohannon shook his head at the thought of Joe Rodriguez. Where Bohannon had respected his brother-in-law as a good man, he now marveled at Joe's mastery of his profession, how he maneuvered their search through seemingly endless avenues of opportunity, almost always choosing the right track that led them to some new piece of the puzzle. Along with the help and guidance of Sammy

Rizzo, Bohannon and Rodriguez began closing in on answers about the mysterious scroll. Accessing the archives of Christian Herald's magazine, published from 1878 to 1992 for information about the Bowery Mission's history and analyzing historic data culled from research among the miles of stacks at the Bryant Park library, along with information available on the Internet, they came to the conclusion that the letter signed "Charles" had indeed been written by Spurgeon to his friend and compatriot, Klopsch.

Primarily in England, there were scores of Spurgeon correspondence extant and in excellent condition. Not only had they accessed the content of the letters, finding great similarities in the style Spurgeon used in his personal writing, they also found original correspondence existing in the Christian Herald records and in the files found in Klopsch's hidden office. All of the sources confirmed not only the manner in which Spurgeon signed his letters but also, even to their untrained eyes, the grand swoop of the capital *C*.

So they were sure of one thing. Eminent British preacher and scholar Dr. Charles Haddon Spurgeon had written a letter to warn his friend and colleague Dr. Louis Klopsch of the danger contained in this ancient scroll written in a Demotic script that was all but extinct.

But that was also where Bohannon and Rodriguez were stopped dead in their tracks. Veiled communication with the University of Chicago's Demotic initiative along with Internet scrutiny of Duke University's collection of Demotic documents had brought the men no closer to having any clue as to what was written in the scroll. It appeared that the manner in which the symbols were arranged, seven distinct columns, each column comprised of three vertical lines of symbols, could be a critical element in deciphering the scroll. But nothing they had accessed, no one they had contacted had offered even the slightest clue of how to unlock this Demotic puzzle.

⸻

Out of the dark, her voice was soft. "How long do you think you're going to wrestle with it tonight?" A rustle in the sheets, and Annie was at his side, her left arm pulling him close to her warmth. The quiet joined with the dark for a few moments. "Any luck tonight?"

"No," said Bohannon, his left hand pulling her arm into a closer embrace. "Sorry I woke you."

"That's okay," Annie said softly. "I was sort of waiting for you, anyway. How are you feeling?"

"Well, my ankle is still sore. The swelling is mostly gone, but being up and around so much really puts a strain on it. Most of the other stuff is healing, and my back doesn't bother me anymore. So all in all, I can't complain."

"You shouldn't complain," Annie said. "Six people on that corner weren't as lucky as you. Seven if you count the driver."

"Yeah, that's true," said Bohannon, thinking once again of the driver, then the man in the subway train. *Odd coincidence.*

Annie broke his train of thought. "How's Joe holding up?"

"We're both pretty tired," Bohannon said into the dark. "But more than that, we're both getting really frustrated. We just seem to be pounding up against a wall. There is so little known about this darn language. It's like we're trying to pick it apart so we can go in sideways or something. It just doesn't make any sense on the face of it. This Demotic doesn't follow the patterns of other ancient languages, and even those few people who know something about it, the information they've given us just doesn't apply to the symbols on the scroll. When we take the letters that have been translated, apply them to the scroll, and use the standard methods that have been suggested to us, we come out with bubkes. Joe's tearing his hair out, and I swear Rizzo's gotten even smaller. I don't know . . . We're not getting anywhere."

Bohannon felt Annie's head nestle into his shoulder, her warm lips kiss his neck. "You know none of this has been some accident, some chance quirk of fate," she said softly. "You know there was a reason you discovered those rooms, a reason you found that scroll, a reason you are here working at the Bowery Mission instead of working on a newspaper somewhere. And if there is a reason for it, which we believe, then God will show you the way to find out what you need to find out. Right?"

Annie Bohannon had an infuriating way of speaking the truth in the midst of uncertainty, of refusing to allow her husband to occupy that place of self-pity that he once found so comforting. She was a real pain in his self-serving attitudes. And he loved her for it.

They had met in their early thirties, an actual case of love at first sight. Bohannon had been married as a teenager—his two adult sons now had families of their own—and he had specialized in messed-up relationships. Annie was still waiting for her Prince Charming. They saw each other, and after that, there was never another who had owned their hearts. Annie had blessed Tom with two more children, a warm and inviting home, a honed edge of common sense, nearly three decades of faithful intimacy, and the courage to make the most important decision of his life.

It didn't hurt that she was knockdown, drop-dead beautiful with a smile that lit up the neighborhood. It didn't hurt that she was hot, her skin was soft, and that she dressed and walked with a totally innocent sexiness that had snapped quite a few necks. For Annie, it didn't hurt that, the first time she looked at Tom, fireworks had been going off in his eyes, that he possessed that imperfect face and physique that was uniquely masculine, a nose slightly askew from some mishap, that his hair was long and curly at the back of his neck, that his quick smile and deep-blue eyes skipped her heart and gripped her stomach.

It didn't hurt that they had loved each other unflinchingly as they matured. They endured career disasters, the deaths of those they loved, and deep disappointment in each other. It didn't hurt that they loved each other unconditionally once they had "grown up," once they could promise their kids that *divorce* was a word that would never enter their world. For twenty-eight years they had stood shoulder-to-shoulder and slept side-by-side, even when they didn't see eye-to-eye. It took many years, until he had finally knocked down most of his walls, before Bohannon could actually say that this woman really was his best friend. And once in a while, he even took her advice.

"Yeah," Bohannon sighed, "I know there's a purpose. I know I'm supposed to be doing this. Knowing is okay, but I need something more than knowing. I need a key. I need to know where the switch is to flip on understanding. I need a clue in order to know where to go. And I'm lost. I don't have a clue, Joe doesn't have a clue, and Sammy doesn't have a clue. We're dead in the water. As much good as it's doing us, the French may as well have never found the Rosetta Stone.

"Aw, I might as well just get some sleep."

Bohannon tried to roll over on his right side, but Annie held him fast with her arm.

"Annie, please, I've got to get some rest if—"

"Tom," Annie interrupted, her voice carrying the hint of a question.

"What . . ."

"Tom, isn't the Rosetta Stone in the British Museum?" Annie asked.

"Yeah, everybody knows—"

"Tom, will you listen to me for a minute?" Annie interrupted again, this time sitting up on her side of the bed. Bohannon returned to his back and looked up at the dark shadow of his wife with a startled, quizzical look on his face. "The Rosetta Stone is in the British Museum, and there are three languages on it, right?"

Bohannon nodded his head at the shadow.

"And one of them is this extinct Demotic, the script that's used on that scroll, right?" Again the nodding shadow. "And you need somebody or something to help you figure out the symbols on the scroll, right?"

"Yes . . . yes . . . and yes," he said petulantly. "I know all that. What's the point?"

Annie gave Tom grace in that moment, consideration for his many days of endless work and limited sleep. She reached over gently, stroked his cheek, folded herself down and back into his body contour.

"Tom, you may already have your key," she nearly whispered to him. "And the key is not far away."

"What . . . what do you mean?" he said, turning to her.

"Richard Johnson," Annie said carefully, lovingly, tightening her grip with her left arm.

"Oh . . . oh, no," Bohannon nearly groaned. "No—no—no. I don't care. If I have to take this to my grave and it's still a secret, I don't care. No, not Johnson. Anybody but Johnson."

Annie Bohannon released his arm and rolled away. "Good night, sweetheart," Annie whispered into the darkness. "God bless you."

Sleep would likely elude him that night. This was a battle that only he could fight, that only he could determine. Tom would have to decide whether the key to the scroll was worth consulting a man he hadn't spoken with in more than a decade.

7

It truly was a beautiful building. Standing across 35th Street late Friday afternoon, waiting for the light to change, Bohannon once again gazed at the strikingly beautiful architecture of the Collector's Club. He had often stared at the building as he walked to his dentist's office, admiring the details of the late nineteenth-century brownstone that housed the club's offices. The club was one of the world's greatest resources on stamp collecting, but Bohannon's visit had nothing to do with the philatelic. He was looking for his old nemesis, Dr. Richard Johnson Sr., former chair of the Antiquities College at Columbia University, fellow of the British Museum and now—in his retirement—managing director of the Collector's Club in Manhattan.

Bohannon banged heads, and egos, with the erudite Dr. Johnson about fifteen years earlier when one of Bohannon's investigative blockbusters for the *Philadelphia Bulletin* claimed millions of dollars had been swindled from investors for phony "rare" antiquities—a scoop Bohannon remembered vividly because it had led to numerous journalism awards, some very generous expressions of thanks from some of those who had been duped, and a bitter castigation from Richard Johnson.

Standing on the far side of 35th Street, Bohannon recalled Dr. Randall Swinton, former antiquities curator of the Philadelphia Museum of Art, who had concocted a plot to pave his retirement. Shortly after aging out of the museum's leadership, Swinton approached several less-than-pure collectors with the deal of a lifetime. Over his two decades with the art museum, Swinton informed his victims, he had managed to "liberate" scores of priceless treasures from ancient civilizations. And he was willing to part with these treasures for only half of their real value, considering the circumstances of the transactions. Only one condition did Swinton place on his buyers: they could never display the items in public, or they would all end up in prison.

It was a masterly deception. During his many trips to the Near and Far

East, Africa, and the Pacific Islands, Swinton had kept a weather eye for masters of forgery, those indigenous and entrepreneurial craftsmen who made a sweet living from preying on unsuspecting tourists, even on some unsuspecting museum collectors. With many of these talented tricksters, Swinton entered into what appeared to be a legitimate business arrangement. "I need the most accurate copies you can make," he would commission them. "Often these most beautiful artifacts are lent to other institutions, and I need something to sit in their place until they are returned. At times, there may be a threat to their safety and it would be wise to have the real item removed for safekeeping and replaced with an identical copy. So give me your best rendition." And the unsuspecting forgers would render for him their best work ever; after all, it would one day sit in the Philadelphia museum, representing the real thing.

Swinton was amazed at how easy it was to swindle those who were less than honest themselves. Within months, he had multiple millions in a Swiss bank account and a sprawling, seaside villa in Barbados. He was lying on a lounge chair on the patio of his island fantasy, shaded by a palm tree, eagerly feeding his slide into soddeness, when it all swiftly fell apart.

One of the beneficiaries of Swinton's largesse had too much ego, and not enough common sense, and allowed several of his rotating girlfriends to hold the little goddess he had purchased from Swinton. Unfortunately for all involved, one of the girls had been the administrative assistant for the *Bulletin*'s editor-in-chief and part of Bohannon's circle of friends at the paper. One phone call to the newsroom, and the wheels of unrelenting discovery began to turn.

It wasn't long after Bohannon's first investigative blockbuster linking Swinton to the theft of priceless treasures from the art museum that the buyers began turning state's evidence in droves. And not long after the pieces were recovered and revealed as fakes, Swinton was found on the patio of his villa, sprawled on a lounge chair, his throat sliced from ear to ear.

Buyers were relieved that they were not prosecuted and that Swinton had spent only a portion of the millions he had swindled. Eventually, restitution was ordered by the courts. And for most, the story went away.

But not for Bohannon.

He had made a mortal enemy in Dr. Richard Johnson, Swinton's colleague and friend, a man who believed passionately in his friend's innocence.

Johnson, more than Swinton, went straight for Bohannon's jugular. In a series of broadside attacks—in professional journals, letters to the editor, and in follow-up stories where other reporters were looking for colorful quotes—Johnson ridiculed Bohannon's ignorance on antiquities, questioned his motives, berated his sources, and defended Swinton.

In the time between the first article and the ultimate discovery that the items were frauds, Johnson dished out an amount of abuse equal to what he believed his friend had received. Bohannon's investigative reports on Swinton's scheme led to journalistic accolades while the vitriolic counterattacks by Johnson ultimately led to a quiet, internal investigation at the British Museum and a conversation between Dr. Johnson and the chancellor of Columbia University. Then Swinton was found, and Dr. Johnson retreated from the public eye, behind the cloak of academia. But he and Bohannon continued the battle, more intensely, outside the earshot of the rest of the world. Johnson believed Bohannon was irresponsible in his journalism and responsible for the death of his friend, in spite of Swinton's crime, and Bohannon was seething at what he believed were unfounded public attacks on his character and integrity.

After fifteen years of near quiet, Bohannon was surprised by just how much turbulence he felt at the mere thought of coming face-to-face with Richard Johnson. Bohannon tried to slow his heart rate and unclench his fists by concentrating on the tantalizing breath of early May rolling up Lexington Avenue. *Might as well get it over with,* he thought, wondering whether, when he left the building, he would walk out or get tossed out.

There was only one way to find out. And it appeared that Johnson was one of the few men in the world who might be able to help them decipher the meaning of the Demotic symbols. He had studied the Rosetta Stone almost exclusively during his many summers of service at the British Museum and had written a few scholarly pamphlets about the amazing complexities of the Demotic language.

In this country, he was their best chance at finding an answer.

Bohannon took a deep breath and walked up the marble steps of the Collector's Club. He had called ahead and made an appointment, noting the quizzical tone to the secretary's voice when she came back to the phone to acknowledge the meeting.

Bohannon's trained observation noted the military carriage of the attendant behind the desk in the foyer, and the slight bulge under his left armpit as the man reached into the small elevator and unlocked access to the top floor. "Go right up, sir. Dr. Johnson is expecting you."

"There sure must be a lot of money in stamps," Bohannon mumbled to himself as the elevator strained to the top floor. The opening doors revealed an elderly, stooped woman wearing a long black dress, her hair tightly pulled into a bun at the nape of her neck. "This way, please," she whispered. A flush of satisfaction warmed Bohannon as he walked along the elegant corridor. *Serves him right*, Bohannon thought, *that he's got an old hag for a secretary.*

Smiling inwardly, Bohannon stepped through the door the elderly woman opened and came face-to-face with a wantonly beautiful blond whose breathtaking curves had been poured into a shimmering, electric-blue dress. Before his heart could start beating again, there was a voice from his left. "Good afternoon, Mr. Bohannon."

Tearing his eyes from the heart attack in blue, Bohannon turned to see Dr. Johnson standing in the doorway to his office. "Please come in," he said, stepping aside as he waved with his left arm. That suspicious part of Bohannon's nature waited for the knife thrust under his rib cage as he passed Johnson, but the smile Johnson shared was disarming.

"Beth, no interruptions, please. I want to give Mr. Bohannon my full attention."

Surprisingly, Johnson's office reflected none of the Victorian opulence on view elsewhere in the building. There was the obligatory oak wainscoting, hardwood floor covered by an Oriental rug, and requisite bookcases. But the space was missing much of what Bohannon had expected, those obvious symbols of wealth and power. Johnson's wooden desk was rather small, and there were no massive, matching pieces. Nor was there a "wall of fame," those ubiquitous collections of degrees, awards, and photos of the famous that give so many in the corporate world the veneer of importance. No, in Johnson's office, the most prominent item was what looked like a sizable draftsman's table over which hovered a powerful lamp and a thick magnifying glass. Bins and drawers stuck out from both sides. Tiny, elaborate mechanisms for securing stamps also hovered on curved arms, waiting to be pulled into focus.

"Please be seated," Johnson gestured toward a leather chair, and instead of taking a position of dominance by sitting behind his desk, he lowered himself into a well-worn leather sofa across from Bohannon. "I must say, you are the last person I dreamed would be sitting in this office," Johnson said, his words dripping with acid as his body sank deeply into the soft cushions in the corner. "To what do I owe this . . . pleasure?" His unflinching stare burned a hole in Bohannon's brain.

Dr. Richard Johnson, educated at Oxford, trained by the British Museum, famous among scientists for his revolutionary studies on Egyptian history, was about as far from the frumpy, poorly dressed academic stereotype as you could find. Johnson was tall, lean, crowned by a thick, silvery gray mane swept back from his considerable forehead and curling around his ears and shirt collar. His suit was finely tailored and looked very expensive, as did his colorful silk tie and gleaming leather shoes. He sat across from Bohannon, appearing relaxed and at ease. But his gaze remained alert, riveted on his past adversary.

Bohannon believed that he had only one chance to make this work. So he took the leap.

"Dr. Johnson," he said, shifting forward in his chair, "I wouldn't be sitting here if I had any other option. For most of the last fifteen years I've hated your guts. To be honest, I still do. And you don't have any reason to listen to me or to listen to the request I have."

Johnson began to rise. "Well then, Mr. Bohannon—"

"But if you don't listen, you will regret it for the rest of your life."

Bohannon watched Johnson waver, halfway between sitting and standing. A red flush had risen from his neck and now engulfed his face, his eyes on fire. Resembling a cobra raising its head and spreading its crown before striking, Johnson unfolded himself to his full height, pushed back his shoulders, and glared down. Bohannon felt as if he were lunch.

"You, sir," Dr. Johnson spat at Bohannon, "you murdered my friend. Just as surely as if you slit his throat, you murdered a man I had known and revered for twenty years. You orphaned his children. You, sir, are a vicious lie-monger and truth-twister, with no regard for decent human beings . . . and I despise you. That, sir, is the only reason you have been received here. And you can die in that chair for all I care."

There was a twitch in the muscle under his left eye. Bohannon slowly elevated himself to Johnson's height, meeting the enemy face-to-face. Unconsciously, he began to size up Johnson, calculating how he was going to beat him into submission. Consciously, he engaged words as his weapon.

"You despise me? You quack . . . what an infantile fool you are." Bohannon took one step toward Johnson and was gratified by the fear that flashed across Johnson's countenance.

"You nearly destroyed me, my family, and my career defending a man who was a liar and a swindler. You engaged in the most vicious public attack I ever experienced. And once your revered *friend,* Swinton, was proven to be a liar and a cheat, you proved yourself a coward by retreating behind ivy walls without a decent apology."

Inadvertently, Bohannon took another step forward, sparking a reaction from Johnson, who stepped back. Bohannon noticed Johnson vainly sweeping his hand behind him, trying to find the telephone handset.

"I don't regret anything I wrote about Randall Swinton. I do regret that he was killed. He was your friend, and you defended him. I can understand loyalty, but I can't understand character assassination and blind defense of a liar who took advantage of everyone with whom he came in contact. He took advantage of you, too. He took advantage of your faith in him. He allowed you to stick your neck way out, even when he knew he had been exposed and had no defense. Is that the friend you're talking about?"

Bohannon felt his anger deflate.

"So, no, I don't regret anything I wrote." He took a deep breath and flexed his right hand, easing the fist. "But I do regret that so many people were hurt. I believe where we differed so passionately was in who should bear the responsibility for that pain."

Johnson, both fear and loathing now removed from his face, stood his ground, his eyes never leaving Bohannon's.

"But Randall Swinton and the feud we engaged in are not the reasons I'm here today," Bohannon continued. He turned his back on Johnson, stepped to the chair, and wearily lowered himself into its embrace. "Maybe, some other day, if you really want to continue this fight—if you still feel compelled to defend a man who abused your good faith—then we can go back and revisit that time. I did what I had to do, what I was trained to do. Swinton deserved to be caught and convicted, judged, not murdered. You? I can't judge you. Only you can judge yourself, judge your motives. But I can't judge you."

Bohannon took a deep breath. The next move was Johnson's. He could sit down, or he could pick up the phone and call the muscle with the gun at the front door.

More ashen, less confident, Johnson edged himself back to the sofa. He fell into the well-worn leather like a wet sack of sand.

Johnson folded his hands together, stared at his knuckles. "There were times I wanted to kill you, have somebody kill you." The voice was dark, a far distance from where they sat. "And there were times when I thought I could have killed Randall myself."

Surprisingly to Bohannon, he began to feel sorry for this man, publicly betrayed by a friend he had trusted.

Johnson's eyes didn't move from his knuckles. "I wanted you to be wrong. God, how I wanted you to be wrong. Randall kept assuring me these were vicious lies. Even after his bogus sales had been revealed, he was passionate about his innocence and certain of your 'collusion,' he called it, with these scalawags who were determined to swindle him and send him to jail. You were the basest of scoundrels, Mr. Bohannon, so easy to hate."

Both of them jumped when the phone rang. Bohannon was trying to coax his heart from his throat as Johnson reached for the handset. "Yes? . . . yes, Beth," Johnson said, looking across at Bohannon. "I'm fine. Yes, you may go home. Thank you . . . yes, I'll see you in the morning. Good night."

Stillness settled.

Finally, Johnson pushed himself up from the corner of the sofa to its edge. "I appreciate your courage in coming here. And I even appreciate your candor about what was, at that time, a very passionate topic for both of us. You were doing your job; I can accept that. And Randall was a crook. I can accept that, too. But he had also been a close, personal friend for many years," Johnson said, sitting back again, wearily draping one leg over the other. "He was wounded, and I was wounded for him. Once you and I collided, I was not about to back down. Pride, I'm afraid."

Once again, Johnson's twisted hands absorbed his attention.

"Still, my friendship with Randall gave me no license to butcher your reputation or, more accurately, to attempt to butcher your reputation in public. It was wrong of me to descend into the realm of such vindictive persecution. And for that, I ask your forgiveness."

Momentarily, a silence separated them, a divide neither one of them could cross. Then Bohannon finished building the bridge that Johnson had just started.

"I forgive you," Bohannon said, standing and reaching out his right hand.

Johnson rose from the sofa and firmly grasped Bohannon's hand with his. "Thank you. You have lifted a weight that I've been carrying far too long."

Knowing grimaces gave notice of each man's disappointments, their clasped hands communicating a message of their own. "Don't thank me too much," said Bohannon. "You may not be as gracious when you see what I've brought you."

Emitting a sigh, Johnson gestured for Bohannon to sit with him again.

"Well, I am certainly quite curious about the purpose of your visit, what it is that could have coerced you to come searching for me."

"First, and I know this may sound ludicrous right now, but first, I need to ask for your word of honor that you will reveal to no one what I am about to share with you. I need to have certainty in your promise to keep this information confidential. Otherwise, we should just end our conversation here."

Johnson's eyes had narrowed slightly, his face taking on a pinched look. Once again, Bohannon could see distrust in Johnson's face. He allowed the silence to hang in the air and waited for Johnson to process what had to be an unexpected request.

"You have my word, Tom. I will protect anything we say and do here today. It will be held in strictest confidence."

"Thank you," he said. "And I don't know if I'll be able to address you except as Dr. Johnson." Reaching into the inside pocket of his jacket, Bohannon pulled out the same folded sheet of paper they had shared with Sammy Rizzo and handed it to the scholar. "Dr. Johnson, do you know what this is?"

Warily, Johnson unfolded the paper while keeping his eyes fixed on Bohannon. As he switched his attention to the sheet in front of him, Johnson rapidly skimmed the symbols on the paper. Arrested, he sat forward on the sofa and carefully examined the columns of symbols. He shot a quick, questioning glance in Bohannon's direction, then got to his feet and crossed to the drafting table, Bohannon on his heels.

Sitting on only half of a high, wooden chair, Johnson leaned into the table. With deft, trained movements, he inserted the sheet of paper into one of the holders, an adjustable, flat surface with clips to hold stamps in place, while with his other hand he switched on the powerful lamp and pulled the magnifying glass into position. For several silent minutes, Johnson poured over the columns of symbols before him. He turned the page upside down. He held it up to the light and inspected the symbols from the back of the page.

At one point, Johnson got up from his perch and, without a word, walked over to the windows looking out over 35th Street. He stood there for a few moments, gazing into the sunshine, then, as silently, returned to the table and began running his fingers up and down each row of symbols.

"You haven't brought all of it to me, have you?" he asked without turning around.

"Well, I—"

"Never mind," Johnson interrupted. "The more important question is, where did you get this?"

"For now, let me just say that it was recently found."

Johnson half turned to face Bohannon, a sly smirk on his face. "Still not ready to bet the ranch, eh? Very well, I understand. So tell me, what do you want from me?"

Momentarily stunned, Bohannon just looked at Johnson. He had expected, if they could settle their feud, that he would hand Dr. Johnson the sheet of paper and the scholar would immediately explain to him not only what the symbols in this Demotic language said, but also what the document meant, some clue to Spurgeon's fear and Klopsch's safekeeping of the scroll.

"Well, I'd like to know if you could tell us what these symbols say, what it all means."

"Us, eh?" said Johnson. "Don't worry, I won't ask yet." Twisting the chair away from the table, he fixed Bohannon in his questioning glare. "Do you know what this is?"

Bohannon nodded. "To an extent. We're pretty sure the language is Demotic. Beyond that, we're lost."

Johnson rocked back and forth in the chair. "Not only is it Demotic, but even this portion, which is clearly part of some larger document, even this portion would be one of the largest single discoveries of Demotic writing outside the Rosetta Stone. This is historic, remarkable, an astonishing discovery.

"At the same time, I need to disappoint you," he said somberly. "I can't promise you that we will ever know what these symbols mean. Demotic is extinct as a language and almost impossible to decipher. I'm intrigued, but I'm not very hopeful. Scholars have been struggling to understand and decipher Demotic for centuries. It's one of the biggest unsolved puzzles in linguistics. Do you know that, depending on the reason for writing, the same Demotic symbols would have different meanings? Did you know that the pattern of inscribing Demotic varied from place to place? That it was essentially a spoken language? A scribe would try to express the language in symbols only when it was absolutely necessary. So as the speech patterns of Egypt changed over a thousand years, the written language of Demotic also changed. It is a remarkably complex problem; therefore one which has enthralled and frustrated scholars. And today, you walk into my office with what may be one of the largest single examples of Demotic that has ever been discovered . . . ever!"

Johnson tilted his head to the right with a wry, twisted smile on his face. "And all you would like is for me to tell you what it means? Well, I am flattered by your faith in me, but I must disappoint once again. Your faith, I fear, is misguided. I don't know if there is a man living who will ever understand what is written here or in the other parts of this document which must also exist.

"Why don't you tell me where, how you discovered this?" Johnson asked, reaching his hand out and resting it on Bohannon's shoulder. "Perhaps it will help us. And I say *us* because, wherever this is going, I'll be going with you."

Tom looked at Dr. Johnson and knew he had to make a decision: either trust this man with all the information and enlist his help, or walk out of the Collector's Club and hope to find another way.

"Let's sit down," Bohannon said.

―᠆᠆᠆᠆᠆᠆

No one had ever dared to call him Dick. It would be like saying to the Pope, "Yo, pal." So incongruous as to be impossible. No, as an adult, he was always Dr. Richard Johnson. Only his most intimate collaborators, those who had known and worked with him for years, felt the freedom to call him "Doc."

Comparing the symbols that Bohannon had left with him to those on a computer printout he generated, Johnson found himself daydreaming about the so-called treasure hunts he would undertake as a boy or the absurdly serious "research" he would enslave himself to as an undergrad. Times when young Richie Johnson would see himself as more adult than his maturity should allow. Like everyone else, though, Johnson possessed that unique place in his consciousness where his growing and his aging had stopped. Something about the human condition made most people oblivious when they stood in front of a mirror. Regardless of the receding hairline, expanding waistline, preponderance of wrinkle lines, and the abduction of color from the hair, they retained an unsubstantiated self-image that they were the same as they had been twenty, thirty, or forty years ago. So it was that the young Richie Johnson struggled into the night, trying to understand those symbols.

As Bohannon had finished the story of the scroll's discovery and Sammy Rizzo's identification of the Demotic language, Johnson's mind had tripped back to Saturday afternoon serials in the movie theaters and his first self-absorbed studies of hieroglyphs. Once again, that unmistakable excitement enveloped his being, that giddy expectation of another treasure hunt. As the adrenalin pumped through his system, he was transformed and transported to his youth.

Johnson felt like a sorcerer about to open a magic box. "Are you sure you want to know what's in here?" he asked Bohannon.

In the ensuing pause, Johnson could discern wheels turning. "Absolutely," Bohannon affirmed.

"Okay, I'll start working on this part right away, but I will need to see the whole scroll as soon as possible. I don't know what's going on here, but my instincts are telling me that I'll have to consider the entire document to begin to understand it. I'll contact you as soon as I think I've got something worthwhile to share," Johnson said, turning the page over and over again in his hands. He turned and began walking back to the table. "Come back tomorrow, if you can."

Bohannon must have left, but the young man in Richard Johnson's brain never noticed. His world was now wrapped up in these columns of beautifully sculpted images. He had been a scholar almost all of his life, chasing the unknown or the inscrutable. He was blessed with an intelligence that immediately brought him both notoriety and social isolation, an exchange with which Johnson was more than satisfied. Permitted, no, encouraged, to indulge his passion, Johnson soon gained a level of fame among the scientific community that was rare and religiously guarded. Johnson had lived in the rarefied neighborhood at the pinnacle of academia for so long that many with less talent and more desire held him in more-than-human but less-than-divine reverence. When the eyes of his mind considered himself, Johnson saw only the twenty-eight-year-old Richie, humbly testing the limits of his understanding.

But for all his intellectual power and prowess, Dr. Johnson often discovered that he was simply a frustrated sixty-eight-year-old man with an unfulfilled pursuit. In addition to secrets and treasures, Johnson had also spent his life in pursuit of meaning and purpose. Sadly, despite his earnest attempts, Johnson found no peace in atheism, Eastern mysticism, or New Age mumbo-jumbo. With all his knowledge, he was still a man seeking truth.

The thought exploded into his mind so dramatically Johnson almost fell off his chair at the drafting table.

"Wait a minute," he said out loud. "Wait a minute!"

Johnson stepped quickly to the coat rack behind the door, fetched his cell phone from the inside pocket of his suit coat, and punched in the numbers Bohannon had given him. Wait . . . Wait . . . Wait . . . "Tom, listen, this is Dr.

Johnson. Sorry to disturb you, but these groupings of symbols, how many are there? Seven? Seven groupings and each grouping has three vertical columns of symbols, correct? And are all the columns the same length? Good. Thank you, that helps me quite a bit. No . . . no . . . there's nothing to report this quickly. An idea just popped into my head, and I wanted to see if it was worth pursuing. Thank you. I'll see you tomorrow? Good. Certainly, 1:00 PM would be fine. Yes, good night, Tom."

Closing the phone and stuffing it in his pocket, Johnson looked at the sheet of paper now taped to the table in front of him. "Twenty-one columns in seven groupings, eh? Well," Johnson announced to the empty room, a wide smile splitting his face, "you certainly are very clever, aren't you?" Looking again at the sheet of paper, he continued speaking into the empty room. "But there is one thing I now have in my favor, don't I? This is a message, isn't it? And messages are meant to be read and understood. So now I know that there's a way in . . . even into this crazy language. There's a way in," he said, sitting back down at the table and speaking directly to the images. "Come on, you know the magic words . . . *Open sesame . . .*" he said with mock seriousness. "Come on, open, says me. Open says me. Open, show me your secrets."

Sometime early Saturday morning, he woke up, his head, arms, and shoulders resting on the drafting table, the rest of him perched in the chair. He tried to stretch and sit up in the chair—and regretted every attempted movement. *Oh heavens, Dick,* Johnson said to his achingly stiff body and the pain that permeated the top half of his torso, *we just can't do this anymore.*

8

By the time Bohannon and Joe Rodriguez arrived that afternoon, Johnson was back at the drafting table, showered and shaved, the aches of the morning massaged out of his joints, meticulously appointed in the finest English pinstripe. Introductions out of the way, Johnson jumped right to the point.

"You've brought the document with you?" he asked.

Bohannon and Rodriguez shot surprised looks at each other. "Well, no," said Bohannon. "We were concerned about bringing it out. It's in a safe place right now, and we didn't want to move it."

His ire piqued, Johnson narrowed his eyes in an accusation.

"But we did bring a copy of the entire scroll," Bohannon said quickly. "And a copy of the letter that was with the scroll."

These amateurs will likely drive me to drink, but for the moment, they are correct about safekeeping. "Here," Johnson said aloud, stepping to the drafting table, "let's see what you have brought me."

Rodriguez moved closer to the table and rolled out what looked like half a piece of poster paper. On it were displayed the seven groups of Demotic symbols. "These first two groupings are what we brought you yesterday, but this is the whole thing. I know there is always something lost in making copies, but I have a colleague at the library who is knowledgeable about languages and also meticulous in detail. He spent many hours transcribing what we found on the scroll. Even though these images are larger than the symbols found on the scroll, he believes this rendering is quite accurate."

Rodriguez turned to look at Johnson. "And here's a printed copy of the letter that Spurgeon wrote to Klopsch. Now you know everything that we know."

"Except," Johnson said archly, "who this colleague is."

Bohannon cut in. "Dr. Johnson, you seemed quite excited on the phone last night, about the twenty-one columns in seven groupings, like it triggered something in your memory. What does the seven mean to you?"

Johnson stretched his body, ran his two hands through the fullness of his silver hair, then clasped his fingers at the back of his head. He leaned back against the table.

"Gentlemen, Demotic, in all its bizarre nature, is a language that is always written on the horizontal axis, right to left. There is no known example of Demotic written on a vertical axis. So, in its uniqueness, this is unique. On the Rosetta Stone, there were several recurring constructions of Demotic symbols that indicated specific connections, or phrases, to the language. None of those phrases are in evidence on the paper you left with me yesterday, and I doubt we will find any of them now that I have the entire scroll.

"Other than Chinese and other Asian languages, no other language is written vertically, certainly not a Middle Eastern language. So whoever constructed this document constructed it vertically for a purpose.

"And," said Johnson, pointing to the drafting table, "those seven groups of columns were also constructed for a purpose. Three vertical lines of symbols in seven columns, there's a reason for it. That's why I'm convinced this is a message that was meant to be read and understood. The recipient would have known how to access the message, despite the language used. So we know there must be a way in, a way to understand what the message contains.

"Now, seven is the number of completeness. There are seven days of creation, seven colors in the rainbow, seven virtues, seven deadly sins, and seven basic notes in the Western music scale. In the Hebrew tradition and in the Bible, there were seven covenants between God and man, seven years of abundance followed by seven years of famine, and the Menorah, the Jewish candlestick used in the temple, holds seven candles. And, every seven years, every cell within our bodies is replaced and renewed."

"Yeah," said Rodriguez, "and there are seven holes in every man's head."

Trying hard not to laugh, Bohannon added, "Yeah, and Snow White had seven dwarfs. She really had her hands full with those clowns."

The middle finger of Johnson's right hand was tapping a staccato beat on the end of the table, his chin pushed up into a scowl.

"Is this humorous to you?" Johnson asked dryly. "Perhaps we should adjourn so you can watch some silly TV sitcoms?"

"Oh, come on, Dr. Johnson," Rodriguez said with an edge. "No harm, no foul, right? Don't stop now."

"All right. Three is just as symbolically important as seven. Three is the number of trilogy—body, mind, and spirit; or father-mother-child; or past-present-future. It is also the number of the three dimensions, or for the process of thought: the thinker, the thought, and the thing. It is also the number for the Trinity of Father, Son, and Holy Spirit. The fact that these symbols are constructed in these vertical rows of three and seven must be significant, otherwise there's no purpose for constructing the scroll in this manner. So, here's what I'm thinking at the moment."

Johnson returned to the drafting table, standing to the side and using his finger as a pointer. "You see this symbol," he said to Bohannon and Rodriguez, pointing to a symbol that looked like a cane or a small hockey stick on a diagonal pitch. "This is one of the seven symbols the University of Chicago has determined in its Dictionary of Demotic that are universally the same in all Demotic writing. That was one of the keys we received from the Rosetta Stone. Even though the written Demotic language was so very unpredictable, there were at least seven symbols, seven we have been able to identify, that are consistent and never change. And that gives us a point at which to start. See, this is another, this another, this another," Johnson said as he pointed to different symbols.

"The odd thing about this document is that even those symbols that we have been able to identify as constants are not used in the same manner as they are used in other Demotic documents I've seen, or on the Rosetta Stone. This symbol, for instance," he said, pointing again to the hockey stick. "This symbol is *F* and it means at its most basic *to fly*. And this symbol over here, the three vertical lines, that is *Y* and it means *sea*. In the Egyptian form of Demotic on the Rosetta Stone, fly is always followed by the sea . . . always. It is a phrase construction that is mostly translated as *the light bearer* or *the bringer of good news*. On these sheets, *F*, to fly, is never followed by the symbol for sea. The symbol for fly is all over these pages, but the symbol for sea never completes it, not once."

Johnson turned from the table to the two men, who were his rapt students. "So, gentlemen, what does this one piece of evidence tell you?"

Silence sat in the room like a third visitor, one that Johnson was quite comfortable allowing to remain. Suddenly, Rodriguez looked up from his hands.

"It means the language is not the message," Rodriguez said confidently. "It means the structure is the message."

Johnson, always a bit too pompous for his own good, was astonished at the exact logic and quick wit exhibited by this tall, Hispanic librarian.

"Well, Mr. Rodriguez," Johnson said with true respect in his voice, "very impressive indeed. You are absolutely correct, sir. This message is not written in Demotic, it is written in a symbolic cipher using Demotic. It may require some knowledge of Demotic to unravel its truth, but our problem is not in the translation of Demotic . . . it is in the translation of this cipher. Gentlemen, I think it's fair to say we're closer to home."

"All right!" Bohannon whooped, punching his brother-in-law on the shoulder, "I knew you would come in handy one day."

"Closer to home," said Johnson warily, "but still a long way to go. Whoever crafted this message was diabolically clever. If someone else, someone without a grounding in Demotic, had found this scroll, they could have spent fruitless months trying to translate these symbols. This use of Demotic is not only a dead-end rabbit trail," he said triumphantly, "but it is also a security device, a firewall, if you will. The author used Demotic not to pass along information but to hide information. We may have passed the first portal, but my instinct tells me there are more portals to come."

With a start, Johnson spun on his heel and took one long step to stand hovering over the two men who, up to that point, had been sitting comfortably in the leather chairs, enjoying Johnson's performance. "Wait a minute . . . wait a minute . . . Tom, where's the copy of that letter that accompanied the scroll?"

Bohannon reached into the soft-sided, black computer bag he had brought along and pulled out a manila folder. He extracted a sheet of paper and handed it to Johnson.

Expectation arm-wrestled with uncertainty as Johnson read the letter aloud. "You may place your absolute trust and confidence in Dr. Schwartzman of Trinity, a true friend of Christ and an able ally for your vital pursuit. Wire me with any revelations. May our Lord and Saviour hold you in His most faithful hands. Charles."

"It appears our English friend Dr. Spurgeon was also a man of portals and security devices," Johnson said. "An able ally for your vital pursuit, eh? Spurgeon was telling Klopsch where to turn, where to get the information he needed to break the code of the scroll. He knew Klopsch didn't understand Demotic, nobody did. But Spurgeon was sending Klopsch to someone who must have had some ability to understand the construction, the vertical columns and the meaning of the three and the seven. Dr. Schwartzman of Trinity—who is this person? That is our next task, who is this Schwartzman and what can he tell us, even when he's likely been dead for more than a hundred years?"

9

An overdue personnel evaluation rested on his cluttered desk, but this morning—more than any other Monday—Bohannon's mind wandered at every opportunity. His head rested in his hands, his elbows propped against the desktop, his eyes closed. The challenges of running a residential recovery program for homeless and addicted men—a facility that provided over a quarter-million meals each year to the hungry of New York City—were far from his conscious mind.

What in the world am I doing? Tom wouldn't admit it to Annie, but his near-death experience on Lafayette Street planted some serious questions in his mind. What was this scroll they'd found in Klopsch's office? What did it mean? Why was Spurgeon so concerned for Klopsch's safety? And—the question that had been eating at him for days—was it mere coincidence that he was confronted by two guys wearing the same amulet, one of whom nearly killed him with a runaway truck? If not, did it have any connection to their recent discovery?

But each time his thoughts wandered over these questions, something even more profound lurked in the shadows of his mind. *What was this all about?* And more importantly, *Why me?*

He didn't want to scare Annie with his concerns. Maybe he was just imagining things. And he was leery of his own judgment. Chasing down the meaning of the scroll awakened all the adrenaline rush of Bohannon's career as an investigative reporter. He loved this kind of chase—the thrill of pursuing the unknown. He was certainly no neutral observer. So he turned to God for guidance.

Bohannon had walked away from his family's faith in his college years, decrying what he perceived as its hypocrisy but actually just wanting to serve his own rebellion. Two years before he met Annie, he ran into a guy, the father of one of his "loves," who talked to him about faith, about the truth of the Bible. For two years, Bohannon had read the Bible like an explorer with half a treasure map, absorbing the obvious, searching for the hidden. After he and

Annie married, he wasn't ready to abandon his heathen living; it was too much fun. Annie, not long out of that place herself, gave him time and walked along with him.

Many who have become Christians later in life can point to that one moment when they surrendered to the idea of a Creator and his eternal plan. Bohannon had no such epiphany. He just realized one day that he believed what he was reading—this whole, crazy, seemingly confusing story of God's love and redemption. Not much changed except that, over time, he became less heathen and more like Christ: kind, forgiving, gentle, hopeful. Certainly not perfect— he was Irish, after all—but better from the depth of his soul.

So he and Annie pursued their faith, pursued their God, while they pursued their lives. They came not only to believe in God's providence but to experience it. And to believe that there was a purpose, there was a plan, for each of them.

Needing answers, Tom Bohannon went to God and sought his plan. What Bohannon heard—that intimate sense of receiving an answer, direction—distressed and confused him even more. He had a job for which he was responsible. A family to care for. A daughter attending Fordham and tuition to pay. And each time, God kept telling Bohannon, *This is my plan for you. I have called you to this time.*

God's voice, or my voice? That was always Bohannon's tripping point. *God's direction, or my own wishful thinking . . . how will I ever know for sure? God, how can I know for sure?*

"Here's the monthly financial statement."

Bohannon nearly fell out of his chair.

Stew Manthey held the package just out of Bohannon's reach, forcing Bohannon to look up as he collected himself. Stew, his mentor and colleague for ten years, was CFO of the mission. He was also a man of wisdom and discernment. This morning, Manthey wore a look of concern along with his pale brown tie.

"Are you okay?" Manthey asked.

Tom stretched and took the packet from Manthey's hand, avoiding his eyes. "I'm fine. How did we do this month?"

"Revenue was good," said Manthey, sitting in one of the chairs that flanked Bohannon's desk. "The repairs to the street outreach truck were unexpected, but other expenses were down. So it was a good month. Marcus and the board will be happy."

"Good," said Bohannon, tossing the packet on top of an overflowing in-box. He tried to turn his attention back to the performance evaluation, but Stew wasn't moving. Reluctantly, Bohannon looked up.

"Stew?"

Manthey got out of his chair, closed the office door, then returned to his seat and faced Bohannon.

"Tom, what's going on? What's wrong? The last week or so, you just haven't been yourself. Ever since the accident, you've been withdrawn, distant. You've been out a lot, and when you are here, most of the time you're only here in body. I'm worried about you."

Stew Manthey was a few months short of retirement, his full, grizzled gray beard a testimony to his hastening transition to gentleman golfer. More than friends, more than coworkers, they had prayed together for this ministry to the homeless and addicted men God placed in their care. Like his wife, Annie, there was little Bohannon could hide from Stew Manthey. He needed to tell somebody.

Twenty minutes later, the sound of singing voices drifted up from the mission chapel below as the morning service began in earnest.

"Wow, that's quite a story," Manthey said, massaging the space between his eyebrows. "What are you going to do, now?"

Bohannon wearily shook his head. "I don't know. I wish I did, but I don't know what to do. What do you think, Stew?" Bohannon grimaced at the pleading in his voice.

"I think you've done the right thing. You've asked God what he would have you do. And it appears you've received an answer." Manthey paused, apparently weighing his response. "Now, I think you have to go tell Marcus and the board what you've found and that you'd like to pursue the meaning of the scroll. See what they say. If God wants you to pursue this, I think Marcus will give you his blessing."

Bohannon's hand was already reaching for the phone.

10

Rizzo liked his office. It contained everything he needed to fulfill his responsibilities as assistant manager of research and authentication. More importantly, he was away from the big kahunas up on the library's main office floor. His space was peaceful, comfortable . . . and private. Now it was crowded.

Rizzo was working on his computer in the curve of the horseshoe desk, while Richard Johnson was to his left, engrossed in the screen of Rizzo's second computer. Bohannon had his laptop at the small, round meeting table, and Joe was at the whiteboard. Each one had taken a different track of Dr. Schwartzman's life and was pursuing anything that might connect the man to the scroll.

Rodriguez was playing the role of quarterback—proposing relevant research portals on the Internet, cataloging each piece of information that was collected, and trying to form a picture that made sense. Thus far, they were encouraged to discover that a Dr. Elias Schwartzman was the eighth rector of Trinity Parish Episcopal Church in downtown New York City. Schwartzman, a native Belgian, had emigrated to America in 1846 after attending seminary in Great Britain. Following five years in the Boston diocesan office, Schwartzman secured a coveted post as assistant rector at Trinity Parish, a haven for the rich and powerful tycoons of America's emerging industrial colossus.

From the limited accounts available, Schwartzman appeared to be a competent parish administrator and an effective preacher whenever he was called upon to step in for the rector, Dr. Warren Dix. Schwartzman also appeared to be quite adept in social and political graces, gradually establishing for himself a high level of visibility and significance in the social life of Manhattan's nouveaux riches. But Schwartzman was certainly no scholar or linguist—so how did he fit into Spurgeon's directions to Klopsch?

"Hey, here's something that tightens the connection," said Rizzo. "Trinity has a history of ministry to the poor and disadvantaged. It began a ministry to African Americans, both slaves and free, in 1705. Can you imagine that? But here's what looks interesting. Back in 1857, in response to the economic panic of that year, Trinity started an outreach center on the Bowery to provide food for needy families when unemployment reached almost forty thousand. Then in 1879, Trinity set up a Mission House to oversee its growing list of social programs. It appears Dr. Schwartzman received a lot of help from Dr. Klopsch in getting the Mission House started. So at least we've confirmed that they knew each other."

Bohannon raised his head from the laptop. "But why would Spurgeon direct Klopsch to Schwartzman?" he asked. "If Klopsch already knew Schwartzman, why would he need Spurgeon's urging?"

"Perhaps Schwartzman possessed knowledge that Klopsch didn't, but which would be critical in deciphering the scroll," offered Johnson, his eyes not leaving the computer screen in front of him.

"Schwartzman sure knew a lot of people," Rizzo joined in, reaching his arms behind his head and stretching out the kinks. "I don't know how he could have time to do any work at Trinity Church . . . hobnobbing with the Astors and the Roosevelts; spending spring in Paris with J. Pierpont Morgan, February and March in Florida with the Audubons; accompanying Edward Elgar on his American tour in 1866. Looks like he spent more time on the road than in the rectory. I wonder—"

Rizzo never got a chance to finish the sentence, or to lower his arms. Without a word, Dr. Johnson launched himself from his chair and, in one fluid move, grabbed Rizzo's arms, spun him and his chair away from his computer, and planted himself in front of the screen. "Edward Elgar? Where? Come on, Mr. Rizzo, make it clear . . . you found a connection between Edward Elgar and Schwartzman?"

The silence of shock circled the room. Rizzo, now in the middle of the room, pushed himself to the edge of his chair, his hands squeezing its arms.

"Doc, I only want to say this once." Rizzo's stomach was tumbling like the inside of a clothes dryer and fury lurked behind his lips. "I may be the size of a child, but I will not be treated as a child or disrespected just because of my size. This is a challenge I've faced throughout my life, and a challenge I've never shirked. I have fought and scraped for the respect I deserve, and I have not given an inch. I am not about to accept such treatment from anyone, certainly not from another academic, who should know better, and certainly not from you, not in this circumstance, where I am carrying an equal weight and responsibility in deciphering this riddle. I assure you, sir . . . treat me with such disrespect once more, and I will prove to you just how well I can defend all that I have accomplished."

Rizzo wasn't sure how he was going to defend himself, but Johnson had reopened an old wound, and he was tired of bleeding in silence.

"Sammy, my deepest apologies," said Johnson, seemingly willing to settle for form rather than substance. Then to Rizzo's relief, he added, "Really, that was a stupid and thoughtless thing to do. Please, forgive me for being so rude. I deeply regret it. You, sir, certainly have my respect. And I ask for your forgiveness."

Rizzo felt outrage wash away in the cooling shower of apology. Bohannon and Rodriguez both cast a furtive glance in his direction.

"Yeah, yeah. Just as I thought," Rizzo growled, leaning closer in Johnson's direction. "You've heard about my black belt and ruthlessness in battle. Well, good. Fear is an effective motivator. So," he said, pushing himself back to his computer, "out of my way. You're not the only one who knows something about Edward Elgar."

Johnson barely escaped Rizzo's speeding chair.

"You think Elgar has something to do with this, eh?" Rizzo asked.

"Well, tell me what you know of Elgar, and I'll tell you what I'm thinking."

"I already know what you're thinking," said Rizzo, his fingers flying over the keyboard. "You're thinking of the Dorabella Cipher."

Johnson cracked a smile, took two steps behind Rizzo's chair, and gently laid his hand on his collaborator's shoulder. "Yes, Mr. Rizzo, sir, yes, I am thinking of the cipher. I will never underestimate you again. But you would be wise to not underestimate this old man, either." Slowly, Johnson's hand moved from Rizzo's shoulder to a pinching position between Rizzo's Adam's apple and the base of his neck. "You should know that I've studied the ancient art of Xiang Shen, or Silent Death, while I lived in China."

"Okay, okay, I surrender," Rizzo said, swatting away Johnson's hand. "We can have our Cage-of-Death match later. But for now, look at this."

On the screen was a picture of two men, both mustached and wearing straw skimmers and high, starched collars. They were facing each other while sitting on a bench, but had turned their faces to the camera. In the distance was the Golden Gate Bridge. A caption to the side of the photo read, *Reclusive composer Edward Elgar was rarely seen in public, even during his infrequent concert tours. This photo, with his friend and traveling companion, Pastor Elias Schwartzman of Trinity Parish in New York City, is one of the very few photos showing Elgar anywhere other than his study in Wolverhampton, England.*

"Elgar and Schwartzman," Johnson said, a trace of awe in his voice. "This is precious. I'm gaining more respect for Charles Spurgeon with every passing minute."

"Excuse us," said Bohannon impatiently, "but what in the world are you guys talking about?"

Rizzo turned in his chair and looked at Johnson. "Dr. Johnson, would you like the honors?"

"No, Mr. Rizzo, no. I believe you have earned the privilege this time."

In tandem and in triumph, they turned to their colleagues on the other side of the room.

"Edward Elgar was one of the most original and inventive composers of the nineteenth century," Rizzo began. "His compositions were intricately inter-twined, actually more like arithmetic formulas than musical compositions. Elgar was a self-taught musician, and in the early stages of his career, his music was not created for the purpose of being commercially or critically popular. Elgar composed music more like Einstein pursued relativity or Pasteur pursued microbes—more scientist than artist, more theoretical technician than seeker of the sublime. He accepted a job as bandmaster in a lunatic asylum for the express purpose of being able to compose out of the public eye. Fame came later, mostly on the popularity of his *Pomp and Circumstances Marches*."

Rizzo caught the looks on the others' faces. He was comfortable sharing his knowledge, grateful for their silently expressed respect. What he wanted was to know more of what they knew.

"While, at first, his audience was limited, it was passionately loyal. Elgar aficionados were almost a cult, the earliest 'Dead Heads,'" said Rizzo. "Such commitment and loyalty, not surprisingly, fostered close connection in the Elgar community. Not only did his followers communicate with each other, they frequently corresponded directly with Elgar himself. Elgar was likely a more prolific letter-writer than he was a composer. And it is one of those letters that has become the most interesting legacy of Elgar to this day."

After a long drink from his stainless steel water bottle, Rizzo continued his story for his increasingly attentive audience.

"Elgar was married in 1889 to Alice Roberts, a former pupil and writer—"

"Mr. Rizzo," said Johnson with a sense of aplomb, "I am quite taken by your grasp of the facts in this matter. Well done!"

"You have my humble thanks, Dr. Johnson. I am only trying to be precise.

"Now, where was I?" asked Rizzo. "Oh, yes . . . one of Alice Elgar's closest friends was Mary Baker, who married the Reverend Alfred Penny, a widower and rector of St. Peter's Church in Wolverhampton. That winter, just before Christmas, the Elgars visited the new Mrs. Penny and her family, and the composer was introduced to the Reverend Penny's twenty-two-year-old daughter, Dora. Those two struck a lasting friendship, perhaps because of their mutual mania about English football. The friendship lasted over twenty years, but its most remarkable moment occurred in 1897. Here," said Rizzo, turning to the computer screen, "let me show you what I'm talking about.

"Elgar's fascination with mathematics led him to experiment with more than just music," Rizzo said as he surfed the Web, the others gathering at his back in the apex of the horseshoe. "One of his greatest fascinations was with mathematical codes, riddles, puzzles, and ciphers. He was quite an amateur cryptologist. And this, my friends, is the birthday gift he sent to Miss Dora Penny on July 14, 1897 . . . the Dorabella Cipher . . . a code that no one has ever been able to break. It remains as much of a mystery today as the day in 1897 when Elgar first scratched out its elements."

Before them on the screen was an intriguing series of semicircles assembled in clusters of varying positions, quantities, and locations. It looked like a series of the letter *c*, or little half-moons, compiled into differing arrangements. Clusters of the same symbol were in groupings of one, two, and three symbols, oriented in one of eight directions, along three horizontal lines. That was it. Bohannon looked at the series of clusters, at the little symbols, and figured Rizzo must have made a mistake.

"This is a code that no one has been able to break?" Bohannon asked. "You've got to be kidding. This is so simple. What could be the problem?"

"The problem," said Dr. Johnson, "is in its simplicity. Where do you start? What can you compare it to? It's not like the codes that were used in World War II, where letters were scrambled in random series, sometimes with some letters designated as triggers that would change the pattern. In those kind of codes, all that was required was deciphering the key, and then the rest of the pattern would fall in line. Time, patience, a natural proclivity to random thinking, and usually those codes broke down.

"But the Dorabella is treacherous," said Johnson. "It isn't what it seems to be. The cipher consists of eighty-seven characters, or groupings, but it appears to be constructed of an alphabet of twenty-four letters. The groupings are aligned in one of eight directions, but the alignment appears to be random and ambiguous. And there is a small dot following the fifth character on the third line, but no one knows why. Even Dora Penny was at a loss. While speaking with Elgar about the cipher, the composer told her, 'I thought that you, of all people, would guess it.'

"Well, Dora Penny died in 1964. She may have been the only living person outside Elgar with the key, but she never deciphered the code. Elgar died in 1934 and never revealed the key. This code has been in existence for over a hundred years. It has been relentlessly pursued by the best cryptographers of each generation. It has been subject to countless computer scans and analysis. It has been assumed to be alphabetical, numerical, geometric, and algebraic. Researchers have applied the Chart of Elements of physics, the DNA formula, Einstein's Theory of Relativity, even the monetary system of world currencies, anything they could think of that has a system or sequence, and no one has yet come up with a solution to this cipher."

Johnson turned from the computer screen, stepped behind Bohannon and Rodriguez, and leaned into the drafting table, studying the copy of the scroll's symbols. "But I believe that Spurgeon sent Klopsch to Schwartzman because Spurgeon knew that Schwartzman possessed the key to the cipher of the scroll."

"How can you be sure?" Bohannon asked with some frustration.

The light snapped on in Rizzo's head so unexpectedly he jolted.

"Because Spurgeon had cracked the code!" Rizzo exulted. "Spurgeon was fearful, remember. From his message, it appears he believed his life was in danger and that Klopsch's life could also be in danger. He wouldn't have sent the decoded message to Klopsch; that would have been too risky. But he would have sent the key. Schwartzman must have had the key to the Demotic symbols."

"Well, okay, Sammy, say all of that is true," said Rodriguez. "Where does it get us in deciphering the scroll? We don't have Elgar, we don't have Schwartzman, and we certainly don't have Spurgeon or Klopsch. How is this going to help?"

The light went out. They were all looking at Rizzo as if he could come up with the magic answer. "Don't look at me," he said, settling back into his chair. "At least I came up with something. You guys got zilch."

Rizzo could feel the spirit draining from the room. It was Bohannon, the hardheaded Irishman who had adopted this adventure as one of his offspring, who grabbed it by the coattails and refused to let it go.

"Okay, we've hit a hurdle, but we're not done yet," Bohannon said to the others. "There are at least two different places we can look for some insight, either into Elgar and his codes or into what Spurgeon shared with Klopsch. I'm going back to the mission and look through every drawer and every scrap of paper in Klopsch's office, but this time for anything that may even look like a code or a key or something, anything that would have to do with Schwartzman or Elgar. Dr. Johnson, how about if you go down to Trinity Parish? I think you might have the best chance of getting the rector to allow us access to the church archives. See what you can discover about Schwartzman, about his relationship with Elgar, and particularly about any contact or correspondence with Spurgeon or Klopsch. We know there is a connection here. We've just got to find it. Come on," said Bohannon, grabbing hold of Joe's shoulder, "let's not give up now. Especially now that we're getting closer."

Rizzo had a momentary vision of a football locker room, players pounding their helmets against the metal lockers.

"Yo, Bo . . . what were you in your youth, a salesman?" Rizzo asked. "Sounds like you want us to go out and win one for the Gipper. And I don't have the foggiest who this Gipper guy was."

"Hey . . . Sammy," snapped Rodriguez, standing up to his full height. "What's wrong with you? Can't you ever take anything seriously?"

Rizzo planted his best snarl on his face as Rodriguez turned to Bohannon. "You're right, Tom, this is no time to back off," said Rodriguez. "I'll go to the mission with you; we'll get through the documents a lot quicker if two of us are working on it."

Rodriguez towered over Rizzo and his chair. "Well, Sammy, what do you want to do? Stay here and keep working the Internet?"

"Actually, I'd rather go to the movies," he said, ducking under Rodriguez's arm and dropping to the floor. "The new Bourne is out, and it's a doozy." Rizzo stepped to the door, then turned around. "But I'd better go along to take care of you two. At this point, I think we're more likely to find something valuable either in Klopsch's records or at Trinity Parish. I agree with Tom, Doc is the man to deal with the rector of that church. And I'm dying to get a look at that scroll."

Rizzo stared as the others failed to move. He felt like a leader with no followers. "So . . . are we leaving?"

11

Rodriguez had the scroll on the table, this time pouring over it with a powerful magnifying glass. Rizzo stood on a chair at his side, while Bohannon slowly sifted through every folder in the filing cabinets.

"Hey," said Rodriguez, continuing his scan, "this language is really wacky. One symbol looks like a mouse, another looks like a scorpion. Some letters look like they stand apart by themselves; others are linked together in strips. And all of them have little sweeps or flourishes at the end like an artist might have been playing mind games. I don't see any kind of pattern here, except that it's all weird. Like this circle here at the bottom of the left column . . . there are no other circles on the scroll. But here's this circle at the bottom of the first column."

"Bottom of the last column," corrected Rizzo. "Remember, Demotic is written right to left, so the left-hand column is the last column. So the circle would be the last thing written."

"What?" said Bohannon, startled out of his search of the files. "What did you just say, the last thing written? Could it be . . . ?

All three at once blurted the same idea. "A signature!"

In less than a heartbeat, they were huddled over the scroll. But Bohannon and Rizzo were at a disadvantage. Rodriguez had the magnifying glass.

"I really hadn't paid any attention to this before," he said, moving the glass up and down, trying to get the clearest view. "It's a circle, but there's something inside the circle, something written or drawn. Get me a piece of paper, will you?"

Rodriguez brought the overhead light down even closer to the scroll and pulled a chair over to the table. Taking the piece of paper and grabbing a pencil, he hovered unmoving like a predator waiting to strike, only inches from the mysterious circle. Slowly, his hand began to move—first a line, then a "v" on its side, intersecting the line. Again he hovered. "This one is tougher to see." Another line at the other side of the circle, then another, smaller "v" attached to the top of the line, looking like a pennant.

"That's it," said Rodriguez, "that's what is inside this little circle."

"So what's it supposed to be?" Bohannon asked of no one in particular. "Those characters don't look anything like the Demotic characters on the scroll. There's no comparison. If it's a signature, if the guy who wrote this message was signing his name, then why didn't he sign it in Demotic? Why go to all this trouble to create this scroll in a dead language and then sign it in something else?"

"Because it's a hallmark," said a voice from behind them. "It's the writer's mark, his seal." Richard Johnson stood in the doorway with his keys in his hand. "Identify the seal, and you will identify the author."

Rizzo snatched up the sheet of paper with the hallmark symbols and jogged over to the computer. "Let's go baby," he said, powering up the computer. "Come on, let's hunt down this shy author."

As Rizzo and Rodriguez peered into the computer screen, Bohannon watched Johnson fall into the nearest chair. "Dr. Johnson, Doc, what happened to you? Are you okay?"

Slowly, as if he were sleepwalking, Johnson turned his attention to Bohannon, a placid resolve on his face, a fearful wildness in his eyes. "Why, why do you ask?" he said from some distance Bohannon couldn't reach.

"You look like you're about to collapse. Doc, what happened?"

Johnson's expression gradually faded from ambivalence to a quizzical uncertainty. "Have you ever seen something but then wondered if that was actually what you saw?" Johnson paused. "I was taking the train back from Trinity, waiting at Rector Street for the 1-and-9 . . . leaning up against a pole near the front of the platform . . . lost in thought about what I just learned from the rector at Trinity. The train was coming into the station, and I looked to my left, you know, to see which train it was. I must have hooked my arm around the pole at the same time, I guess. I'm not sure . . ."

Johnson fumbled through the story, and Bohannon's mind sorted out the pieces. As Johnson had turned to identify the number of the incoming train, there was a commotion behind him. To his right, two voices exclaimed. Reflexively, Johnson had pressed closer to the pole and quickly pivoted himself to the right. A rushing body brushed past his, a hand glancing off the edge of his right shoulder. The body—it was a man, in workman's clothes—flashed past. The man appeared to stumble, twisting and turning toward Johnson, his hands outstretched, as he fell in front of the oncoming train. Screams, the screech of brakes, and the smell of oil burning against hot metal filled the platform.

"It all happened so fast. It was terrible. I can still see it and still hear it, the thud and the screeching of metal-on-metal brakes at the same time. It looked as if, at the last moment, he changed his mind and was trying to save himself. And I'm wondering, could I have gotten my arm out in time, somehow, to hold him back? Was there something I could have done?"

A sadness as blank as snow in fog covered Johnson's countenance. "I could have saved him . . . I should have saved him."

Bohannon squatted down in front of Johnson's chair, coming eye-to-eye with the doctor, putting his arm on Johnson's shoulder. "Doc, listen to me, look at me. This was not your fault. It's not your fault this man took his own life. He was obviously determined. Even if he had a doubt at the end, he was the one who sent himself running across that platform. There was a split second of time; no one could have reacted fast enough to save that guy, not you, not a professional athlete. Come on, don't beat yourself up with guilt. Sadness at a man's meaningless death? Sure. Shock at being so close to death? Yeah, I know about that. But guilt? No, Doc, that's not yours to carry. The guilt was carried by that man as he threw himself in front of that train. It was his sin, not yours."

Johnson's eyes softened with gratitude and relief.

"You're right . . . You're right, Tom. You know, I've got to admit that I have never believed in sin. Foolish idea. We're just here, doing our best. Sure, there's right and wrong. But sin? In order to have sin, there has to be a God to sin against. Foolish idea. There's just no proof," said Johnson, turning to include Rizzo and Rodriguez. "But today, I saw sin. I saw sin flash behind me. I saw sin as a man threw away his life in front of a train. He had no right to do that. Who did he leave behind? Who will be grieving for him tonight? That's wrong; that is sin.

"And I just can't get that last image out of my mind," said Johnson. "The man's face, looking at me, his eyes wide, his hands outstretched. He was closer to me than you are. I could hear his breath escape. And as the train flashed past, that necklace, a cross of some kind, with a lightning bolt going through it, hanging motionless in the air, then gone, snapped away with a crushing force."

Bohannon felt as if his face, his head, his body was being sucked right into Johnson's eyes, into his mouth, into his brain. He was losing contact with the present.

"Wha . . . what did you just say?"

As Bohannon finished his tale of the runaway truck and the two men with the odd-looking crosses around their necks, a heavy stillness entered the room. The four of them sat around the table cluttered with forgotten work. Now they knew they were hunted. Bohannon feared Johnson was close to shock. Having someone try to kill him could do that. There were predators out there, a cabal of killers who obviously were determined to protect the scroll's secret, whatever it was.

"Any luck at Trinity?" Bohannon spoke the words softly, gently, but they broke explosively into the silence of men considering their own mortality.

"The rector was helpful," Johnson responded hesitantly, "more than accommodating, really." Gradually, the color came back into his cheeks as he warmed, physically and emotionally. "We had a wonderful discussion about the early history of New Amsterdam. But alas, no significant light was shed on Elias Schwartzman. At least not information we need, even though we searched the church archives. Plenty of documents have not been archived, so there may still be vital information available from the church, but that would be a formidable project. One I thought best to put in abeyance until we exhaust every other avenue."

"Speaking of archives," Rizzo chirped from in front of the computer screen, "I've uncovered a Web site that will search hallmarks. Just trying to draw . . . hmm . . . got to get this right. Trying to draw the symbols inside the circle. Okay, looks good. Let's go fishin'."

The hard drive jumped into motion, whirring and clicking as it raced around the world of cyberspace, looking for a match to the interesting symbol. Rizzo anxiously watched the screen.

"If this search doesn't work, what do you think our next step should be?" Rodriguez asked. "I don't know—"

"*Bingo*," Rizzo barked. "Gotcha, sucker. The letters are Phoenician . . . 'aleph' and 'resh' . . . and they've matched to a hallmark."

He was quickly surrounded, each pair of eyes trying to read the screen faster than the others.

Abiathar—leader of a Jewish religious community in Palestine in the eleventh century.

"That's it?" said Rizzo, stunned at the brevity of the message. "That's all they know about this guy? A multibillion-bit world system, and all they've got is one sentence? Criminy, we're still skunked."

12

Rizzo ran into Joe the following morning at the corner coffee-monger, the portable, stainless steel stalls that dotted hundreds of corners in Midtown where men with accents rapidly dispensed coffee, tea, bagels, and attitude, this one conveniently situated on Fifth Avenue, just outside the Humanities and Social Sciences Library.

"Hey, Godzilla, I've been thinking," said Rizzo.

"You aren't even awake yet."

"Yeah, but listen . . . I've been trying to come up with some way to unlock information about this Abiathar, our mysterious author. Last night I whipped through the Internet and uncovered several Abiathars, but nearly any of them could have been our man. We ain't gonna find out scratch that way."

Rizzo scrambled up the ramp to the side door of the library, Rodriguez climbing the stairs beside him.

"We need an expert," said Rodriguez, "someone with a broad knowledge of early Middle Eastern history. There's George Pappadoukus in the Reading Room."

Rizzo nearly dropped his Lipton with lemon. "Make me barf," he squawked. "I wouldn't talk to that Greek geek if he was my only ticket to Mariah Carey. He wanted my job, and it feels like he wants me to die from paper cuts anytime we're in the same room. Stuff that one."

Walking toward the staff elevators, Rizzo grasped for other options.

"There's another guy over at Columbia, where I got my master's," said Rodriguez, "but this guy is years removed from 'feet on the ground' experience, and that's going to be critical."

Rizzo felt his heart flutter and his gut twist. "Maybe I have an answer," he said, getting on the down elevator while Joe continued on to the periodicals room.

Kallie Nolan was a dicey choice, one fraught with anxiety for Rizzo, but the only one he could come up with at the moment. Nolan was studying at Tel Aviv

University for her doctorate in biblical archaeology and, almost as difficult a task, to earn the rare and highly coveted title of "garden guide." With the heavy workload she was already carrying, asking her to join in a wild-goose chase to track down some information on this Abiathar guy was asking a lot. But Rizzo didn't know where else to turn, so he typed out a quick e-mail and hoped for a positive reply.

———⁓⁓⁓———

Just about a week later, on a Tuesday, Sammy was knocking on Joe's office door, the bottom of his New York Jets' Brett Favre game jersey dusting the marble floor.

"Joe, open up, you've got to read this," Sammy shouted through the mail slot at the midpoint of the door to Rodriguez's office. "C'mon, this is good stuff."

Rizzo nearly fell on his face as the door jerked open. "It better be good," Rodriguez snapped. "I was up all night, my wife is getting really sick of this schedule, and yesterday I fell asleep on my desk for two hours. One of these days, I've got to get some work done."

Sammy bounced from foot to foot with anticipation, and finally, Rodriguez got the point.

"What is it?" he barked.

"I was wondering when you would come to your senses," said Rizzo, climbing into a chair. "Here, it's a printout of an e-mail I just got from Kallie. We're starting to put the dots together."

Rizzo had met Kallie Nolan several years ago when Kallie was doing archaeological research in the library and had become a regular denizen of the stacks. She became lost in the labyrinthine hallways one day, and Rizzo came to her rescue. After that, she would often stop by Rizzo's office for hot tea and interesting conversation. The relationship became strained after Rizzo made a pass at her, so there had been no telling if she would respond or just ignore his request. It had taken several days, but Kallie had responded to Sammy's initial e-mail with almost nine pages of information.

Rodriguez took the printout, stepped around his desk, and sat in the specially designed ergonomic chair that relieved the constant back pain from too many years of competitive basketball. Rizzo looked forward to his visits to Rodriguez's office. It was so much warmer and more inviting than Rizzo's sterile glass-and-steel enclosure in the underground stacks. Just off the periodicals room of the massive Humanities and Social Sciences Library, a room that could have fit perfectly in any Tudor mansion in England, Rodriguez's office was a bibliophile's dream—floor-to-ceiling oak bookcases on three walls, leaded glass windows dominating the fourth. His desk and filing cabinets were in matching oak, as was the floor, all complemented by an authentic Persian rug. Rodriguez had inherited the office and its furnishings when he'd been promoted, and Rizzo accorded him great credit in that he had changed nothing during his tenure except the desk chair that kept his back pain in check. Rizzo loved this office, and often daydreamed himself into its confines. When Rodriguez took a quick, questioning look at Rizzo, he impatiently waved Joe back to the text of the e-mail:

Sammy,

I've done some research on the name you gave me, Abiathar, and he turns out to be a very interesting character.

First, I've got to tell you this request of yours was a blessing. I've been struggling to find an appropriate subject for my doctoral thesis, and you dropped one in my lap. Below is what I've found out thus far, and I hope it's what you're looking for. I hope the form is okay—I've already started work on the thesis, so I cut and pasted a copy of what I've written so far. It reads a little bit like a fourth-grade geography text, but this is the preliminary draft, framing information from a mishmash of sources before I fill in with a lot more historical background. I've included all the information because I think it will help make more sense of Abiathar's story.

***

Faced with Jewish rebellion against Caesar, Roman legions swept into Jerusalem in 70 AD, destroyed and dismantled the temple, Herod's Palace, and any vestige of Jewish sovereignty. Every Jew who remained alive was banished from the city and all the areas near the city. For nearly a thousand years, Jewish elders desperately tried to hold together a community that had lost the center of its universe.

Jewish life up to that point had been based on Jewish law interpreted by Jewish scholars.

In this new world, one of the greatest challenges to scholars was how to deal with a law centered on a temple and a priesthood that no longer existed. Much of this original, biblical law dealt not only with temple life, but also the life of a community wholly independent of non-Jewish governance.

To compensate for this loss of temple and priesthood, the Jews created new structures of governance (the Academy) in place of the Sanhedrin and new, hereditary leaders (the Exhillarch in Babylon; the Gaon in Palestine) in place of the high priests.

Though exercising significant power in their communities, these Jewish "officials" still served solely at the pleasure of the ruling monarchs. There was an Exhillarch in Babylon—ruler of all the Jews in Persia and Palestine—who could trace his lineage to the royal line of David. The Exhillarch exercised his power through a pair of lieutenants, the Gaonim.

Early in the eleventh century, wearying of the Jewish "rulers" who interfered with his authority, the caliph of Babylon had them executed, and he abolished the positions. Left without a hierarchical leader, the Jewish community in Palestine established its own hereditary position of Gaon. In 1046, Solomon Ben Judah was appointed Gaon of Palestine, in Jerusalem, and Jewish communities throughout the East were now under his authority, but not always under his control. Financial offerings intended for Palestine were often siphoned off to support Jewish interests in Spain, North Africa, and Egypt, weakening Solomon's position.

Solomon died a few years later, having chosen his son Joseph to be Gaon and his other son Elijah to occupy the office of "Av Beit Din" (head of the court). Both Joseph and Elijah were worthy candidates, having studied Scripture and Jewish law and writings since their early childhood. They were "scholars"—students for life who did no other work but to study, understand, and try to interpret the Jewish law. When Joseph died suddenly in 1054, it wasn't his brother Elijah who ascended to the position of Gaon, as would have been expected.

After a long wandering, David Azariah, from the house of the former Babylonian Exillarchs and the line of King David, unexpectedly entered Jerusalem. How or why he garnered favor is a mystery. Perhaps it was some good but undeserved reputation that followed him. But after Joseph's death, David was appointed Gaon and ascended to the highest Jewish authority in the East.

The people of Jerusalem quickly learned how wrong their choice had been. David proved a nasty judge and spoke ill of both Solomon and Joseph. Stricken by a terrible, unshakable disease in his second year, David Azariah suffered for six years before he died in 1062. Finally, Elijah could step up to the place rightfully intended for him by his father, Solomon, and brother Joseph. Elijah was gladly received as the new Gaon and remained in power for twenty-two eventful years.

Arguably one of the most widely accepted scholars among the Jewish people since the closing of the Talmud in 500 AD and generally showing a preference for a natural (as opposed to miraculous) redemption for the Jewish people, Elijah had studied with some of the ancient world's most renowned scholars. Influenced by the rationalist school of thought, and perhaps by the experience of having his rightful title usurped by another, when Elijah was installed as Gaon in Jerusalem in 1062, he established a rational and practical governance for the Jewish community.

In 1071, centuries of relative peace and calm in Jerusalem came to a sudden, smashing end when Islam finally broke through the Byzantine western borders and a new group of converts rose to power. They were known as the Seljuk Turks, and their brand of Islam was extremist. Their soldiers were assassins, and their eyes were on Jerusalem and Egypt. Overtaking the stable but sleepy Abbasid Empire, the Seljuk Turks marched on Jerusalem with all the fierceness and wrath of bloodthirsty new converts. Always a rationalist, Elijah gathered the Academy members and the Jewish community and fled to the coastal town of Tyre just as the Seljuk swept into Jerusalem.

For eighteen years, the Gaon Elijah—and his son Abiathar after him—held their exiled community together in Tyre. While

free of the Seljuk, Elijah was not free from conflict or controversy.
A much revered scholar, judge, and human being, Elijah found
himself thrust into leadership of a group steadfastly opposed to
another fraud.

David Ben Daniel, another descendant of the Davidic dynasty,
wandered into Egypt and laid claim to the title of Exhillarch.
Meborak, the highest official of the Egyptian Jewish community,
supported David's claim. David, though authentic in lineage,
was not loyal in heart and mind. Threatened by the powers of
Meborak, the Nagid, he then used his high title to end the office
and remove any higher authority than himself. Meborak, a much-
loved physician, fled in fear of his life to Spain. Over thirteen years,
David deposed every legitimate Jewish ruler except Elijah. When
the Fatimid Dynasty of Cairo overthrew the Seljuks in 1089,
David, his power now extended beyond Egypt by the Fatimids,
stripped Abiathar of his title and authority. But the Jews, still loyal
to their Gaon, returned to Jerusalem, where they openly resisted
David's tyranny.

It took another five years before Meborak, the legitimate
Nagid, ruler of the Jews in Egypt, and Abiathar, ruler of the Jews
in Jerusalem, wielded enough power and influence to remove this
usurper from office. In gratitude, Abiathar penned a "Megillah"
(or scroll) detailing the turbulent events of his reign, his rise and
fall and reinstatement. This was sent to Meborak Ha-Nagid in
Egypt for safekeeping. Meanwhile, the Jerusalem to which the exiles
returned was scarred, having long ago fallen into disrepair, and was
now dilapidated. The Fatimid government had little interest in the
city, concentrating instead on the important coastal cities and their
harbors. A very small retinue of Fatimid soldiers was left to guard
the walled city.

For ten years, the Jerusalemite Jews lived and worked freely,
occasionally contending with their Muslim neighbors, many of whom
preferred the extremist Seljuks to the more liberal Fatimids. During
this time, Abiathar remained in close correspondence with leaders
of the Jewish communities in Constantinople, Damascus, and Egypt
and was one of the first to identify a new threat growing in the West.

Constantinople's emperor was calling to Europe for help. The Byzantine emperor was frustrated by the constant onslaught of Muslim invasion and by the Egyptian government's hostility to, and harassment of Christian pilgrims visiting the Holy Land. Both the pope and the emperor were beating the drums of war.

As an army of Christian crusaders crossed west toward Constantinople, the Egyptians failed to reinforce Jerusalem. When the crusaders finally marched on the Holy City, they met only minor resistance from a small, badly armed retinue of guards and soldiers.

Now, with the Christian takeover of Jerusalem imminent, anticipating his fate and the fate of all "unbelievers" once the crusaders breached Jerusalem's defenses, Abiathar again implemented his plans to escape the city with his followers, as his father had done before him. Abiathar's plan was the same, to find refuge in one of the fortified coastal towns and wait for a safer moment to return to Palestine.

It wasn't long before the crusaders swept into Jerusalem, riding a wave of butchery, killing every Muslim and Jew in the city— along with an uncounted number of fellow Christians.

The European conquerors established the Kingdom of Jerusalem and reigned for 159 years. Abiathar, meanwhile, vanished from the annals of history. There is no record of Abiathar or any exiled Jews from Jerusalem entering Aker, Tyre, or any other fortified Muslim coastal city . . . and in those times, the arrival of a band of Jews from Jerusalem would most certainly have been recorded.

Over the span of time, Abiathar is wiped both from the pages of history and from the memory of the Jews. His name is not only obscured; it is forgotten. It is shocking to discover that a man of his ancestry, importance, and education disappeared without a trace after the fall of Jerusalem.

***

Sorry, but that's all I have for now. I am totally fascinated by this Abiathar character, and I intend to continue searching for any further evidence of his life after the crusader invasion.

This is going to make a great thesis! Thank you for handing me something original.

And Sammy, you may have been reluctant to ask, but I forgave you a long time ago for making that move on me. You were a great friend then, and I hope you will continue to be a great friend now. I've missed you, and I've got so much to share with you. But that will wait for another time.

New York . . . Jerusalem . . . wherever, I hope to see you soon.

Kallie

"Do I read this right?" Rodriguez asked. "Is Kallie saying that Abiathar was the head man of the Jewish community in Jerusalem when the crusaders first captured the city in 1099? Our Abiathar? This is the same guy?"

Rizzo wriggled happily, clapping his hands together. "Yessiree . . . that's our guy," he hummed gleefully. "'We got the motive, which is murder and we got the body, which is dead!'"

Rodriguez looked blankly at the little man opposite him.

"Rod Stieger—you know? *In the Heat of the Night*?" Rizzo watched, but the blank look remained. "What did you do with your youth, Rodriguez? Yes, he's our guy! The author of that crazy scroll was Abiathar, leader of Jerusalem's Jewish community over a thousand years ago. Isn't that great? Now we can really get someplace."

"Not so fast, Sammy." Rodriguez's voice was heavy and resigned as he rested his forehead in both palms, his elbows atop his disaster of a desk. "If that scroll is from the leader of the Jews to somebody else, why was it written in a language that had been extinct for nearly six hundred years? Why wasn't it written in Hebrew or Greek or Aramaic? No, it still doesn't make sense. What does Abiathar know about a language that represented the spoken word in Egypt one thousand years before he was born? No, Sammy, Abiathar may be the author, but we're no closer to understanding this message than when we found it.

"And I'm getting a bigger headache. I'm going home."

13

Two days later, the band of four sat in Dr. Johnson's apartment on Central Park West, soaking up the warmth of well-aged brandy and finely brewed, hazelnut coffee.

"Hey, Joe," Rizzo said over his snifter, "I renounce my claim on your office. I'll just allow Dr. Johnson to bequeath me this apartment. I could force myself to live here."

Mellowed both from the fine dinner Johnson had prepared and the hypnotic effects of the brandy, Bohannon glanced around the study. Beautifully preserved, leather-bound books occupied a majority of the study's bookcases and competed with mementos memorializing Johnson's many overseas adventures. *Now, this is the guy I expected to meet.*

Johnson's apartment—stunning to the others who lived in typically cramped New York City apartments—boasted twelve huge rooms with soaring ceilings. There was a Victorian opulence in the design of each room: hand-carved wooden moldings framing each fireplace, each doorway, each set of windows; pocket doors and leaded, stained-glass windows, lamp shades and ornamentals; custom-made stone columns and floors, treasure after neck-turning treasure. In addition to some stunning, original oil paintings that strategically adorned the walls, and the seemingly haphazard placing of priceless antiques, perhaps the rarest and most beautiful vision was available on the twenty-foot wide terrace that ran the length of the sixteenth-floor apartment and directly overlooked a sprawling vista of Central Park.

Tucked into a sumptuous leather club chair, Bohannon wondered how Johnson had come to reside in an apartment that could only, in the superhot real estate market of Manhattan, be afforded by multimillionaires.

"It's not mine," Johnson said, so startling Bohannon that he had to grab his glass with both hands. "My elderly aunt owns this apartment. Her husband worked closely with George Eastman in developing the process for mass producing roll photographic film. He became one of the officers of the Kodak Company that Eastman launched, acquired thousands of shares of Kodak stock for pennies, cashed out at their peak, and was still filthy rich after he bought this apartment for cash many years ago. My aunt is now ninety-four, living in the most opulent assisted-living facility you've ever seen, and keeping me guessing about her future plans for this more-than-adequate home."

Bohannon caught Johnson looking directly at him and understood the unspoken message . . . no, this apartment was not purchased with the proceeds from looting a museum or selling forgeries like Randall Swinton. Bohannon could feel the burning in his cheeks as they reddened, a physiological reaction that he had never learned to control.

"Well, gentlemen," said Doc, breaking the stupor and sitting up in his chair, "what do we know, and what do we do next?"

Bohannon seized the moment and automatically slipped into reporter mode. "We know the scroll is a message, sent by Abiathar, Gaon of Jerusalem. We know, with fair certainty, that the message was likely dispatched prior to 1099 when the crusaders captured Jerusalem and butchered its inhabitants. That the message is written in Demotic, a language that is unknown and was extinct hundreds of years before Abiathar was born. We know that the message was written in twenty-one vertical lines, grouped together in sets of three to form seven columns of Demotic script, and that there is no other existing example of Demotic being written in vertical, rather than horizontal, lines. So, we also know that the message is most likely in code and that understanding it will not require translating the Demotic but will require a cipher to unlock the code.

"That message is obviously important, and we know that Charles Spurgeon must have found a way to understand the message since he warned Klopsch about its contents. Spurgeon urged Klopsch to contact Dr. Schwartzman at Trinity Parish, and Schwartzman was a close friend of composer Edward Elgar, who was fascinated with codes, ciphers, riddles, and other forms of puzzles. We know that 110 years ago, Elgar sent a letter to Miss Dora Penny with a cipher that has never been broken, that Miss Penny's father, Alfred, was rector of St. Peter's church in Wolverhampton, and that Alfred was acquainted with Dr. Schwartzman, a fellow Anglican priest from America. Dr. Schwartzman traveled with Elgar to California on one of Elgar's rare concert tours, thus there was an overlapping relationship between Elgar, the Penny family, and Schwartzman.

"And we know there was, or is, a group of men here in New York City, ready to kill, willing to die to prevent us from uncovering the truth of the scroll," said Bohannon.

"Maybe we should call the cops," Rodriguez suggested.

"Hey, Joe—you getting senile?" snapped Rizzo, sloshing the brandy high along the sides of his snifter. "We call in the cops, and one thing is certain. We'll be out of the code-breaking business in a New York minute. I think we just keep our eyes open and a roll of quarters in our fists. That's what I know—lethal hands. What do you think, Tom?"

Foreboding failed to dampen Bohannon's enthusiasm for the chase.

"*I* think that Sammy Rizzo has terrible taste in clothes," Bohannon said, stifling a grin.

Bohannon watched as Rizzo looked down at his black, Hawaiian shirt with yellow palm trees, the red-and-green-plaid Bermuda shorts, and his pink, hi-top Converse sneakers. Rizzo seemed perplexed as the others chuckled behind their snifters.

"And we also know that no one will believe anything about what we have here." Bohannon's voice sounded more calm than he felt. "I, for one, will be looking over my shoulder at every corner, but we can't stop now." The rest of the team nodded.

"Come on, now, what else do we know?" said Johnson. "That was a great summary, Tom, but it was only a summary of what we now know conclusively. Look under the surface; search for a crack or a connection; what *else* do we know? The answer has been before our eyes. It must have been. Or Spurgeon had access to something we don't."

Sitting up suddenly, Rodriguez got their attention. "Well, one thing we can be pretty sure of is that the Penny family and, therefore, Elgar and Schwartzman would have known about Spurgeon, the most renowned Christian preacher in England. And that Spurgeon would likely have heard of Elgar, who was extremely popular the last decade of the nineteenth century. They were famous contemporaries in a close-knit society. Spurgeon probably knew all about the Dorabella Cipher since it was the rage of England. You know, I—"

Rodriguez suddenly jumped out of his chair, holding fast to his brandy.

"Doc," he said with an infectious urgency, "where's your computer?"

Johnson half turned and pointed to a corner, "It's over there, behind—"

Rodriguez was already flinging open a pair of three-paneled oak doors, revealing a well-equipped media center.

"Quick, your password," Rodriguez flipped over his shoulder as he fired up the computer.

"First you'll get my password, then you'll get my bank account," said Johnson. "I don't—"

"Yo, Doc, c'mon all ready," Rodriguez complained. "I've got an idea, and you're just slowing things down."

"Rosetta Setter," Johnson spelled out, "but you could be more civil."

"Yeah, yeah, maybe some other time," said Rodriguez, hunched over the keys. "But not . . ." The printer punched out a page.

Rodriguez stood up, gazing down at the paper in his hand. "Holy Christmas," Rodriguez said, turning to his partners. "Will you look at this? Holy Christmas! It's the Dorabella Cipher. It's three lines."

"Of course it is," said Johnson, dismissing it with a backhanded flip of his hand, "but the lines are horizontal. That can't help us."

"You're right," said Rodriguez, a tone of triumph in his voice, "until you turn it on its side—like this. Then," he said, holding the sheet in front of their faces, "then, the lines are vertical, aren't they?"

"Yes, but—" Bohannon started, but Rodriguez cut him off.

"Look, it's logical to conclude that Spurgeon, Elgar, the Penny family—they were all in the same social strata, all churchmen, all in the public eye, and with homes less than one hundred miles apart. It's logical to conclude that they not only knew *of* each other, but certainly could have known each other. Doc, Schwartzman didn't know the key, Schwartzman *was* the key. He was the link, the common denominator between Spurgeon, Elgar, and the Penny family. Schwartzman was social, outgoing, a climber in society. What did Spurgeon's letter say of Schwartzman? *'An able ally for your vital pursuit.'* There's no one else Klopsch could have contacted who would have provided the connection between Spurgeon, Elgar, and the Penny family. Schwartzman brought them together. He was the key."

By now, Rodriguez was pacing back and forth in front of the large bookcases, from windows to fireplace and back again, his left hand wrapped in the thick, black hair curling behind his ear, while the other three stood, propped against chair or table, taking in his train of thought. "Spurgeon didn't know squat about Demotic, wouldn't have mattered anyway. So, how did he know what was in the message? But . . . but . . . Elgar was perhaps the preeminent cryptographer of his time. Would it not have been logical for Spurgeon to have at least shared this strange document with Elgar, a man who named his first major orchestral work *The Enigma Variations*? Spurgeon had an ancient document that was absolutely baffling, more so if he had shown it to any linguists, who would have been as stumped as he was. Who else would he turn to?"

Rodriguez took a breath but kept pacing. Into the quiet, Bohannon slipped an unsettling question. "But Joe, even if Spurgeon did show it to Elgar, what good would that do? The scroll was written eight hundred years before Spurgeon and Elgar lived. Even if Abiathar used Demotic as a code and not a language, what good would the Dorabella Cipher be to us now, trying to unlock this scroll? They were written eight hundred years apart."

"You are making one critical, but erroneous, assumption," said Johnson, crossing the floor to Rodriguez and requesting the sheet of paper. "You're assuming the eight hundred years separating the two documents negates any possible connection."

Johnson turned to Rizzo and Bohannon and, with Rodriguez in his wake, stepped over to an elaborate side table bearing a Tiffany lamp. Johnson opened a drawer in the table, withdrew another sheet of paper, and held them both under the light.

"Imagine, for a moment," said Johnson, "that Elgar composed the Dorabella Cipher *after* he saw Spurgeon's scroll. What if this Dorabella Cipher is a result of Elgar's introduction to, or involvement with, Spurgeon's scroll? What if," Johnson said with a note of awe, "Elgar helped Spurgeon crack the code of the scroll, and then used the scroll's code as the basis for writing the Dorabella Cipher?

"Here, look at these two sheets of paper. On the left is the Demotic alphabet. On the right, the Dorabella Cipher. What do you see?" asked Johnson.

Looking over Johnson's shoulder, Bohannon nearly fainted, his blood rushed so abruptly to his head. The first Demotic letter looked like two lower-case *c*'s, turned backward. The second letter was one lower-case *c*—the exact same building blocks Elgar had used in creating the Dorabella Cipher.

Quiet reverence thickly filled the room. Bohannon felt a lump in his throat, an incalculable hope in his heart, and a reluctance to break the spell.

"YAAAHHHOOOOO!" Rizzo split the silence at the top of his lungs. Looking like a crazed leprechaun who had just discovered his pot of gold, Rizzo began leaping and dancing about the room with an uninhibited abandon. The golden palm trees, swaying and leaping in time to the wacky plaid shorts, precipitated a sudden burst of common hysteria.

Johnson grabbed the brandy bottle, took a deep swig, passed it on, and joyously joined Rizzo in his wild gyrations. Soon, hidden behind the sedate walls of the Upper West Side, all four of these reserved professionals were whooping and hollering; leaping and dancing around the elegant confines of Johnson's study.

"If my aunt walks in now," said Johnson, catching his breath, "I'll be disowned."

"YAAAHHHOOOOO!" screamed Rizzo, and the four of them launched again, crazy men in a lunatic asylum who knew they had just discovered the key to freedom.

Tomorrow, they would discover what the key unlocked.

14

Midafternoon the next day, Friday, the four men climbed the ladder that now led to the scaffold and gathered in Klopsch's office. Rodriguez rolled out the cushioned, protective covering and turned on the strong, overhead lamps while Bohannon entered the combination and opened the huge safe. It had been a pretty simple decision to leave the scroll in the safekeeping of Klopsch's office and the massive vault. If it had been safe there for one hundred years, it would likely be safe there for a few more weeks.

Bohannon could see the anticipation in Johnson's eyes as he was about to get his first look at the scroll container and the complete scroll. Bohannon felt like a presenter at the Academy Awards, about to disclose the Oscar winner. Resting the mezuzah on the table, atop the protective covers, Bohannon grasped the metal rod in his left hand and, maintaining a gentle pressure, began unrolling the scroll from the container. Within moments, the entire scroll rested before them. Quickly, they laid upon the scroll the enlarged copies they had made of the Dorabella Cipher. Like a medical team entering into a challenging surgery, the four men approached the table and began scanning scroll and cipher, cipher and scroll, looking for any sign of connection.

Eight hours later, all four of them were on the floor, their backs leaning against the walls of the office, their eyes dulled, their enthusiasm dampened. They had applied alphabetic sequences, musical scales, mathematical formulas, even chaos theory, but nothing had resulted in a better understanding of the scroll. Their hope, however, had not faded. The Dorabella Cipher, when turned on its side to make the lines vertical, made for fascinating comparison to the Spurgeon scroll. The most obvious comparison was that the lines were nearly identical in length when the symbols or characters were enlarged to approximately the same size. Unfortunately, it was hard to tell if the number of individual characters in each line was the same. Elgar's cipher was frustrating on many levels, but one was that it appeared to be impossible to determine if each combination of miniature arches was an individual character or, as in many languages or codes, some characters were connected or linked together to become one character.

"I know it's there," Dr. Johnson said almost to himself, rubbing a hand over his weary eyes. "I know it's there. What are we missing?"

"You know," Bohannon said, thinking back on all the times he had lost his keys, or his wallet, or his watch (it was a common occurrence), "the answer is probably very simple. We're the ones who are making it difficult. What would be a simple way for Elgar to connect his cipher to the scroll? What could link this ancient Egyptian language to Elgar's little squiggle-pictures? The answer is probably so obvious as to be ludicrous."

"Or so bloody obvious that I should kick myself!"

Johnson jumped to his feet and crossed to the computer. Pounding on the keyboard, Johnson continued his soliloquy, mumbling to himself, "How could you be so stupid? What a dolt. What are you waiting for: somebody to smack you over the head with the obvious? Some scholar . . . some scientist." Shaking his head back and forth, Johnson finally pulled up what he was looking for, and the printer cranked up to speed. He turned around with a chagrined look upon his face. "You're not going to believe this," he said, reaching down for the printed page. "So stupid. I can't believe I'm so stupid!"

He crossed to the table, put down the sheet of paper, and stared silently for a long moment.

"There it is," said Johnson, the sound of resignation in his voice. "There it is."

Johnson turned away from the table, leaned against the wall in his custom-tailored suit, and stretched his lean body, releasing a long sigh.

With a wary eye on the doc, Bohannon crossed to the table and looked down at the scroll. Sitting between the Dorabella Cipher and several columns of the scroll was a much enlarged photograph showing lines of symbols. Rizzo crawled onto a chair beside Bohannon; Rodriguez pulled up behind them. "What is this?" asked Bohannon. "It doesn't look like anything we have here."

Detaching himself from the wall, Johnson returned to the table. "Come on, now, think of all the history lessons you've received in the past week or so. What is this?"

Each man looked at the photo, searching for clues. But they barely had time to register what they were seeing.

"It's the Rosetta Stone," said Rizzo, becoming more agitated with each word. "That's the Egyptian hieroglyph next to the Greek. I can't tell what part of the stone it's from, but this is the Rosetta Stone. I'd bet my BBs on it."

Everybody started talking at once, asking questions, seeking answers. Johnson raised his hand for quiet.

"Tom, you provided the final clue when you mentioned comparing the Egyptian language to Elgar's scribbles. I should have thought of it a long time ago. There was only one way for Spurgeon and Elgar to discern the message on this scroll. First, they had to identify the Demotic language. Then, they had to identify that the message was not to be found in the Demotic language, but in a code using Demotic symbols. The only source of Demotic available to Spurgeon and Elgar would have been the Rosetta Stone, in the British Museum. This is how they deciphered the scroll . . . Greek, hieroglyphs, and Demotic. The Rosetta Stone gave them the solution to the code. They compared Greek to hieroglyphs to Demotic in this scroll, and it revealed the pattern in which the scroll had been written, the structure of the cipher. That structure, when compared to the Rosetta Stone, would have given them the scroll's message in Greek, and with the Greek, they would have been able to decipher the scroll. Then Elgar used the scroll's same structure to construct his famous Dorabella Cipher. Granted, none of us are Elgar. But all we need to do now is find the pattern. And that shouldn't be too difficult since Elgar has already completed all the hard work."

They were immediately back around the table, continuing with the surgery, confident in their ability to save the patient.

15

Bohannon had never appreciated ethnic comments about the Irish and drinking, but he liked his beer. Beer ran as plentiful as water in his home. From his late teens onward, that first long, cold drink was something he always savored.

Even while attending Penn State, when money was tighter than a warped door, Bohannon had been sure to pinch as many pennies as necessary just so that he could visit the My-Oh-My on College Avenue. At the My, the hot dogs were cooked in beer, the sauerkraut was cooked in sherry, and the hot dog buns were individually steamed for each order. They were so hot, soft, and tasty that the dogs were often done in three bites, leaving a desire for more.

The best part of the My, at least in 1973, was that with the dogs at twenty-five cents and the one dollar drafts, you could leave with a full stomach and a nice buzz for less than five dollars.

Tonight, the Guinness never tasted so good, and the waitress had been dispatched for four more pints as soon as she put down the first round.

They had finally left the mission around 9:00 PM and grabbed a cab to the Old Town Bar on 18th Street, just uptown from Union Square. The Old Town, in continuous operation since 1902, hadn't changed since the day it opened. A favorite haunt of the young and upwardly mobile, it got crowded and loud in the evening, particularly on a Friday night. But Bohannon steered his quartet up the steep stairs just inside the door to the much quieter and less-packed dining room. Tucked into a booth by the front windows, the team was weary, wary, and thirsty. First, it was Guinness all around, then the Old Town's famous cheeseburgers (sautéed onions and coleslaw on the side, of course) and crispy spuds. They inhaled the burgers as the fixins dripped through their fingers, and poured creamy black Guinness Stout down their throats.

When they finally came up for a breath, Rizzo, twirling a spud in a mound of ketchup, asked the question each of them wanted answered. "Well, do you think it's true?"

No one said a word.

Bohannon drew *the* sheet of paper out of his shirt pocket, opened it up, spread it in front of him. It had taken a couple of hours to get the entire scroll decoded, the process moving more quickly the more they got used to the cadence of the code. First they decoded each symbol literally. Once through the entire scroll, they went back through the decoded text, filling in gaps in the language so that it read smoothly in English.

The scroll was, in fact, a message. More precisely, it was a letter from Abiathar, the Gaon and leader of the Jewish community in Jerusalem, to Meborak, the Ha'Nagid of Egypt . . . the only remaining, legitimate Jewish authority in the East and the leader of the Jewish community in Alexandria. The message was a simple one—simply astounding and simply impossible.

Abiathar, Gaon of Jerusalem, son of Elijah, son of Solomon, to Meborak, Ha'Nagid of Cairo, most excellent of rulers—greetings, and may the God of heaven and earth, the God of our fathers, the most exalted God of Abraham, Moses, and David bless your house, guide your ways, and give you wisdom in abundance.

Grief overcomes me and fear attempts to destroy my faith. It is with broken heart that I must inform you of the imminent fall of Jerusalem into the hands of the Christian invaders. These Europeans have swept aside what feeble resistance the Fatimids mounted and are at this moment assaulting the walls of Jerusalem. They will, no doubt, enter the Holy City tomorrow.

Tonight, I will attempt to lead as many of our community as possible through the tunnels to the Kidron Valley, around the far side of the Mount of Olives to bypass the Christian camps, in the hope that some remnant of us may reach safety. We pray for the Lord's blessings.

But another, more urgent, matter I reveal to you, my most esteemed Meborak.

Thirty-seven years ago, my beloved father, Elijah, came to a realization that changed his life and the lives of all Jews to come. Recognizing the impossibility of building the Third Temple of God on the heights of the Temple Mount—because Islam had stolen the sacred place to erect the Dome of the Rock and the Al-Aqsa Mosque—my father decided if we could not build a temple on the Temple Mount, he would lead the construction of the Third Temple under the Temple Mount.

For nine years, Elijah and a small band of workmen secretly carved out a great cavern in the limestone under the Temple Mount and began making preparations for constructing a replica of Zerubbabel's Temple. The unexpected invasion of the Seljuk Turks in 1071 forced my father and the Jewish community to seek exile in

Tyre. Before they escaped, the cavern was sealed and the tunnel entrance to the cavern was collapsed.

Elijah died during the eighteen years we survived in Tyre, but he had instilled in me both a passion for righteous governance and a determination to see the temple completed. Once the Fatimids drove the Turks from Jerusalem, our community returned and soon set about the work of secretly constructing the Temple of God under the Temple Mount.

Our work was completed not long ago. Then the Christians came.

Jehovah God has kept our secret thus far, but to keep the infidel from desecrating the Holy of Holies, we have once again sealed the temple and blocked all entrances. Most excellent Meborak, you have proven yourself a steadfast brother in the past. Guard this scroll with your life, and treasure it until the day when the cavern can be reopened, ritual sacrifice will be possible in the Temple of God, and our Messiah shall come. Look to the Prophets for your direction.

May the Lord bless you and keep you; may the Lord make His countenance shine upon you and be gracious to you; may the Lord turn His face toward you, and give you peace.

Shalom,

Gaon Abiathar, Jerusalem

The four men around the table looked at each other with a mixture of disbelief and uncertainty, the same way they had responded just a few hours earlier when they first deciphered the scroll's secret. None of them knew where to start.

"Can this really be possible?" Rizzo asked again. "Is it possible? What do you think, Doc?"

Johnson pushed back his shoulders, bending his head first left, then right, trying to stretch out the tension of the last few hours and weeks. Opening his eyes, he threw a cold towel over any simmering sparks of hope.

"I don't see how there is any possible way for this claim of a secret Third Temple to be true," Johnson said slowly. "Look at it realistically. First of all, how could anybody excavate a cavern, a cavern big enough to hold the massive size of the Jewish temple, under the Temple Mount and keep it a secret? What did they do with all the debris from digging the cavern? How did they get regular or daily access to the area under the Mount? How, in God's name, could they have assembled all the granite, marble, cedar, gold and silver, and everything else that was required, and get it under the Mount and into the cavern without anyone finding out? Where did all the workers come from, the artisans, the skilled craftsmen? What did their families know? What did their families think when they didn't return? And no one breathed a word of it for a thousand years? How can that be possible?

"But even if that was possible, are you going to tell me that there has been a huge, secret cavern under the Temple Mount, containing a completely rebuilt Jewish temple, for over a thousand years and, in one of the most archaeological active areas in the world, this huge cavern has never been found? That would be ludicrous."

As Johnson finished his assessment, coffee and apple pie arrived, briefly blunting the conversation.

"So, what is this thing?" Rodriguez asked. "If you're right, Doc, and I'm in the same boat with you, I don't see how it can be true . . . but if you're right, then what is this scroll, this code, this message? Why was Spurgeon so fearful? Why did someone go to such incredible lengths to create a scroll like this, dig up an extinct language to write it in, develop an amazingly intricate code to protect its contents, and then send it off to the only legitimate Jewish leader in the East for its safekeeping? Why go to all that trouble if it's all a lie? That doesn't make any sense, either."

"You're right, Joe, it doesn't make sense," said Bohannon. "And you're right, Doc, if a temple was under the Temple Mount, it doesn't make any sense that it hasn't been found. So, we have two opposing theories, neither of which makes sense. And yet, there has to be an answer."

Bohannon shook his head. "You know, I read a lot of Sherlock Holmes books as a kid and one of the things that Holmes always said was, *'When you have eliminated the impossible, whatever remains, however improbable, must be the truth.'* I think the next thing we have to do is to eliminate the impossible, and then try to grasp the truth, even if it is improbable."

Bohannon looked up at the other three.

"Can you repeat that again, this time in English?" Rizzo deadpanned.

"No, Tom's right," said Rodriguez. "Either this is a crazy scam, or it's true. It's much less likely that it's something in between. Remember Kallie's e-mail? She told us that Abiathar had written one scroll, a Megillah, to Meborak already. Why couldn't he have written another? I don't know about you guys, but not only am I fascinated by this crazy scroll, but after all the time and effort we've already invested in it, I'm not inclined to stop now just because it doesn't seem to make any sense. As our first task, we need to figure out whether it's even possible for a temple to be down there. Let's see if we can get an answer to that question, and that will tell us the next place to go."

"I know the next place I'm going," said Bohannon. "I'm going to bed, and I'm going now. You've got the check, right, Doc?"

<center>~~~~~</center>

Bohannon was bone weary and wanted to get home, so he was first out of the Old Town Bar. He turned west on 18th Street, bound for the 6 train station at Union Square. Normally, crossing 18th Street meant looking to the right to check for oncoming traffic, but for some reason, when he was halfway across, Bohannon also glanced to his left. That's when he saw the man.

He was dressed in dark clothes—jeans, a rough jacket—a black, knit watch cap pulled down on his head in spite of the mild spring evening. Bohannon thought he saw a hooked nose, mustache, and Middle Eastern features. He couldn't be sure. But his heart began to race. His New York pace quickened.

Left on Broadway, Bohannon had only one short block to cover before crossing 17th Street, where he would enter Union Square. Another sixty yards, and he would reach the subway entrance.

Broadway was still bustling with pedestrians. Feeling foolish, Bohannon peeked over his left shoulder as he reached 17th Street. His breath froze. The man was close behind. He seemed to be staring directly at Bohannon.

Tom was anxious to get across the street, but he self-consciously held himself back from the edge of the curb. Even before the light fully changed, Bohannon hustled across the street and quickstepped through the crowded asphalt area of Union Square, home to the weekly farmer's market, hoping to leave the man in his wake.

Suddenly, Bohannon stopped at the top of the stairs to the Union Square station. He stepped aside, halted by indecision. Should he go into the station or stay on the street? What was safer?

A quick glance to his right, and Bohannon saw the man moving toward him. Only two pedestrians and a few yards separated them. The man, clearly Middle Eastern, was looking daggers through Bohannon's skull.

Tom turned on his heel and walked quickly past the subway entrance. Union Square Park beckoned on his left, but it was dark, the pathways twisting. Too isolated.

Quickening his pace, reviewing his mental map, Bohannon hurried south on Union Square West, crossed 14th Street, and continued down Broadway, that long, diagonal slash that cuts across Manhattan from Houston Street on the south to 106th Street in Harlem. Then he remembered the substation that NYPD staffs 24/7 inside the Union Square Station. *A couple of turns, and I'll double back.*

At the corner of 13th Street and Broadway, in front of the Union Square movie theater, Bohannon hazarded a look behind him. The man was there, closing fast, his eyes on Bohannon—and his arm raised. Bohannon stifled a scream, pushed himself back against the wall of the theater, and raised his fists. The man smiled.

"Aliah," he said, waving his arm.

The man brushed past Bohannon, walked up to a woman with a scarf over her head, gave her a polite hug, and kissed her cheek. "I'm sorry I'm late." Holding the woman's hand, the man turned around, leading her past Bohannon and into the door of the movie theater.

Bohannon's shirt was soaked, his breathing ragged and shallow. His fists, still held in front of him, began to shake. People were looking at him, but avoiding eye contact. Nobody in New York City messed with crazy street people.

16

Johnson was grateful for the invitation to the Bohannons' Memorial Day family picnic. Holidays are difficult for the single. *And friendless,* Dr. Johnson thought.

Rodriguez was also there, with his wife, Deirdre, and their children. Rizzo, as was his habit, kept everyone loose and laughing.

But no matter how hard Johnson tried to be "normal," he continued to hear the Siren call of the search seducing him, in spite of the paranoia that often dogged his days and the nightmares that regularly plagued his nights.

From the glances he exchanged with his associates, their excitement about Abiathar's message was a shared collusion. Stuffed with meatballs, baked ham, and Tom's revered, secret-recipe potato salad, and too preoccupied to participate in the family ritual of "do you remember when," they eagerly followed Bohannon into his study.

"What do you think we should do?" Rodriguez asked, almost as soon as the door found its jamb. No small talk, no pleasantries. "Do we keep going with this, or—"

"Or quit?" Johnson interrupted. He looked at the men in the room and knew their thoughts. Somebody had to speak it.

Bohannon turned on the TV and tuned in to the Indy 500, but nobody paid any attention to it. "I'm frightened," said Johnson. "I won't deny it. The memory of that incident in the subway haunts me. I feel like a fool saying it, but I feel like my life is turning into a bad spy movie."

There were understanding nods from Rodriguez and Bohannon.

"The other night when we were leaving the Old Town," said Bohannon, "I thought I was being followed. It scared the living daylights out of me. I gotta tell ya, I'm beginning to wonder what we're doing here."

"I was wondering that, too," said Johnson. "There is certainly reason for us to question whether we should continue with our quest to understand this message on the scroll. And I am concerned . . . concerned about the welfare of us all. But then, I realized something very important."

"What's that, Doc," said Rizzo, "that your tailor is stuck in the Middle Ages?"

It suddenly struck Johnson that Sammy's barbs carried a profound purpose. He was helping them all laugh in the face of fear.

"No, my dear Mr. Rizzo," Johnson bowed in his direction. "I realized that I want to do this. And that neither terror nor threats have diminished my desire to understand the message of the scroll. Nor has it deterred my determination to discover whether this message could in fact be possible. There is no question I'm uneasy about our situation. But I'm not scared, and I don't want to give up. Not now."

Nobody moved, or objected.

"Well, it looks like we're all in," said Rodriguez.

Johnson crossed the room and stood by the window, gathering his thoughts and switching gears. "I've been doing some research—called a few friends, sent a few e-mails—tried to come at this thing from the edges without making it too obvious," said Johnson, swirling his martini. "I haven't been able to find anything yet that would either confirm or deny the possibility of something unknown existing under the Temple Mount.

"What I did find is that Abiathar's family, including his grandfather, Solomon; his uncle Joseph; his father, Elijah; and Abiathar himself, could trace their history directly to Ezra, one of the prophets of the Bible's Old Testament. They were 'Aaronites,' or from the family of Aaron, the brother of Moses, making the men priests.

"And it was the priests who would have known how to rebuild the temple— what the measurements should be, where things were placed. It was only the priests who could consecrate the temple once it was built, only the priests who could enter the 'Most Holy Place' in the middle of the temple, only the high priest, one man, who was permitted to enter the 'Holy of Holies' where the Ark of the Covenant would reside, and only once a year.

"So if Abiathar had not been a priest, it really would have cast a great deal of doubt on the veracity of the scroll's story. That he was a priest," said Johnson, "doesn't prove it's true. It only means that we should continue looking for a clear answer, one way or another."

Johnson, who was still standing, wandered over to Bohannon's bookcases. "One other bit of family news was interesting. Abiathar's brother Solomon fled Jerusalem for the Egyptian town of Suez when he and his brother were first informed of the European Crusade. After some time, this Solomon was appointed Gaon and continued a line of 'Gaonim' in Egypt, serving under the Nagid. We can assume, then, a rather strong connection between Abiathar and Egypt. But there is still no concrete evidence . . . no, not even a suspicion . . . that a temple was erected under the Temple Mount."

"How can we know whether it's possible or impossible until we tell some-body exactly what it is we're looking for?" asked Bohannon, sitting down heavily in an old, tattered but extremely comfortable recliner. "We can look from now until the fifth of Umptober, and we're not going to get any closer to the truth until we talk to somebody who has firsthand knowledge and tell them every-thing we've discovered thus far. Until we risk opening up what we know, we're just flying blind."

"I guess you're right," said Rodriguez, opening up his bottle of Bud and pouring it into a nice, frozen mug. "I've been scouring the Internet and prowling through all the archaeology and ancient history periodicals in the library's vaults, and even though there've been millions of words written about the Temple Mount, about the first and second temples, about the archaeological finds in and around Jerusalem, I haven't found a single word or conjecture that there could actually be a Third Temple sitting, waiting to be found under the most fought-over piece of real estate in the world. But one thing all the writers agree on is that no one really knows what exists under the Temple Mount platform."

Bohannon kicked off his loafers and stretched out the recliner to its full length. "So who are we going to find who is going to have all the information we're looking for? Who is going to share it with us and not turn us in as nut cases, or steal the information and go looking for the temple themselves? Who do we trust?"

Drawn to Tom's collection of books squeezed into every available space, Johnson began slowly rolling over the Rolodex in his memory, looking for a connection with wisdom, resources, and good character—a person of integ-rity, who could keep a secret. Flip . . . flip . . . flip . . . the cards kept flipping, revealing name after name with no response.

He had taken note of Bohannon's taste in reading. It was an eclectic grouping, nothing remarkable, but generally good, foundational literature and the requisite professional reference material.

"There are plenty of scholars who have the knowledge," Johnson said, con-tinuing his mental catalog, "but there are very few I would trust with informa-tion that is incredibly valuable on so many different planes."

Turning to a new bookcase, Johnson's pulse quickened, and his admiration for Bohannon skipped to a new level. First edition, numbered set, nineteenth century, illustrated complete works of Shakespeare . . . First edition, complete set of Victor Hugo . . . wow!—autographed copy of *Last of the Mohicans* displayed under plastic, with the front cover opened to the autographed flyleaf. *That is rare, probably should be in a museum*, thought Johnson. "You have a nice collection here, Tom," he said, continuing his inspection. Signed copy of *The Great Gatsby.* "Very nice."

"It's a hobby," Bohannon said from his prone position, "something to fill the time with value."

Johnson turned quickly on his heel, breaking away from his bibliophilic reverie. "Bohannon, you never cease to amaze me. A hobby. Once again, I think you may have uncovered the answer."

"What?" Bohannon mumbled from the edge of sleep.

"No, not *what, who*: Winthrop Larsen. I've been wracking my brain for a professional I could trust, but I never thought of Winthrop. He's a teacher here in New York. Teaches social studies to middle school students, even though his family is "Old New England" and old money. But Winthrop has an interesting *hobby*, Mr. Bohannon. Saying Winthrop is an avid archaeologist would be like calling the *Titanic* a rowboat. Winthrop brings a passion to his study and dedicated study to his passion, along with a wealth of resources which allows him to apply the most sophisticated and modern technology to his efforts. He's blessed with a schoolteacher's schedule and spends every summer either on a dig somewhere in the world or in the bowels of the British Museum, increasing his knowledge.

"I've known Winthrop for more than a decade," said Johnson. "Several summers, we collaborated on our assignments at the museum. And there are two things that make Winthrop Larsen remarkably important to us: He has a genuinely sincere heart and is of the finest character; and he is an expert on the history and archaeology of Jerusalem . . . authored a monograph on the debated discovery of the first wall of David's palace, parts of which were published in the *American Archaeology Review.* If Winthrop can't help us, perhaps no one will."

"Hey, Doc." Johnson turned to his left. Rizzo leaned against a low table that flanked Bohannon's recliner. "If this guy Winthrop is rolling in dough like you said, what's he doing teaching public school? Why not ride the money train and spend his life digging in the desert?"

Rizzo may enjoy playing the roll of class clown, but his mind was quick and his logic flawless. To Johnson, intellect was a saving grace.

Johnson leaned his shoulder against the end of the last bookcase. "It's likely a combination of things, but primarily, Winthrop doesn't want to live either on his family's name or on their wealth alone. I don't know if it's rich man's remorse, but Winthrop refuses to accept privilege. He wants to earn his own way, and he is determined to spend his life personally helping those who do not enjoy privilege. To live off his family's wealth and only pursue archaeology . . . well, it would betray his own soul."

"So," said Bohannon, "let's go. Where does he live?"

There was a knock on the door, followed by Annie's head peeking into the room. "Come on, you guys, the family is out here. You're not going to spend another day holed up in a cramped room. Dr. Johnson, there are some children out here who want to hear more stories of knights and dragons. Sammy? And you two, get out here and pay some attention to us."

Johnson saw the knowing glance pass between Rodriguez and his brother-in-law. "C'mon, Tom," said Rodriguez. "It's a wise man who knows when to say, 'Yes, dear.'"

"Doc?" Bohannon asked.

"I'll call Winthrop tomorrow," said Johnson, joining the exit, "and see if we can get together as soon as possible."

—∿∿∿—

They came in from Freeman Alley without a sound. Now that only two remained, they were much more careful. Two dead, and no closer to the scroll.

On Friday at the end of his shift with the renovation crew, Ishmael had slipped a wooden wedge between the latch and the frame of the Bowery Mission's back door, the one with the deadbolt lock.

They pushed past the trash bins, silent in their soft-soled shoes, and raced up the backstairs to the first landing. It was well after midnight Sunday night, and the mission was quiet. Monday was a holiday, so no workers were expected. Mukhtar needed only moments to unlock first the door to the volunteers' dorm area, then the lock to the men's bedroom, and finally the last locked door, leading to the storage area that flanked the space behind the organ pipes . . . and Klopsch's hidden office.

Two weeks ago, Ishmael had watched as the men climbed through the reno-vations and entered the previously hidden space. Twice before, they had tried to gain access, twice before they were nearly detected.

Their leader demanded the scroll, regardless of the risk. So they tried again.

Ishmael grasped the thin penlight in his teeth and climbed the old, wooden ladder. Mukhtar followed with the tools.

The bellows room was the size of a large closet, but only half as high. It smelled like damp dog and mouse droppings. Every surface was plastered with the dusty grime of decades. Ishmael crawled to a corner of the room, his nos-trils immediately clogged with a foul powder. He reached back his hand, and Mukhtar filled it with the pry bar. With the caution of a safecracker trying to pick a lock next door to a police precinct, Ishmael eased the bar under the edge of a board and slowly applied pressure. With a pop that stopped their hearts, the board snapped free of its nails. There was no other noise.

"More care," Mukhtar whispered. "Their security will do rounds."

Ishmael stifled a string of Arabic insults, keeping the penlight in his mouth and his attention on the next board. This one moved more easily, as did the next. The opening was narrow, blackness on the other side. Ishmael listened to the blackness, then tucked his head into the opening.

He swept the room with the intense beam, leaning his head in farther, tilting it left and right. Ishmael swore and nearly dropped the penlight.

The surface of the table in the middle of the room was unoccupied. The doors of the safe were slightly ajar. The shelves were empty.

Ishmael's fist pounded the floor of the bellows room, catapulting dust. He pulled his head back through the hole in the floor, pulled the penlight from his mouth, and rested his back against the wall.

"It's gone," he said to Mukhtar. "Everything is gone. The safe is empty. The books and documents are gone. The scroll has been moved."

Ishmael felt Mukhtar's eyes on him, and the unspoken question hung in the darkness.

"There is another way . . . a way to convince these infidels to return the scroll," said Ishmael. "A way that will bring the leader to his knees." Mukhtar picked up the pry bar and returned it to the tool bag. "Tomorrow, we begin to watch."

17

The Wednesday after Memorial Day was the kind of spring day that revived hope in the weary and warmed the bones of the aged. The sky, a cloudless cobalt prism, so magnified the sun's heat and light that Joe and Sammy flinched and shaded their eyes as they exited the side door of the Humanities and Social Sciences Library. It took a long breath to adjust.

Then Sammy Rizzo smiled, his eyes closed, his face lifted to the sky. "Oh, God . . . this is wonderful." Standing on the top step of the stone stairs leading down to 42nd Street, he turned to look up at Rodriguez. "Let's eat in the park, eh?"

The mismatched pair crossed 42nd Street in the middle of the block while the lights were red, dodging the odd car, and entered their local Chipotle restaurant, McDonald's Corporation's successful diversification into Mexican fast food. Sammy loved Chipotle, not only because its fajita burrito was out of this world, but also because it was so huge he would have half remaining for dinner. He also got a kick out of the questioning glances he intercepted as he trotted alongside the tall, long-striding Joe Rodriguez. *Let 'em scratch their heads. I've made my way in a big man's world.*

Bryant Park, the square-block green oasis between Fifth and Sixth avenues behind the library building, had been resurrected during Manhattan's rebirth. Once a dark den for drug deals and muggers, it was now a brilliant, thriving oasis—an outdoor Midtown magnet both day and night. The gravel pathways surrounding the big, open green were a midday riot of alfresco lunchers resting on the park's dark green chairs while they munched on their sandwiches and downed their health food.

Rizzo's favorite spot was on the south side, near the carousel. He loved the sound of children's laughter.

This day, they were fortunate enough to score a table in the mottled shade of a just-blooming plane tree.

Rizzo's hands wrestled with the oversized half burrito, escaping salsa sliding down his fingers. He didn't come up for air until he was nearly half done.

Rodriguez was chuckling at him. "Have you eaten in the last two days?"

"Funny man," Rizzo smirked, swabbing his hands in a pile of napkins. "I happen to have a big appetite."

"To go along with your ego?"

"To satisfy my hyperthyroid, dunce. It goes with the whole package."

Rizzo backhanded a mangled napkin in Joe's direction. "You . . . you eat like a sissy ballet dancer. Salad is not a man's meal."

"I've got to watch my figure . . . Deidre likes me lean and mean."

"You wuss."

Rizzo went back to attacking his burrito but stopped in mid-chomp.

"What does Deidre think about this treasure hunt we've embarked on?"

"I haven't told her much about it." Rodriguez looked up as the carousel began another circular voyage. "I'm not sure where this is going . . . and I don't want to worry her needlessly. I don't know . . . I don't know if that's the right thing or not."

Rizzo had known Joe Rodriguez a long time, more than ten years. He knew Joe and Deirdre enjoyed a powerful, committed marriage, that Joe was devoted to his wife and family. And he was confused.

"Joe . . . why are you doing this?"

"Huh? Doing what?" Rodriguez turned back to Rizzo.

"Chasing down this scroll, that's what. *Doing what!* You moron. Who knows what we're getting ourselves into? It seems like we've got a bunch of whacko terrorists trying to track us down, we've come up with this scroll's message that could have worldwide impact, and our next stop could be in that secure little resort of Jerusalem. So, yeah . . . why are you doing this?"

Rodriguez's smile was weighted, its burden pulling down the corners of his lips. He looked off in the direction of the carousel once more, the long, black curls on his head silently nodding affirmation to some unspoken summons.

"My father died several years ago. We really didn't have a relationship. He was the macho Hispanic male, ruler of his world. He didn't have time for me or much interest in me." Rodriguez pulled his eyes from the painted horses. "So when he died, to be honest, there really wasn't much to miss. Then last year, I was visiting my sister. She told me there was something she wanted me to have, and she brought out this small, wooden jewelry box. Dad's jewelry. She opened it and took out a ring. 'Here, I think you should have this.'

"It was a gold ring with a large, square, rounded red stone encased in the gold. I remembered my dad wearing the ring. And I was so proud to get it. It was the only thing of his that I possessed.

"The ring was too big for me," said Rodriguez, "but I wanted to wear it. I wanted people to ask me about it, so I could tell them, 'This was my dad's ring. It was given to me.' I wanted to have a legacy. I guess I wanted to belong to him, be the son who is bequeathed the king's ring."

Rizzo watched pain rise and fall in Joe's eyes.

"I knew I either had to put a ring guard in it or get it sized smaller, but I procrastinated. Kept telling myself, 'You've got to get this ring fixed.' And then I'd think, yeah, okay, I'll get it done.

"About two weeks after I got the ring, I was on the F train and got to the Bryant Park stop. By the time I got to the top of the station stairs, I realized the ring was not on my finger. I raced back to the platform, but the train was long gone."

Bryant Park was crowded, but only the calliope music from the carousel interrupted the silence around their table. Rodriguez pulled in a deep, sighing breath.

"I can only assume my dad loved me, because he never told me so himself. I didn't think I wanted any part of him. But then I got the ring. And I was proud to be his son."

Rodriguez looked up, stepped out of his memories.

"I've regretted losing that ring ever since. I've regretted my indifference and resentment of my father. Who knows what he had to live through, who knows what made him the man he was? And I've regretted my laziness and my foolishness for being so cavalier with a precious gift."

Rodriguez held up his hands and looked at his fingers.

"Part of me died that day. I don't know how else to express it. I had a chance to live a fuller life, and I lost it, squandered it.

"I've been looking for something, something I couldn't define, for a long time, Sammy. Maybe this is it. I'm not sure. But I know I'm going. I'm not going to live with any more regret. And besides . . . somebody will need to keep you in line."

"Me? *Me?* I'm the perfect traveling companion."

"You're a perfect pain in the butt." Rodriguez leaned his elbows on the edge of the small table. "Look, Sammy, you're one of the brightest guys I know. You're a critical thinker with excellent logic. You're a great asset to this team."

"But?"

"But . . . sometimes you really turn people off. I know you're just being a wise guy; it's part of the personality that makes you unique. And I'm used to your comments. But others aren't. Some of the things you say, or do, can seem pretty childish . . . immature. I don't want to hurt your feelings, Sammy, but if you want to be taken seriously by these guys, if you want to really be part of this *team*, then . . . and this is just my opinion . . . then tone it down a notch. Okay?"

Rizzo felt the burrito turn in his stomach. He wrestled with his defenses. *Keep it hidden. Keep it buttoned up.* He heard the children's laughter.

He felt like his heart was going to leap from his chest and go running down the gravel path.

"At least you had a dad." *Don't cry!*

"Sammy, I . . ."

Rizzo held up a hand. "It's okay. Looks like this is the time for True Confessions."

He pushed the soiled napkins in circles around the table. *It's okay . . . it's okay.*

"My parents were normal-sized people," Sammy said, his eyes still on the napkins. "I'm a dwarf. There's some medical name for it—some one-in-a-thousand shot. But it was a shot my dad couldn't take. Maybe he thought it was his fault. Maybe he couldn't take the comments. I'll never know. He left when I was two. Never seen him since."

Rizzo grabbed a bunch of the napkins and squeezed them in his fist, unconsciously depicting the ache in his heart. "It nearly killed my mom. Most of my early memories are of her crying. First, I felt it was my fault. As I got older, I realized just how much her heart was broken by my dad."

Sammy remembered the small apartment in Brooklyn where his mom always kept the shades drawn. How the blankness of her soul had slowly taken possession of her face.

"So I became the clown. I was the dancing elf with the endless wisecracks . . . the only one who could make her laugh." Eyes on the tabletop, Rizzo's hand went to his mouth, rubbed down and over his chin. "It was that way until she died." He sniffed, and held his breath.

"I'm sorry, Sammy."

The carousel stopped.

Another deep breath.

"I know, Joe . . . thanks." He waited a moment to gather himself, then looked up at his friend.

"I've known other short people who are really angry . . . really angry," Rizzo said. "They blame everything on big people. They've got some score to settle. Well, I came to peace with that a long time ago. I'm not anybody's fault. I just am. Sometimes, unfortunately, part of who I am is that dancing elf with the endless wisecracks. It's in there and just comes out. So thanks for the attitude check, Joe. I really want to be part of this team. So I'll try to keep my mouth in check. But no promises, eh?"

Rizzo forced a smile onto his face.

"Why do *you* want to go, Sammy?"

Sammy felt his smile warm. "Now you're really digging." He laughed. "You're going to think I'm even weirder."

"Impossible."

Rizzo picked up the intact half of his burrito and stuffed it back into the Chipotle bag. Then he looked at Joe.

"You remember Kallie Nolan?"

"The archaeologist . . . the one you said you put a move on, right?"

Rizzo nodded his head. "Yeah, a really bad move." He leaned into the table. "I'd go anywhere if it gave me a chance to see Kallie Nolan again. She was . . . special. She treated me like a normal guy. It was like she never noticed anything different about me. I never had a woman friend before, somebody I felt so comfortable with. And of course, being a guy, the hormones kicked in. One night when we stopped at her place after doing research at the library, I went over the edge. Way over. She kicked me out. Didn't talk to me much after that, then went back to school and on over to Jerusalem to study."

"Didn't you ever apologize?"

"I did . . . I tried . . . but after that night, it seemed like I could never break through. Like she was determined to wear a mask."

Rizzo's attention was drawn by the carousel. "I'd seen that mask before," he said. "It was the same one my mother used to wear to hide her pain. That's why I have to see her again, Joe. I need to make sure the mask is gone."

Rizzo grabbed the lunch bag, slid off his seat, and headed down the gravel path back to the library. "C'mon on, you sack of sweat. You'll make me late with all your sob stories."

18

"Excuse me, guys," Larsen said, his mind reeling from what he had just heard. "Let me get this straight. You found a scroll you believe to be a thousand years old, in an extinct language, in code. Somehow you broke the code, and the message claims the Jews built the Third Temple of God under the Temple Mount. All of this has remained secret for a thousand years, and no one has found this temple in the most archaeologically active six square miles on earth. And you are asking me if it's a hoax?"

The men sitting across from him looked like they had just been caught stealing hubcaps. Larsen's summary made their findings appear ludicrous.

"Yeah," said Rizzo. "Sounds pretty stupid, doesn't it?"

"Actually," said Larsen, his voice picking up, "no, it isn't stupid at all. I don't know if what is written on the scroll is true. But it certainly is possible."

"What! What are you saying?" exclaimed Bohannon, echoed by the others in the room.

"Oh, yeah, it could be there," said Larsen, leaning his elbows against the small conference table to close the distance between him and the others. "And it's not far-fetched to believe that, if it is there, no one has ever found it."

Recently slipping into his forties, Winthrop Larsen was medium in many ways—medium height, medium weight, medium features. His wire-rim glasses and short, auburn hair added to his bookish look. But there was nothing medium about the thrill Larsen felt, the adrenaline rush that had his body buzzing. He may have been standing in a small conference room on the third floor of the Humanities and Social Sciences Library on New York City's Fifth Avenue, but his heart and mind were trying to pierce the mysteries of the Temple Mount.

"Winthrop, I'm stunned," said Johnson. "Obviously, your comments are encouraging, although I never really expected anyone to take any of this seriously. But how can this message be possible?"

The team members each arranged for half a day off so they could have a late lunch and meet with Larsen in a conference room at the library. Now he was going to test their endurance. "Get comfortable," said Larsen, "because this will take a little bit of time.

"The entire area around Jerusalem, including the Temple Mount, is comprised of Cenomanian limestone. It's a sedimentary rock that behaves very strangely when water and pressure are applied. In laymen's terms, it melts. This result is called *karstic*. When rainwater seeps into the ground, the limestone melts, though ever so slowly, with a honeycomb of tunnels and caves forming naturally.

"In the nineteenth century, Charles Warren discovered a large, vertical shaft that went deep underground in the City of David, the rocky crag upon which the ancient city of Jerusalem was founded. Recent excavations discovered another karstic cave adjacent to Warren's shaft, which is big enough to hold twenty to thirty people.

"The Gihon Spring," said Larsen, warming to his lesson, "ancient Jerusalem's main water source, is also a karstic spring. The route that Hezekiah's tunnel followed was originally formed by an underground karstic stream.

"Basically, karstic caves, tunnels, and cisterns played a significant role in Judean antiquity, and it's likely that the Temple Mount is riddled with these things. Hang on to that thought, because it's important.

"The interior of the Temple Mount is a source of hundreds of legends, but little concrete scholarship. There is a great boulder in the center of the Dome of the Rock, the foundation stone. Jews believe the foundation stone is the point from which the entire world was created. Muslims believe the foundation stone was put in place by the angel Gabriel and is home to the 'well of souls.' It's all a mystery because the Muslim Authority—the Waqf—won't allow anybody underneath the Mount."

Rodriguez interrupted Larsen's lesson. "Winthrop, if the Temple Mount is really a mass of tunnels and caves, how in the world did it support a massive Jewish temple when it was there? How does it support the Dome of the Rock and the Al-Aqsa Mosque and the thousands of people who come there in pilgrimage? Why doesn't everything just fall into a huge sinkhole?"

"That's a good question, and one that the Jews would have had to answer before they could ever erect a temple as large as the one that was there in Jesus' time.

"The answer," said Larsen, "is that the temple of old and the Islamic shrines of today are not actually constructed on the Temple Mount. They are actually constructed on a huge, stone platform that was built by King Herod two thousand years ago."

He stepped to the whiteboard and began to sketch his explanation. "Herod's platform is three hundred feet wide, in its time, the largest in the world. If the platform was supported by Mount Zion only, it would tip over once anything of size was built on it. So Herod constructed a series of arches under the platform and also built four huge, stone, retaining walls to support the outer edges of the platform around the existing, natural hill. Then he filled in the area between the walls and the hill with stone, rocks, dirt—anything they could find and squeeze into the space.

"Herod was also extravagant in his use of water," said Larsen. "Herodian cisterns were man-made and elaborate, not only meant to capture drinking water for Jerusalem, but also to gather enough water for Herod's swimming pools, decorative pools, and fountains."

Larsen turned from the board and leaned against the edge of the conference table. "In Judea, collecting water and saving water were a matter of life and death. Torrential rainfall in Israel can fill a lake or create a rushing river in a matter of minutes. In the desert, one significant rainfall can supply a small town and irrigate its crops for nearly a year. Creating cisterns, whether plastering over existing karstic caves or carving out man-made, decorated pools, was critical. So we know that the Jews of the eleventh century, like their ancestors long before Christ, had the engineering and construction skill to create cisterns, caverns, or causeways of almost any size they desired."

Larsen paused, making sure he had everyone's attention. It was an unnecessary tactic.

"Gentlemen, it is certainly possible that the Jews of the eleventh century could carve out a great cavern in the limestone under the Temple Mount. But what is more important is that they probably didn't have to. In a region that already has many natural caverns, it might be much wiser to use an existing one, or at least enlarge a smaller one. There would certainly be a lot less debris to discard.

"Your research—Spurgeon's letter, Schwartzman's connection to Elgar, Abiathar's history, not to mention the violent opposition you have encountered in your search—appears to validate the authenticity of the scroll. So it's my belief," said Larsen, "that the only remaining question is not whether the Jews could have created a place for the Third Temple. The question is, does it exist?"

Bohannon smiled. *This is like the Fellowship of the Ring. Something tells me we're about to embark on a journey.*

Larsen was engaged with other members of the team in speculation about the Mount, tunnels, and other topographical information. Bohannon remained in the background, observing the group, sifting through what he had heard thus far, replaying the message of the scroll in his mind, and trying to connect the dots.

"Winthrop, I have a question for you," Bohannon stated over the conversation. The chatter stopped, and heads swiveled in his direction. "And there is really only one question. How do we get ourselves under the Temple Mount to find out if anything is hidden there?"

Uncertainty joined them in the room. Uncertainty about the implications of what they were hearing, its cost and its consequences.

"There is only one way for us to discover whether the message of the scroll is true or a hoax," Bohannon announced. "We need to go and look. And we can't leave this search for somebody else. Only God knows what might happen if the temple exists and it were manipulated for political or personal agendas. That could be a disaster.

"I don't know about these chaps, Winthrop, but I'm expecting to take an extended vacation in Jerusalem at the earliest possible moment. What do I need to know, and where do we go from here?"

Immediately, all the mouths were speaking at once.

⸻≈≈⸻

An hour and a half later, after Rodriguez had gone to the deli across 42nd Street and returned with pastrami and Swiss on rye and a variety of Snapples, they were once again gathered around the whiteboard as Larsen tried to give them a visual of what they were up against.

"You are facing a very difficult challenge," said Larsen, gathering up several different colors of dry erase markers, "actually, many difficult challenges. First, you have to get into Jerusalem. Not a difficulty in itself for men traveling on business. But, men with a load of underground equipment may draw some attention. And attention is going to be your enemy.

"How do you get near the Temple Mount? How do you investigate the Temple Mount? Greater yet, how do you get under the Temple Mount without drawing attention to yourselves? I won't even bother to address how you're going to get out, or what you're going to do if the thing is there. But let's just say you get yourselves under the Temple Mount somehow through one of the tunnels. Then what? Where do you go? How do you find your way around, assuming you can get around under there? How do you locate a temple that's remained hidden for a thousand years?"

Larsen shook his head. "I just don't know." He gazed thoughtfully at the whiteboard for a minute. "But perhaps we can narrow things down a bit.

"For what you are considering, perhaps the most important event came in 1867 when the Turkish/Ottoman authorities gave permission to a British archaeologist and explorer, Charles Warren, to explore the few tunnels they already knew existed beneath the Temple Mount. Their conditions were that he would work only during the day and only under the supervision of their officials. And that he would reseal each tunnel, close up every hole, once he concluded the dig.

"But Warren was a very ambitious young man," said Larsen. "He bribed his guards to give him freedom at night and, without the knowledge or consent of the Turks, began his own, independent search under the Temple Mount. From inside the existing tunnels, Warren and his assistant dug new tunnels under the Temple Mount. To avoid detection, they closed the tunnels behind them as they went."

"Yo," snapped Rizzo, "that doesn't sound very healthy. Sounds like they were trapping themselves underground. Not too bright, if you ask me."

"Unfortunately for his assistant," said Larsen, "that is exactly what happened. The man died in a cave-in during the process, and Warren was forced to leave his body where it lay.

"Warren, however, uncovered two points of curiosity," said Larsen. "Now, you must remember that nearly two thousand years of history passed from the time of Herod and his great temple to the time of Warren. Jerusalem was sacked, destroyed, and rebuilt several times. So what was ground level in Herod's time was now underground in Warren's.

"His first discovery is called 'Warren's Gate.'" Larsen began to sketch the inside of a tunnel. "It is a small gate or window sealed shut with stone bricks and mortar. Warren concluded that the gate led to the underbelly of Herod's Temple. Nearby, Warren made his second discovery—an alcove or cave, which he theorized was adjacent to the Holy of Holies of Herod's Temple. During Muslim control of Jerusalem, the alcove was used by Jews seeking a place of prayer near to the now-destroyed temple. Somewhere in time, both the alcove and the gate were sealed by authorities, and eventually, their existence forgotten . . . until Warren.

"Over the last hundred years, Warren's Gate and its alcove were not only the subject of numerous theories but also the flashpoint for many crises. Rumors abounded in 1911 that British excavators had secretly tunneled underneath the Dome of the Rock and uncovered and absconded with the temple treasures. In the early 1990s, an attempt by archaeologist Dan Bahat to secretly make an opening in Warren's Gate nearly caused a major war.

"Now, beyond history, what makes Warren of such interest to you," said Larsen, turning back to his rapt listeners, "is that Warren made a series of maps from his time in these tunnels. Today, it is clear that rather than spending most of his time burrowing beneath the Temple Mount as he thought, Warren actually discovered the continuation of the Western Wall. Warren reached bedrock at the northwest corner of the wall, and that's where his digging was forced to stop. But those maps are still in existence, and at least it's a place to start. Of all the spots in the tunnels that honeycomb Mount Zion, Warren's Gate is the one most pregnant with possibility."

As he looked at the "class" arrayed before him, Larsen spotted the tell-tale signs of information overload.

Joe Rodriguez stretched to the full length of his six feet and four inches. "Okay, so it looks like there's at least one way in and probably others," he said. "But there's something that I just haven't been able to figure out.

"This temple was a pretty big place, I gather. So the cavern the Jews needed to create would also have been a pretty big place. And from what Tom has been telling me lately, the Bible is very specific about the dimensions of the temple and about the material that is to be used to construct the temple—cedar and gold and bronze and cut stones—and all the artisans that were needed. How could these guys manage to get all this material underneath the Temple Mount without anybody putting two and two together? And this cavern would have to be huge, right? Where would they put the debris? I'll tell ya, it still sounds like the movies to me. It's a good story, but it doesn't make any sense."

Bohannon turned to squarely face his brother-in-law. "Yeah, the whole thing does sound like a movie, and it is hard to believe. But we've got one thing that appears to guarantee it's all real." He waited a moment. "If this is some fancy, elaborate hoax, why are people trying to kill us?"

Rodriguez grimaced and slowly nodded. "Listen, I need a break," he said, stretching his shoulders. "How about if we take ten minutes and then get back at it?"

19

Bohannon caught up with Joe in the hallway, even though it was only a few yards between the conference room and the director's lounge.

"Listen, Joe, how much have you told Deirdre about everything we're doing?"

"Not a lot," said Joe, as he ushered Tom into the lounge, following the wonderful aroma that had invaded their deliberations in the conference room. "And probably not as much as I should have. I don't think she would be very happy if she discovered that your 'accident' was a deliberate attempt to kill you, or that another one of this killer tribe tried to push Doc under a train. Or that the bunch of us are seriously considering embarking on a treasure hunt under the Temple Mount in Jerusalem. Geez, Tom, Deirdre and Annie would flip out if they realized everything that we're keeping from them."

Bohannon ignored the room's fine furniture and books and followed a finer smell into the kitchen, where some fresh-baked cookies—chocolate chip and oatmeal raisin—beckoned.

"Mmm, they're still warm," Rodriguez cooed. "An afternoon ritual around here. One of the assistants pops some Otis Spunkmeyer in the oven. Good thing we're just next door. These won't last long."

Bohannon set to work scooping cookies onto a plate, while Rodriguez loaded a tray with mugs of coffee and tea.

"I've told Annie about finding the scroll and trying to figure out what it meant. But not much since. She thinks we're just trying to identify the message because it will be of more value to the mission once we understand what it means. But Joe, what am I going to tell her? Keep your eyes open when you go out because somebody may try to kill you? I don't know," he said, shaking his head wearily. "I don't know. Sometimes I feel like I have to keep all of this from her. Other times I feel that if I don't tell her, then I'm not protecting her. That she would probably be safer if she knew to be careful. I don't know."

Bohannon caught Rodriguez's concerned look over the steaming mugs.

"There was a long time in our marriage when I wasn't honest with Annie. I had a secret thought life. But after twenty years of marriage, God gave me the strength to be honest with her."

Bohannon saw alarm in Joe's eyes.

"Yeah, you can imagine what life was like then," said Bohannon, shaking his head. "But over time, we worked through it, and Annie forgave me. And for the first time in our marriage, we could be honest, vulnerable, transparent with each other. You know what I found out? I used to believe that if Annie ever knew who I really was—you know, that guy that all of us have hidden under the surface, the one we never want our wives to know about—if she knew that guy, she would never be able to love me. How could she? I didn't love myself. But you know the amazing thing? The more Annie knows me, all of me, the real me, the more she loves me. I'll tell you, Joe, I don't get it at all. But it's the truth."

Bohannon hung his head for a moment, allowing the fullness of his emotions to be recorded and felt. "Ever since that day, our marriage has gotten better. Not every day is great, but over the last ten years, our life has been great, like we're kids on our honeymoon. And you know why? Because even when I screw up, I know I need to be honest with Annie. Most of the time, I can do it. Sometimes, I fail. But we have a new life together, and we both work real hard to keep it safe and make it work.

"And Joe," he said, rubbing the heels of his hands over his bloodshot blue eyes, "I can't keep this truth from her any longer. I just can't. Being honest is not an option anymore; it's a necessity.

"So be forewarned. Annie is going to know all about this tonight. And I'm going to tell her that we're going to Jerusalem as soon as we can figure out what we need and where to go. You can do what you want with Deirdre. I just didn't want you to get blindsided at home."

Bohannon looked up, and he was alone in the kitchen. Glancing to his left, he could see the retreating Rodriguez turning out of the doorway and into the hall, an urgency to his normally aggressive gait. Glancing to his right, he saw the tray of mugs, abandoned on the counter.

Good man, thought Bohannon. *Good man.*

"So that's the whole of it," Bohannon said. "I'm really sorry I didn't tell you all of this before. I never expected for it to turn into this huge . . . thing . . . and to be honest, then I got scared when we realized there were people after us." Bohannon rested his chin in his right hand, shaking his head as if the weight of the world rested on his neck. "I don't know. This has all been pretty crazy. But regardless, I should have filled you in on all the details long before this, and I'm really sorry that I didn't."

They were sitting in Paesano's, their favorite restaurant in Little Italy, at the little table tucked into a corner by the front window, giving them a clear view of the endless pedestrian traffic on Mulberry Street. It was a busy Thursday night, the weather was good, the Italian restaurants had once again invaded the sidewalks for the *al fresco* dining tourists loved, and Mulberry Street was closed to motor vehicles, giving the strolling throngs more room to study menus and listen to the pitch of headwaiters and a strolling brass band wearing red, white, and green caps.

Even in Little Italy, Paesano's was unique. While all around it, restaurants modernized, Paesano's was the quintessential, old Italian restaurant from 1940s movies. Chianti bottles hung from battered oak beams along with potted plants and fake grape arbors, and antique opera posters decorated the white plaster walls. There were no red-checked tablecloths. But Frank Sinatra, Dean Martin, and Perry Como crooned from the speakers; good, inexpensive pasta was served; and patrons enjoyed a nice view of the street without being out in the middle of the crowd.

Bohannon tore apart a piece of bread while he waited for Annie's reply.

"I forgive you," she said with no trace of rancor. "I wish I had known before; I would have known how to pray for you—even though these guys with the lightning bolt crosses are pretty creepy."

Bohannon knew his wife well enough after nearly thirty years that he, finally, was able to tell when there was something lingering behind those pretty blue eyes.

"What is it?"

"There's only one thing I need to know," said Annie, searching his face. "Why you? Why not let Dr. Johnson take this scroll to the British Museum and let the archaeologists try to figure out if a temple could be under the Temple Mount? Why should you or Joe be involved any further?"

That's the big question, isn't it? The one I've been asking myself.

He reached out his hand to hold hers. "I've been praying about this for a long time, trying to understand—not what I want to do, but what God wants me to do." He looked into her eyes. "Annie, each time I struggle with this, each time I bring it to God, I keep getting the same answer . . . *This is what I'm calling you to do.* Honestly, it doesn't make any sense. I've got my job to take care of. Shoot, I've got you and Caitlin and Connor to protect. I shouldn't be getting mixed up in something crazy like this. But . . ."

Bohannon's voice trailed off with his thoughts.

"But God's told you . . . called you, right?" said Annie. "Well, Tom . . . really . . . I'm not surprised."

Bohannon's head snapped up. "What?"

"Look, Tom," she said, stroking the back of his hand, "you've never been one to back down from a challenge. That's what made you such a great investigative reporter. Even under the hammering you took over the Swinton case, you did what you knew was the right thing to do."

Annie looked out the window at the strollers passing by, took a deep breath, and turned back to her husband. "I don't know why God picked you, but I know why I would pick you. You're honest, and you're trustworthy, Tom. You're not out to make yourself a million bucks. If this message is true, the world will need someone of character and integrity—someone they can believe in—to be sure it's not a hoax or some bad practical joke gone terribly wrong."

"But why me?" said Tom. "I don't want to be a hero."

"You are a hero," said Annie. "You just don't know it yet. You're made of the stuff of heroes. You and Joe, you're the kind of men who have always made the difficult choice to be heroes."

Bohannon shook his head in disbelief.

"No, I'm serious," she said. "You would have been the guys to build log cabins in the wilderness; you would have been the guys riding the Pony Express; you would have been the guys holding the line at the Battle of the Bulge. Why did those men do it? Why did those men take such risks? Because they were called to it, they were built for it, and they had the courage to overcome their fear and do their duty."

Bohannon felt heat rush to his cheeks. Annie smiled.

"I don't know why God's picked you for this," she said. "But in one way or another, he's been preparing you for this moment all of your life."

Annie waited until Alejandro, their favorite waiter, deposited their pasta in the appropriate locations.

"So what do you do now?" she asked. They both knew the answer.

Twenty minutes later, they were scooping up the remains of their shared *tartuffo*. Silence had been their companion.

"Tom, I know you've got to go . . . honestly, I do. I can't imagine you not following through. God has chosen you for this time, for this job. We know without a doubt that God brought us to New York, without a doubt that you were to work with the Bowery Mission. There are no unexpected circumstances in God's kingdom. Remember how often we earnestly prayed that we would be in the middle of God's will for us, no matter what his will was? You know that, once you seriously ask God to fulfill his will, the rest of it is his responsibility to work out. Well, I think God is working out his will in your life right now. And, Tom . . ."

She waited until he lifted his eyes from the ice-cream mess on the plate.

"I'm proud of you."

This was huge.

"I'm really proud of you," she continued, "because of how you have allowed God to work in you, heal you, change you. And how, for the last several years, you have never allowed one thing, not even failure, to deter you from pursuing God's will in your life.

"I'm proud of your character and your integrity, Tom. And most important, I fully believe that God will protect you and enable you to fulfill this work he has called you to."

Bohannon's mind stalled. This was overload. This was abundance of blessing. This was . . .

"Come on, hon," Annie said, pushing back her chair and rising from the table. "Let's go home and cuddle."

Bohannon's smile lit up the night outside. And Alejandro was surprised by an unusually large tip.

20

Seven thirty in the morning comes late in New York City. Commuters by the tens of thousands are on the move by five o'clock in order to reach Manhattan before the bridges and tunnels get clogged, before the Long Island Railroad and Metro North trains are turned into sardine cans on wheels.

Only a few leaden-eyed stragglers from Friday morning's first wave remained in the coffee shop on Third Avenue, just a few blocks off Grand Central Station, when Bohannon stumbled through the door, looking like he was still half asleep, the last to arrive.

Winthrop Larsen believed the coffee shop must have been modern in some earlier life. Now its chrome was dull, the plastic seats in the booths cracked and broken. But it smelled of fresh brewed coffee and toasted bagels. And that was good enough.

The location was ideal because it was close to the Bryant Park library for Joe and Sammy, Tom could walk over from Grand Central after exiting the subway, and it was convenient to Winthrop's hotel. Doc was needed at the Collector's Club, so it was just the four of them.

Winthrop was in the middle of a debate when Tom joined the others in a spacious, corner booth.

"You've got to admit, this story of yours is hard to believe," Larsen said. He rubbed his forehead. *How do I get through to them?*

"So we've got some major hurdles to clear." Joe threw up his hands. "But yesterday even you said it was possible for a temple to be under the Temple Mount."

"I also said it could be bogus," Larsen volleyed, his index finger punctuating each word. "Just because something is plausible, or possible, doesn't mean it's real."

"Hey," Bohannon interrupted, "can I get some coffee before we start duking it out?" Tom waved down a waiter, got a cup of coffee, and added on his order for blueberry pancakes.

"Look," said Larsen, "you guys believe there's a hit squad out there waiting for you, determined to wipe each one of you off the face of the earth. Now, I agree that the Doc and Mr. Bohannon have had some close calls. So it's understandable that you could feel there is some force out there opposing you.

"But it's also possible that this cross with the lightning bolt is the new punk rock symbol and six million have been sold around the world. And it's possible for men with Middle Eastern features to be feeling a bit tender when they are accused of doing some evil thing in New York City. And it's also possible that the message on the scroll is a fabrication."

Larsen was divided. Half of him wanted to believe this unbelievable story while the other half was laughing at his own naïveté. A divided mind was unacceptable for a scientist.

"Joe, listen . . . if we're ever going to take significant steps toward discerning the veracity of this temple claim, then we have to do it from a position of independent, unbiased observation, not assumptions. We need to test everything we believe, as much as possible."

"Okay," said Bohannon, "so yesterday, based on your understanding of geology and the history of Temple Mount archaeology, we agreed it was possible to find or create a space beneath the Temple Mount that would allow construction of a Third Temple."

"But that still leaves us with a lot of questions," said Rizzo, taking his bowl of oatmeal and bananas as the breakfasts arrived.

"The piece of this puzzle that's been driving me nuts," Rizzo continued, "is how eleventh-century Jews could accumulate the materials necessary to construct the temple and get those materials through a tunnel, under the Temple Mount, without being discovered. Right?"

Heads nodded.

"Well, I think I may have an answer," said Rizzo. "Look . . . I was checking this out last night."

Rizzo moved some of the dishes around, making space in the middle of the table, and laid down a piece of copy paper. On the paper were drawn a series of rectangles of different sizes. Each rectangle contained a protruding "tongue" on one edge and an indented "groove" on another end, but the location of the tongue and groove were different on each block.

"I think the greatest challenge the Jewish builders faced was preparing and transporting the stones needed to erect the temple," said Rizzo. "In most of the construction from that era, mortar wasn't used to keep the stones connected. Instead, builders cut each stone specifically to fit in its exact position relative to the other stones around it. Each 'tongue' was in the right place and fit perfectly into each 'groove,' supplying the building with stability and strength."

Bohannon looked up from his pancakes. "So how did the Jews get all of these huge, perfectly matched building stones under the Temple Mount without anybody getting suspicious?"

"They didn't!" Rodriguez held a chunk of omelet suspended over his plate. "That's what you figured out, right Sammy?"

"Bingo! Go ahead . . . fill in the blanks, Joe."

"Okay. The primary building material in Palestine is the one thing they have in abundance, limestone. The Jews needed to enlarge a cavern in a limestone hill," said Joe, "and they needed to cut limestone blocks to build the temple. One plus one equals two. There was no need to sneak huge blocks of stone through a tunnel and under the Temple Mount, and there was no debris. Once the location was identified, they just cut the stone blocks they needed right there, enlarging the cavern as they went along."

Rodriguez and Rizzo slapped high fives across the table, grinning at each other like prospectors who just hit paydirt. "You da man, Sammy."

But Larsen must have been wearing his doubt like a spring jacket. "What is it, Winthrop?" asked Bohannon.

Winthrop Larsen could have been anything that he put his mind to. More importantly, Winthrop Larsen could have been nothing at all and still lived a life of privilege and wealth that few other Americans could imagine. Winthrop's most endearing trait, though, was his unflinching honesty and candor, and the analytically questioning mind upon which that discovery of truth was most often based. Spawned from New England shipbuilders and traders, Larsen was as stable as Vermont granite, and often nearly as immovable.

"Gentlemen, these are theories," Larsen admonished. "Plausible, perhaps even likely, but theories nonetheless. Sammy, that was a fine analysis, but it's not verifiable truth. If we're thinking about going to Jerusalem to find out whether the temple in this message actually exists—and we all have to admit that's where this discussion is going—then we need to base our decisions on the most complete gathering of facts possible."

Larsen could see that his deductive process was about as welcome to these guys as a toothache. They clearly wanted action.

"So, I have a theory of my own to propose."

"All right, Winthrop," hooted Rizzo, "now you're gettin' with the program."

Larsen acquitted himself well at Yale, not only as president of the honors society, but also as captain of the rugby team and an Ivy League champion sculler. Throughout his life, Winthrop remarked that the nicest compliment he had ever been paid was that he "was just a regular guy." Now he found himself enjoying the camaraderie of these other guys more and more.

"If we accept that Elijah and Abiathar could have quarried their limestone from under the Temple Mount while at the same time enlarging their cavern, that still leaves the problem of the monumental engineering feat that would be required to dig out, and stabilize, a cavern big enough to construct a temple the size of Solomon's or Herod's that existed on the Temple Mount . . . huge, imposing structures, right?"

Heads nodded in reluctant agreement.

"Wrong!" Larsen snapped. "First of all, trying to construct an exact replica of Solomon's Temple would be a challenge since no one has any idea what it looked like. Drawings from the Middle Ages portray it as a massive citadel or cathedral. But, historically, this is not very believable. Today we are used to massive monumental structures. The ancient Levant was a much more modest place. Palaces, public buildings, cultic areas, and fortresses were the size of today's smallish cabins. Towns were the size of moderate Beverly Hills estates. The ancient city of Jerusalem, the City of David, was so small an area that it took a thousand years to convince the Christian world of its location."

Larsen's listeners devoured every word.

"An Israelite temple of Yahweh, contemporary with Solomon's, was uncovered at Tel Arad. It's slightly larger than a modest master bedroom. In the days of Ezra, the prophet, the crowd who saw the original Second Temple wept because it was so disappointing in comparison to Solomon's Temple. Now, their disappointment may have been with its grandeur, rather than its size. But when Herod refurbished the Second Temple, which was most likely also refurbished in the Hasmonean period, he not only built a much larger one, but he supposedly erected the new temple around the older one, while it was still being used, and only dismantled the older temple when the newer one was complete.

"So," said Larsen, looking over the expectant faces, "how big was Solomon's Temple? How big was Zerubbabel's Temple? How big does Abiathar's Temple have to be? Think small . . . small, elaborate, and decorated with gold, certainly.

The temples that adorned the surface of the Mount were surrounded by courts and other buildings. But to build a temple under the Mount, the space need not be massive, not by modern standards anyway.

"They would have needed some cedar—poles, planks, beams—but that would not have aroused any suspicion. And they certainly needed a good amount of gold and silver, but that could have been smuggled inside of sacks."

Larsen dropped his gaze to the table and scratched the stubble on his right cheek while his listeners waited patiently. Looking up, he took a deep breath.

"Gentlemen, I will be the first to admit that we are building theory upon theory. But I believe we have built a strong enough theoretical case to suggest a high level of probability that a Third Temple could possibly exist under the Temple Mount."

Larsen weighed the magnitude of his next words in the time it took to drain his cup of coffee. "I think there is only one way to know for sure. I think somebody has to go to Jerusalem and poke around under the Temple Mount . . . without getting shot."

21

In normal circumstances, Johnson would have been in heaven. He found comfort in the dusky richness of old leather that mingled with the smell of oil soap and wood polish. The warming scents of a library, a thick, rich carpet under his feet, a battered but friendly leather chair waiting to wrap itself around his tired bones.

But these were no normal circumstances. The five members of "the team" had converged on Rodriguez's office that cold, gray, rainy Saturday morning.

A few hours ago, they had cleaned off the desk, covered it with a large, topographical map of Jerusalem, then huddled around the desk, intensely investigating the map and sharing theories and suggestions.

Johnson wondered whether his compatriots also wrestled with personal doubts and fears. He seemed to be getting inexorably drawn into a task he did not feel equipped to undertake. Academic research? . . . An archaeological dig? . . . These he could handle. A search for the Third Temple of God? At that, Richard Johnson's heart grew faint. Johnson had found no peace in atheism, Eastern mysticism, or New Age mantras. To now put himself into the middle of an age-old religious conflict seemed . . . well . . . sacrilegious, like he was daring God to prove himself. And how did the others feel? Rodriguez, a lapsed Catholic; Larsen, raised a proper Episcopalian but now properly nothing at all; Rizzo, God only knew what; and Bohannon, a Bible-believing Christian with many unanswered questions. Was this ill-conceived quintet really thinking of taking on this investigation themselves, an investigation that could trigger seismic change for two of the world's great religions? Were they worthy? Were they capable? Were they crazy?

Johnson caught a questioning look pass from Rodriguez to Bohannon.

"Tom, whaddaya think?" Rodriguez asked.

"I know what I think," said Johnson, jumping in quickly. "We call the State Department the first thing Monday morning—the office here in New York—and ask for the man in charge."

Johnson plunged forward, not allowing an opening for debate. "We get an appointment to see him, tell him the story, show him the scroll, the letter, and the message, and get him to set us up for a meeting in Washington with someone who will know what to do with this information."

⌇⌇⌇⌇

Feeling the irritation of sleepless nights and annoyance at Doc's interruption, Bohannon cut off Johnson's argument. "Look, Doc, if—"

"Stop, Tom," Johnson flared.

Bohannon felt the burn at the back of his neck, heat rising through his cheeks, wrapping around his temples.

"This is an international diplomatic bombshell," Johnson continued. "If everything we've discovered is true, and there is a Third Temple sitting under the Temple Mount as we speak, and the world finds out about it before the State Department can huddle with the Israelis, the Palestinians, the Saudis, the Egyptians, the Jordanians—and probably the Syrians and Lebanese—well, when people say 'All hell will break loose,' they're speaking about this situation."

"C'mon, Doc . . . you're not lecturing to a bunch of undergrads, now," Bohannon complained. "You're blowing this up a bit—"

"No, no," said Johnson, throwing up his hands and forestalling budding objections, "you've got to be crazy to even think of continuing with this search. We were in this to find out what the scroll said, then we were in it to find out if its message was possible. But now, gentlemen, this is all beyond us. Do you think you can ignore the fact that two of us have nearly been killed in the last few weeks in what appears to be purposeful attacks?"

"We're not ignoring anything." Tom heard his voice rising, powerless to quiet it. "We're still not sure what we've got . . . if it's true."

"These people don't need true, don't you understand that?" Johnson challenged. "Look at what happened just recently. An earthen bridge leading to the Temple Mount was washed away by severe weather. When the Israelis tried to repair the bridge, the Muslim community erupted. Claimed the Israelis were trying to undermine the Dome of the Rock and the Al-Aqsa Mosque. There were riots in the streets of the Old City."

Johnson got out of his chair and stood over the map, pointing his long, bony finger directly at the Dome of the Rock. "That, gentlemen, is a ticking dirty bomb," he said with emphasis, his finger thumping on the position. "Something stupid or inconsequential could set off a feeding frenzy of violence that would shock the world and threaten peace for all of us."

Bohannon buried his head into his hands, shaking it back and forth. "Another doomsday prediction? Is that what you have for us?" Jackhammers pounded at his temples. "Look, Johnson, you were wrong about Swinton, and you're wrong about this, too."

Tension shimmered through the room. Bohannon raised his head. The others were still, staring at him. Johnson, standing next to the desk, oscillated at the wavelength of rage, purple fury painted on the flesh above his collar.

Bohannon could taste the air, that metallic scorch that followed on the heels of lightning.

"Still the bully, Mr. Bohannon?" Johnson, his voice hollow, tremulous, looked like he wanted to step toward Bohannon but didn't trust himself to lose his grasp on the desk. "Strike first, think later—is that not the journalist's mantra?"

Bohannon's heart clutched his throat. Old wounds—and a new betrayal— lay like a shroud over the window to Johnson's soul. *Oh, God . . .*

—⁓⁓⁓—

"What," Johnson asked, his voice trailing down to a whisper, "would the resident madmen of the Middle East do if, because of some inadvertent slip one of us makes, one morning next week they tuned into Fox News and discovered that the Third Temple of the Jews was ready and waiting for ritual sacrifice, and the coming of the Messiah, and none of the governments of the Middle East had any idea this was going to hit the radar screen?

"Moving forward with this now, on our own, would be madness."

Johnson set both hands on the desk in front of him, covering a significant section of the map, and tried to hold his emotions in check. He was determined. The others must understand. They must see his logic, must accept his argument.

"Taking this information, traveling to Jerusalem, attempting to gain access to the underbelly of Temple Mount, searching for a hidden temple—gentlemen, this is a death warrant. Trained, covert operatives would be putting their lives in danger trying this same stunt. But there's a more important consideration than our lives, than the lives of seven million Israelis and countless followers of Islam."

Johnson steadied his voice. "We may be pushing the button for the end of the world."

Johnson waited for Bohannon to erupt once again, for a barrage of objections. But none came forth. Johnson figured he knew why.

Ever since they had unlocked the code and deciphered the meaning of the scroll, Johnson wondered in the back of his mind about the discovery of the Third Temple, and what that would mean to the eschatological history of the world. He expected the others were wondering the same thing.

For more than two decades, Johnson had wandered through the world's religions, looking for something that made sense, that had some meaning for him, that struck a supernatural chord. He hadn't found it yet. But he picked up enough knowledge to know that the temple had something to do with the Antichrist, Armageddon, and the end of the world. He didn't know exactly what, but he did know that this was very explosive information and that it needed to be handled by experts.

This was not the time for a bunch of amateur archaeologists to go bumbling around Jerusalem and start World War Last.

Johnson looked at his compatriots, who appeared wilted like last week's lettuce. Only Larsen entered the void. He took Johnson's arm and led him out of Rodriguez's office.

"Doc, you make a strong argument," Larsen said quietly as they stood in a corner of the Periodicals Reading Room. "There certainly is a lot at stake. And we may get to a place where we need to step away and let the professionals deal with the possibility of a Third Temple. But I don't think we're there yet. Sure, we've got the scroll and the secret message, and we all believe the message is real. What we don't know is how it could be possible. How is it possible that a temple is under Temple Mount and has never been found? What do you think any government officer would do if we went to him with what we have so far . . . a half-formed theory with little factual support? We may, someday, need to face the doomsday scenario you fear, and that will force us to make some tough decisions. But making that decision now is a bit premature."

Larsen's argument was logical.

"Look, why don't you and I look into the question of the Mount? These guys can go home to their wives and their jobs and rest for a bit. Let's you and I see if we can put together a strong argument—a realistic, supportable argument—that eleventh-century Jews could have accomplished this amazing feat. If we can do that, along with translating the message of the scroll, maybe then we have something to take to a government official. Until then, well, I'd feel a little foolish trying to spin this yarn to the State Department."

Johnson knew Larsen was right.

"Okay. Tomorrow morning, my office. But if we get closer to this thing, we're heading to Washington, not Jerusalem. I'm too old to die now."

Turning away from Larsen toward Joe's office, Johnson came face-to-face with Bohannon. There were tears on Tom's cheeks.

"Doc, I'm so sorry. That was rude . . . mean-spirited . . . cruel to bring up Randall." Bohannon's eyes were pleading. "I'm sorry, Doc. Please forgive me."

Johnson opened his mouth, but no words came. He offered his right hand to Bohannon. And found himself in a warm, earnest, shaking hug.

22

The walls and bookcases of Johnson's Collector's Club office were covered with huge, blown-up copies of ancient and modern maps of Jerusalem. They included topographic studies of the Temple Mount, enlarged drawings of walls, gates, and steps, plus ancient documents, like those sketched by Charles Warren, which suggested routes for tunnels and other water sources in and around the Temple Mount.

Winthrop Larsen caressed the polished oak of the bookcases like the back of a long-lost love. He stood just inside the door and allowed the room to embrace him, his gaze absorbing every detail of Johnson's occupancy. He lowered his books to the table with care.

As he settled himself in the chair next to Johnson, Larsen caught himself fiddling with the Italian silk tie that hung incongruously around his neck. The tie mocked his familiar faded blue jeans and battered Top-Siders. Thankfully, he hadn't worn the same color or design as Johnson's.

Johnson and Larsen, both with letter-sized pads of paper, began taking notes, jotting down questions, and making lists as they tried to work themselves through different alternatives. Johnson had a fistful of his favorite writing instruments stashed in a coffee mug to his left—new or fairly new Ticonderoga #2 pencils, each sharpened to a precise point.

"The first question we need to answer is where to look," said Larsen, who tried vainly to breathe through his apprehension, the familiar stage fright that always accompanied his deliberations with Johnson. "It's a huge area to be investigating underground. The top of the Temple Mount is thirty-six acres by itself. The base of the mountain will be a great deal larger. Doing a random search, even if it were possible, could take us a year, and we still wouldn't find anything."

Johnson looked up from his pad. "We have one advantage," he said. "We're not the first ones to face that problem. Abiathar and his Jews would have faced the same issue, how and where to get access without being observed. They obviously had a way in and a way to get access to their cavern. It's possible that they used an existing tunnel or some other method of entry to get under the Mount. And it's likely that it would not have been a tunnel that anyone else would have normally used. So it's got to be obscure, or abandoned by the time of the tenth or eleventh century."

Larsen got up and crossed to the poster board taped to the front of a bookcase, upon which were pasted ancient drawings of tunnels, gates, walls, and waterways. Then he crossed the room and stood before a massive map of ancient Jerusalem with more than a dozen other views and cutaways framed around the edges. *Perhaps this is what all the study was about,* Larsen thought as he ran his mind over the Jerusalem terrain. *Perhaps this is what all the training, all the trips, all the research has led to. Thank God it's led to something. Perhaps now my father will find some value in my life. Perhaps now he will understand. Perhaps Richard will . . .*

"Richard, you've gathered a great deal of valuable information here in a short time," Larsen said as he turned away from the maps. "I congratulate you. But there are other significant possibilities that we should consider, perhaps add to these maps. First of all, we need to remember that there were at least five gates, the Huldah Gates, in the lower reaches of the southern wall. Herod built the wall to support the platform on top of the Temple Mount, and at least two of those gates led to underground tunnels that ascended up through the mountain and exited on the platform near the entrance to the temple." Larsen picked up a red grease pencil and began to mark locations on the map of ancient Jerusalem. "The gates were here," he said, making small squares, "and exited here."

"Yes, I remember," Johnson said, pointing the deadly end of his pencil at the map Larsen marked. "We took a group from the museum to examine those gates about ten years ago. The most western gate, the Double Gate, has a double-arch entryway and a double-section lobby once inside the gate, while the most eastern one, the Triple Gate, has a triple archway on the front, which is now blocked, and a lobby of three rooms behind the entrance. General archaeological opinion is that there were two and three passages, respectively, leading up from the gates. But no one knows what is behind the other three gates."

Larsen turned from the maps and walked back to the table where Johnson was making lists.

"Don't you think it strange, Richard, that there has been so much archaeological interest in Jerusalem and the Temple Mount, yet there remains so much that is completely unknown?

"I recently saw a quote from Hershel Shanks in *Biblical Archaeology Review*," Larsen said, as he flipped to the article. "'The City of David, a long, narrow ridge extending south from the Temple Mount . . . was home to Jerusalem's earliest settlers. But how much do we know about this crucial site? Despite, or perhaps because of, its claim to being the most excavated city in the world, Jerusalem continues to confound, and sometimes delight, archaeologists as recent excavations force them to rewrite the history of the ancient city, its fortifications and its water system.' It appears as if every week science is finding out more and more about Jerusalem, about the placement of its walls, the variety and security of its water systems, the spread of the city."

Larsen jumped as Johnson slammed his Ticonderoga into the wooden arm of his chair, shattering the pencil. "It's not strange that we know so little of the Temple Mount," said Johnson, "it's absolutely criminal!

"Winthrop, you have just touched on one of the things that absolutely drives me nuts"—Johnson waved the shattered remains of his pencil in Larsen's direction—"the arrogance of the Muslims and the incompetence of the Israelis in their stewardship of the most vital historical site in the history of the world.

"For thirteen hundred years, since the Caliph Abd al-Malik captured Jerusalem, Islam has maintained control over the Temple Mount, remarkably, even after Israel regained sovereignty over all Jerusalem following the '67 war. Even then, the Israeli government allowed Muslims to control the Temple Mount. But what have they done with such control? Absolutely nothing of value, and," Johnson said, stomping his foot, "most likely an incredible amount of harm."

Larsen returned to his seat. Experience told him his mentor was only getting started.

"Through all this time, the Muslims have virtually shut down access to the Temple Mount, even for legitimate research and the world's most renowned archaeologists. It's virtually impossible to get near the Mount unless you are an Islamic worshiper. And it is impossible to gain permission to do any kind of exploration primarily because the Muslims are frightened that evidence may be uncovered that verifies the existence of the Jewish Temple on the Mount, something they refuse to acknowledge even today.

"But that's not the worst part," Johnson said, wagging his finger in Larsen's face. "The most infuriating thing is that the Waqf is simply raping the Mount with impunity and destroying irreplaceable artifacts. Again, I believe it is a blatant effort to destroy any evidence of a Jewish temple, and therefore any Jewish claim, on the Temple Mount. Do you know that in the last few years, the Waqf has had the audacity to bring bulldozers—*bulldozers*—into the area under the Mount that some have called Solomon's Stables? And the bulldozers have dug out thousands of yards of dirt, poured it into dump trucks, and hauled the dirt to a dump, all without any oversight or supervision from international archaeological agencies. Random searches through the dump have found significant pre-Herodian masonry, portals and lintels and columns, strewn among the dirt and trash. Some of the artifacts have been recovered, but they have been thoughtlessly ripped from their contextual resting place, destroying any opportunity science would have had to make sense of their importance.

"And the Israelis?" Johnson scoffed. "The Israelis sit placidly and ignorantly on their butts and do absolutely nothing to stop this outrage." Johnson quickly got out of his chair and crossed to a corner of the room, digging through a pile of periodicals. He came back to Larsen with a magazine in his hand. "Here . . . here, read this. It's absolutely disgusting."

Larsen obediently reached out to take the magazine, a 2000 edition of *Biblical Archaeology Review* that Johnson had opened to an article entitled, "Furor Over Temple Mount Construction," by Steven Feldman, and then, with effort, ignored Johnson's pacing while he read:

> The furor stems from a construction project undertaken by the Waqf, the Muslim religious authority that controls the Temple Mount, to create a second entrance to the al-Marawani mosque, located under the southeastern quadrant of the Mount in an area popularly, but mistakenly, known as Solomon's Stables.
>
> The huge underground mosque at times attracts thousands of worshipers, so there was no question that a second entryway was needed for safety reasons. But the Waqf's decision to simply haul material from the area and to dump it, in the dead of night, in the nearby Kidron Valley has been attacked as irresponsible destruction of an archaeological site. Israeli archaeologists say the area should first have been subjected to a controlled excavation. Now personnel from the Israel Antiquities Authority (IAA) can only sift through the dump in the Kidron Valley in hopes

of gaining some raw, but context less, data about ancient Jerusalem.

Solomon's Stables served as a storehouse and stable in the 12th century A.D. for the Crusaders, who assumed that King Solomon had used the vaulted cavern in the same way. But the site actually dates to the reign of Herod the Great (37–4 B.C.), who greatly expanded the Temple precinct.

"It is one of the most important sites in the country, and they've gone at it with a bulldozer," Jon Seligman, Jerusalem region archaeologist for the IAA, told BAR. Seligman was appointed to his position at the very end of 1999, in the midst of the controversy—"Dropped into the boiling oil," as he put it—though he had served as Jerusalem district archaeologist since 1994.

Seligman said that the IAA has been examining the dumped remains, primarily pottery shards, coins and even some nails. About 40 to 45 percent dates to the Byzantine (fourth to seventh century A.D.) and early Islamic (seventh to eighth century A.D.) periods; about two percent dates to the late First Temple period (seventh to sixth century B.C.)—"The background noise of Jerusalem archaeology," in Seligman's words.

Seligman added that the dump was not his primary concern. "The issue is the Temple Mount," he said. "The dump is a side issue."

"This was an opportunity to learn about the site," Ronny Reich, an IAA archaeologist and a specialist on the history of ancient Jerusalem, told BAR. Now, according to Reich, that chance has been lost forever. Reich added that the material hauled away from the Mount might even have contributed to the debate on whether Jerusalem was a significant city in the tenth century B.C., the era of King David.

By destroying the historical context of the remains, the Waqf's action violates Israeli law, which requires the IAA to conduct excavations before construction can begin at any historically significant site. Relations between the Waqf and

Israeli authorities have been greatly strained, however, since 1996, when a decision by then-Prime Minister Benjamin Netanyahu to open an exit at one end of a tunnel running alongside the western wall of the Temple Mount led to widespread and deadly rioting by Muslims.

Israel's attorney general, Elyakim Rubenstein, admitted that law enforcement authorities had lost de facto authority over the Temple Mount. "The remnants of the history of the Jewish people are being trampled," he said. "The Waqf must be told that we have tolerance for their worship, but they will not be allowed to kick aside our history." Rubenstein acknowledged that "the issue there is a very sensitive one. Every Muslim home boasts a photograph of the Al-Aksa Mosque, part of which lies over Solomon's Stables."

Given the volatility of the situation, Shlomo Ben-Ami, Israel's internal security minister, announced in December that no forceful means would be employed to seal the new entrance. "I don't want to put on a show of force that will cause the entire city to burn," he said. Indeed, on December 6, Ahmed Tibi, an Arab member of the Knesset (Israel's parliament) and a confidant of Palestinian leader Yasser Arafat, warned, "If someone has the nerve to close the entrances, he is declaring war on the Muslims!"

At press time, the situation had become quieter, thanks in part to the Muslim holy month of Ramadan and to heavy rains that have hampered construction activity. Seligman told BAR that the work at Solomon's Stables was near completion in any case. But it seems only a matter of time before the issue flares up again elsewhere on the Temple Mount.

This is not the first time the Waqf has destroyed archaeological features on the Temple Mount. In the 1980s, an unauthorized trench dug to relocate utilities uncovered an ancient wall thought by an archaeologist who briefly saw it to be from the time of King Herod. It was probably a wall of one of the courts of the Second Temple. The wall was 6 feet thick, and a length of over 16 feet of it was exposed, but it was quickly removed and the area covered before it could be studied.

In 1993 the Israeli Supreme Court handed down a decision in a case that had been brought to prevent the Waqf from continuing to destroy archaeological features of the Temple Mount (see Stephen J. Adler, "The Temple Mount in Court," BAR, September/October 1991; and "Israeli Court Finds Muslim Council Destroyed Ancient Remains on Temple Mount," BAR, July/August 1994). The court found the Waqf guilty of 35 violations of the antiquities law that involved irreversible destruction of important archaeological remains. Even during the pendency of the lawsuit, however, the Waqf continued to destroy ancient features on the Temple Mount.—S.F.

Larsen put the magazine down and turned his head to look again at the immense map of the Temple Mount area of Jerusalem.

"Richard, couldn't this whole thing, the arrogance of the Waqf and the indifference, or incompetence, of the Israelis, couldn't that prove invaluable to us?"

"Are you kidding me?" Johnson blurted, snapping the point off another pencil. "Why they—"

"Doc, wait a minute, think," Larsen cautioned. "I'm not saying it's right. And anybody with any sense would never let it continue. But think about it at least from our perspective. First of all, this article tells us that there is already a mosque situated under the Temple Mount, another argument that it's possible for a temple to exist there. And, as you've noted, the Muslims have prohibited almost any exploration, either on top of or under the Mount. The only known study under the Mount was conducted by Warren, in secret, at night. But the dearth of information about the underbelly of the Mount has also prevented anyone from stumbling upon Abiathar's Temple. Lastly, we know there are several documented tunnels and cisterns either at the base of, or under, the Temple Mount, correct? Well, how many other tunnels are in existence that no one has ever discovered? And they could be tunnels that are easily accessible if you knew where to look, but have never been officially uncovered."

Larsen reached out his hand and placed it on Johnson's arm. "Look, don't let your righteous anger ruin your perspective. If we can find a way into the Mount—or should I say, once we find our way into the Mount—if we do it right, we won't have to worry about a bunch of archaeologists or a bunch of tourists tripping over us. Nobody gets under there. Once we do, we'll have the place to ourselves. It will make the search much easier knowing we have free access and don't have to worry about making noise."

Johnson looked at Larsen as if he had two heads. But his face softened, and his reason returned. "And I thought you were the student," he said respectfully.

Larsen blushed, then tried to hide his delight behind a light chuckle. "Well, since you're in a receptive mood, I've got a few other thoughts for you. I think I may have identified three potential entrance points for us, entrance points that may not be under constant scrutiny by the authorities."

Tossing aside his ravaged pencil, Johnson capitulated.

"The first," Larsen said, returning to the map of the Temple Mount and pointing to the areas he had identified, "would be in the area of the southern wall we've already been talking about, the Huldah Gates. The second would be an area around the Gihon Spring. And the third would be the recently uncovered King's Garden Tunnel." He looked to Johnson for rebuttal or release.

"Press on, my friend, you have my interest."

"Okay, let's take the Huldah Gates first," Larsen said, buoyed by Doc's encouragement. "As you said, most pilgrims entered the Herodian Temple Mount area through either the Double Gate on the west or the Triple Gate on the east. A Herodian entry chamber, which is only partially preserved, exists inside the gate and leads to tunnels through which the worshiper could walk up to the level of the Temple Mount esplanade.

"Now, there were two *mikva'ot*, or ritual cleansing basins, on either side of this tunnel's exit. The pools provided the last opportunity for worshipers to cleanse themselves ritually before entering consecrated ground. In their surveys late in the nineteenth century, Charles Warren and Charles Wilson identified two subterranean cavities beneath the Temple Mount. Recently, other researchers have claimed these cavities were the Jewish ritual baths that were situated at the end of the tunnels from the Huldah Gates. But the main point for us is that what once could have been cleansing basins on the surface of the Mount were already, over a hundred years ago, well beneath the surface.

"It's possible that when we get to Jerusalem, we may be able to access these cavities, as Warren called them, or other cavities or caverns that are underground, and find an entry point to the tunnels that at one time led from the Huldah Gates to the surface of the Temple Mount," he explained, returning to the assembly of maps and charts. "Perhaps along one of those tunnels, we could find some clue to the whereabouts of Abiathar's Temple. This is a possibility, but not, I believe, our best possibility."

"Okay, professor," said Johnson, with a patrician's bow of the head, "what is our best possibility?"

Addressing the map of Jerusalem at the time of Jesus, Larsen again took the red grease pencil and drew a small square near the base of the escarpment upon which the city rested, at the edge of the Kidron Valley, southeast of the Temple Mount. He then drew another square, outlining an area at the very southeast corner of the city, directly against the city wall, at the very end of the City of David. Pointing to the squares in order, Larsen stated, "The Pool of Siloam, just inside the Tekoa Gate at the southeast tip of the City of David and . . . the Gihon Spring, across from the Mount of Olives at the base of the escarpment." He looked over at Johnson.

Johnson nodded. "Right. Hezekiah's Tunnel carried the water from the Gihon Spring to the Pool of Siloam," said Johnson. "Since the Gihon Spring was inside the city walls, Jerusalem's water source was protected in the time of siege."

"Ah, that's what we were taught," said Larsen, turning away from the map and resting his hands on a nearby chair, "but now it appears that what we were taught was completely wrong.

"For years, the most educated and accepted theory of Jerusalem's walls was that they could only be built at the top of the escarpment, both because of engineering difficulties and also because any lower position would have left the city within range of enemy archers standing on the other side of the Kidron Valley. So it was theorized Hezekiah's Tunnel was constructed to bring freshwater from the Gihon Spring to the Pool of Siloam, inside the walls.

"But Reich and Stammers have unearthed a fourteen-foot-wide wall that predated Hezekiah, that runs along the base of the escarpment, and completely encloses the Gihon Spring. The remains of the wall reveal the existence of two huge towers on either side of the spring, obviously designed to protect the spring from attack."

Larsen watched Johnson as he absorbed the new information. "So, why the tunnel?" Johnson asked.

"Exactly, why the tunnel?" Larsen responded. "Why cut a fifteen-hundred-foot tunnel when it was not necessary to keep the water supply safe? And," he said, turning back to the map, drawing a serpentine shape along the face of the escarpment, "why start the tunnel from both ends at the same time? Wouldn't that make the chance of meeting in the middle nearly impossible? And why this highly irregular 'S' course? Contrary to popular lore, this was not an engineering marvel where the two teams miraculously converged. From both directions there are numerous dead ends, obvious starts and stops, as the teams tried to find each other. But the most important question is, why build it in the first place?"

"Do you think it possible that Abiathar may have used the Siloam Tunnel as his point of entry to the lower reaches of the Temple?" Johnson asked, tracing the course of the tunnel with his finger. "That perhaps, if we could gain access to the tunnel from the Gihon Spring, we may find a hidden point of access that would lead us farther under the Temple Mount?"

Larsen stretched for a moment. "Can I get you a cup of coffee, or tea?" He walked over to a sideboard that Johnson had set up with a small coffee urn and carafes of very hot water. Johnson was expecting a long day.

"Tea, please . . . sugar and lemon," said Johnson, looking at the maps rather than at Larsen. "Winthrop, I really appreciate all of your insight. But there's something that bothers me about each of the first two possibilities."

"Go ahead, poke holes in them," Larsen said, stirring the mugs. "I have issues, too."

"Well," said Johnson, "I think the Huldah Gates are interesting, but they are too close to the Mount itself to really be a 'secret' entrance for Abiathar to be constructing a temple. There would simply be too much activity, too close to the Mount, for it to be kept a secret.

"The second possibility, the tunnel to the Gihon Spring, is very curious, particularly now with the information of the wall existing around the spring. It's farther away from the activity of the central city, both ends of the tunnel would be close to a gate, and at night, in darkness, I could see the tunnel being very accessible to a priest who could have handpicked the guards who were on duty. But the challenge I have is the direction the tunnel runs, primarily from north to south . . . if you start at the Gihon Spring, away from the Temple Mount area. And the spring itself is already several hundred yards south of the Mount enclosure. It's just an assumption on my part, but I think Abiathar and his father would have planned to erect their Third Temple as close as possible to the location of Herod's Temple, at least to the foundation of Herod's Temple. I would think proximity to the Holy of Holies would have been critical to the Third Temple."

Larsen startled Johnson, whose attention was thoroughly engrossed in the map, when he placed the steaming mug of tea in front of him. "Sorry," Larsen said, placing his hand on Johnson's shoulder. "Your reservations are the same as mine. Either one is possible, but neither one seems perfect. Which brings us to the third possibility."

Setting his own mug down as he again approached the map, Larsen's adrenalin surged. "There is another, recently discovered candidate. A few years ago, archaeologists uncovered several yards of a wide, underground passage that they speculated had been used for either sewage or drainage during the Second Temple period. The passage runs under Tyropoeon Street, directly along and parallel to the Western Wall of the Temple Mount. So far, all the sources I have checked report that the excavations have not yet penetrated beneath the Kotel, the Western Wall itself. It is believed by most researchers that this passage was used by many Jewish leaders for escape during the Roman conquest of the city. This passage also runs north to south, but in following the Western Wall, it also passes extremely close to where we believe Herod's Temple was located and about as close to the Holy of Holies as one can get. From what I can determine, this drainage tunnel must be very close to Warren's Gate.

"In addition to being in close proximity of the Second Temple's location, this passageway empties out into the lower part of the Kidron Valley, where the Kidron meets the Himnom, in an area known as the King's Garden, just below the Pool of Siloam. Now, that would have been a very long walk, from the southeast corner of the city, under Siloam, all the way up to the Temple Mount area. But this passage is wide, it's high, and it could have easily been used to transport material to a building site under the Mount." When Larsen turned away from the map, he nearly bumped into Johnson.

"That's it," said Johnson. "I'd bet my stamp collection on it. That's it!" Johnson threw his arm about Larsen's shoulders and turned him back to the map.

"Well, even if the King's Garden Tunnel isn't the way Abiathar made his way into the Mount," said Larsen, relaxing now that he had his presentation out of the way, "we've now got at least one route that would give him access that is more than a possibility; it is an active probability. Doc, I know you think we need to give this to the government. And I understand the potential danger we face here in New York and once we get to Israel. But think of this for a moment. If you are worried about a leak from our small group, what might happen if we share this information with the government? Talk about a leaking sieve. Right now, all we have is a letter in an unknown language and a hunch. Is that enough valid information to bring in the State Department? Is this enough information to risk the Washington press corps getting a hold of it and stampeding off to speculation after speculation?

"I don't think so," said Larsen, as they both returned to the table. "Doc, I believe we must go to Jerusalem and see if we can discover whether this Third Temple really exists. If it does, then we take it to the State Department. If it doesn't exist, no one is hurt, and we are the only ones who are disappointed."

Larsen saw the strained look on Johnson's face, watched while he ran his hand through the silver mane and rubbed the back of his neck.

"Let me throw two other items into consideration," said Larsen. "If we all decide this is the right step for us to take, I'll finance the entire operation, and we won't lack for anything, or any possibility. And before we go, I'll speak to my uncle."

"The general?" Johnson asked, raising his eyebrows.

Four-Star General Ethan Allen Larsen—thirty-year veteran of the military service; twice winner of the Silver Star—was the chairman of the Joint Chiefs of Staff, under the authority of the commander in chief, the president, leader of the entire military might of the United States of America. While Winthrop's father had been disappointed in his son's choice of a profession, Uncle Ethan had been one of Winthrop's most steadfast allies, a man he could trust and on whom he frequently relied for good advice and wise counsel. The general also played a wicked game of squash, but not with the same reckless abandon or skill as Winthrop.

"Uncle Ethan's over at the Pentagon now. I'll ask him to get us a thermal imaging scan of Jerusalem, particularly the Temple Mount area, from one of his spy satellites, along with some high-res, close-up photos of the entire Temple Mount area. I can also ask him for an up-to-date and complete 'threat assessment' for Jerusalem and the Temple Mount and a capabilities assessment for the security forces of the Waqf and the Islamic Authority. I'll tell him it's for my doctoral thesis. I think he'll buy it.

"If we go, Doc, one thing is certain. We will be prepared."

Johnson's eyes remained locked on Larsen's. "I hope you are right, Winthrop. For all of us, I hope you are right."

⸺⁓⁓⸺

"What's wrong with you, boy? You expect me to believe that sack of spit? Was I born under a rock in some cave?"

Winthrop Larsen's ears were burning. "Listen, Uncle Ethan, I was just asking a question about—"

"Your doctoral thesis my Aunt Nellie's patoot. Don't try to play me, Winthrop. Thermal imaging sat photos, I can buy that if you're looking for an underground tomb. But why are you asking me questions about an encrypted satellite phone? What are you up to, Winthrop? And don't give me that thesis bull."

Winthrop was so comfortable talking to his uncle that his question about the encrypted satellite phone slipped out before his brain could catch it. But Uncle Ethan caught it . . . Ethan Allen Larson, chairman of the Joint Chiefs of Staff, missed very little. Winthrop scrambled for a satisfactory answer.

"Uncle Ethan, I'm sorry. Forgive me, sir. I didn't mean any disrespect."

"Then what in Sam Hill is going on?"

"I will be looking for hidden tombs in the Kidron Valley. But there's something else I'm looking for and . . . well . . . I thought it best you not know the details, sir. I wanted you to have deniability. Let's just say I'm going to be out of the Israeli zone for a while. And a satellite phone that can't be picked up might come in handy."

There was a long silence on the other end of the phone. Winthrop held his breath, trying to grasp control of his racing heart and rising anxiety. He was telling his uncle the truth . . . sort of . . . at least so far, and he wanted—

"Boy, you worry me sometimes."

Winthrop didn't know how to answer. He couldn't implicate the general in what they were planning.

"Who's going to have your back?"

"Sir?"

"Who's going to have your back? Wherever you're going, the best plans can turn into a snake pit in seconds. Who's going to save your sorry rear end if this escapade of yours blows up?"

"Well, I . . ."

"Button it, Winthrop, and listen sharp. I'm going to give you a phone number. In ten minutes, you call this guy. Tell him what you need, then do what he tells you. But two things, Winthrop."

"Yes, sir?"

"Don't ever jerk me around again, boy."

Guilt and regret cackled in Winthrop's spirit. "Yes, sir."

"And Winthrop, don't worry. I've got your back."

"I—"

"Slap a lid on it, boy. You get your butt in the wringer over there, you call this guy. I'll know how to contact you, too, if necessary."

Winthrop's love for his uncle caught in his throat.

"Thank you, Uncle Ethan. I'm sorry . . ." Larsen ran out of words.

"Winthrop, you're like my own son." The general's voice had lost all its edge. "I forgive you. But I won't forgive you if you get yourself hurt over there. Just don't do anything foolish. You listenin' to me, boy? Keep your powder dry and your head down. Now, tell me everything about this cockamamy plan of yours and then give me ten minutes, got that?"

"Yes, sir." Winthrop felt like saluting. *I don't deserve that man.*

23

Sunday night was quiet in the house. Bohannon sat in the old, ugly recliner in his study. In his lap he held a heavy pile of paper—printouts from Web sites, articles, and information about Jerusalem and the Temple Mount. Now that they were actually going to Jerusalem, he felt compelled to learn as much as he could about the city. Preparation and a sharp memory had been his greatest allies as a reporter, and the habit was tough to break.

Thus far, Bohannon had discovered that the Temple Mount was the central, historical focus of Jerusalem, both in ancient and modern times. The site was home to Solomon's Temple, to Zerubbabel's Temple that was built by the returnees from the Babylonian Exile, and to the enlarged and spectacularly refurbished Temple that Herod the Great constructed around and over the existing structure before dismantling it. What remained on the thirty-six-acre Temple Mount platform today was the result of two major building efforts: the first begun about 20 B.C. by Herod the Great and the second occurring under the Umayyad caliphs in the late seventh century.

———

Sunday night was quiet on the Fordham University campus. Many students were still home for the weekend, others sleeping off the weekend or cramming for finals. Caitlin Bohannon left the library carrying three books and a knapsack and headed cross-campus to O'Hare Hall, the five-story dormitory that was her August-to-May home. Her thoughts were on her psych final, not on the man who emerged from the shadows of the construction site on Martyr's Lawn.

Slipping past Larkin Hall, on the west side of the old Duane Library, Caitlin was aware of the fact that few people were about. She was a junior, and a girl didn't survive for long in New York City—let alone on a college campus in the midst of the Bronx—without developing urban radar, an early warning system for potential danger. But Fordham was relatively safe, emergency call boxes were stationed throughout the campus . . . and psych was dominating her thoughts. She walked on the west side of Thebaud Hall, skirted the grass meadow of Edwards Parade, and entered the tree-lined path that flanked Keating Hall—Fordham's most recognizable landmark.

That's when she noticed the person behind her—short, huddled into a burgundy, Fordham hooded sweatshirt, probably another student sweating the finals. She could not be aware of the second man, hidden under the trees of the pathway ahead.

—⁓⁓⁓—

Prior to his study, Bohannon only knew of Herod from the biblical Christmas stories: the mad, jealous king of Judea who ordered the massacre of all male children in Bethlehem. He didn't know that King Herod was a master builder on an unprecedented scale.

In addition to his soaring palace at Masada and the deepwater port he carved out of the coast at Caesarea—including a 3,500-seat amphitheater—Herod initiated a project to expand the temple area of Mount Zion by creating a vast level platform bordered by a massive retaining wall.

Herod more than doubled the size of the previous Temple Mount. His enlarged enclosure constituted the largest sacred space in the whole of classical antiquity. By comparison, the area dedicated to the goddess Athena on the Acropolis of Athens, including the Parthenon, occupied barely a fifth of the area of its Jerusalem counterpart. Herod's glorious sanctuary was destroyed in 70 A.D. when the Romans conquered and burned Jerusalem, effectively ending the first Jewish revolt against Rome.

—⁓⁓⁓—

A dark shape moved out of the shadows ahead, into the path. Caitlin stopped. She turned her head. The student behind her was closing the distance quickly. An ally, perhaps? Someone to walk with?

She glanced quickly to her left—the shape was moving toward her—and swung back to the right. The "student" looked much too old.

"Excuse me, miss, but could you—"

The psych book was her heaviest. Dropping the other two, she hit the "student" square in the face, spine first, with her right hand, pulled the pepper spray from her pocket with her left hand and let fly toward the closing shadow on her left. Without waiting to check out the results, Caitlin spun on her heel and raced across the broad, open expanse of Edwards Parade.

⸻⸻

It was late. Bohannon wasn't surprised that he had nodded off over the stack of papers in his lap. He drank some of the water by his side, poured the rest in his hand, and rubbed it on his face.

He had been surprised to discover that, after the destruction of 70 A.D., the Temple Mount remained largely unoccupied for seven hundred years, until the late seventh century when the Umayyad Caliph Abd al-Malik and his successors reclaimed the site and established what exists today: the splendid Dome of the Rock on a raised platform in the middle of the esplanade, and the Al-Aqsa Mosque at the esplanade's southern end. The Muslims renamed the sacred enclosure al-Haram al-Sharif, "the Noble Sanctuary."

⸻⸻

As Caitlin sprinted south across the flank of Edwards Parade, she pulled out her key ring, put the oversize whistle in her mouth, and blew with all the breath remaining in her lungs. Before she reached the campus security office to the west of Thebaud Hall, two security officers were running in her direction and a security vehicle—lights flashing—was circling behind her.

Ten minutes later, an officer brought her bloody psych book into campus security. Finally, Caitlin wept.

⸻⸻

The only surviving part of the temple complex from Herod's period, Bohannon discovered, was the incomplete circuit of the enclosure wall, the south, west, and east sides, its distinctive masonry leaving no dispute to its Herodian lineage. On the south, the ancient masonry had now been laid bare along the entire length of the wall, which was also the southern wall of the Haram al-Sharif. The western

Herodian wall was also uncovered along its entire length, the southern part of it the Jewish devotional section known as the Western Wall, formerly the Wailing Wall. Like the southern wall, the western wall of the Temple Mount was also the western wall of the Haram al-Sharif.

If they were going to succeed, Bohannon and his team would have to get under, over, or around those walls without being detected.

The phone rang. *Who can it be at this hour?*

———⌇⌇———

Joe Rodriguez sat on the sofa. Annie and Deirdre were upstairs with Caitlin, safely entrenched in the warm confines of the master bedroom. Caitlin was safe, unharmed. Joe looked ready to tear the guts out of a rhino. Tom had all he could do to keep his hands from shaking.

Bohannon didn't know how long they had been sitting in silence.

"This changes everything."

Tom could barely hear the words.

"I bet it was them," Joe muttered. "I bet it was them. I'll kill them if I ever get my hands on them."

"Get in line." Tom looked up at Caitlin's high school graduation picture on the mantle. He twisted his hands together and set his jaw. His insides felt like a hundred pounds of wet concrete.

"You know," Bohannon's voice was a whisper, "for most of my life, I've told people I believe in God. Until Annie and I got married, that was basically what it was, words. Then I began to see the depth of her faith and experience its impact on our life together. It's been a long journey"—Tom swiped his right hand through his hair—"but there have been moments when God's presence, his love, have seemed so real, so close."

Bohannon got out of his chair and crossed the room to take Caitlin's picture in his hands.

"Annie and I have spent a lot of time talking about this so-called adventure of ours and praying about it as it became clear that someone would need to find out if Abiathar's letter is true."

Tom lowered the picture and looked at his brother-in-law. "Joe, I'm afraid I may never see my wife or my kids again. I'm scared that I may never come home, and so is Annie, even though she's trying carefully to hide it. I've been feeling like I have to go to Jerusalem. I can't explain it any better than to say I've felt 'called' to do this.

"But now . . ." Bohannon walked over to the sofa and handed Caitlin's picture to Rodriguez. "Now, we're going to find this thing, shove it down their throats, and let them choke on their lightning bolts."

24

Late Friday night the fifth of June, the team met at Richard Johnson's office in the Collector's Club for their final review of preparations. They were booked on a 6:00 AM El Al flight the following morning. Bohannon felt they all needed some rest, but none of them were likely to sleep that night. So it was a blessing that they had something to keep their minds occupied: gathering, examining, practicing with, and packing their survival gear, spelunking gear, and a miniature, mobile video camera with catheters for probing under the Temple Mount.

When they needed a break from packing, they reviewed the satellite photos provided the day before by Winthrop's well-connected uncle and the small assortment of electronic gadgets Winthrop had purchased from Uncle Ethan's shadowy contact—a satellite phone with an encryption option in a padded, metal carrying case; a pair of high-end GPS units; and a small, square item about the size of a laptop computer battery.

"What's this little do-dad?" Rodriguez asked.

"It's called Siren," Larsen answered, "and it is a very sensitive and effective tool to detect sound. This little device just may save someone's life."

Rodriguez and Rizzo had been busy packing a medical kit on Johnson's conference table at the corner of the room, but they were also following the conversation between Bohannon and Larsen. "Winthrop," Rodriguez asked, "why would a sound detector be so valuable?"

The maps and drawings of Jerusalem still hung from the bookcases. Larsen crossed to one close-up of the Temple Mount. "You see these walls," he asked rhetorically, pointing to the massive walls that supported the Temple Mount platform. "They may look strong, but they are far from it. The walls supporting Herod's Temple platform, after two thousand years, are crumbling before our eyes."

That got everyone's attention.

"All of the walls have at one time or another collapsed in part or in whole," said Larsen. "The Romans, after conquering Jerusalem, spent an entire month systematically tearing down the Temple and its retaining walls, dumping the debris into the surrounding valleys until the fill reached the level at which they were working. The south and east walls were probably collapsed to the last few courses by the Roman soldiers. By late in the Roman occupation of Palestine, it is believed that the Mount was somewhat restored in order to construct a pagan temple on the platform.

"Of one thing we're sure," Larsen continued. "During the early days of the Muslim occupation, the entire area was beautifully restored. Many of the stones from the retaining walls were placed back in line, and extras were used to construct two elaborate palaces along the southwest corner. But then in 749, a transitional period between the Byzantine Empire and the Muslim rule, the southern wall collapsed completely from a massive earthquake. Another, more destructive earthquake devastated the Mount in 1546, swallowing up the Al-Aqsa Mosque, damaging the Dome of the Rock, and destroying the dome of the Church of the Holy Sepulcher.

"Now, all of that would simply be a history lesson," Winthrop stressed, "except that the two walls that remain the most vulnerable to collapse are the southern and eastern walls. These are the highest walls and the ones that run farthest down into steep valleys below. The primary danger remains earthquakes. Jerusalem is only a twenty-five-minute drive from the most active seismic area in the world, a fault area that records three hundred measurable events each year."

Winthrop walked over to the outside wall of the office, turned on the device, and held it against the wall. "Today, right now, the southern wall is in a state of possible collapse," he said. "During the Intifada uprising in 2006, Muslim authorities illegally carried out a radical digging project along the southern wall, emptying out the interior of the Mount's southeast corner. The Muslims kept no record of what was done structurally. It is possible, more than likely probable, that retaining features inserted by Herod and designed to stabilize the integrity of the wall were removed. The wall began to buckle and now is curving outward and leaking water after rainfalls. The last information I received is that the Israelis had agreed to allow the Jordanian Waqf to send Muslim engineers to inspect and repair the wall.

"But the engineering crisis remains," Winthrop said, turning to face the room while he held the device against the wall. "If the worst happened, Joe, and you were trapped on the other side of this wall, I think you would be very happy if one of us had this dandy little trinket in our back pocket."

"Yeah," said Rizzo, "maybe we could use it to order a pizza."

—∿∿∿—

Winthrop looked at the small device in his hand. It was far from high-tech, but it might be the most important piece of equipment they were carrying with them. The object was simple, but sturdy, essentially a motorized video camera about the size of a thin cell phone mounted on a narrow, steel plate. The plate was welded to a pair of axles and a small electric motor that drove four, independently suspended, mini tank treads. The entire unit was painted a flat gray and was no more than five inches long, a couple inches wide, and about two inches deep.

"Sewer Rat. It's an apt name."

Dr. Johnson had come up behind Larsen and sat down next to him. "I wonder how engineers ever checked the integrity of pipe installations before this little guy was invented," Johnson marveled.

"The remarkable thing to me," said Larsen, "is not only that they use something like this to inspect underground sewer and gas lines, but they can also use it inside major conduit to inspect the integrity of telephone or fiber-optic wire systems. It has proven very reliable. Between the Sewer Rat and the video-head catheter systems we got through medical supply, we should be able to penetrate just about any area under the Temple Mount. At least," said Larsen, looking over at Johnson, "I hope so."

"Well, Winthrop, if this most unlikely of expeditions is successful, we will all owe you a great debt of gratitude. Your generosity and your uncle's assistance have provided just about anything we could have dreamed."

Larsen self-consciously nodded his thanks and looked to his left. He was surprised to find Johnson staring at him. Johnson's steel-gray eyes were alive with concern, not excitement, an intensity that unsettled Larsen's equilibrium. He held Johnson's gaze and waited.

"Winthrop, why are you doing this?" Johnson asked in a low baritone, trying to keep the conversation private in a very animated room. "Why are you willing to risk your life on what may be a wild-goose chase? I understand why I'm going." Cradling his coffee cup, Johnson leaned against a door frame and closed his eyes. "I would shoot myself if I couldn't go on this adventure," he whispered, his head slowly rolling back and forth. "God or no God, Temple or no Temple—this could be making history, not just reading about it or teaching it. And it's time I made some history."

Johnson's eyes opened abruptly as he continued. "We both know why Tom and Joe are going. I'm told Rizzo also has some powerful, personal motivation. But you, Winthrop, don't you realize how much you are risking here?

"You've got your whole life ahead of you. You're brilliant, you've got more money than most governments, and you're good looking enough and good natured enough to find a woman who's going to love you for you. Why take a chance on something as whacky as this? You agree that some group appears to be intent on stopping us. You know that if the Israelis, the Waqf, or Islamic terrorists get wind of what we're trying to do, they will try to stop us. I doubt they will be acting with any restraint. This is serious, and it's dangerous, and you don't need it."

Johnson moved closer to Larsen, whispering in his left ear. "Go home, Winthrop. Leave this alone. It's bad enough that four of us who know better are willing to do something stupid. Please, don't take this risk."

For years, Larsen had revered Dr. Johnson and longed to live a life like his. Engulfed in a wave of Johnson's genuine concern and apprehension, moved by the passion and pleading in his mentor's voice, Larsen momentarily felt his resolve waver. As he raised his head to look at Johnson, his eyes swept across the thermal imaging scan of the Temple Mount. His heart pounded, his breath caught in his throat, a ripple of electricity cruised across the muscles of his shoulders. When Larsen's eyes met Johnson's, his decision had already been carved into will.

"Doc, thank you for caring so much about me . . . about my safety and well-being. I appreciate it; I really do. It means a lot to me to hear such concern and caring in your voice."

"Then, why—"

Larsen firmly put his hand on Johnson's arm. "Doc, there have been eight generations of Larsens living on these shores since the first one stepped into what they believed was a virgin wilderness. More than two hundred years separate me from those men and women, but each day I walk in their shadows. There's not really all that much that a Larsen has been required to do to become successful, at least not for the last one hundred fifty years. All the work was done long before my great-great-great-grandfather was born. The only question left is whether you will work in the family business, or whether you'll choose a life of luxury and boredom, or both. It wasn't easy walking away from the temptation to be a Larsen. But there was something I wanted more than money. It was self-respect. And once I got the opportunity to work and study at the

British Museum, once I met you and others like you who were dedicated and determined to bring value to the world instead of just taking valuables out of it, I knew that was the life I wanted to live."

Winthrop dipped his head a few degrees to the right, just enough to get under Johnson's eyes as they stared toward the floor. "Doc, I decided a long time ago not to live the life of a Larsen. That decision has already been made. So I don't have that life waiting for me. But even if I did, Doc . . . even if I did"—he paused, making sure he had Johnson's attention—"this is the kind of decision that will define a man's life. For some reason, I'm not even sure why, the men in this room have become my family, not the Larsens. If I were to walk out now, I would be walking out on everything I cherish, everything that holds value for me: trust, honor, respect, commitment, faithfulness. The things that define a man's character. That's what this is about, Doc, about living out, walking out the character I hope lives in me."

Larsen searched Johnson's gaze. "Does that make sense? Do you understand?"

Johnson stretched out his right arm and gently placed his hand on Larsen's shoulder. He didn't say anything, just nodded his head and held his gaze, until Rizzo reminded them of his presence.

"Are you two lovebirds about to break this up, or are you going to make me puke?"

"Rizzo, you've got all the manners of a sow."

"Thanks, Doc," Rizzo chirped, "I think you're swell, too. But listen, how about if we cut out the cutesy cuddling, get this gear packed up into the van, and go home to get some sleep? How about that for an idea, eh?"

Rizzo struck his Ninja pose and Larsen was suddenly frightened that Johnson might actually strike Rizzo, a fine start to what would inevitably be a difficult enough task, even with the best of team spirit.

"All right," said Larsen, getting up to grab his jacket. "Let me get the van, and we can load all this stuff. Doc, the van's across the street, should I just double-park out front?"

"No, there's a small driveway between our building and the hotel on the corner," said Johnson. "It's protected by an iron gate, so you wouldn't have noticed it. I'll disengage the electric lock, and the gate will be open. Back the van into the driveway, and we can load the gear right out of the elevator on the bottom floor."

"Okay, be back in a minute."

First there was the flash. Milliseconds later, the windows imploded. The deafening roar and battering shock wave of the explosion were hurled into the room, propelling a shower of glass shards that impaled every visible surface.

A moment earlier, Rizzo had been leaning his chair against the back wall, checking messages on his Blackberry. Rodriguez was in the restroom, Bohannon was carrying two duffels out to the elevator, and Doc Johnson was stashing all the rolled up maps, charts, and photos into a small storage closet behind his office door.

With the rattle of falling debris still filling the office, Bohannon burst into the room, thousands of window splinters crunching under his feet. He saw Joe across the office, picking himself up off the floor of the restroom. Doc Johnson, who had been caught in a door-sandwich, was sitting groggily on the floor, a purple knot rising on his forehead while he rubbed what was clearly going to be a badly bruised forearm. Sammy was on his back, on the floor, both he and the chair knocked backward by the blast. The sparkle of broken glass dotted the bottom of the chair and the bottom of Rizzo's shoes. There was no blood, but Rizzo laced the air with impassioned profanities. "Tom," he squawked, "find Winthrop."

Bohannon turned and sprinted to the elevator, Rodriguez on his heels, hoping he was not going to discover his fears blown all over 35th Street. The front doors of the Collector's Club were askew on their hinges, hanging like drunken soldiers against the marble pillars. Pushing through the broken doors, Bohannon ignored the cacophony of car alarms, his eyes riveted to the smoking hulk that was once a white van. Bohannon reached out for something to keep himself from falling and found Rodriguez's arm. Neither one of them could— at that moment—gather up the courage or the will to venture any farther. The doors to the van had been blown out and Larson's body, parts of it, had followed, thrown against the wrought-iron fence. Larsen's right leg, from the knee down, was missing, as were his right arm and shoulder. His back, what was left of it, was pressed against the wrought-iron fence. His body was charred, still smoking, and a half-dozen glass spears were embedded in his skull. Winthrop's startled and lifeless gaze failed to see Bohannon's tears.

25

Several hours later, Rory O'Neill, accompanied by his omnipresent bodyguards and a squad of uniformed officers, walked into Johnson's mangled office.

Tom, Joe, Sammy, and, for much longer, Doc had been downstairs in the library, talking to detectives, going over and over the same story until they felt they were going to scream. The homicide detectives knew they were hearing only part of the story. But Bohannon had pulled Rory O'Neill's business card out of his wallet—the one with O'Neill's private office number and his nearly secret home number written on the back in O'Neill's own hand. It was almost a "Get Out of Jail Free" card. But not quite.

The card was powerful enough for the detectives to grant Bohannon's request that he would only speak to O'Neill.

Rory and his wife, Vivian, regularly volunteered at the Bowery Mission on Thanksgiving, when 850 volunteers helped serve twenty-five hundred meals to the poor and homeless. It was through that long-term relationship with the O'Neills that Bohannon had earned the privilege to request the commissioner's presence at the Collector's Club that night. So here was the police commissioner of New York City, a man who controlled a uniformed force of thirty-six thousand highly trained officers, larger than the armies of most countries, and he was making a personal, not professional, visit to a crime scene.

Bohannon was out of his chair and walking to the door as soon as he saw the commissioner walk in. "Thanks for coming, Rory. I really appreciate this. I know it's probably way out of line and not the normal protocol. I hope you don't take any heat because of it. I didn't know what else to do. We desperately need your help."

O'Neill was relatively short, with a boxer's build. In spite of the power, prestige, and pressure of leading a small army and trying to protect the world's greatest city from predatory radical terrorists, O'Neill was a sweet, soft-spoken man who often purposely retreated to the background when accompanying the mayor, world dignitaries, or his wife.

"Tom, that's okay," said O'Neill, leading Bohannon over to a pair of chairs. "I know you wouldn't have asked me to come if it wasn't absolutely necessary. And I'm sure you understand that I'll help where I can. But there's only so far I can, or will, go. Now, why don't you tell me what this is all about? Start from the beginning. But I need to know why a man died tonight, okay?"

Bohannon's face revealed the relief and gratitude he felt, but not his growing unease. Anything they hoped to accomplish in the future would depend on how well, and how fully, he told their story. "This may take awhile, Rory, but I'll tell you everything that I know and then leave it up to you."

Over the next forty-five minutes, Bohannon laid out the entire story for the commissioner, and he seldom missed a pertinent detail. At intervals, O'Neill would interrupt Bohannon's narration to ask probing questions, but it didn't take the commissioner long to understand why Bohannon had been such an excellent reporter.

When Bohannon had finished his narrative, O'Neill looked at him impassively. Friendship and police work never mixed well.

"And you want me to let the four of you get on that plane tomorrow?"

"No, Rory," Bohannon said, shaking his head. "Not tomorrow—but once the funeral is over, then yes, more than ever, I want you to let us go, let us leave the country, go to Jerusalem, and find out if this thing is real. Because now, I'm convinced that it is."

O'Neill ran his right hand over his naturally slick dome. "What if the guys with the necklaces leave New York with you and follow you to Jerusalem? You won't be any safer, and we won't have any suspects. But if I keep you here, your attackers will also stay here, and we'll very likely pick them up—because they will try again to get the rest of you."

It didn't make any sense to let them go. O'Neill's job was to find and apprehend the men responsible for this homicide and what was probably a multiple-homicide at the newsstand on Lafayette Street. Having Bohannon, Johnson, Rizzo, and Rodriguez close at hand would make that job much easier.

"Rory, you've got us for the next three or four days, at least," Bohannon said, obviously scrambling for a convincing argument. "And for the next three or four days, our friends with the lightning bolt will also know exactly where we are, or where we will be. We'll give you the next week. But, Rory, after that, I'm leaving. And I'm sure the others will be leaving with me. You understand the implications for the Middle East—the implications for right here, for New York City? If the temple is under the Temple Mount, the whole dynamic in the Middle East changes. Maybe there's peace—"

"And maybe there's war," O'Neill interrupted, frustrated by his own indecision. "Why you? Why do you have to go? Why don't I lock you up in witness protection, tell the State Department everything you've told me, and let the government take care of it?"

Bohannon looked O'Neill dead in the eye.

"I don't know why, Rory, except that I'm confident this is not a coincidence. I'm not here by accident."

"You're going to get spiritual on me, aren't you?" said O'Neill.

Bohannon shot him a crooked smile.

"Rory, you've been around us long enough. You know what we believe." Bohannon sounded earnest. "We believe in a personal God. It's a simple theology, but terribly difficult to live. Probably got something to do with my dad being so distant when I was a kid, but I've always had a hard time believing that God was interested in me. Taking care of everyone else? Sure. But me?" Bohannon shook his head. "I don't know. I know what I'm like, what I think, how I act. Why would God want to know a guy like me?

"But that's the Christian faith, that's what I'm trying to live. I used to think that if Annie knew the guy I really was, she'd dump me. But she got to know the real me, and she loves me anyway.

"I kinda think that's what God is like. He knows all about us and still loves us. Is still interested in us." Bohannon fell silent.

O'Neill wasn't sure that Bohannon had answered his question. Doubts peppered his thoughts, interfered with his natural ability to evaluate and act quickly.

"I don't know why me, Rory, but I've got to do this. This is my assignment, my responsibility. I have to go to Jerusalem. Doc, Joe, Sammy . . . I believe they have their own reasons, but they also believe this is something they have to do. For me, there is no other choice. I don't understand it, but I believe this is something God is asking of me. I need to go to Jerusalem. And I'm asking you to let me do that."

O'Neill scowled as he got up from his chair and turned to the precinct captain who had accompanied him.

"I want two uniforms on each of these guys, day and night, no excuses. In their homes, with them at work, with them in the bathroom. And I want an unmarked at each of their homes, their offices, and plainclothes like glue on every member of their families. The suspects in this bombing have made other attempts on their lives and will probably try again. I'll give the sergeant a full description of the suspects at the precinct. This case gets the highest priority and the highest net of confidentiality. The explosion was a ruptured gas line. Three-sentence press release. Everything else gets a lid on it. Bill, it's absolutely critical that you keep your men in line. I want no leaks. There's no margin of error on this—got it? Okay. I'll be sending in two teams from Special Ops. One here tonight to clean up the mess. The second one to the station house tomorrow. They will work directly with your detectives, shadow them at every step. But they will be under my command. Are you okay with that?"

"Yes sir," said Captain Reilly. "No intention to pry, sir, since it's clear this case has more to it than I'm aware of. But is there any more you can tell me, sir, anything that I can share with my detectives that will help them in protecting these four or in apprehending the killers?"

"I'll give you everything I can Bill, you and your detectives, back at the station. But I can tell you this is very serious stuff. If we're going to keep these four guys alive, there is absolutely no margin for mistakes of any kind. Choose your best men, Bill, and your most trustworthy. I'll see you back at the house."

O'Neill pulled out his cell phone and alerted the two Special Ops squads, one of which was "wheels moving" in less than two minutes. Then he turned back to Bohannon and walked him over to the table where Rodriguez, Rizzo, and Johnson still sat silently, vacantly, looking out the ragged hole that used to be a window. "Captain Reilly will be providing each of you with a ride home. The unmarked car will remain outside your homes, and the uniformed officers who accompany you will remain with you for your protection. This is not a request. Before you return to your homes, all four of you will come to the precinct station house, and we will try to pin down the descriptions of the men with the lightning bolt necklace and look at some mug shots from Interpol. Then you'll be free to go for the time being. Okay?"

There were nods, but that was all. O'Neill, still trailed by his two body-guards, turned to leave the room. Passing his captain, he lowered his voice. "Bill, get a doc in here—and a psych. These guys may be in shock."

26

They had accompanied Larsen's body back to Rhode Island and were swallowed up by the countless masses who turned out to honor one of their leading citizens. Then they went back to Manhattan and tried the best they could to insulate themselves from the horror of recent events, the uniformed officers escorting each of them home. Four days had passed. There had been no arrests, no more attempts on their lives, nothing but the numbing knowledge that a good man who had quickly become a good friend, a companion in a quest, had been brutally murdered by these predatory phantoms with the lightning bolt amulet.

Bohannon had arranged for a leave of absence from the Bowery Mission in anticipation of the trip to Jerusalem, but with the delay, he was unwilling to sit at home with his thoughts, doubts, and growing anxiety, so he sat in his office with his thoughts, doubts, and growing anxiety, filling his time with some mindless filing. He was kneeling on the floor in his jeans and chamois shirt, stuffing manila files into hanging folders, when he glimpsed a pair of impossibly spit-shined shoes followed by the bottom edges of two trench coats. The commissioner had come to visit. "Hi, Rory," Bohannon said before he stood up and turned around.

There was no hint of a smile on O'Neill's face. "C'mon," he said, "we need to talk." O'Neill closed the door behind Bohannon, leaving his two menacing companions flanking the portal. O'Neill turned the two leather office chairs so they were facing each other, rather than allow Bohannon to retreat behind his desk. An alarm was going off in Bohannon's brain.

"Tom, after the explosion, we went back to the morgue, pulled out the corpse of that truck driver, and gave him a much more thorough work over," said O'Neill. "After that crash, we had no reason to think it was anything more than a terrible accident. For us, he was just a 'John Doe' we were still trying to identify. This time, we really put forensics to work. The dead guy was an

Egyptian, Sayeed Farouk, and he was in this country illegally. He showed up on INS files about a month ago, entering on a cargo ship from Cairo. His passport and entry visa were forgeries."

O'Neill shifted in his seat, and Bohannon tried hard, but fruitlessly, to remain calm.

"You know we have teams of officers and detectives stationed around the world, working with Interpol and other governments to try and stay ahead of terrorists." O'Neill leaned forward, hands folded between his knees, forearms resting on his legs, eyes full of knowledge and warning. Bohannon could barely breathe. "Through our contacts in the Middle East, we tracked down this guy Farouk and, just this morning, got a report from Egypt, through the State Department. Farouk is an Egyptian nonentity, a stonemason from the city of Suez with no record, no apparent connection to any terrorist organization, no political flags at all. Apparently, just a hardworking family man. So our guys in Egypt are wondering why this 'everyman' from Suez was driving a truck in New York City that was ticketed to take you out.

"Our guys dug deeper . . . talked to his coworkers, his neighbors. All they could find out about Farouk, other than that he was a talented mason, was that he had an interest in ancient Egyptian history, spent a lot of time in the library, and belonged to a historical society in Suez."

Bohannon's mind raced around pyramids and pharaohs until he was suddenly brought up short by O'Neill's silence. "So, that's it?" Bohannon asked.

O'Neill reached into the pocket of his jacket, pulled out his hand, and held it, palm up, in front of Bohannon. "Ever see anything like this before?"

Resting in O'Neill's hand was an amulet, a Coptic cross with a lightning bolt slashing through it on the diagonal. Bohannon's insides began to churn, a taste of bile rising in his throat.

"Yeah, I've seen it twice, within minutes of each other," said Bohannon, shifting uneasily in his chair. "Once on the subway, I thought the guy was trying to pick my pocket. And then, again, on the driver who crashed his truck into the magazine store at Spring and Lafayette, nearly killing me. And Doc Johnson also saw one on a guy who tried to push him in front of a subway train and ended up dead instead." He looked up at the commissioner. "What is it, Rory? What does it mean?"

O'Neill's fingers traveled up, down, and around the amulet, as if his senses could glean some clue from the burnished metal.

"We don't know much about these guys. Nobody does, because they've got no history. Up to this point, they've simply been a bunch of Egyptians interested in ancient documents. Suddenly they show up here in New York trying to take out a team of guys who are headed for Jerusalem to search for a hidden temple. Didn't you tell me the other day that the scroll you found had been sent to Egypt for safekeeping and had remained there for nearly eight hundred years?"

"Yeah," said Bohannon, perking up, "the letter indicates that it was to be delivered to Cairo, but Doc believes it may have ended up somewhere else in Egypt because there is absolutely no record of it in any of Cairo's ancient libraries and, because of its unusual composition, it certainly would have drawn some notice."

"Could it have ended up in Suez?" O'Neill asked. Bohannon didn't answer, and O'Neill did not wait for a reply.

"I told you our contacts in Egypt tried to track down Farouk and interviewed a lot of people in Suez. They came across something they didn't understand, but which they passed along as part of the report. Farouk was a member of what appeared to be a group of historians whose name, in Arabic, would be translated *The Prophet's Guard*. The group apparently was formed about 1100 A.D. Records are sketchy, but it appears for approximately the first 750 years of its existence, the group was called the *Temple Guard* and it was composed of Coptic Christians."

O'Neill had been sitting back comfortably as he shared this information. But he suddenly pulled himself closer to Bohannon. "Tom, did you know that Egypt was a mainly Christian country for more than a thousand years? I never knew that," he continued, not waiting for an answer. "Mark, the guy who wrote the gospel of Mark in the Bible, he preached in Alexandria, died there, and started the Christian church in Egypt—the Coptics. Even though the Muslims conquered Egypt in six-something, Egypt didn't become a Muslim country until the twelfth century. And there is still a strong Christian church in Egypt.

"Well, for many years, the Christian protectors of the scroll, the Temple Guard, held their meetings in a building now called the Bibliotheca Historique de L'Egypte in Suez, which has some of the rarest documents from the ancient Middle East. They met at the library in a room that was completely off-limits to anyone who was not a member of the group, a room that was removed from every other part of the library and was locked down tight when the group wasn't there. The Temple Guard appears to have been all but unknown outside of that library. Then, around a hundred fifty to two hundred years ago, everything changed.

"The library's records show there was some radical turnover in the group. It suddenly became controlled by Muslims, and the name was changed from the *Temple Guard* in Coptic to the *Prophet's Guard* in Arabic. Oddly," said O'Neill, "not long after the name was changed, the Prophet's Guard abandoned the room and never returned to the library. When the staff looked in the room, it contained a table and an open chest sitting on top of the table. That was it. There was nothing else in that room.

"And here's the pièce de résistance—It was called the Scroll Room."

Bohannon sat, dumbfounded. *If Larsen hadn't been killed, none of this would have come to light.*

"Tom, my gut tells me these Coptic Christians had the scroll and were either hiding it or protecting it until a little more than 150 years ago. From what you've told me, the Temple Guard probably knew where the scroll came from. They may have known what some of the message contained—there's got to be some reason why they protected it so faithfully for 750 years. But then the Muslims got control of it, probably not a friendly takeover, either. And not long after that, it disappeared . . . and so did the Prophet's Guard. For the last 150 years, I think the Prophet's Guard has been searching for this scroll, trying to get it back, trying to keep it out of the wrong hands. And right now, you guys are the wrong hands.

"I don't know how they found you or found out that you possessed the scroll," said O'Neill, fingering the amulet once more. "It really doesn't matter because now they've got you dead in their sites, and clearly, they are not going to stop until they've recovered the scroll, all of you are dead, or both."

O'Neill looked once more at the amulet, then casually tossed it to Bohannon. "Do you know the meaning of that symbol?"

Bohannon shook his head.

"It's meant to represent 'Death to Christians.'"

O'Neill allowed Bohannon time to process that bit of information.

"Tom, you were wondering if I would prevent you and your team from leaving for Jerusalem. The way I see it, you don't have a choice. If you stay here, you will still be a target and so will your family. They probably are already, yours and Rodriguez's. It won't matter how much police protection we provide for you. If these guys really want to get to you, and it's pretty obvious that they do, we won't be able to stop them forever."

Reaching across to put his hand on Bohannon's arm, O'Neill's voice softened. "Tom, the best way to get these madmen to take their eyes off your family is for you and the other three characters to get out of the country, quickly. While you're doing that, we'll get your families out of their homes as a precaution and keep them safe until you get back. But there's one more thing I want you to do."

Fearful that his family could be harmed, enraged that his friend was dead, and determined to carry on with what appeared to be God's plan, Bohannon tried to shake off his warring emotions and focus on the commissioner's words.

With a voice more somber than he had expected, Bohannon responded to the commissioner. "What do you need, Rory?"

"Here," said O'Neill, handing Bohannon another of his business cards. "I want you to call this guy at the State Department, Sam Reynolds. His dad and I joined the department when we were discharged from the Marines. I've known Sam all his life; he's a good man. And he can help you, where you're going. Talk to him today, before you leave. Give him some idea of what you're planning. He could be an asset when you need it. You said Larsen had gotten you a satellite phone? Well, use it to stay in touch with Reynolds. He'll keep me updated."

O'Neill got out of the chair and put on his coat. "Use your head, Tom. Find a way to get in and get out quickly." O'Neill extended his hand. "Come home alive, Tom. Make sure you come home."

PART TWO

CITY OF GOD

27

JERUSALEM

Bohannon stepped out of the plane, into the Jetway, and immediately thought of that line from Neil Simon's *Biloxi Blues*, uttered by Matthew Broderick on his first day at Paris Island. "It was hot . . . heat hot . . . jungle hot . . . Africa hot."

Walking up the Jetway to the terminal in Ben Gurion Airport, outside Tel Aviv, his pampered Western body was once again embraced by man's artificial climate control.

The four of them cleared customs quickly—scholars and amateur spelunkers on a trip to explore some Israeli caves, a trip sanctioned through Kallie's connections at Tel-Aviv University. And they were blessed to find their luggage waiting for them on the carousel, El Al's legendary effectiveness proven once again. While the luggage may have undergone security scans of many stripes, none of them was concerned about tripping an alarm because the only things in their bags were personal items. The cave-exploring gear was shipped separately to their hotel.

So carrying his bags out of the baggage claim that mid-June Saturday morning, why did Bohannon feel more like a spy than a tourist?

I am a spy, he suddenly thought to himself.

Another thought was beginning to form in his mind in response to the first one, when the desert attacked again. It took only one step through the sliding pneumatic doors, and Bohannon's rebelling body began to soak the short-sleeved oxford—the signature blue cotton button-down that he wore with unfailing regularity, except when he wore a white one. Immediately, he regretted the poplin suit. Jealously he looked at Rizzo's green and blue plaid shirt over fluorescent green, nylon running shorts—garishly glaring, but disgustingly more practical than anything Bohannon was now sweating through.

"It's hot," said Rodriguez, now at his side. Bohannon resisted comment.

Other than Rizzo constantly pestering the attendants, there had been very little conversation during the trip. Bohannon was lost in his own thoughts, and the others appeared to be suffering in their own pain. Prior to the trip, Bohannon had not noticed how alike he and Johnson and Rodriguez were in makeup. In the face of grief, each of them retreated to a safe place, behind the protection of well-constructed walls. It was there, also, that Bohannon wrestled with the forces of fear that he could seldom understand or describe.

Rizzo, who had brought only a backpack and kept it under the seat in front of him, preceded the others out of the airport and into the heat, a head-turning neon apparition. The other three looked the part of who they were, experienced travelers who packed light and kept themselves mobile. But none of them had dressed correctly for this heat. Even though it was early June, each was beginning to visibly wilt in the desert's midday swelter. Then Bohannon saw her winding her way through the knots of people waiting for shuttles or waving down taxis. Rather, he saw the hat . . . broad-brimmed straw Stetson, western style, the sides tied up tight under a leather thong. Even more distinctive was the green and blue tartan ribbon wrapped around the base of the hat's crown.

As she drew closer, Bohannon made observations below the hat. "Sammy Rizzo, you dirty old man," Bohannon whispered with admiration.

Kallie Nolan was wearing a fairly standard archaeologist outfit: khaki shorts, short-sleeved khaki safari shirt with the sleeves cut off at the shoulder, and well-traveled leather boots. But it wasn't the clothes that drew Bohannon's attention. It was how the clothes wore Kallie. Golden bronze, the fitness of a runner, Nolan was a stunning, healthy, well-built, thirty-something who was all legs, arms, golden strawberry ponytail, and dazzling emerald eyes that overflowed with a joy of life that infected all who entered her orbit.

Everyone was watching Kallie, but she wasn't watching anyone except this little guy in the fluorescent green shorts. Sammy stopped in his tracks and stood open-mouthed, staring at Kallie as she approached.

Putting his bag down, ignoring the catatonic Rizzo, Bohannon took two steps toward Kallie and grasped her outstretched hand.

"Kallie, it's a pleasure to meet you," Bohannon said sincerely. "This is Doc Johnson . . . and Joe Rodriguez. And that guy . . ."

Before Bohannon could turn toward Sammy, the plaid and green flashed past his eyes and landed in Kallie's open arms.

"Kallie . . . it's your kissin' cousin, home from his travels," Rizzo crowed, wrapping his arms around Nolan, who had dropped down to one knee, and hugging her close as she hugged him right back. Bohannon then realized that Rizzo's shirt was the same tartan design that Kallie had wrapped around her Stetson.

She unwrapped Rizzo from her neck and held him at arm's length. "It's good to see you again, Sammy Rizzo. And good to see that you are still in one piece. I've been worried about you." She looked up. "About all of you. Your last few messages were frightening. I was so sorry to hear about Mr. Larsen."

Rodriguez and Johnson both shook her hand with the same warmth and sincerity as Bohannon. But she quickly turned her attention back to Rizzo, who hadn't left her side.

"I was beginning to think that I would never see you again," Kallie said to Sammy, who was soaking up all of the amazed stares that were directed his way. "I didn't think I'd have the opportunity to tell you how much I respect you and how much I have valued your friendship."

Bohannon watched in amazement. For the first time in his memory, Rizzo had morphed from the master of wisecracks and put-downs into a man of gentle sincerity.

"Thanks, Kallie . . . I've missed you, too," Rizzo said, looking into her eyes as if there were not a thousand people within earshot of his comments. "Thank you. I don't think I'm worthy of your respect, but I'll take it, gladly."

Rizzo the gentleman gave Nolan a tender embrace.

But it was Rizzo the instigator who turned toward his three companions.

"So, you human sweatbands, I would say I've just hit a grand slam, eh? Rizzo, four—the rest of you clowns, zero." Taking Kallie's hand in his, Rizzo turned away from the terminal. "So, one of you can carry my bag. Lead on, my beauty."

Bohannon, Rodriguez, and Johnson began to evaporate in the heat. "Come on," said Kallie, over her shoulder. "I've got the university's van over in the parking lot. Let's get you guys to the hotel. Then we can talk."

All felt their spirits lift: air-conditioning!

"Sorry. The van's not air-conditioned. But the hotel's not too far. And we can keep the windows open."

It was hot . . . heat hot . . . jungle hot . . . Africa hot. The windows were not going to help.

—〜〜—

The one thing they had talked about on the trip over was that they would keep Kallie Nolan out of this project as much as possible. If nothing else, just to protect her. Who knew where the Prophet's Guard would turn up next.

Now in Israel, the obvious slapped Bohannon silly. What they had been trying to avoid thinking about for weeks was all around them, living, breathing, and speaking. Men in robes and head coverings; women with veils over their faces; men in uniform, automatic weapons cradled in the crook of their arms; women in uniform, their eyes relentless, always on guard.

This was not America, not even post–9/11 America. *Israel was not even like New York City*, thought Bohannon, *where the scars were deepest and the expectation of "again" the highest.*

Life in New York City had changed forever. More and more buildings had surrounded themselves with flower planters—those huge, concrete, reinforced planters that doubled as car bomb protection and fooled no one.

Downtown, the precautions were even more draconian. Streets around the New York Stock Exchange were still blocked with police barricades and uniforms with automatic weapons. But it was around the federal buildings that New York looked more like Baghdad. The streets were impassable, secured by thick, metal, pneumatically controlled barricades that were lowered only after presentation of highest security clearance ID, and only after the vehicle was subjected to a thorough search.

Grand Central Station was constantly patrolled, not only by the NYPD but also by roving squads of military in their camo, each entry under heavily armed guard. Subway stations now routinely, but randomly, were under close surveillance by squads of specially trained NYPD officers. Most New Yorkers were aware of, and thankful for, these heightened security measures. But what most New Yorkers failed to notice was the "army of the normal." New York's antiterrorism squads had been well publicized. No one spoke of the spooks: the taxi drivers; UPS deliverymen; street vendors; moms with baby carriages . . . the hundreds of plainclothes disguises that made up the thousand officers who comprised Rory O'Neill's "army of the normal."

Daily reminders of how life had changed were dotted all over the New York City landscape.

Yet the flow of New York had not changed.

There was no fear. Concern, but no fear. Millions still rode the A train or the N/R from Queens without a second thought. They ate in restaurants, went to work in ridiculously tall buildings, raised their children. The city continued to grow, rents continued to climb. And people moved from place to place, building to building; neighborhood to neighborhood, city to city, with few worries. America remained an open society even in the face of unseen warriors fighting an unconventional war against Western civilization.

Being driven out of Tel Aviv Airport, past fortified checkpoints, Bohannon realized just how much freedom was being taken for granted in his home city. Israelis were serious about security; they had to be. They were all targets, and their enemies surrounded them. At times, their enemies were right in their midst. In New York, Bohannon admitted, the soldiers made him feel safer, more at ease. Here in Israel, the soldiers made him feel like a suspect, as if they were just waiting for a wrong move. And his guilt was magnified by the secret he carried with him.

28

Kallie turned the van east on Highway 1, pointing it toward Jerusalem and trying to gain enough speed to bring some relief to these guys who were looking pretty damp. Rizzo was riding shotgun and appeared to be enjoying the scenery . . . Kallie's legs. Bohannon, Johnson, and Rodriguez each sprawled across one of the bench seats, the luggage stuffed in the rear.

"I've confirmed the arrangements you made," said Kallie, her eyes straight ahead and both hands firmly on the steering wheel. But the aging van had a mind of its own, rapidly drifting right at any slip in concentration. "Hotel Tzuba is confirmed, a nonsmoking suite, and the rental car will be there, waiting for you. It took some convincing for the rental company to find and supply the kind of big SUV you requested. There's not much demand for big cars like that over here—gas is so expensive. If you hadn't been so specific and so insistent with the company, I doubt you would have gotten what you were looking for. By the way," she said, trying to sound nonchalant, "why will you need such a large vehicle?"

Bohannon turned in his seat to look at her. "Kallie, I thought we had an agreement."

"Oh, come on!" A sudden shift in posture, and the van began tracking for the shoulder, so Kallie had to return her effort and attention to controlling the beast. "Do you guys actually think I'm going to allow you to come here on a quest for antiquities and leave me sitting home while you have all the fun? Who's the archaeologist here? Who's the one who dug up the information on Abiathar when you needed it? So you're tracking down something that has to do with Jerusalem at the time of the crusader conquest, you won't tell me what it is, and you won't let me help you out, right? Well, that just stinks. I've got half a mind to drop you off right here and let you walk the rest of the way."

"Where is here?" a sleepy Rodriguez asked from the depths of the van.

"We're just coming into Latrun," said Kallie, trying to relax her forearm muscles for a moment. "There're the ruins of a crusader castle over there on the right—the Castle of the Knight. You could practice your treasure hunting over there while you are waiting for some schlump to pick you up."

"Schlumps? Yeah, that's us," said Rizzo. "A bunch of schlumps from Schlumpsville. Hicks on a hunt."

"Aw, come on you guys. I know you're up to something that has adventure all over it. Do you know how absolutely boring it is to be an archaeologist? Ninety-nine percent of the time we're using a paintbrush to move dust one particle at a time. There's not much adrenaline rush in this business. Except for this stupid van," she said, trying to wrestle it into submission.

She felt a gentle hand come to rest on her right shoulder. "Kallie, it would be an honor for us to include you in this project," Johnson said quietly. "In one way or another, you've been a part of this almost from the beginning. Including you would be the right thing to do. With all that being said, don't you understand that there must be another, overriding, reason why we are trying to keep you at arm's length?"

Nolan kept driving, the clenched muscles of her jaw losing traction against common sense.

"We are all traveling in uncharted waters here; we have no idea how, when, or where this will end up. It's possible," said Johnson, "that we could get ourselves into some significant trouble. And, Kallie, none of us are willing to put you in that position, even though you are more than willing to sign on. I'm sorry, dear, but you're just dealing with three old, overly protective academic types who are scared of our own shadows and our dear Mr. Rizzo, who doesn't have an ounce of sense in his diminutive body."

Rodriguez and Bohannon had the good sense to remain quiet.

"Listen, Kallie," said the reasonable Rizzo, sitting to her right, "in spite of Doc Johnson's inaccurate diagnosis of my capacity, everything else he is saying is right. We don't know what we're getting into, honestly. But none of us are willing to allow you to take the same risk."

Muscling the van into a right turn at the Mevasseret Zion interchange, Kallie turned south, on road 3965. "Yeah, you guys are scared and I'm the Queen of Sheba. I can see it on your faces. I see it on other faces all the time. The thrill of the hunt, the adrenalin of the unexpected, the chance to uncover treasure: you are clearly on a mission that has your passions and your curiosity inflamed. I just want a chance to be part of that action."

"I'm sorry, Kallie, I really am," Johnson said, his gentle voice nearly sucked out the window. "But that just won't happen."

Silence settled in the van. They drove past a quarry on the right, then circled the Sataf roundabout, bearing right on road 365 to the Kibbutz Tzuba. None of the men knew exactly where they were heading. All Kallie had e-mailed them was that she had arranged for them to stay at the Hotel Tzuba, outside of Jerusalem but close enough to have easy access. Driving through the main gate, Kallie pulled up in front of a quaint-looking country inn, square in the middle of a kibbutz.

"Welcome to Hotel Tzuba," Kallie said wryly of the sixty-four-suite hotel with great views of the Judean hills, only fifteen minutes from Jerusalem. "Whatever you guys are up to, it's unlikely anybody is going to look for you here."

⌒∿∿⌒

That evening, the Jewish Sabbath complete, four men slid into the black SUV with the tinted windows and continued their drive down Highway 1 into the fabled city of Jerusalem. Over her strenuous objections, Kallie had been dispatched back to her apartment. Johnson knew they were fortunate the SUV didn't get into a wreck or kill any civilians, because none of them were looking at the road, not even Bohannon, who was driving. They looked more like bobble-head dolls, bouncing and twisting this way and that, trying to see everything at once. Kallie had wrangled them invitations to a university reception that was to be held in the courtyard and gardens of the Citadel, known as David's Tower, located just south of the Jaffa Gate.

Johnson, who was now the closest thing they had to an expert on Jerusalem and its history, was constantly surprised by how different the real thing was from the "book" thing, or the "picture" thing, or the "Internet" thing. The group was stunned into silence by the beauty and history, but Johnson coped with the magnitude of the city by telling the others the history behind the sites.

"This has been the weakest point of Jerusalem's defenses since one thousand years before Christ," said Johnson as they entered into the Citadel's grounds. Johnson and Bohannon wore light pants, open collared shirts, and light, poplin jackets—fairly standard reception wear. Rizzo was out of character in a pair of Dockers and a navy blue golf shirt. Rodriguez, on the other hand, had descended on the kibbutz store and was arrayed like a fashionable Israeli . . . simple, wide-lapelled safari shirt, kibbutz shorts, and boots.

"Every major change in government has added to, improved on, or extended this fortress," said Johnson as they walked through the gardens. "Herod the Great added three massive towers; the Romans used it as a barracks after destroying the temple; it was the last part of Jerusalem to fall to the crusaders; and it was the seat of the king of Jerusalem. The Ottoman Turks added that dominant minaret, and the Citadel served to garrison Turkish troops for four hundred years until the British, under General Allenby, took control of Jerusalem in 1917. Once the nation of Israel was formed in 1947, the fierce and feared Jordanian Arab Legion took up position in the Citadel to defend the Old City because it had a dominant view across the armistice line into Jewish Jerusalem. And so it continues. The Tower of David—which has nothing to do with King David—still dominates Jerusalem's skyline and is master of its sight lines, even more than the Dome of the Rock."

Turning to his friends, Johnson smiled. "And tonight, it is the best place for us to be, with an unfettered view of the Temple Mount and two sides of the Mount itself. Hopefully, it will show us a way in."

Wine flowed, talk flowed, self-importance flowed all around them that evening, but as the moon rose over the Mediterranean, the musketeers from New York remained huddled by themselves, at the far eastern wall of the Citadel, trying not to look too obvious as they diligently studied the Mount and its surroundings.

What had struck Johnson unexpectedly was the palpable force he had experienced the moment the team had exited the SUV. It was more than a feeling. This was a weight, a presence, a reality that he was experiencing mentally, physically, and emotionally—and if he were willing to admit it, Johnson would have to say spiritually, though he wasn't sure what "spiritual" really meant to him. Jerusalem exuded a dominating presence, a power of its own, as if it were a living, breathing entity.

Perhaps, because he had visited Jerusalem before, the presence overwhelmed Johnson more completely than his three friends. He tried to shake it off at first. During the reception, he tried to ignore it. But as he stood on the ramparts, looking out over this ancient city, Jerusalem's call became too insistent.

"This city is alive," Johnson said softly. Rizzo was by his side, but his words barely gained the attention of Bohannon and Rodriguez. "I never thought I'd hear myself say this, but there is something living here that is spiritual and not human. Clearly, it's not a circumstance of history that the three religions that dominate this world, each of which believes in a single deity, look upon that hill over there as the most holy site of their faith. It's not the hill that's holy. It's what is under the hill, or in the hill." Johnson shook his head, violently. "Oh, I don't know what I'm talking about."

"That's okay, Doc," said Rizzo, more subdued than usual. "I understand where you're coming from."

Johnson's silence stretched across the roofs of ancient buildings, straining to touch the Mount. Both Bohannon and Rodriguez turned toward the silence.

"If there is a God," said Johnson, with an accent of reverence, "and if this God can be known by man"—Johnson put both of his hands on the round, metal railing at the top of the rampart and leaned far over the wall, getting himself as close to the Temple Mount as was physically possible—"then that is where he lives."

29

Self-consciously trying to look like tourists, they strolled down David Street, one of the few straight, direct streets probing deeper into the Old City, in the direction of the Western Wall Tunnel. The reception had been winding down, and they had done as much reconnaissance as possible from the tower's rampart. Evening had passed with a cooling breeze, and the night had great promise of clear sky and moderating temperatures. Impulsively, they decided to take a walk, with the Western Wall as their target and espionage as their goal.

Who would notice? They were four tourists interested in the Western Wall. They would be lost mingling among the other tourists, the shoppers, the steady flow of humanity up and down David Street. At least, Bohannon was hoping that was true.

—⁓⁓—

Levin detested night duty. With his years of service, his seniority, his connections, he should never have to neglect his family like this. Besides, this was poker night, and for the first time in three years, he had been on a winning streak. Levin detested night duty.

But his senior lieutenant was in a nasty automobile accident and would be in the hospital for at least another week. His duty sergeant was on vacation in Majorca. That left Levin with five nights of duty this week, and he was as coiled as a scorpion's stinger.

Captain Avram Levin had served with Shin Bet for a dozen years, carefully selected out of the main Israeli army corps in the second year of his service. Tall, broad, muscled—the body of a competitive volleyball player, a striker of confounding accuracy and deadly power. A defender who once stepped into a Levin "kill" was knocked unconscious for ten minutes and never played the game again. For many years, Levin held hopes of gaining a berth on the Israeli

Olympic volleyball team. A knee injury sidelined him once, the Intifada sidelined him the second time. Now, his only "kills" were the days when his team of spooks nailed a carrier. Now, it was nights, also.

Shin Bet, the domestic Israeli security service, had a tougher job than Mossad, the international security service, though a lot less visibility and fewer accolades. But every Israeli citizen knew, respected, and was grateful for Shin Bet, because Shin Bet kept the streets, the busses, the cafés as safe as possible, as safe as could be expected, when it seemed the entire Palestinian population was being trained as suicide bombers.

One of the main weapons in Shin Bet's arsenal was the unobtrusive surveillance cameras that continuously scanned nearly every street in every major city in the country. Here in Jerusalem, the concentration of cameras was even denser, the attention to monitors more widespread and more diligent. This was Levin's domain. He was Watch Commander at Shin Bet's Aleph Reconnaissance Center in the Old City. The men in his command called him "The Hawk," an appellation he coveted and nurtured.

With a striker's aggression and immediate decision making, Levin was legendary in his corps for swooping in behind a monitor, stabbing his index finger at the screen, and demanding "target status" for someone who triggered his intuition. Levin intercepted more carriers, terrorists intending to become suicide bombers with explosives taped around their midsection, than any other officer. He missed once in a while, but by experience, when The Hawk pounced, every soldier in the security station elevated their surveillance to red alert.

There was a prowling, predatory Hawk circling the security station that night.

⹦⹦⹦

Bohannon and his coconspirators reached the entrance to the Western Wall Tunnel just after 9:00 PM. The tunnel had become an instant Jerusalem tourist must-see attraction almost from the moment it was uncovered. But they were surprised to see that the tunnel's ticket office was still open (a half-dozen people bought tickets in the few minutes they stood by the entrance), and would remain open most evenings until 11:00 PM. Surprised, also, to read that "guided tours are available for booking at any time of the day or night."

Clearly, this would not be an entry point for their search.

This was a disappointment for Bohannon, primarily because he remained ignorant of so much about the Old City, the Temple Mount, and its surrounding areas. During the weeks of preparation, he had been briefed by Doc, Sammy, and Joe on the basics of Jerusalem topography, the layout of the Old City and its walls, plus the physical dimensions and orientation of the Temple Mount. Telling was one thing; seeing was another. And the more he saw, the more doubtful Bohannon was of being able to fulfill their plans.

For one thing, while Jerusalem was no New York City, the human activity around the Temple Mount, even at night, was significant and discouraging. Bohannon often imagined the Temple Mount as being off by itself, outside the mainstream of Jerusalem's urban bustle, a quiet, secluded location that would be all but deserted in the wee hours of the morning. What he found was a city intricately entwined with itself. While the Old City and the Temple Mount were certainly different from and separated from New Jerusalem on the west, the whole place was a thriving metropolis of which the Old City and the Mount operated more like the hub of wheel spokes going in all directions. It was certainly not isolated.

Bohannon looked wistfully at the entrance to the Western Wall Tunnel. *How convenient that would have been.*

⁓⁓⁓

Glancing at his watch, Captain Levin barked an order to his men, who were already kicking themselves for getting posted on night duty with Levin. "Sweep the Mount and the Western Wall," snapped Levin. "Do it now." Hands moved, dials twisted, keyboards were punched, and backs straightened. It was going to be a long night.

⁓⁓⁓

"Warren's Gate is inside that tunnel, isn't it?" Bohannon asked, knowing the answer, his eyes still on the entrance. "We're never going to be able to use that for an entrance. And Warren's Gate is supposed to be the closest to the Holy of Holies, right?"

Nobody tried to answer; nobody looked toward Bohannon. They just stared at the tunnel entrance, wondering where, how they were to find an opening like this that would allow them access to the underbelly of the Temple Mount.

Standing not far from the Western Wall, with the Temple Mount rising above them, despondency began to build like storm clouds. Bohannon's voice was a bit plaintive. "How are we going to do this?"

—⌇⌇⌇⌇—

Without explanation, Levin abruptly stopped his restless pacing and perched himself on a high stool, with a small, straight back. Looking over the shoulders of his squad, he took a much-maligned pipe out of his shirt pocket and began gnawing on its stem. The taste of tobacco was still there, but that was all the vice he allowed himself since the first spot was discovered. Which didn't matter here since this watching post was strictly nonsmoking, a rarity in the Israeli military, but a necessity to maintain the integrity of their highly sophisticated equipment. And this was not a detail where any of them would have introduced any distraction. All of their families lived in the city.

"Daniel, hold that position," Levin said quietly, the mangled stem still in his mouth. His eyes remaining on the fifth screen, the one in the middle of the bank. Levin lowered himself from the stool. "Bring it up." Like an unfolding telescope, the picture on the screen narrowed its focus over and over, pulling the small knot of men into closer relief. There were four of them, three Americans by the look of them, one of them very short. But it was the cut of the fourth man that initially caught Levin's interest. The fourth was dark, rather tall, dressed like a native. But he just didn't look "right." And "not right" was what had been drilled into Levin and all of his men so often that they thought about it in their sleep. "Not right" was always dangerous, often deadly.

"Can you hear anything?"

"No sir, they're not speaking."

"Well, they certainly don't look happy. If they look any harder at the tunnel entrance, they'll bore a hole through it. Are you making a second copy of this for print?"

"Yes, sir."

"Send it to the Avina Station as soon as it's complete. Request they let us know if they come up with any matches."

"Yes, sir."

Levin put his left hand on the soldier's shoulder and leaned in closer to the screen, where the four men were still gathered close together. They were speaking, but so softly the sound could not be recorded. Yet their eyes remained on the opening to the Western Wall Tunnel. "The old one dresses like an academic. From the cut of his clothes, he could be British," said Daniel Stern, a recently commissioned lieutenant who had come up through the ranks. "The second one is clearly American, but he looks more like a businessman on holiday than anything sinister. The small one? . . . dark features, perhaps Italian, but the dress is American, also."

Levin inclined his head toward Stern, but kept his eyes on the four men at the tunnel entrance. "It is not the Brit nor the Yanks that I'm concerned about," said Levin. "It's the tall one, the dark one, the one who looks like a local. And what those three are doing with him . . . and what the four of them are thinking about."

"I think we had better get moving," said Rodriguez. "If we stand here any longer looking at that tunnel entrance, somebody could think we're up to no good."

The men turned to their right, walked back through the Wailing Wall plaza, and stood at the southernmost point of the Old City. For years, the Wailing Wall had been the only exposed section of the Temple Mount's Western Wall, a sixty-foot-long exposed section of one of Herod's great walls. A narrow walkway ran in front of the Wailing Wall, a space where only a few at a time could come face-to-face with the stones that supported the Temple. After the Six-Day War in 1967, when Israeli soldiers captured East Jerusalem—including the Old City—and united the city for the first time in nineteen years, General Moshe Dyan ordered the immediate bulldozing of an entire neighborhood, creating the huge plaza in front of the Wailing Wall, which now allowed thousands of Israelis to come and pray at any time.

"Back to the hotel . . . or more snooping?" Rizzo asked, rubbing his hands together.

"For me," said Rodriguez, "I think if we keep hanging around out here at night, we're just asking for somebody to take an interest in us. Let's get some sleep and come back tomorrow when the place is crawling with tourists."

Contact was lost as the four men passed the Wailing Wall plaza and turned north, along the very edge of the Old City. Trees, hillocks, and buildings blocked the view, and there were no navigable streets in that area—thus no cameras looking for car bombers.

"Copy it and send it. I want multiple images of all four men, different angles, and I want them posted in here immediately, so all the watches will have them fresh in their minds." Captain Levin chewed on the stem of his pipe and suddenly longed for more than the taste of tobacco. "There may be nothing wrong with these guys, but they just feel wrong," Levin said to the room, turning away from the monitors. "Somebody get some coffee in here. Reuven, increase the frequency of all scans. Daniel, call command. Recommend a higher level of alert. All right, gentlemen, let's stay sharp."

The Hawk went back to his chair but remained standing. Both his pipe and his talons were in restless motion. His instincts were telling him this was going to be a long week.

30

It was not quite midmorning Sunday when they met Kallie for breakfast at the Crowne Plaza Hotel, near the convention center and not far from Jerusalem's central train station.

On the ride home the night before, Bohannon had convinced the others that they needed more information, and more help, from the archaeologist. Although Sammy was adamantly opposed and none of them were happy about the risk she would take, Kallie was all for it. All of them knew they might as well pack up and go home if they didn't have somebody they could trust, somebody who had the information they needed and who would be willing to help them in this seemingly crazy scheme.

It was another bright, sunny morning, with cobalt blue sky and a menacing promise of withering heat. With a light morning breeze still on the air, they sat on the patio, under a large umbrella, luxuriated in the luscious local fruit, and tried to avoid fixating on Kallie, whose flowered summer dress had become the central point of several orbits. *Perhaps she was oblivious to the attention,* Bohannon thought, as he watched a young waiter nearly fall over an errant chair. Or perhaps, she had gotten so accustomed to it that she didn't notice anymore. It was clear Kallie relished this opportunity to share as much information as she possibly could and that she was determined to prove just how invaluable she was to their purpose, whatever that purpose was.

Popping in pieces of melon as her punctuation points, Kallie attacked Dr. Johnson's question.

"Even though they are linked now, Warren's Gate and the Western Wall Tunnel are two different stories with two different histories," Kallie explained. "I'll try to give you the condensed version, but if my passion begins to overwhelm our time, just give me a wave.

"So, you know some things about Warren, but," she said, pointing with her fork, "did you know he was suspected of being 'Jack the Ripper'?" That stopped everyone at the table, cups in mid-delivery, food spared the final spearing. "Weird, eh? After stirring up all his controversy here, Warren returned to London and became the city's police commissioner. He was one of the key investigators during Jack the Ripper's bloodletting, and when the murders continued and no viable suspect turned up, rumors and speculation became more vocal that someone *on the inside* or someone with *privilege* was the Ripper and was being protected by the police. Some thought the Ripper was a member of the royal family. Other speculation was that it was one of the investigating detectives, perhaps the commissioner himself. Of course, we still don't know."

Kallie took a moment, resuming her attack on the fruit salad. Seizing the break, Johnson stepped in to get back on point. "But how did Warren get such unfettered access to make all the finds that are attributed to him?"

"In 1897, Warren and his associate Charles Wilson gained the approval of the Muslim Authority to embark on a series of exploratory digs in the areas around the exteriors of where the Temple Mount walls were surmised to exist. Warren was a lieutenant in the Royal Engineers and a member of London's Palestine Exploration Fund. Leading a team of engineers and with financing from the PEF, Warren and Wilson began exploring along the walls of the Mount.

"He discovered a series of tunnels beneath Jerusalem and the Temple Mount, some of which were directly underneath the headquarters of the Knights Templar. Various small artifacts were found which indicated that the Templar order had used some of the tunnels, though it is unclear who exactly first dug them. Some of the ruins that Warren discovered came from centuries earlier, and other tunnels that his team discovered had evidently been used for a water system, as they led to a series of cisterns. On one of his nightly forays, Warren uncovered what was a small, stone archway with a lintel. It was clearly an entrance, or exit, for something, but the archway had been sealed shut with stones and mortar.

"What has since become known as Warren's Gate is shrouded by legend and surrounded by mystery." Kallie abruptly stopped her breakfasting. "Most archaeologists and temple experts believe there is a high probability that Warren's Gate is just outside the location where the Holy of Holies from Herod's Temple would have been located. The Holy of Holies, or most inner court of the Temple, was home to the Ark of the Covenant, which held the stone tablets containing the Ten Commandments; a container of manna; and the staff of Aaron, which budded before Pharaoh. Also in the Holy of Holies was the mercy seat, the location where the Jews believed the glory of God, his presence, resided.

Only one person, the Israeli high priest, was allowed to enter the Holy of Holies, and that was only once a year. If you believed that, then Warren's Gate was the closest you could get to God on this earth."

"Dangerous stuff in this neighborhood," Rizzo chirped, finishing off the remnants of his oatmeal.

"That's for sure," Kallie resumed. "Warren's Gate became a lightning rod for conflict. Tradition claims the Muslims, when they gained control of the Mount, flooded a cistern that is supposedly on the other side of the gate, to keep anyone from gaining access to the Holy of Holies."

The others finished their breakfast much sooner than Kallie, so she waited while a waiter cleared the table and then jumped into story number two.

"For over one hundred years, the only way to reach Warren's Gate was through a narrow shaft, and access to the shaft was severely regulated. But in 1967, the Israeli Ministry of Religious Affairs approved an archaeological dig that took twenty years and uncovered the foundations of the Western Wall for hundreds of yards to the north of the Wailing Wall. Ignoring the impassioned complaints of the Muslim Authority, the Israelis carved out this tunnel to follow the path along the wall. In 1996, Prime Minister Netanyahu ordered that an exit for the tunnel be cut from the Struthion Pool out into the Via Dolorosa. The Western Wall Tunnel now gives everyone access to some of the most fascinating historical locations in the Old City, including Warren's Gate and a series of massive Herodian foundation stones for the walls upon which the Temple Mount platform was constructed. These foundation stones had not been seen for nearly two thousand years."

Each had gotten the obligatory small cup of sweet diesel fuel the Israelis call coffee and sat quietly for a moment, waiting for it to cool.

"Devout Israelis have someone sitting in front of Warren's Gate, praying, twenty-four hours a day," said Kallie. Bohannon saw her glance up at him, then look at Dr. Johnson. "So, if you were thinking of using Warren's Gate to get under the Temple Mount, you can forget that option. You've got to look for another way in."

The twinkle in Kallie's eyes indicated that she knew she had guessed correctly.

Bohannon shot an accusing look at Rizzo.

"Hey, I didn't say a thing," Rizzo objected, rattling his chair with his denial. "Tell them, Kallie. I'm not a rat."

Kallie's smile was encyclopedic. It exonerated Rizzo, defended her honor, and acknowledged the depth of her insightful wisdom, all without a word. "Sammy didn't reveal your secrets," she said. "I can put two and two together . . . Warren's Gate and the cave-exploring equipment that was waiting for you at Tzuba."

A thoughtful, appreciative smile creased Bohannon's cheeks. "I can see why Sammy is smitten with you, Kallie. Doc, why don't you fill in our new teammate. Let her know what brings us to Jerusalem."

〜〜〜

Twenty minutes later, they were in Kallie's modern apartment in a high-rise building on Bar-Lev Road, across the road from the Ammunition Hill national memorial and not far from Hebrew University, where she was completing her studies. As the temperature rose on the Crowne Plaza terrace and the intensity of the conversation grew, Kallie had suggested a change in venue. She was proud of her apartment. It was bright, sunny, and full of graceful touches that held deep meaning for her . . . the decorative, metal, mini Eiffel Tower that reminded her of her favorite city on earth; a framed print of Prague's Charles Bridge at sunrise; and dozens of framed, family photos. She loved her family with a granite-hard passion that fueled her.

She grabbed a pitcher of iced tea and plunked it on the glass-topped coffee table along with some sturdy glass tumblers. But Kallie wanted to get down to business and wasn't thinking of entertaining etiquette. While they were in the restaurant, she had to fight to keep from screaming at these knuckleheads as they unwrapped their incredible story.

At one point, Johnson, seeing the emotional outburst brimming just under the surface, had reached out and placed his hand on her arm. "Not here, Kallie," he had whispered. "I know . . . I know. Take a breath. Hold on."

Somehow, she made it through their story and had gotten out of the hotel without exploding. On the twenty-minute drive to her apartment, she remained silent, sifting the amazing story, stifling her anger at not being completely informed earlier, and measuring the apprehension that was growing in her heart. Now she could wait no longer; she had too much to say.

"First of all, I am really ticked off at you guys for keeping this from me. I know," she said, warding off Johnson's attempt to explain, "I know you didn't want to put me in danger. Don't you know how ridiculous that is? Anyone who chooses to live in Jerusalem, almost anywhere in Israel, does it with the knowledge and acceptance that danger is a reality of daily life. I could be picking out peppers in the market, sitting in class, or just walking down the street, and a random suicide bomber could snuff out my life. So that's a bogus excuse.

"Second, I'm really ticked off at you because you don't know how foolish you are and how your foolishness could have already put me in danger."

Kallie looked at their innocent, questioning eyes, and some of her frustration escaped into the afternoon. *They weren't stupid,* she thought, *just ignorant.* But whether ignorant or stupid, they had placed themselves in the crosshairs of Middle East conflict and, by arriving in Jerusalem with their avowed purpose, were inviting, almost requiring, an obligation on both sides to wipe them out. An obligation that would now extend to her if either side discovered the real purpose for the investigation and research she had undertaken for them over the past few months.

"Look, what you have just told me is a death warrant. Each one of you," she said, deliberately pointing her finger at each, "is a dead man. And you pulled me into this without understanding the risk. I'm not talking about the guys with the lightning bolt crosses, that's a whole different issue. What I'm saying is neither the Arabs nor the Israelis can allow you to leave this country alive. If they knew what you were planning, they wouldn't allow us to live through the night. Dr. Johnson, I'm surprised that you, at least, didn't understand the reality of the situation here in Israel and what your intentions would stir up."

Unwilling to wait for an excuse or to give anyone else the floor, Kallie picked up her glass and her warning at the same time.

"To begin with, you are never going to get permission to dig anywhere on the Temple Mount. Excavating in Israel requires a license from the Department of Antiquities, which is granted only after very serious reviews of credentials, monetary and scholarly backing, and an approved site. All excavations must meet with the approval of the department. But that doesn't help you at all because excavations cannot, under any circumstances, be carried out under or upon Temple Mount. Near the Mount is also problematic. Only one area is approved for exploration, the Jerusalem Archaeological Park, just to the south of the Temple Mount, and that area is already under the full authority of Israeli archaeologists.

"Did you really think that a group of Americans with some bags full of equipment could wander around the Temple Mount without raising any suspicion? The Temple Mount is under an intense amount of surveillance, day and night, and that includes all of the areas immediately around the Temple Mount. Don't you think the Israelis and the Muslim Authority haven't considered the possibility of intruders on the Temple Mount for any number of reasons? Don't you think they both understand the intense emotional upheaval that will ensue if anything broaches the delicate and precarious balance of power? The Israelis have already experienced the street riots that erupted on the basis of rumors. How did you think they were going to respond once they discovered your plan to poke around under the Temple Mount? It's impossible. Neither side can allow that to happen.

"Listen to me, Palestinians don't exactly love Americans to begin with, but the four of you start investigating access points to the base of the Temple Mount and the Palestinians will immediately come to one conclusion: that you are planning to undermine the Haram al-Sharif—the Noble Sanctuary, containing the Dome of the Rock. That, for whatever reason, you intend to collapse the holy mosque. To the Western mind, this is a true overreaction. To the Middle Eastern Muslim, this is a natural and automatic conclusion.

"Alarms would be going off all over the place. The Waqf, both in Jerusalem and in Amman, Jordan, will approach Israeli authorities, demanding explanations, promises, and guarantees. The Islamic Movement, a group of radical Israeli Arabs, will once again sound the cry that 'Al-Aqsa is in danger!' There will be riots atop the Mount, stone-throwing youths, angry Jerusalemite Palestinians. Word will sweep across the Arab world in minutes with cries for help and threats of war."

Stabbing into the brief space when Kallie took a breath, Johnson asked, "Are you talking about Hamas or Fattah?"

Shaking her head and her strawberry curls, Kallie dismissed the question with a backhand wave. "Hamas would not be in the picture. Their base is in Gaza and Ramallah, and access to Jerusalem is denied and cut off. Fattah, after their near civil war with Hamas, is relegated to the West Bank, and they have been severely weakened. Both will threaten and gesture, but this holds little weight in Jerusalem. What you will have to worry about are the local Jerusalemite Arabs. They have access, and they will use it. They are not very well organized, but there is a dangerous splinter organization of the Northern Islamic Front—En Sherif—that comes from Umm El Fahum, the headquarters. They do have contacts in east Jerusalem and are very radical in their paranoia over Jewish designs on the Temple Mount. If the Northern Front ever got a sense of what you were trying to prove, they would exercise no reluctance in slitting your throats.

"That's one side," she said, then drained her iced tea. "But should the Israeli authorities catch wind of your plans, they will immediately suspect that you are one of two things—foreign radicals intent on bringing about some biblical calamity or fulfilling some strange, messianic urge. Or they would suspect you were acting together with the Jewish Underground, a banned Jewish terrorist organization committed to blowing up Muslim structures on the Temple Mount.

"Whoever you are, the Israelis would be swift in deciding on a course of action. If they had even the faintest hint that you had designs on excavating the Temple Mount, you wouldn't be investigated; you would be immediately arrested, thoroughly interrogated, and then dumped into a jail cell until they could arrange an unceremonious removal from the country and the revocation of any future right to enter the State of Israel."

Kallie's neck was getting stiff, both from tension and from the fact that she was punctuating her words with emphatic thrusts of her head and hands. "But," she said, rolling her head back over her shoulders, sitting back in her chair, "if any of them dreamed that you were searching for the Third Temple, if they understood that you guys believe it exists, you'd be squashed like bugs, me along with you. A Third Temple? That would mean war, all-out war. The Israelis would probably have to go nuclear to hold off the Arabs. Your lives, my life, they would mean nothing to either the Israelis or the Arabs as a price to prevent a nuclear war."

Kallie had closed her eyes at the thought of nuclear war. If Israel went nuclear against the Arabs, someone would go nuclear against Israel . . . Iran, Moscow, perhaps even the North Koreans.

Opening her eyes, she watched in silent contemplation as each of her guests weighed the implications of her words and recognized, for the first time, the enormity of the outcome should their information prove correct.

"What do you think, Joe?" Bohannon asked.

"I'm beginning to wonder," said Rodriguez, "not only about our chances of finding the Temple, but also our chances of surviving the next few days and returning home in one piece. Maybe it would make sense to leave the backpacks of equipment at the hotel, hightail it to the airport, and get out of Israel as fast as possible. Why not leave now?"

"Because the 'lightning bolts' are still looking for our sorry rear ends," Rizzo answered.

"And because they are still looking for the scroll," added Johnson. "We can't go home now. Your families would still be in danger, and we would be in danger. Our lives are at risk whether we stay here or go. But here, it's only us at risk—us and Kallie. We go home without determining whether the Temple is real or not, the risk returns with us. The lightning bolt guys are after the scroll. They know it exists. It was likely in their possession at one time. They may not know all that it means, but obviously, they believe it's important enough to kill for it. Perhaps this is the same group that Spurgeon feared. Who knows? And it doesn't really matter. We've got this scroll, we know its message, and it's up to us to find out if it's true. That's all we have control over at the moment."

Joe Rodriguez ran his hand through the thick, black curls on his head. "Maybe next time we go walking around the Mount, we should wear disguises."

The stiff throbbing at the back of Kallie's neck intensified. Too many long days hunched over digs in small pits, meticulously sweeping away grains of sand with a toothbrush. "What do you mean, next time?"

Kallie saw a momentary flicker of understanding in Rodriguez's eyes. "After the reception last night, we walked down David Street to the Western Wall Tunnel. We stood there for a while, talking about Warren's Gate and the Foundation Stones. Then we walked over to the Western Wall. We were wondering if maybe we were there too long."

"You didn't go into the Western Wall Tunnel?" she asked.

"No," said Dr. Johnson, "we just stood there and watched for a while. I was surprised how many people were still entering the tunnel so late at night. Kallie, what is it?"

"How long were you standing there?"

The four of them looked at each other, each now exhibiting a growing anxiety. The others deferred to Bohannon.

"We might have been standing there for twenty or thirty minutes," he said. Bohannon got out of his chair and stepped toward one of the apartment's sunny windows. "We're in trouble, aren't we? We made a mistake."

None of them needed to hear the answer.

"There are thousands of hidden surveillance cameras all over Jerusalem," said Kallie, suddenly feeling empty inside, "and hundreds scattered around the Temple Mount. As a society living with the constant threat of terrorism, Shin Bet's internal security apparatus is incredibly effective. The city is reduced to sectors, and each sector has a sophisticated communications center monitoring the feeds from all of the cameras in that sector. If you were standing outside the Western Wall Tunnel for thirty minutes last night, Shin Bet has you on tape. You may already be under surveillance."

31

"Do you know these men?"

They were inside a low, stone building. Once a family's dwelling, but now caught in the no-man's-land between Jordan and the land the Jews stole in 1967. The floor was dusty, the tabletop was dusty, the air was dusty. The Imam looked down at his once spotless white robe now coated in gray.

Mahamoud drew closer to the photo. It was clearly a copy. But the four men were visible, their features distinct.

"No. I don't know who they are."

"Shin Bet is concerned," said the Imam. As the iron-willed leader of En Sherif, the outlawed faction of the Northern Islamic Front, the Imam had cultivated many impeccable sources of information. "They are running the photos through facial recognition and have reached out to Interpol. As yet, they know nothing. Only that these four stood at the entrance to the Western Wall Tunnel for thirty minutes."

"Who is the one?" asked Mahamoud, pointing to the one in the shorts. "Israeli? But if Israeli, why would Shin Bet be concerned? Unless . . . unless he was a rogue . . . Jewish Underground, perhaps?"

"I don't know," said the older man, his kaffiyeh hanging down past his long gray beard. "But I am also concerned. Leonidas has proven his value again. We pay him well; we will continue to need his service. But for now, alert Yazeer. Get his team activated. Find these men. Find them quickly."

⎯⎯∾∾⎯⎯

Rizzo was at Kallie's computer, pulling up Google Earth while Kallie was huddled around the kitchen table with Bohannon, Rodriguez, and Johnson, two maps overlapping one end of the table, four thick reference books stacked on the other.

"I've been doing some of my own work while I was waiting for you to get over here," Kallie was saying as she pulled open one of the huge books. "I thought . . . well . . . I thought you guys were doing a treasure hunt. I Googled all of you when Sammy first got in touch with me. And, Doc, forgive me. I saw there was this big stink in the past about selling counterfeit antiquities, and well, I don't know, for a while I was worried that you might not have legitimate motives. I'm sorry about that. But it didn't take long for me to put that aside and turn my energy to figuring out why you were coming all the way to Israel.

"So I started taking the few pieces of information that you shared with me combined with what I knew from the research I did for you, and I began running down every thread as far as I possibly could.

"Sammy," Kallie said through the doorway, "have you zeroed in on that area and pulled up that interactive map of Israel?" When Rizzo grunted an affirmative, Kallie addressed the table again. "Come on, I'm going to show you something interesting."

Rizzo made room for Kallie at the computer. He hopped up on another chair to remain by her side. "Okay . . . here's the Temple Mount . . . you can see the Al-Aqsa Mosque, the Dome of the Rock, even some of the walls. Now, the satellite photo can't get us close enough, so let's pull up the map of Israel and Jerusalem. Okay, here, on the right of the Temple Mount is the Kidron Valley. Down there is the Gihon Spring and the City of David. I figured if you were going to find a way under the Temple Mount, one that wasn't closely guarded or overrun with tourists, it would have to come from around Gihon. There have been several interesting discoveries there recently by Israeli archaeologists. It had always been assumed that King Hezekiah built his water tunnel from Gihon to the Pool of Siloam to protect Jerusalem's water supply in time of siege. But they have just discovered the foundations of a wall much farther down the slope to the Kidron Valley, a wall that would have enclosed the Gihon Spring. It even had guard towers on either side of the spring, obviously for protection. So Hezekiah's Tunnel was not to supply water.

"That's one of the amazing things about Jerusalem, how little has been done archaeologically over time and how limited our information is. Why, just recently a team uncovered a tunnel that was totally unknown—"

"The King's Garden Tunnel, right?" asked Johnson. "Larsen and I also believed that would be a possible point of access. It runs in the right direction, passes very close to where archaeologists have theorized the Holy of Holies exists, and is large enough to have been a conduit for the material needed to build the Temple. That would be my guess."

Nolan was nodding her head in agreement. "You're right, Doc. That is exactly where I was looking. I figured the only challenge for us would be initially getting into the tunnel. Now that it has been discovered, security has been increased in that area. But I've been checking it out over the past several weeks, using my garden guide status to visit at different times of the week, different times of the day or night. And there is good news. The tunnel entrance is nearly hidden from the Old City and the Temple Mount, on the down slope of a hillock, surrounded by high bushes. It has not been opened to the public, so there are no tourists. And most importantly, it's not guarded after midnight."

Bohannon's heart skipped. "That's great!" he blurted. "Right?"

"It's good," Kallie said calmly. "It's good. It's a place to start. But there is no guarantee. And there is a second good possibility, Zechariah's Tomb. Joe, would you get that book from the table for me? Thanks."

She flipped a few pages and then turned the book around for the others to read. "This is the family lineage of the Jewish priesthood, from Aaron through the seventeenth century. It goes on for several pages. Turn over two pages, look at the one on the left, about halfway down."

Rizzo spotted it first. "There's our boy, Abiathar, son of Elijah."

"Okay," said Kallie, "now track his lineage backward about two thousand years. Look for the prophet Zechariah. Found it? Okay, now look to the side. What does it say?"

Rodriguez followed the lineage lines from Zechariah to a line that ran parallel through generation after generation. "It says Zechariah was from the priestly family of Beni Hazir."

"Okay," Kallie continued, "go back to Abiathar."

Rodriguez flipped the pages. "It says Abiathar was also from the priestly family of Beni Hazir. Is that normal? Are all priests from Beni Hazir?"

"Doc?" said Kallie.

"No, all priests are from Aaron, but there were several other family lines over time that were differentiated primarily because of theological differences. Families that became known for a different interpretation of the Torah. So, tell us, what's the link to Beni Hazir? You've taken us here for a reason."

Kallie swung around to again face the computer screen and passed the book to Rizzo. She moved the mouse so that the cursor returned to the King's Garden Tunnel. "Okay, so here's the King's Garden Tunnel, at the base of the Kidron Valley.

"But look to the right, on the other side of the Kidron Valley. Do you see that notation, 'The Tomb of Zechariah'? Watch this." Kallie mouse clicked on the "I" info icon next to Zechariah's Tomb.

Up popped a small info balloon, with a pointer to Zechariah's Tomb. Inside the balloon it said, "Believed to be the burial site of the prophet, one of a series of tombs belonging to the priestly family of Beni Hazir."

"How clever," purred Johnson. "That is an interesting connection. I'm impressed. So, Kallie, since you are clearly the expert here, what do you think?"

Kallie's voice was low, little more than a whisper. "Abiathar needed a way, he needed an entryway to bring in his men, his material, and he needed a way that would not draw attention to itself, even if the coming and going were min-imal. During his lifetime, or his father's, no one would question a few workmen coming or going from the tombs, carrying wood beams to shore up new tombs. And even though we don't know much of anything about the King's Garden Tunnel, it may also have been a common access point."

She turned her chair around to face the men, who had in the space of a few hours irrevocably changed her life. "What's my hunch? I think we've found Abiathar's entrance. I don't have any evidence, but it seems to me, from all the possibilities you have been reviewing and all the possibilities I have been researching, if there is a secret passageway that would lead to a cavern con-taining the Third Temple, it would come from one of these two locations. If I had to place a bet, I'd wager on the King's Garden Tunnel. Until a few months ago, no one knew it existed. Zechariah's Tomb has been open for hundreds of years, and it is so much farther away. I think the King's Garden Tunnel has to be the first place we look."

"Hallelujah," cried Rizzo, dropping the book off his lap.

Doc Johnson turned on his heel and paced toward the window. "Yes . . . yes . . . Tom!" Johnson turned again, facing the room. "This all makes sense. Remember what Winthrop was telling us about the Mount and the bedrock. Yes . . . yes . . . this all makes sense. Kallie, you're . . ."

Nolan waited patiently in her computer chair, arms folded across her chest. Doc Johnson must have read her face, and the adrenalin spike drained from the room.

"Which leaves us one final, major hurdle," said Kallie. Doc sat down at the table and Bohannon ran a hand through his hair.

"How do we get into the tunnel without notice?" Rodriguez took a deep breath, held up his two hands, palms upward, and shrugged his shoulders.

"Not only how do we get in," said Kallie, "but also how do we determine if there is an access point that may take us under the Temple Mount? And how do we figure out where to look if we do get under the Mount? God knows how many caverns and tunnels and caves may be under there."

"Your use of the pronoun *we* may be a bit premature," said Johnson, dryly.

Nolan pressed on, addressing Bohannon directly. "Tom, the only question that remains to be determined is whether we go there during the day or during the night. Can we trust going there during the day? Can we discover what we need to discover during the night? Whatever the answer is, before we commit ourselves to either of these locations with all our equipment for what will likely be several days, we need to know if there is a likely tunnel, or an entrance to a tunnel, that could take us under the Temple Mount.

"And it's going to be *we*, Doc, because the four of you, by yourselves, will appear suspicious and out of place if anyone were to take the time to look. But if you happened to be in the care of an official garden guide, such as myself, then all anyone would see would be a small group of tourists . . . affluent tourists. And they wouldn't give you a second thought. And then we can take as long as we like trying to find the way in. That's why *we*."

Kallie was in.

Then all eyes were on Bohannon.

"To answer one of your questions," he said, "we expect that in some way the scroll will guide us once we get under the Temple Mount. Abiathar would not have left this most important part up to chance. We believe the answer will be in the scroll."

"Wait a minute. You've got it here?" she asked, incredulous. "This scroll may be priceless, and you're carrying it around in your luggage? Are you guys out of your minds?"

"What else were we going to do with it?" snapped Rodriguez. "Leave it at home? The New York police commissioner told us to get our families out of town. Do you think the scroll would have been safe anywhere we could have left it? Besides, I agree with Tom. I'm confident we're going to need it again before this thing is over. As far as looking suspicious, we thought of that, too. All of our equipment is in backpacks, and we've all come prepped with our Merrell hiking shoes and chamois shirts. We'll look like backpackers who are visiting the sights. But it would probably help to have a guide along."

Rodriguez waited for his brother-in-law. It was his call.

Kallie felt a shiver start at the bottom of her spine. Bohannon was looking at her like a professor about to give a failing grade. She willed her heart to slow.

"We'll be here at seven to pick you up," Bohannon said to Kallie, his voice somber. "Be in your guide uniform and ready to go. We'll need to risk it during the day just to get a reasonable sense of what we're facing. I want to get to the Gihon Spring as early as possible, before anyone happens to be wandering around."

"Then make it five thirty," said Kallie. "Jerusalem wakes up early. I'll be by the front door, waiting. And you guys, make sure you look like tourists. You got that, Sammy? Hiking shorts if you have them, and rugged shoes. This will be no Sunday stroll."

—∿∿∿—

Bowing deeply from the waist, a slow extravagance of submission, he stopped when the upper half of his body was parallel to the floor. The cross and lightning bolt amulet hung straight down from his neck. "Welcome, Effendi."

"How did you discover them?"

No greeting in return, no sharing of compliments. This was rude behavior, but this was the Prophet's representative. A very holy man, recently arrived from Egypt. Perhaps he had no time for courtesy.

"A mere chance, Effendi. My cousin, he is a waiter at the Crowne Plaza. Often, he brings us bits of conversations, bits that prove to be valuable in furthering the cause."

"Prove to be valuable in lining your pockets, more likely. Stand up."

"Yes, Effendi."

Rasaf straightened his back slowly, ignoring the pain, determined to present himself as a worthy disciple. This was his great opportunity, after all. Bad manners would not spoil this chance for him. Only the old man's face was visible. That was enough. His skin was very dark, heavily creased by sun and wind. His face was framed by a thick, jet-black beard that oddly seemed both trimmed and wild. Rasaf took in all of those elements quickly. But he could not escape from the old man's eyes. They were fierce, two discs of flaming onyx, consuming Rasaf. They spoke to him in songs of Jihad. They called him to great sacrifice. They filled him with ancient hate. Rasaf trembled.

"Where are they?"

"They drove to an apartment building on Bar-Lev Road near the university. We are watching."

"Good. Continue to watch. Take no action, but stay with them without fail. We will allow them to lead us. For now."

"Yes, Effendi." This *would* be his great opportunity, Rasaf exulted.

"Rasaf, do you have children?"

"Yes, Effendi," Rasaf said, beginning to smile at his good fortune.

"Fine. It is good to have children."

The eyes were burning pits, harbingers of mayhem. Rasaf began to bow under their relentless power.

"Don't do anything to make them orphans."

Startled, Rasaf stopped bowing and looked up. And he was alone.

―――∾∿∾―――

When they returned to the Hotel Tzuba that night, Johnson pulled out the thermal imaging photos that Larsen had gotten from his Uncle Ethan. Johnson still marveled at the thought of having the chairman of the Joint Chiefs as an uncle. The power of the Larsen family was staggering, yet appeared to be directed only to service.

Even with a magnifying glass, Johnson could detect no significant change in image along the Kidron Valley, no indication of the King's Garden Tunnel, let alone any other tunnel branching off from it or extending from Zechariah's Tomb toward the Temple Mount. It would have been heartening to find some evidence of a tunnel, but the lack of evidence didn't disprove its existence. It was as he had expected. The only way they would truly know would be to go inside and find out for themselves.

And hope no one was watching.

32

Lieutenant Daniel Stern ached. Every part of his body ached. His eyes hurt, and especially, his neck hurt. Yet he would not consider leaving his post. He stayed for The Hawk. But he also stayed for his wife and children, now two and five. The sun was up, only barely, yet its unmistakable message was that it would be another withering day. And Stern had no idea when it would end.

The Hawk was on duty, sitting atop his perch. He had been on duty for nearly thirty-eight hours without sleep. Captain Avram Levin was losing his patience and getting cranky. For his squad, many of whom had joined him in the vigil, this was the most anxious time. The Hawk was a good man, a good leader, an inspiration to his men. But his talons were sharp when time and circumstance failed to follow his orders.

Levin's team was perhaps Shin Bet's best. That is why they were assigned to the Aleph Reconnaissance Center to protect the Temple Mount. Not to protect the shrines from tourists, but to protect Israel and its future from terrorists of any stripe.

Since the moment they focused on the four men at the entrance to the Western Wall Tunnel, the Aleph team had intensified its sweeps. In addition to its normal timetable and procedure, The Hawk would routinely, and randomly, call for a sweep of any area that popped into his consciousness, even areas that were outside of his zone.

"Command, give me a sweep of David's Tower, then down David Street. See if we can pick them up again. Stern, roll down the Kidron Valley. If they are coming back, they will be coming back soon."

~~~

Mahamoud pulled out the cell phone and hit the speed dial button.

One ring only. Leonidas was on the other end.

"Nothing yet . . . be patient . . . I will call you when information arrives."
The phone connection went dead.

—∿∿∼—

Kallie guided the large, black SUV into the tourist parking lot at Bev Shaloan.
She popped out quickly and put on her official bucket hat with the garden guide
logo so prominently stitched to the side. The bucket hat, the logo, she could
abide those. The rest of the uniform was typically Israeli, stern and simple. Leaf
green, short-sleeve, button-front shirt along with rolled-up shorts of the same
color. The winter uniform was just a longer version of this. No, it wasn't the
uniform. It was the stupid, little "G/G" pennant, held aloft from the brim of her
bucket hat by a long, stiff wire. *It makes us look like targets in a shooting gallery,*
she thought. So the hat always went on last.

"Gentlemen, I would like to show you one of the more interesting and
rarely visited sites in the Old City of Jerusalem."

"Negotiating for a bigger tip, eh?" said Rizzo, getting a head start up the
pathway. Rodriguez also strode past Kallie and began consuming the path with
long, athletic strides. Like the others, he had on his backpacker outfit, including
a wide-brimmed hat all of them were wearing for protection from the sun.
Only Rodriguez was still wearing the kibbutz shorts he had purchased at Tzuba.
"They are just so much more comfortable than the ones I brought from New
York," he told the others.

Kallie looked at the other two. "We'll walk along that pathway, around to
the other side of the hill. Would either one of you like me to share my training,
give you a more detailed, historical description?"

The two men looked at each other, looked at Kallie, and then looked along
the path.

"No offense," said Tom, taking her arm, "but let's go. The only thing I want
to know is out there, underground. And for it to look right, you need to lead
us. So, lead on."

Kallie shook her arm free, spun on her heel, and, with the abhorred pennant
bouncing with every step, led the men along the path to the hill, behind which
was the partially obscured entrance to the King's Garden Tunnel.

Kallie presented her identification and garden guide credentials to the
guard and, after a small gift for his family was arranged, led her clients around

the barrier with "No Admittance" written in Hebrew, Arabic, and English and into the tunnel.

⸻

"Nothing, Captain," said Stern, reviewing all the screens. "It's still pretty early. Only a few tourists out, trying to beat the heat. Some shoppers, some at the Wall, a garden guide showing a few the entrance to the King's Garden Tunnel. Nothing yet."

The Hawk was rocking on his chair. They had lost track of these men, and he wasn't happy.

⸻

Rasaf's car was so old, it barely held itself together. A Subaru wagon some affluent Westerner had abandoned, its fenders were of mismatched colors, only one door opened, and the air-conditioning had long since vanished. But it was reliable, the engine and drivetrain still running strong. Already dusty from following the black SUV into Jerusalem, Rasaf sat in his car at the far edge of the car park, just south of the Western Wall. He held a small, collapsible telescope to his eye, trained on the hill behind which was the King's Garden Tunnel, while in his other hand he held a cell phone to his ear.

"Yes, Effendi, the guide just took them into the tunnel entrance. No, Effendi, I cannot see the entrance. Yes, Effendi, they are searching." Rasaf listened carefully to the instructions coming through the phone. "Yes, Effendi. I will call them. We will be prepared. Yes, Effendi, tonight."

Rasaf clicked the phone shut and stuck it in his pants pocket. Like his car, his clothes had seen better days. They were as nondescript as Rasaf, the pants a dull, dust color, his shirt only a vague reminder of its original green. On his head sat a round kufi of worn, sweat-stained brown leather. In the morning air, he still wore a light, faded blue jacket. Even with the jacket, and the temperature inching up, Rasaf shivered at the demands of the old man.

Allah preserve us, he thought. Then he sat back in the creaky seat, and waited.

⸻

Midday had passed, and evening was well upon them. The Hawk was now pacing at a feverish tempo. The day had escaped with no further contact with the four men who had raised their suspicions the night before, so Levin released Stern from surveillance and assigned him to review all the tapes they recorded that day. With three screens rolling at the same time, it didn't take Stern long to see something that had been missed earlier.

"Captain, look at this," and Levin was immediately at his shoulder. "Remember those tourists we noticed going into King's Garden Tunnel this morning? Well, here they are, coming out. Sir, look at the time."

"Roll that back again, Stern," Levin whispered. Levin was gnawing on his pipe and berating his caution. *Immediately, I should have acted immediately.*

"Here, sir, you see? The four tourists with the garden guide."

Checking the running time at the top left of the video, Levin spoke, as if to himself. "Ten thirty, and they entered just after six this morning?

"Four hours . . . more than four hours," Levin said. "How could they be in there for four hours? There is not that much to see. Only the entrance is accessible. Not even a garden guide would have access more than a few meters into the tunnel. Stern, zoom in. I want a better look at those people."

Stern moved his mouse and used the scroll button to zoom the picture in closer. A female garden guide and four men, or three men and a child, the guide clearly identifiable because of the pennant on her hat, the men less so because their wide-brimmed hats obscured their faces. Stern could feel both Captain Levin's hot breath on his neck and his growing anxiety. "Closer, Stern, closer on that man on the left." Again the mouse scrolled the zoom, bringing the image closer, but beginning to lose its resolution. Without warning, Levin's strong hand was on Stern's shoulder, digging into the meat with a sudden fierceness.

"Print that . . . pull back two clicks and print that, also."

The Hawk moved swiftly to the other side of the room and ripped last night's photo from the bulletin board. He swept past the printer, snatched up the two photos, and spread the three images on the desktop next to Stern's computer. Experienced, knowledgeable veterans of surveillance, Levin and Stern looked at the images, then at each other. The man, the kibbutz shorts, the visible features, they were the same.

"Pull up the records starting at 10:30 this morning, and get it on all the screens. Follow the trail of that SUV. They've got a ten-hour lead on us, but we should still be able to find out where they went. That black SUV will stand out like a beacon. All of you," The Hawk said, pulling away from Stern's monitor, "work with Stern. Follow his directions." Two quick strides, and he was at his desk, grabbing the phone. First, Surveillance Command, no greetings, no pleasantries. "This is Levin. I want full Vehicle Tracking on line immediately. We need to track a vehicle from this morning. Stern will give you the specifics in a moment." His finger stabbed the Cancel button and then speed-dial number two to Shin Bet headquarters. "Lubich, this is Levin. Ready four squads; full gear. And get a bird in the air. I'll come back to you with a target."

Hovering again over Stern's shoulder, Levin tried to focus on all three photos at once. "Is that a child or a midget?" he said to the back of Stern's head.

"He moves like an adult, not like a child," said Stern.

"The other two," Levin asked, "English or American?" Stern snapped a quick glance to his left. "American . . . this one could be British. But the other is clearly American," he said. "It's the same men as last night." Looking back to his screen, Stern was relieved. "Here, see, the black SUV. All of them got in it. Pulling back onto the Ha-shilo'akh Road. North," he called across the room, "10:37 and heading north."

Stern froze the image on his computer screen.

"Got it," said Levin, who was already moving. "Keep going after them."

Speed-dial number two. "Lubich . . . black, Toyota SUV . . . late model . . . plate number IV 3-77AY. No, they had no bags, no backpacks going in or coming out. It was reconnaissance. We get them, we don't have to worry about the tunnel. Stern," he snapped, pulling the phone away, "what have you got?"

"They looped around the Old City, heading west on the Bar-Lev. We've still got them going west. Looks like they may be headed for Highway 1."

"Still west . . . I know if they leave the city, we'll lose contact. I know, Lubich, I know."

The handset slammed into the cradle. Levin looked at his watch . . . 20:15 . . . be getting dark soon. How would they find these men?

"Captain." It was Sergeant Ehud, across the room. "The guides say they have no record of anyone being hired this morning for a visit to the tunnel. And the Toyota is rented to an American from New York City. They gave their local address as Hotel Tzuba."

Speed-dial number two. "Lubich . . . forget before . . . Hotel Tzuba . . . get the bird in the air to look for the black SUV . . . alert two squads and get them moving toward the kibbutz, but carefully. No sirens, no notice. Keep the other two on hold for now."

Speed-dial number three. "Major? Yes, we have a bird up and two loaded squads en route to the kibbutz, two in reserve. Yes, at least one is positive as an American. Stern has e-mailed you all the details for you to share with the consulate. No, not sure of the others, but one certainly looks like a local. Yes, sir . . . the King's Garden Tunnel. Yes, sir, if the Toyota SUV is there, the squads will be in place in an hour. Yes, sir, no sirens. Yes, sir . . . we're all still on duty. Thank you, sir."

Captain Levin turned on his heel, took a deep breath, and once again thanked God that he worked for a commander who understood his work and his men. While The Hawk was ripping up his own insides for failing to move more quickly, the major was only complimentary. "Good work, Stern," said The Hawk, a much gentler hand on the lieutenant's shoulder. "Good work, men. The major sends his gratitude and compliments. But we need to remain vigilant. We're still not certain where these men may be, or what they may be planning. Stick to it, and question everything."

The Hawk returned to his perch. His face was a steely mask, reviewing the images on every screen. Inside, he was furious at his own blunder. *I had him. Last night, I had him.*

━∿∿━

Mahamoud immediately recognized the voice of Leonidas. "Hotel Tzuba . . . in the kibbutz. The vehicle has been positively identified, and Shin Bet has two armed squads en route, probably thirty minutes away. But they have no orders yet to engage. They will likely stage at the Mevasseret Zion interchange awaiting orders. You don't have long."

The phone line went dead.

Mahamoud had gotten the earlier report from Leonidas and passed it along to the leader of En Sharif, the renegade arm of the Northern Islamic Front. Shin Bet had recorded the four men entering the King's Garden Temple and had now tagged them as suspected terrorists. But no one knew their allegiance. And the Imam's instructions had been clear. "Alert Yazeer and his team. I want these men eliminated tonight. They must never come near the Mount."

Now, the last remnants of light fading in the western sky, Yazeer was at his right, his two men in the back seat, as they sat in the deep shadows of an olive grove just off the Sataf Roundabout.

"Shin Bet will move the reserve squads to control the intersection at Highway 1 and move the other two squads into Tzuba," said Yazeer. "We can't fight Shin Bet . . . too many, too well armed. If they capture these men in Tzuba, there will be nothing for us to do." Yazeer rested his head in his hands. "We are in Allah's hands." Turning to the back seat, he looked at his men. "Take your vehicles farther down this road, away from Highway 1. About four kilometers south, the road ascends over a hill and then drops down to the right on the far side of the hill. Take your vehicles to the base, on the far side of the hill, one on each side of the road. Remain out of sight. Only move when you receive my call."

—⁓⁓—

Kallie was filling a fourth backpack with bottled water, trail mix, and peanut butter and jelly sandwiches. Johnson was checking their lanterns and flashlights and packing extra batteries while Rizzo was filling a backpack with their caving gear. Rodriguez had the toughest job, making sure the thin arthroscopes didn't get crushed by the small, tanklike, pipe inspector and that all of the monitors and control cables were secure and undamaged. Bohannon was stowing the mini cameras and recorder, extra CDs, and the communication equipment when he nearly had a heart attack. He had just placed the satellite phone in the backpack when it lit up like a pinball machine and started spitting out its annoying beeps. Bohannon didn't know whether to answer it, or hit it for scaring the living hoots out of him. Gingerly, he picked it up, realizing he didn't know how it worked. He put the receiver to his ear. "Yes?"

"Tom, is that you?" The voice sounded as if it was in the next room, not halfway around the world. "Tom, listen, this is Sam Reynolds at State. We don't have time to chat. Mideast desk just got a flash from Shin Bet. They know where you are and they have some very unpleasant ideas about what you are up to. Two squads of their counterterrorism unit are staged at the Highway 1 interchange, just north of you, waiting for the 'go' order. The only thing holding them back was to notify us they were about to pick up a very suspicious American and the three men he's traveling with.

"I'd say you have less than five minutes to get out of there and get lost, or you will be inside an Israeli jail cell within the hour. Get out . . . get out now."

The lights went off, the phone went in the bag, and Bohannon was yelling for his partners to move.

⹊⹊⹊

The Israeli pilot had not yet seen his relief on the radar screen and was beginning to register a little anxiety about his dwindling fuel. For this job, he couldn't just hover in place. He had to remain some distance away, downwind, flying gentle loops that generated the least amount of noise. He was beginning to stir up some righteous indignation toward his dispatcher when the door to the hotel room swung open, no lights showing, and five people raced to the black SUV, each one toting an overstuffed backpack.

"Targets are running . . . say again . . . targets are running." No longer concerned about stealth, the pilot swung his chopper hard to the left and accelerated as the Toyota came to life and bolted past the kibbutz gates. "Intercept is moving," came the disembodied voice from his radio.

"Target vehicle is moving at high speed toward the Sataf Roundabout," reported the pilot.

"Understood. We'll be on them shortly."

⹊⹊⹊

The phone rang. "Mahamoud, they are moving. They are coming to you. Shin Bet will not be far behind." Yazeer already had his automatic weapon at the ready.

⹊⹊⹊

The phone rang. "Effendi, they are moving. We are ready. The others are just below us."

"Very well, Rasaf. You know what to do."

Rasaf bit his lip and shifted the dirty leather cap on his head. "But, Effendi. We have seen watchers from the Northern Front. They also pursue these Americans. These Muslim brothers of ours may interfere. Of course, we would kill the infidels to recover the scroll. But our brothers? How—"

"Fool," snapped the voice in his ear. "Anyone who stands between the scroll and the Prophet's Guard is an enemy. For the first time in over one hundred years, we have a chance to recover the scroll. Do not allow anyone to stand in your way. Not anyone. Do you understand me?"

Rasaf held his breath to quiet his heart. "Yes, Effendi. We are ready."

⚬⚬⚬

The phone rang. In the back seat, Johnson dug it out of the backpack. Bohannon was driving at a ridiculous speed, and Rodriguez, riding shotgun, was vainly trying to spot potholes in the distance. "We're coming to the roundabout," said Rodriguez. "Slow down. Tom, slow down!"

"Yes . . ." Johnson listened, then turned to Bohannon. "Shin Bet has two squads coming down 3095 right now, two more at the interchange, and a helicopter on our tail."

"Faster," Rizzo shouted. "Come on . . . faster!"

⚬⚬⚬

The black SUV careened past them, wildly ignoring the laws of physics. Two wheels clung to the asphalt as it hurtled round the circle, then all the weight shifted to the other two wheels as the black monster headed south on the 3095.

"Now, Mahamoud. Now," called Yazeer as he crawled halfway out the passenger-side window. "Call them."

⚬⚬⚬

"Target vehicle gaining speed. Just turned south on the 3095," reported the pilot.

"Roger that," said the voice.

"Wait," the pilot stammered. "Another vehicle just came out of the trees at the roundabout and is pursuing the SUV, also at a high rate of speed. No lights. It appears they are trying to intercept."

"Say again?" came the voice. "Is this two hostiles?"

"I have no clue," said the pilot. "What I do know is that my fuel is getting very low."

"Understood. We're minutes out."

⸻∿∿⸻

Five sets of eyes were on the road ahead. None of them saw the dark shadow closing fast from behind.

⸻∿∿⸻

Rasaf had placed his men on the hill. He had chosen wisely. He had good sight lines in many directions, overseeing the 3095.

⸻∿∿⸻

Noise like firecrackers. Thuds against the steel gate on the back of the SUV. Headlights burning to life just behind them. Sensory overload for the flash of a second. Then he knew they were being fired upon. Bohannon floored the SUV as it climbed the crest of a hill, then almost lost control as the road on the other side fell away to the right.

⸻∿∿⸻

The pilot realized that he didn't know the guy's name. "Ground," he snapped, "we have hostile fire on the target vehicle. Say again, hostile fire on the target vehicle."

A momentary pause, then the voice came back. "What?"

⸻∿∿⸻

"Now," Yazeer yelled into the night, the Uzi in his hands ripping into the Toyota's rear gate. "Now, close it off."

⸻∿∿⸻

Hanging on for life and praying for deliverance, Bohannon saw two cars emerge, one on each side of the road, and form a roadblock at the bottom of the hill. Men got out, pointing something at them. "Oh, God!" blurted Rodriguez.

⚮

"Now," said Rasaf.

⚮

"Mahamoud, why are we shooting rockets at the SUV?" Yazeer screamed from the window. For the shortest instant, Mahamoud turned to the voice. And saw the trail of light coming toward them.

⚮

Nolan, Rizzo, and Johnson were on the floor in the back, Rodriguez was holding on to any handle he could find, and Bohannon was looking for a way out when it whooshed past the Toyota's right side and homed in on the cars in the middle of the road. A blinding flash of light.

⚮

"Ground! Ground! Acknowledge. There is rocket fire. I don't know who's shooting at who. Two cars formed a roadblock ahead of the SUV, but they've been blown away by an RPG round . . . God, there's another RPG. It just took out the pursuing vehicle. Rocket fire is coming from the hill to the west. Target vehicle is—Oh, no. My fuel alarms are going off. You're on your own, ground. Shalom."

"Understood," said the voice—not very convincingly.

⚮

"Floor it," yelled Rodriguez at the top of his voice, swamped by flashbacks from his youth in the Bronx. "Floor it. Don't you dare slow down. Bust right through them."

⚮

The two squads of Shin Bet troopers pulled up to the carnage on the 3095, each Hummer cautiously closing in on one of the burning heaps of metal. Two troopers, now on foot after being dropped off, closed in on the hill from the other side.

They didn't find much. Charred bodies in the mangled wreckage, RPG casings on the hill sitting beside flattened grass in the shapes of bodies. Few answers for all their questions, no sign of the black Toyota SUV, and no helicopter to track it down.

⸻

One of the other men was driving the battered Subaru. They were headed west, intending to make a big, lazy loop before heading back to Jerusalem. Rasaf was on the cell phone. "Yes, Effendi, the scroll is safe. We were successful in helping the Americans avoid the ambush, and Shin Bet stopped to deal with the wreckage on the road. No, Effendi, we could not follow. But we will be waiting for them at the King's Garden Tunnel. Be assured, Effendi, the scroll will soon be returned to the hands of the Prophet's Guard. And then we may all return home. Thank you, Effendi. I am blessed that you are pleased."

Rasaf closed the phone and leaned his head onto the seat back. It was only then that he realized he had somehow lost his leather hat.

⸻

The phone rang in Aleph Reconnaissance Center. Captain Avram Levin knew it was Shavuot. Much of Jerusalem was closed and quiet. But security never sleeps. This weekend, neither would he.

Levin had been on duty for three days. So had his team at the computer terminals. None of them were thinking about leaving. Their replacement details had been reassigned to other tasks, a good thing since the threat alert had been elevated, leaving Levin and his detail to deal with ensuring the security of the Temple Mount and the Old City of Jerusalem.

The phone rang again. The Hawk reached for the handset.

"Yes?"

Stern had turned away from his computer screen to watch Levin. He would have to be reprimanded for that. Yes, it was three days. Yes, Stern had a family. But there . . .

"Yes," said Levin, no change of inflection in his voice. "Yes . . . I see . . . and forensics will gather any clues? Yes, all right. Thank you."

The Hawk carefully replaced the handset. Stern waited for his voice. As the silence stretched, hope deflated.

"Threat level has been elevated once more. We are now at Threat Level Red. The Americans escaped. They escaped from Shin Bet, they escaped from two hostiles in a car who attacked them with automatic weapons, they escaped from an additional group of hostiles who attacked them with rocket-propelled grenades. Four men are dead, apparently all Muslims, apparently all part of the first group of hostiles who attacked the Americans as they fled Kibbutz Tzuba. And apparently, this first group of Muslims was killed by a second group of Muslims, those with the RPGs. Why all of this has happened, we have no idea. Why the Americans are in the company of one who appears to be an Israeli, we have no idea. Why these two groups of Muslims are pursuing the American group, we also have no idea."

Levin sat on his stool, his eyes closed, and allowed the silence to build in the room. The Hawk was not opposed to the dramatic.

"We have no idea where they are. But we do have one advantage, isn't that right, Stern?"

"Yes, sir. We know where they are going," said Stern. "They are coming to us."

"Yessss," hissed The Hawk. "And we will be ready to welcome them."

33

Kallie Nolan was on the ground, barely balanced on all fours, retching and crying at the same time. Johnson had pulled out one of the blankets and draped it over her back. Bohannon and Rodriguez were sitting on the ground next to the building, Rodriguez rocking back and forth from his waist up. Bohannon had his hand on a large wad of gauze, pressing it against Rizzo's bicep, trying to stop the bleeding. Approaching the building, Johnson could actually feel the menace of restrained aggression.

For a long time, no one spoke.

It was later, but none of them knew how much later. It was farther away, but none of them knew for sure how much farther away.

Bohannon had driven like a maniac for miles, making random, rapid turns onto one road and then another, without thought, without direction. He heard the nearly silent sobbing coming from behind his seat and knew that Doc was holding and comforting Kallie. He stole a glance at Joe and was not surprised to see panic in his eyes, yet a dangerous resolve locked in his jaw. "Sammy's been hurt," said Joe. "Something caught him in the arm, and he's bleeding."

"And I ain't got that much blood," came a strained voice from the back.

After an interval that could have been thirty minutes or three hours, Bohannon slowed the car and shut down the headlights. They were on a thin ribbon of road, darkness all around them. For quite some time, they had seen no other vehicles in either direction. Descending a hill, the road bottomed out into a flatland that appeared to be farms. Guided only by the faint light of moon and stars, Bohannon carefully navigated the middle of the road, his eyes searching ahead. Suddenly, but slowly, he turned the Toyota to the right and flicked on the switch for the four-wheel drive. The large SUV rocked down a short embankment at the side of the road. There was silence in the car as Bohannon gingerly picked his way along what he hoped was a dirt track. His hope was soon fulfilled.

There were no lights. As quietly as possible, Bohannon steered the Toyota alongside a building that had appeared on their right. It looked like a barn or a storage building for machinery. Beside it was a huge cypress tree. Bohannon stopped the SUV in the blackness under the tree, hard against the side of the building.

Spilling out of the car, Kallie scrambled into the distance to relieve the upheaval in her guts while Joe helped Rizzo to the side of the building and Tom dug a first-aid kit from one of the backpacks.

Out of the darkness, Bohannon heard Johnson's voice. "There must have been three groups, right? Or were there four?"

There was quiet again.

Kallie's spasms subsided, and she sat back, resting on her haunches. Johnson got up and crossed to the tree. Gently, he put his arm around her shoulders, helped her to her feet, and guided her to the wall where the men were sitting. Though her back rested against the wall like the others, her head and shoulders had slipped to the right and were cradled in Johnson's arms.

Bohannon cleaned Rizzo's wound, despite his protests that he was fine. Something, shrapnel or glass, had ripped into his right bicep, nearly halfway through his arm. No arteries were cut. Bohannon couldn't tell about anything else. They got the bleeding stopped and wrapped the arm in a huge wad of antiseptic-covered gauze.

"Yeah," said Bohannon, his answer, like his thoughts, moving in slow motion, "there must have been three different groups out there. The Shin Bet squads, but I don't think we ever saw them. Then there were the guys who came up behind us. I think they were connected to the guys with the roadblock."

Bohannon's lips stopped as his mind tripped back. Sataf Roundabout . . . down the road . . . a car behind them . . . over the hill . . . the road blocked . . . then light, fire, explosions all around them. Everything was noise. His mind replayed the noise over and over again. Rizzo's voice brought him back to the wall.

"But who shot the rockets?" asked Rizzo, propped against one of the backpacks, his eyes closed.

Silence sat as thick as the blackness. Bohannon began to think there would be no answer.

"Not rockets, RPGs," said Rodriguez, his voice low, but sculpted with rage. "Rocket-propelled grenades. Smaller, easier to transport, as easy as shooting a gun. One of the gangs in New York got their hands on some RPGs when I was a kid. Blew apart the house of a rival gang leader. Killed four little children. That's all, just four innocent kids. I was walking down the street, saw the smoke and fire trails, just like tonight. Nobody ever paid for that house, for those kids. Just got away with it."

Bohannon realized that they couldn't stay where they were for long and somebody had to make some decisions—give them some purpose—before they all became unraveled.

God, why have you given me this burden? his spirit cried. *I'm no leader. I don't know what to do.*

But then, he did.

—⁓⁓—

"Yes, Major. Two squads, out of sight, flanking the King's Garden Tunnel. Another two squads at the Citadel, in reserve. One squad south, one squad north on the Soueyvet Road to close off escape. All cameras are working, all avenues of access covered." Levin listened for a moment. "Yes, sir . . . yes, we are all tired. And I would agree with you that we need to be relieved, that we need to have a fresh squad on duty. But, sir, please, give us a few hours. Give us until daylight. I can tell you that none of us are going to leave until we apprehend these men. My squad and I would prefer to finish what we've started." Again, he listened. "Yes, sir, you have my word. If we lose our edge, our effectiveness, we will immediately stand down. Yes, sir . . . and thank you, sir."

Levin rested the handset in the cradle, wondering if his request was prudent or prideful.

"Thank you, Captain." It was Lieutenant Stern standing at his computer. Sergeant Ehud, the rest of the squad, were also standing. "Thank you for your faith in us. None of us are willing to give up now. We're in this with you. And we won't let you down."

The Hawk leaned against his chair, too tired to sit. What had he ever done to deserve men like these? It was just past midnight. A new day. Perhaps, now, their luck would change.

—⁓⁓—

Bohannon shared the bottle of water with each of them, not for drinking, but for pouring on their faces, for rubbing on the back of their necks. They needed to snap back.

He walked over to Joe, who was inspecting the riddled Toyota.

"The car is okay, Tom," he said to Bohannon. "Nothing vital was hit. The rear gate is full of holes, and one taillight is shattered. Otherwise, it looks okay.

"But you know, I don't think they were trying to disable the car. Otherwise, they would have shot out the tires, ruptured the fuel tank, or blasted out all the windows. I don't think they were trying to kill us, at least not initially. I think the guys behind us were just trying to drive us into the roadblock and trap us there."

Rodriguez looked at his brother-in-law. There was steely resolve in his eyes. "They were after the scroll, Tom. The Prophet's Guard. That's why they didn't try to wreck the car. They know we have it with us. If Shin Bet nailed us, the 'bolts' never would have gotten their hands on the scroll. So they had to act fast, stop us, and get the scroll before the Federales showed up. Which means there are more of them out there waiting for us to show ourselves again."

"But who were the other guys?" Bohannon asked, rubbing the back of his head. "I was all set to agree with you, but think about it for a minute. The Guard wants the scroll back. They don't care about us, except we have the scroll. And they will protect the scroll at all costs. We saw that in New York. So who was protecting the scroll tonight? The guys with the guns and the roadblock? Or the guys with the RPGs who took out the guys who were trying to take us out?"

Bohannon put his hand on Rodriguez's shoulder and led him to the huge trunk of the cypress tree. "Joe, if the Israelis spotted us, if they believe we intend to pull off some terrorist plot to destroy the Temple Mount, that would be one adversary. But what if the Waqf, or the Northern Front, or some other radical Muslim group also found out about us? That would be a second adversary. Both of those would do everything in their power to keep us from returning to the Temple Mount. Different reasons, but the same objective. The Guard doesn't care about the Temple Mount. They care about the scroll. The Guard would have protected the scroll at all costs, even if it meant wiping out some of their Muslim brothers."

"Or wiping out a couple squads of Shin Bet commandos," said Joe. "We don't know how many RPGs they had up on that hill."

"What we do know," said Tom, "is that now we have three different groups out for our blood, the scroll, or both. We have a car that's obviously been identified and will draw cops like a magnet." Bohannon looked at his watch . . . 12:15 AM. "We don't have many hours of darkness left, and our original idea of getting lost in the Muslim Quarter just got thrown out the window. We've got to get ourselves underground quickly; there are no intermediate steps anymore. We need to get into that tunnel, unseen, in the next few hours or it's all over. We can't take Kallie any farther, and Rizzo needs a doctor. We've got to get them out of this, and fast."

"Tom, I think I may have a way for us to get into the city. But what about Kallie? What if they know who she is?"

⌁∿∿⌁

Bohannon and Rodriguez squatted down in front of the rest of the team. Bohannon, particularly, wanted to look into Kallie's eyes, find out what he saw there. He was surprised. Kallie was panicked, she was feeling the effects of shock, she was pale, but her eyes were clear and angry.

"Okay. This is what we're going to do . . ."

34

Rodriguez was driving a truck on a circuitous route to Jerusalem.

Earlier, he had dropped Kallie and Rizzo at one of the many roadside bus stops. With Rizzo's wounded arm wrapped in bandages and covered by a jacket, they had gotten on the late-night bus from Jerusalem to Tel Aviv. Carrying two of the backpacks, now mostly empty, they would take another bus from Tel Aviv to Beirut. If all went well, before midday they would be out of Israel. By late that afternoon, they would be registered in a Beirut seaside resort hotel, Rizzo would have seen a doctor for his arm, and their only concern would be buying some toiletries, a bathing suit, and a good book, and then waiting for Bohannon to call while watching Israeli TV to see if Kallie was a wanted woman.

Kallie would arrange for two one-way tickets, first-class, open reservation, from Beirut to Manhattan. She had the key to Doc Johnson's apartment in her pocket. If they were looking for her, she wouldn't hesitate. Get on a plane and out of the Middle East immediately, dragging Rizzo with her.

Bohannon and Johnson, meanwhile, were in the black SUV. Avoiding all main roads, they planned to zigzag through the farm country to a small village, southwest of the outskirts to Jerusalem, where they would find a place to conceal the Toyota. Bohannon and Johnson would then walk out of the village, one kilometer east, and be waiting in the shadows by the side of the road when Rodriguez rumbled to a stop. At least, that was the plan.

The truck was slow. That couldn't be helped. It was an ancient something-or-other, but all discernable markings had worn off long ago. Joe had found it in the machinery barn and jumped the wires easily. Better fortune was that the truck bed was more than halfway full, tobacco packed into burlap sacks. But the best fortune of the night hung in a corner of the building: a half-dozen sets of well-worn farmworkers' clothing—overalls, straw hats, and sleeveless shirts, plus dirty, stained kaftans and keffiyeh.

Rodriguez was behind the wheel, looking every bit the nondescript farmer on his way to market. Johnson and Bohannon were now in the back of the truck, lying on top of the tobacco sacks, wrapped up in their robes, pretending to be asleep.

But only a few hours of darkness remained.

━━∿∾━━

He was not happy being awakened at such an hour. He was even more disturbed by the report he received. Mahamoud's wife was at the door to the mosque. She wanted to know where her husband was. Her children, hanging onto her skirts, were crying. She *had* called Yazeer's home, she told the porter, and Yazeer's wife didn't know where he was, either. She wanted the Imam. She wanted to know where Mahamoud was and why he wasn't home at such an hour.

The Imam looked at his watch . . . 2:10 AM. Why didn't that idiot go home? Could he and Yazeer be out celebrating their great victory? He would take a finger from each if that were the case. Mahamoud had many vices. In that way, he could not be trusted.

The Imam turned to the porter. "Tell her to go away, to go home. We will find Mahamoud and send him home." Stepping away from the door, he reached into a drawer for his cell phone. The number was well known.

"We may have a problem," he said with no preamble. "Neither Mahamoud nor Yazeer have returned home. I will check on Yazeer's men, discreetly. But I am concerned. Call me the moment you have news. In the meantime, I will begin to sound the alarm."

Leonidas, on the other end of the call, said nothing. He already knew all of the answers. Making the Imam wait longer to receive the answers would make them all the more valuable. Life in Jerusalem was about to get more interesting.

━━∿∾━━

Rasaf was again alone in his car. The mutilated and multicolored Subaru was nearly invisible in the mottled shadows of the overhanging trees. He looked at his watch in the dull ash-glow of his hand-rolled cigarette . . . 2:33 AM. His men had been gone for thirty minutes. No bother. This was a good crew: disciplined, respectful of a leader. They had handled themselves well at the roadblock.

He had made his decisions, but he was less sure of himself now than he had been on the hill. The Effendi had been correct. Northern Front did try to intercept the Americans. But now? Who could be sure of what would happen next?

Rasaf staged his team at obscure, high points dotted along the Kidron Valley and instructed them to watch. The Americans had been here once; they would return. They were looking for something, something to which the scroll had led them. It was also clear they didn't know exactly where it was or exactly how to get it.

Treasure? wondered Rasaf. *Gold from the Temple, jewels from Solomon? It must be something very valuable.* Good, let them search. Let Shin Bet search; let Northern Front search. Rasaf knew what he wanted, and he knew where it was. It was coming to him. He would not allow it to slip through his fingers.

Rodriguez drove the truck along the Ma'ale Ha Shalom to the Derech Ha'ofel, coming north to the Old City. At 3:12 AM, they rounded the curve below the southeast corner of the Temple Mount area. No other vehicles were on the road. Rodriguez felt naked and exposed. Well into the distance, he could see the gleaming gold of the Dome of the Rock. He didn't know if they would make it. The truck's engine was wheezing and sputtering with each increase in altitude. They had decided to drive up the Ha'ofel, past the Gihon Spring, then loop back to the south, turning onto the Jericho Road just south of the Lion's Gate. At the junction with the road leading to the Church of the Ascension, a smaller road cut off to the right from the Jericho Road. Here, just above the Valley of Jehosephat, Rodriguez pulled into a narrow wadi under a grove of heavy-limbed trees and cut the engine. All of them were watching, furtively, looking for evidence that the area was under heightened surveillance. But the main reason for bypassing the area around Gihon was more practical than tactical. It would be easier to carry the sacks downhill, rather than uphill.

Rasaf lifted his nose to the breeze in the wake of the lonely truck's passing. "Tobacco, rich, too. Those farmers will do well."

"Stern, come on. Talk to me. At least let me know you're still awake."

"Nothing, Captain. And unfortunately, I am still awake." Stern turned in his chair, facing Levin. "Nothing on the roads, sir, and nothing in the streets. It's been totally silent for over an hour. One farmer's truck struggling up the causeway. Never stopped. It'll be light in"—he looked at his watch: four twenty—"just over an hour. If they are going to make a move on the tunnel, it will have to come very soon."

The Hawk picked up the phone and checked, once more, on the units staged and waiting for action.

———∿∿∿———

"That is very bad news, Leonidas, but thank you, nonetheless. We will provide for the families and, of course, for you. What of the Americans?"

While his voice remained cordial, the Imam's eyes had become blazing torches. *Kill my men? There will be retribution,* he vowed. But first, the Americans. First, the safety of the Noble Sanctuary, the Haram al-Sharif, must be assured.

"What? No, they cannot have vanished. You are telling me," his voice rising, "that Shin Bet has lost them, has no idea of their whereabouts?"

A moment to listen.

"No," the Imam shouted. "No—that is not acceptable, Leonidas. Not acceptable."

The connection severed, and the line went dead. The Imam looked at the screen: Signal Lost. *No,* he thought, *we are not lost.*

Quickly, but without a whisper of sound, he descended the curving steps and entered the porter's office. "Awaken the faithful. Awaken them now."

———∿∿∿———

Rodriguez led the way, three farmworkers making a delivery. Each had a heavy burlap sack hoisted on his right shoulder. They began walking down the path alongside the road. To his left, from the east, Bohannon could see the first glimmer of pink.

———∿∿∿———

Rasaf was getting restive. None of his men had reported. Which meant none had seen anything. Even though he was deep under the trees of the car park, he still had a clear view of the Mount and the entrance to the King's Garden Tunnel. His men were also stationed with good lines of sight. But the blackness of the night had lost its luster. Dawn was not far off. Where were they?

⌁⌁⌁

Captain Levin nearly fell off his stool when the major walked through the door, unannounced. By reflex, he and his men quickly snapped to attention. "Be at your ease; stay at your stations," said the major, crossing to Levin's perch, welcoming hand extended. "Avram, it is a pleasure, my boy." Levin received the earnest warmth in the major's eyes and began to relax his alarms. "What do we have?"

The alarms reengaged. "Nothing, I'm afraid," he said, offering the major his chair and feeling emasculated in his acceptance. "In the last two hours, only four vehicles have been on the road past the King's Garden Temple: two automobiles traveling south; one automobile and one farmer's truck traveling north. None of the vehicles slowed down, let alone stopped, anywhere along the Derech Ha'ofel. Since midnight, the pedestrian traffic has been almost nonexistent. A few drunken tourists, about 2:00 AM, but they were Russian—now they are in jail."

He turned to the major, and away from the screens. "But nothing, nothing on the Americans."

⌁⌁⌁

This was it. Bohannon, Rodriguez, and Johnson had momentarily stopped in the shadows of an outcropping. Stepping out would put them in full view of anyone who might be watching, and Bohannon knew there were many who could have taken on that responsibility: Israelis, Muslims, the lightning bolts, maybe others. He looked into the faces of the other two, sweating under the weight of the burlap sacks. "Tom," said Rodriguez, "we're screwed. Whether we walk out from behind this rock or not, we're screwed. We're never going to get out of this mess except one way. And that way," he said, pointing with his elbow, "is out there. C'mon. We've got to take the chance."

Before Bohannon could react or respond, Rodriguez was walking out of the shadows, stoop-shouldered, his back bent to the weight, his feet slowly picking their way down the path. He was hiding in plain sight. The trump card was played. Bohannon, then Johnson, followed.

—⁓⁓⁓—

"Rasaf, there's movement."

Flicking away the cigarette, Rasaf grabbed the wireless phone. "Where?"

"On the streets to the Temple Mount."

"Fool," Rasaf growled into the speaker, "I don't care about the streets to the Temple Mount. What's happening on the road, or down by the tunnel entrance?"

"Fool," mocked the voice on the other end, "you should care about the streets to the Temple Mount. There are thousands . . . thousands . . . of Muslims coming down every street."

—⁓⁓⁓—

"Captain, look at the streets," yelled Ehud, embarrassed by the volume of his alert.

Levin and Major Mordechai scrambled to the screens. The streets around the Temple Mount were overrun with Muslims. They were pouring into the huge square atop the Mount and spilling over its sides. Mordechai was already on a phone. "Dispatch all the police . . . keep the guard in reserve."

Levin was about to grab a phone himself, but Stern grabbed his hand instead.

"Captain, we've found something. Swinging cameras around to the Mount, we found this on the other side of the valley, under a grove of trees, just off the Jericho Road."

Levin remembered the truck chugging up the hill to market. Weren't there two men sleeping on the sacks in the back?

A bitter-tasting bile rose in his throat. "Not again." The Hawk didn't hear the hint of fatalism in his own voice. He was moving too quickly.

—⁓⁓⁓—

Rodriguez slid on the loose gravel and nearly lost his balance. They turned away from the main path and to a much steeper path, short, leading to the corner of the entrance, but covered with loose stones. All three of them shifted the sacks to their left shoulders and reached out to the towering boulder on their right for balance and support. Rodriguez stopped to peer around the boulder, and Bohannon crashed into his back, falling awkwardly into the thick brush on his left.

"Tourist," Bohannon growled.

"C'mon," said Rodriguez. He turned the corner, and was gone.

—〰〰〰—

Levin ignored the phone and grabbed the walkie-talkie. "Squads one and two—move, now! Squad three—cross the valley, just opposite the Golden Gate. One kilometer to the east, a farmer's truck. Secure it. The rest, follow the path down to the tunnel. Be careful. We haven't located them yet."

Levin was inclined to dispatch his two reserve squads from David's Tower to help with the worsening situation on the Temple Mount, but they were his backup: all he had in case something else went wrong.

—〰〰〰—

He saw the movement at the same moment his wireless phone squawked.

"Rasaf, soldiers are converging on the entrance to the King's Garden Temple."

"Yes, I can see them."

"What would you have us do?"

Rasaf thought for a moment. "Have you seen any other movement near the tunnel entrance, have any of you?"

No one answered.

Rasaf had failed to lift his finger from the transmit button. "Something is wrong here." The words were meant for himself, not for his team. "Something is very wrong here." He saw the transmit key depressed. "Stay alert. This doesn't make sense."

—〰〰〰—

After Johnson helped him get up, Bohannon stepped around the boulder and joined Rodriguez at the entrance. There was a chain across the entrance with a warning sign attached, but Rodriguez had hoisted the chain, allowing Bohannon, then Johnson, then himself to get into the foyer and under cover.

⸻⸺∿⸻

"Rasaf . . . there is movement at the entrance."

⸻⸺∿⸻

Ehud had the growing demonstration on the Temple Mount, another of the squad remained zeroed in on the truck, but Levin and Mordechai were draped all over Stern, straining to see what was happening at the King's Garden Tunnel in the half-light of early dawn. "Kick up the resolution," snapped Levin. "This is the worst time of day to get a clear visual."

Stern tried to tighten the image.

"There's movement by the entrance," said Stern, watching dusky shadows slip into the tunnel entrance.

"Yes, but who?" Mordechai looked down at Stern. "Who is that?"

⸻⸺∿⸻

Standing on a rooftop, mostly hidden by a parapet, the Imam watched as the demonstration, apparently random, unfolded below him. He was not interested in the masses swarming the courtyard of the Dome of the Rock. The Imam was watching intently those to whom he was connected by the walkie-talkie in his hand, the fingers of demonstrators who were spilling over onto the sides of the Mount. He was following information, and so far, the information had proven to be accurate. They were down there somewhere, he was sure. They intended to destroy the Dome or the Mosque, of that he was also sure.

His cell phone rang, forcing him to put down the walkie-talkie. He knew the voice. He didn't expect pleasantries.

"Have you heard of the Prophet's Guard?"

"No."

"An Egyptian group, Muslim, based in Suez City. For the last nine hundred years or more, they were the guardians of something they kept in a secure vault.

Whatever it is, it is no longer there. Now, these men are out in the world, trying to retrieve what they have lost."

A momentary pause, while the Imam sifted through the information. "And why do you tell me this?"

Leonidas allowed the question to float, unanswered, for several long moments.

"These men, the Prophet's Guard, are the ones who killed Mahamoud and Yazeer. You can identify them by an amulet they wear—a Coptic cross intersected by a lightning bolt. Many of them are in Jerusalem at this moment."

The call disconnected. And the Imam threw his phone onto the rooftop.

⌇⌇⌇

"Anwar . . . Aphek . . . come down the hill, through the crowd, and pass by the tunnel entrance. Tell me what you see."

Rasaf felt his pockets. No more cigarettes.

⌇⌇⌇

Once past the chain, fear and adrenaline smacked into gear. Quickly, at a brisk trot, they crossed the main visitors' area and stopped at an iron-gate barrier that covered the entrance to the main tunnel. All three of them dropped their sacks, untied the burlap, and pulled out their backpacks. While Johnson and Bohannon were strapping into their backpacks, Rodriguez pulled a small bolt cutter out of a side pocket and deftly snapped the lock. The bolt cutter and the snapped lock went back in the side pocket and out came another, identical lock. Johnson swung open the gate, Bohannon picked up the loose burlap sacks, and both headed down the main tunnel. Rodriguez closed the gate behind him, snapped the new lock in place, and hustled to catch up, jogging into the dark.

⌇⌇⌇

The sergeant and the rest of his squad had engaged their night-vision goggles. Gefen wasn't comfortable with the goggles. He believed it restricted his range of vision. But whatever you were directly looking at was certainly clear.

Gefen held his squad in place while he peered around the boulder at the tunnel entrance. A chain stretched across the entrance, with a "No Admittance" sign. Past the chain was a visitors' area and off the visitors' area appeared to be side rooms—four of them. He detected no movement, no sign of anyone inside.

Twelve heavily armed, antiterrorist commandos swiftly and silently poured through the entrance in a ballet of brute force. Four peeled right without a word. Four peeled left, covering every opening. Four flared out in a crescent, dropping to one knee, across the main visitors' area and waited for reports. "Clear One . . . Clear Two . . ." In addition to the tunnel entrance, there were three possible points of exit from the visitors' area. Right and left had been cleared. Gefen stood and turned to his troops. Four fingers, and Gefen pointed his men toward the tunnel entrance in front of him, and the gate that was closed over it.

35

He prayed to control his fury. Here on the rooftop, without his prayer rug, he had gotten down on his knees in the spreading light of dawn and pleaded with Allah for vengeance on this Prophet's Guard, Muslims who would kill Muslims. Just as he was about to do.

It had begun to rain. His once pure white robes, now dirty and caked with mud, no longer helped project the image of master. But he still had his voice.

"Da'ud." His most trusted student responded immediately.

"Yes?"

"Leave the demonstration in Famy's hands. Take two of your best men, your most trustworthy men. I am about to bestow on you a great honor."

—∿∿—

Rodriguez was running blind until Tom turned the blue light in his direction. It was another of the little gizmos that Winthrop Larsen had supplied. A blue-light lantern that would completely illuminate the direction in which it was pointed, but would give off no light behind. As long as they kept the blue light pointed down the tunnel, no one behind them could tell they were there. Rodriguez thought it was pretty cool when he first saw it in operation. Now, it only added to his anxiety, reminding him that others may, at that moment, be giving chase.

"Keep moving," said Rodriguez. The other two didn't need any encouragement. Despite the weight of their packs, the three men set off at a brisk pace, following the tunnel deeper into the earth.

—∿∿—

The gate was locked, but one of Gefen's men made fast work of cutting it loose.

A locked gate did nothing to ease their concerns. Anyone could lock a gate from the inside.

Gefen motioned two men in, entered himself, and had the other two follow.

Using universal sweep techniques, Gefen's squad moved along the tunnel. Deftly trained, they moved quickly, confidently. But there was no movement or light ahead of them, nothing unusual picked up in their night-vision goggles.

Gefen estimated they had advanced several hundred meters when they came to a junction. The current tunnel continued straight ahead, and a new tunnel opened at a ninety-degree angle to the right.

The squad converged on Gefen, waiting for orders.

They had passed the first junction without any incident, continuing straight ahead. But now they could see a second junction, and this one had five spokes breaking off from the main tunnel. They stopped cold in their tracks.

It only took a moment to decide. Gefen tapped three of his men and pointed to the right. The other man remained with him, and moved straight ahead. Gefen figured he was better than any three of his men put together, so one with him was plenty.

He held up a fist, then snapped a finger to the right. The three commandos poured around the corner without a sound. Immediately, Gefen and his companion sprinted across the junction and into the tunnel on the far side. One hundred meters into the tunnel, they skidded to a stop, their weapons at the ready.

"Aleph Center, this is Gefen. Acknowledge."

"Gefen, this is Major Mordechai. Report."

"Major, this is one major foul-up."

For a moment, Mordechai wasn't sure if it was a joke. Levin, for his part, was about to rip out Gefen's adenoids.

"Sergeant Gefen, come again?"

"Major, my squads have got this place covered. There is a main tunnel, and about a thousand meters in, there is a junction with a second tunnel branching to the right. We have both tunnels secured."

Mordechai looked at Levin. Clearly, something was missing.

"Sergeant Gefen, is that your entire report?" asked the major, allowing his increasing frustration to come clearly through his voice.

"Yes, sir," said Gefen, "because there is nothing else to report. These tunnels don't go anywhere. They just stop . . . a hundred . . . a hundred fifty meters in from the junction, the tunnels just stop. It's a dead end. Nobody is going any-where in here. And the rest of the place has been swept. It's clear, it's all clear. Yes, sir, there is nothing else to report."

Bohannon and Rodriguez were sitting cross-legged on the floor, waiting. Ear-lier, Johnson had driven a climbing piton into the wall, pulled out a ball of twine, and gone off to explore each of the five forks. Now, Doc was back, care-fully inspecting each of the five possible portals. It was taking him forever, and they would have long ago lost their patience. Except for one thing.

There was no noise coming from behind them. No light. No muffled thump of jogging feet.

Both of them were still perspiring, and neither one of them could resist looking back up the passageway once every few seconds. Fear was still with them, anxiety was still with them, adrenalin was still pumping. But the edge was coming off.

"One thing I don't understand," said Rodriguez, scratching little designs in the dirt. "Why did the Israelis make such a big deal out of finding the King's Garden Tunnel, when it doesn't go anywhere? That doesn't make any sense."

"Perhaps the Office of Antiquities knows something we don't," Bohannon answered. "Maybe there's more to the King's Garden Tunnel than is obvious. But I sure am glad we took the time to check it out before piling in there with all our equipment."

Bohannon looked back up the tunnel toward the entrance to Zechariah's Tomb. "You've got to give Kallie some credit," he said. "She's a lot more devious than she looks."

Rodriguez allowed his mind to slip back to yesterday—was it just yesterday? Kallie had led the team into the King's Garden Tunnel, but it didn't take them long to discover it was a dead end and that Zecheriah's Tomb was the only remaining possibility for them to find a way underground. But Kallie's mind was working overtime. She pointed out to the men that Israeli security cameras most likely had the entrance to the King's Garden Tunnel under surveillance. If they were already on Shin Bet's radar, someone would eventually pick them up entering the tunnel. But instead of exiting immediately, what if they didn't come back out for hours? Where would Shin Bet look if they finally disappeared?

Rodriguez shook his head. "That's probably where Shin Bet's SWAT teams are at this very minute, wondering how we managed to evaporate into thin air. Hey, remind me never to play poker with that woman."

Rodriguez heard him before he saw him. Doc Johnson came sauntering back to where they were sitting, a beatific smile stretched across his face.

"My friends, you are so fortunate to have me with you." With a sweep of his arm, he bowed gracefully from the waist. "There is such a great value in a fine education, don't you think?"

Rodriguez was about to hit him with a rock.

"Follow me," said Johnson. "Not only can I lead you to Zechariah's Tomb, but I can also lead you to the tombs of the Beni Hazir. And from there, I believe we may encounter our old friend Abiathar."

Rodriguez looked at Bohannon. "Clearly, the adrenalin rush has gone to his head. He better recover soon, or he's in for a big hurt."

All three strapped on their backpacks. "By the way," said Johnson, "when we get back, remind me to congratulate Kallie. She was right. Zechariah's Tomb is the right way in."

36

"Well, you tell the Antiquities Commission for me that I think they are a bunch of idiots. It's amazing this nation still exists with such fools in positions of responsibility."

Major Mordechai slammed the handset into the telephone receiver with such force that Levin knew he would have to order a new unit.

"Incredible stupidity, incredible," the major moaned as he began pacing through the Aleph Center. "They didn't think it was important. Didn't think it was important! By all that's holy, what's wrong with these people?"

All Captain Levin could do was wait until the major had expended his anger and frustration. He sat on his stool, chomping on the stem of his pipe, and waited. Eventually, the major came over, leaned against a railing, and filled in the missing pieces for Levin.

"When the King's Garden Tunnel was discovered last year, at least the entrance down by Gihon, it didn't take much excavation for the Antiquities Commission to discover that it had hit a dead end. So, they began plotting what they expected were reasonable courses for the tunnel to follow and, at one of their possible terminus points, they found a similar tunnel entrance. But it also culminated, after a few hundred meters, in a dead end."

"Another Hezekiah's Tunnel?" asked Levin.

"Exactly. They figured it was begun at both ends at the same time and, like Hezekiah's Tunnel, it would have scores of dead-end shafts. But the commission didn't have the funds in its budget to excavate a new tunnel. So they decided to announce the King's Garden Tunnel to the world, set up the entrance down by Gihon, and charge admission fees to tourists until they got enough money to excavate the full length of the tunnel. But they kept that information to themselves." Mordechai just shook his head.

"Then there's another entrance," said Levin. "One we don't know about."

The major's eyes narrowed to tiny specs. "They've gotten in, haven't they?" he said. "They've gotten under the Mount."

—〰〰—

Before leaving from New York City, Johnson had spent many hours planning and mapping out how the team would approach their search under the Temple Mount.

Using all of the existing information from Warren's digs, the Israeli Antiquities Commission, contacts at the British Museum, and every scrap of evidence he could find on the Internet, Johnson began to compile a notebook full of Temple Mount lore—fact, fiction, and frivolity. Sifting through the available information, he also began to construct a grid of the Mount and its environs, a grid that existed both above and below the Mount.

His intention was to divide the space above and below into corresponding sectors. He then applied all of his accumulated data to the sectors. Using colors, symbols, and hunches, Johnson began to discern what he believed were the most likely sectors for where Abiathar may have erected the Third Temple. One factor was discerning where the original Temple was located. Another was trying to discern Abiathar's point of entrance to the dark halls of the Temple Mount's belly. Neither was certain.

Contributing to uncertainty was the fact that, like all ancient archaeological sites, the Temple Mount had grown in height over the past two thousand years, each civilization building its foundations upon the ashes of its predecessor. Like most tells in the Middle East, the slice of civilization Johnson was searching for now rested under layer upon layer of latter days.

Johnson's problem was a three-dimensional one, not only length and width, but depth as well. In order to minimize his possibilities, Johnson slaved over his homemade grid, exercising his brain and his resources to their maximum potential.

In the midst of that exercise, Johnson had a critical revelation. The scroll must accompany them.

Throughout the chase to find the meaning of the scroll, all of them agreed that, prior to leaving for Jerusalem, they would secure the scroll in a bank's safe deposit box. They also agreed that, just in case they didn't return, they should leave a letter and the key to the safe deposit box with Johnson's attorney. The scroll would be presented to the British Museum in return for a hefty contribution to the Bowery Mission.

But the more Johnson studied the pieces of information he managed to find, and the more he thought about the cleverness with which Abiathar had communicated his secret, the more he became convinced that the mystery of the scroll had not been fully unlocked.

"Gentlemen, please, use your heads, not your testosterone," Johnson pleaded that day in his office. "Look at this scroll. It's a message, not a language. The cipher Abiathar created was incredibly complex. This man went to extraordinary lengths not only to send this message, but also to hide this message. Do you then think it reasonable that anyone who could decipher this message and find an entryway under the Temple Mount would then be empowered to walk right up to where Elijah and Abiathar had spent decades, and countless lives, to construct the Third Temple? Don't you think it would be more likely that the closer anyone would get to the Third Temple, the more complex the problem of finding it? After all, neither Elijah nor Abiathar could afford the possibility that some fool Bedouin could stumble into a cave that would lead under the Mount and that, by sheer dumb luck, he could stumble upon the completely finished Third Temple of the Jews. They wouldn't allow that to happen."

Johnson was grateful for the reluctant nods around the table, but frustrated with the denseness that still remained.

"Gentlemen, there must exist, yet to come, puzzles, riddles, ciphers, something that will need to be solved, something that will be directly connected to this scroll, this key, which will give us access to the location of the Temple.

"We must," Johnson said with emphasis, "we must take the scroll with us. The scroll, not a copy, or we will simply be wasting our time." Suddenly, Johnson was drained. He hadn't realized how impassioned he was about this search.

Now, standing under the Temple Mount, Johnson looked at the grid in his hands. He hoped he had gotten it right.

———∽∾∾———

Anwar and Aphek, cousins and bricklayers, followed Rasaf's orders to walk downhill within sight of the entrance to the King's Garden Tunnel. But that also put them into the midst of the Israeli soldiers stationed all around the tunnel's entrance. They were scruffy enough to be of no consequence to the soldiers, some standing idly in the rain, some running back and forth on unknown errands. As a result of the demonstration on the Temple Mount, other civilians were also walking up and down the hill in the early morning half-light.

The cousins took no notice of the three men who passed them, dressed in kaftans, stern looks on their faces. They were focused more on the movement of the soldiers. The knives that pierced their necks were so thin, so sharp, that neither felt anything amiss until hands grabbed their shoulders and pulled them into the darkness at the side of the road. They felt nothing as sharp, bloodied knives silently sliced the leather thongs around their necks, the amulets slipped inside kaftans for delivery to the Imam.

⌒∿∾⌒

What Johnson hadn't expected was the complexity of the labyrinth they now found themselves exploring. None of his research had prepared him for this.

At the five-pronged fork in the bowels of Zechariah's Tomb, Johnson overcame his first hurdle. By exploring different forks, and the tunnels that ran from them, Johnson found the tombs were a crisscrossed mishmash of low-ceiling tunnels, some flanked by burial racks stacked like bunk beds along the walls, and some tunnels leading to individual burial crypts. All of these different tunnels spread out from the five-pronged junction, heading in numerous directions for unknown distances. Now he knew why there was a locked iron gate over the Tomb's entrance.

Under closer inspection, Johnson discovered small inscriptions at the upper left corner of each prong's portal. The inscriptions were generally in Hebrew or Aramaic and appeared to be listing the family names of those buried in that particular tunnel. That was how he discovered the corridor of the Beni Hazir. And that was how their search began.

Johnson estimated it would take no more than forty-eight hours to determine whether the message of the scroll was true or just a fairy tale. From the outside, he had anticipated an initial period, perhaps twelve to twenty-four hours, of exploratory searching, using the same tunnels or corridors that Abiathar and his workers must have used. From there, Johnson expected the task to become more difficult. From what they knew of Abiathar, the scroll, and the cipher, the old priest would have carefully protected the path to the Temple and, ultimately, was likely to have sealed the existing route altogether. Perhaps in more than one location. But Abiathar would not have wanted to hide the Temple completely. The scroll's purpose was to eventually lead the Jews back to the Temple when it was safe.

So Johnson surmised there would likely be several critical junctures where choices would have to be made, choices guided either by the scroll itself or by some signal or cipher that Abiathar would have left behind. Depending on the complexity of identifying and unraveling these clues, Johnson had anticipated an additional twelve hours. Throw in some time to sleep, rest, or eat, within forty-eight hours they should either have found the Temple or concluded this was all a hoax.

Drawing on their field experience, in consultation with Larsen, they agreed to provision themselves for three days. If they hadn't solved this puzzle within seventy-two hours, they would have to come out and try again. And Johnson knew, now, there would not be any second chance. Too many people were determined to stop them. They had gotten lucky, this time. There would not be another time.

⁓〰⁓

They sat in the dark, in the damp, in their thoughts. Supposedly a time of rest, it became more a time of rising anxiety.

Johnson's mind was running at warp speed, trying to figure out how he could bring the order and certainty he felt in New York City into the dark chaos that was now stripping away his hope.

Johnson and Larsen had planned to use the Mount's geology as part of their strategy. The Temple Mount was constructed on a long series of ridges, often called Mount Moriah in Scripture. At the northern end was the Damascus Gate; at the southern end the City of David. Mount Moriah was sloped, descending from north to south. When King Herod erected the platform upon which the Temple was built, the northern end rested on the bedrock of Mount Moriah. It was at the southern end of the platform that the bedrock fell away steeply, and there, Herod had constructed a series of arches and pillars to hold up the platform.

It would be fairly reasonable, Johnson and Larsen had surmised, to find an entry point from the south and to continue to move northwest through existing arches and caverns. While many considered the area between the Dome of the Rock and Al-Aqsa Mosque as the most likely site for the Temples of Solomon and Herod, there was an alternative, south of Al-Aqsa, recently proposed by Tel Aviv architect Tuvia Sigva and gaining support from scholars. It was here they planned to begin their systematic search, as much as the mountain would allow.

In New York, it made sense. Here, in the cold and dark, an oatmeal clamminess encasing his entire body, Johnson was beginning to experience anxiety, leaning dangerously toward fear. *I can't let this get to me,* he lectured himself. *I'm the one who's supposed to know the way. These guys are depending on me. But where do we go now?*

Johnson searched the blackness for inspiration, and found only blackness. And it was heavy.

For a time, they followed the tunnel leading from the "five forks" as they called it. There were no highways in the limestone, but the tunnel from the Beni Hazir ran generally in a westerly direction, gently sloping downward as it continued for several thousand yards, becoming more narrow as it descended.

Johnson was not a fan of caves. He didn't like the air. The lower they descended, the warmer and more fetid the air became. The cave smelled of old, wet dirt. And decay. The rot of flesh, long completed, seemed to ooze from the rock like deathly sweat. At intervals, shallow, bone-filled chambers had been hollowed from the sides of the tunnel. And always, out beyond the edge of their lights, came the faint scratching of claws against stone.

They came to a second junction. Only two choices, they took the one to the right, the one that appeared to be going more in the northwesterly direction they desired. As he had at the "five forks," Johnson took a small, fluorescent yellow, adhesive dot from one of several sheets he carried. He stuck two small circles near the tunnel floor, just inside the tunnel they were entering and on the opposite wall of the tunnel they were leaving. He had pasted one spot inside their choice at "five forks" and would attach three at their next point of choice. That way, if they doubled back on themselves and found a mark, they would know exactly where they were. And the dots, which they could retrieve, would also direct them to the way out.

This second tunnel was quite short. Soon, they stepped out into a large cavern about forty yards wide and thirty yards deep. Facing them were two dozen arches, twelve stacked on twelve, supporting what appeared to be a natural limestone ceiling. A tunnel opening appeared at the mouth of each arch.

"Yes!" Johnson trumpeted as he ran into the cavern. "Yes. This is it."

He stopped suddenly, aware of his impulsive reaction, and turned to face his two bewildered colleagues.

"Look," Johnson said, half turning with a sweep of his arm, barely able to control his elation, "look, these are Herodian arches. See the way they are built up to support the ceiling." Breathless, he turned back to Bohannon and

Rodriguez. "We must have crossed under the Kidron Valley much more quickly than I imagined. The way these arches are built . . . their height . . . this must be the southern edge of the Temple Mount platform."

Johnson turned once again to gaze at the arches. "This," he said, his right fist pounding on his thigh, "is a great stroke of luck."

"Ah, Doc?"

Rodriguez's voice pulled Johnson from his celebration. "Yes, yes. What?"

"Sorry, Doc, but the GPS doesn't agree with you."

Johnson spun on his heel as his stomach settled into the seat of his pants. He crossed to where Joe was resting on one knee, his backpack on the ground, the GPS device in his hands. Reluctantly, he looked over Rodriguez's shoulder, Bohannon joining them on Joe's other side.

"See, we're here," said Rodriguez, pointing to their position on the map, "at the bottom of the slope, but still on the far side of the Kidron Valley. We've still got a long way to go before we hit the edge of the Mount's platform."

A long, deep sigh escaped from Johnson, who rested his forehead in the palm of his right hand. "I thought we were so close."

"Guys . . . I think we have a bigger problem," said Bohannon.

Doc looked up and saw the light from Bohannon's helmet sweeping across the arches on the other side of the cavern.

"Which of these tunnels do we take next?"

⌇⌇⌇

To conserve their resources, they had agreed to use their power-cell lanterns only when on the move. But the darkness had a different plan. It was so black, it had a living presence—isolating, crawling, invading. They began to hate the darkness.

Three times, they returned to the cavern of the arches after hitting dead ends in one of the tunnels. Twice more, they came to the cavern, coming out from an arch that was different than the one they entered. Several of the arches led not to tunnels, but to something more like fissures in the limestone, tight, confined cracks. With the gear they were carrying, it was hard work moving forward. Each time they returned to the cavern, they were moist with perspiration. Because the air was so damp, they never dried.

They had invested four precious hours and had come no closer to their goal. Cold, damp, tired, and frustrated, they sat in the dark. And waited for inspiration.

———〰〰———

Major Mordechai was on the phone again, his generally pale complexion now mottled red.

Captain Levin was amazed the telephone still functioned after the beating it had taken from Mordechai's frustration.

"No, General, we can't send troops out now, poking around the Temple Mount, not with thousands of Muslims already staging a demonstration in the courtyard. There are so many of them, they are sprawling over the edges of the courtyard and down the sides of the Mount. If we put any more soldiers out there, it would be a provocation that could spark all-out riots."

Levin looked again at the monitors. The rain continued.

"No, sir, we don't know where they went. Yes, sir, I know. We've got extra details of men in here right now, we're poring over every inch of videotape from the last two days, from the first moment Captain Levin became suspicious of these three men."

Mordechai looked at Levin as he listened to the general on the other end.

"General, I was here in the Aleph Center continuously from late last night. I can assure you that Captain Levin and his men did everything humanly possible to track and capture these people. They've been on duty for days." Another pause. "Absolutely not, sir. If I believed any of them were impaired, I would have pulled this squad off-line immediately. These men have performed admirably. Yes, sir, I agree. We missed something. And we are determined to find out what it was and how it happened. But I can tell you without a doubt, General, there's no fault to be found here. We all know none of these systems are perfect. But I also know Levin's squad has done the best they could, the best anybody could, to get these men into custody."

Mordechai fiddled with the phone cord while he listened. "Yes, sir . . . yes, sir, I understand."

The major settled the handset into the cradle much more gently this time. Then he turned to face Levin.

"He doesn't care," said Mordechai. "The general said we will find those men, and we will do it quickly, or someone else will have this job."

—∼∽∿∼—

Arch eleven rescued them from the cavern and restored some portion of hope.

Bohannon had checked his watch on the way into the cavern. Now its hands mocked his expectations. The explorers had spent twelve costly hours deadlocked in the cavern of the arches, and it nearly broke their spirits. Finally, Rodriguez picked up a rock, threw it over his shoulder at the wall of arches, and, following the rock, they found what appeared to be, so far, the way out. Even though it was less than six feet high, causing them to stoop painfully, this route was truly a tunnel, sections of it clearly carved out with tools.

Johnson was in the lead again, pressing forward with the dogged determination of a man on a mission. They passed through a sea of smells—the bitter sweetness of animal urine, like old apple cider turned to vinegar; the wooly musk of ancient dead—and plunged deliberately to the edges of darkness.

Two hours later, his energy sapped, Bohannon pushed himself forward, closing the gap with Johnson. "Doc." The sound of Bohannon's voice was a shock. The last few hours in the cavern they had all been quiet, unwilling to speak for fear of sounding retreat. Now his one word bounced off the walls and brought each of them to attention.

"Doc, we've got to stop soon and get some sleep."

In the glare of his lamp, Bohannon saw two eyes that were not yet registering comprehension.

"Doc, all of us have been awake for nearly forty-eight hours. We've got to stop and get some rest."

Bohannon felt as if his words had popped an adrenaline balloon. Suddenly, all three were on the floor, sprawled into a small alcove that had widened the tunnel slightly.

"We should all get into some dry clothes before we pass out," said Rodriguez. Rapidly, the three men stripped to the skin, put on dry underwear and socks, and crawled into their sleeping bags. Propped against his backpack, Bohannon began to rifle through some of its side pockets and resurrected some trail mix. As he turned with an offer, both Rodriguez and Johnson were already asleep. *Not a bad idea*, thought Bohannon. He stretched himself out and was snoring before the trail mix bag hit the floor.

37

Captain Levin had never been in Central Command's Operations Complex before, as if he needed anything else to add to his anxiety. Wednesday morning, he was now three days without sleep. Both he and Major Mordechai had been summoned by General Moishe Orhlon, Israel's Defense Minister, for a face-to-face explanation of what had occurred since Levin first spotted these men Saturday night, more than three days ago. Levin wondered if his military career had come to an end.

They were ushered past the sprawling, electronic operations center to a meeting room dominated by a large table, dominated by Orhlon. The general looked like a man who had bet his life savings on a sure thing and lost. The ashtray in front of him was overflowing with cigarette butts, like the one dangling from his lip. To his right stood Levi Sharp, director of Shin Bet. Levin prepared himself for the blast. But it was Mordechai who stepped into the line of fire.

"General Orhlon," he said with a salute. "Aleph Reconnaissance Center is my command. We failed in our mission. Our men, they were relentless, but we failed to intercept the Americans. We believe they have found a way to penetrate below the Temple Mount. Their purpose is unknown, but we fear terrorism. I take full responsibility."

Just inside the door, Levin looked at the back of Mordechai's head and was once again filled with respect for his commander. Mordechai had trained his subordinates in the credo of the military: there is no excuse; only responsibility. And Mordechai had the courage to put his butt where he held his beliefs. Levin, shaking his head, knew he could do no less.

Unable to speak out of turn, without his superior's request, Levin also took a pace forward and snapped a firm salute. His eyes searched neither Sharp, to whom Mordechai and Aleph Center reported, nor Orhlon, to whom they all reported. Rather, he searched the far wall, stood silently, and hoped for recognition.

It was clear that, long ago, Orhlon had surrendered in the battle for fitness. He was obese, hypertensive, borderline diabetic. The scuttlebutt filtering down to Levin was that Orhlon probably had lung cancer. But he was no less the warrior.

Orhlon's eyes burned into Levin's skull. He allowed silence to dance on the table.

"You have something to say, Levin?"

"General, I am honored by Major Mordechai's loyalty, but the responsibility for what has happened is mine, not his. We spotted these men, what, two days ago? I should have acted then. Everything that has happened since, sir, must be laid on my shoulders."

Orhlon looked slowly at the two soldiers, both still at salute.

"That is exactly what I want to know," said Orhlon. "Exactly what *has* happened since the first time you saw these men. Every detail, important and unimportant. I want it fast, I want it straight, and I want it now," he snapped.

Levin detected a quick glance pass between Orhlon and Sharp. "So, at ease. Sit down. Levin, you start."

—∿∿—

When Johnson and Rodriguez awoke, "breakfast" was muesli and water, followed by an energy bar. For now, they allowed Bohannon to sleep.

While they chewed, Johnson alternately consulted the maps he and Larsen had sketched out prior to departure and the handheld global positioning unit. He was not encouraged.

"What do you think, Doc? Any idea where we are?" Rodriguez was still halfway into his sleeping bag, admittedly reluctant to relinquish the warmth.

"I'm not sure." Still staring at the maps, Johnson tried to process his thoughts. "I think I know, but I'm not sure. The GPS works fine at times; then, at other times, it just quits. At those times, there must be something between us and the surface. Right now, I can't get a signal. But I think we're here."

Johnson tapped the eraser of his pencil against the section of map illuminated by his headlamp. When there was no response, he turned toward Rodriguez, bringing the map with him.

Blessed with a trio of GPS positions he had recorded the previous day, Johnson took what he knew and applied it to what he surmised. From Zechariah's Tomb, they had progressed in a generally northwest direction until hitting the cavern of arches. From that point on, Johnson knew, charting direction was dubious.

"I think we're along here," Johnson said, tapping a triangle he had drawn on the map. "If we're at the southern point of the triangle, then we still have a long way to go before we reach the perimeter of the Temple Mount area. If we're closer to the midpoint or the top of the triangle, then we've come more than halfway to the Temple Mount perimeter. Until I get another reading, I just won't know."

Rodriguez looked at the map. "Even supposing we're halfway to the perimeter, we would still have a long way to go. We still have to clear the Kidron Valley and cross under the Pool of Siloam. Probably another mile, as the crow flies. But I haven't seen any crows down here. Looks to me like we're going to have a tough time getting this done in three days, assuming we can even find Abiathar's cavern."

The words were confirmation of what Johnson feared. He had hoped this would be the easy part, that the entry portal would lead to a clearly discernable, easily navigated series of tunnels that Abiathar's workmen would have used to import the materials they needed. He expected difficulty later, once they pierced the underbelly of the Mount itself. Like Rodriguez, he now seriously questioned their chances of finishing in the three days allotted. He responded to Rodriguez with a scowl.

"Perhaps we should begin to conserve our water," Rodriguez floated, picking up the pencil and tapping it against the map. "Doc, let me ask you another question. The night we were on David's Tower, you were talking about the power, the presence you felt here in Jerusalem."

"Yes, the sense of an emanating presence was, well, I felt I could almost touch it," Johnson replied.

"What about now, now that we've come down here?"

How could Johnson explain what he was feeling? In some ways, it felt like anxiety, an emotion with which Johnson was well acquainted: a heavy, pushing weight on his chest; labored breathing; an invasion of his consciousness, pushing other thoughts to the fringes. In other ways, it felt like euphoria: a lightness of being; a sense of peace; elusive, but somewhere in his psyche, a sense of joy.

He could feel it, but he didn't understand it. And he wasn't sure if he wanted to describe it.

"Yes, it's stronger. It's definitely stronger. And it gets even stronger the closer we get to the Mount."

Johnson turned his light toward Rodriguez's face and saw the question in his eyes, a question neither one was prepared to ask.

"I don't know, Joe. I really don't know."

⌇⌇⌇⌇⌇

Dampened by the rain, dispersed by the Imam's henchmen, the demonstration on the Temple Mount ended without major incident. The amulets now rested on the table in front of the Imam. They did little to ease his growing concern, though his lust for revenge had been satisfied.

Da'ud stood before him, eyes downcast, shifting his weight from foot to foot, clearly uncomfortable. There had been no information for more than twenty-four hours. The Americans appeared to have vanished. Most likely, they discovered an entry point and were now underground, perhaps under the Mount itself. *Impossible*, his mind declared. "We cannot allow this to happen." Rage began to rise again.

"Da'ud, gather fifty men, trustworthy, competent, obedient men. Gather them immediately. Separate them into five groups, and take them into the Stables." The Imam began to pace behind the table, considering his strategic possibilities. "Position one group under the Dome of the Rock; position another group under the Al-Aqsa Mosque. Station them in a way to protect the buildings from all sides. They are to protect those shrines with their lives, if necessary."

He didn't look at Da'ud; his eyes were off into some distant place. "Direct the other three groups into a systematic search of the tunnels. Find these men and kill them. Find them before they can even attempt their plot."

Abruptly, he spun on his heel, strode to the table, and swept up the amulets in his hand. "Find them," he shouted with uncontrolled violence, his outstretched arm pointing to Da'ud, the amulets, speckled red, dangling from his hand, "before this fate becomes yours as well."

38

Initially, the tunnel in which they slept led them in a general northwesterly direction, without incident, for more than an hour. The tunnel was easily passable. They were making good progress. Bohannon was encouraged.

But then conditions changed, significantly. The tunnel had been gently sloping downward since they entered, but suddenly the slope became more severe with each step. Bohannon's boots twice skidded on the damp floor. Fifteen feet in front of him, Johnson gave a yelp, lost his footing, and landed heavily on his backpack. He was easily convinced that Rodriguez, the strongest and most athletic of the trio, should take point.

Rodriguez quickly perfected a safer way to descend this slippery slope. Each of them was wearing the spelunking gear they had purchased: shirts with padded elbows; pants with padded knees; thin, form-fitted thermal gloves with textured palms; and hard hats with attached spotlights. Rodriguez leaned his body into the rough wall on the right, using his padded right elbow as a fulcrum, and pressed his boots against where the left wall met the tunnel floor. Supported by both sides of the tunnel, Rodriguez inched himself forward, followed by the other two, who tried to mimic his every move.

After half-an-hour of painstaking progress, Bohannon was worn out by the contortions necessary to navigate the tunnel and wondered where this plunging slope would take them.

"Whoa!"

Rodriguez's exclamation stopped Bohannon and Johnson dead in their tracks. Bohannon had been concentrating so heavily on his footing and on maintaining his leverage against the walls he hadn't even noticed that Rodriguez was stopped in the middle of the tunnel, standing upright on a flat, level surface. "Joe, what's wrong?"

Rodriguez turned his head to look back up the tunnel. "C'mon down and see for yourselves."

Bohannon didn't like the disgusted tone in Rodriguez's voice, but he still took his time to navigate the final portion of the slope, then turned to offer Johnson any help he might need. Bohannon and Johnson both turned to Rodriguez in the same moment and both felt their stomachs sink.

The three men stood on a flat ledge, about four feet wide and fifteen feet long. The ledge, and the end of the tunnel, overlooked a subterranean lake. Other than the ledge they occupied, the rest of the walls were smooth to the water's edge. The lake was at least two hundred yards across, and almost as long. There was no way around it. Across the lake, in the distance, above another small ledge, were several openings in the wall.

Bohannon dropped to his haunches and slipped off his pack. "Oh, God, now what?" It was a prayer.

—⁓⁓—

The cigarette smoke hanging in the air between Sharp and Orhlon failed to obscure the serious nature of their situation. And its absence, when cleared by the heavy-duty ventilating system of Central Command, failed to reveal any solutions.

"Levi, this is one awful mess," said the general, as he squashed another butt into the already-full ashtray. "These guys have been under the Mount for thirty-six hours, God knows doing what, and we sit here scratching."

Orhlon got up and went to the sideboard, pouring more black coffee into his mug. Returning to the table, he lit another cigarette before his khakis hit the chair.

"The prime minister hasn't given us clearance to launch any action that might take us under the Mount."

A young aide came into the room and handed a single sheet of paper to Sharp while Orhlon emptied half his coffee mug in a thunderous gulp.

"Other than that, we don't know squat about who these guys are, what they're doing here, what they're planning, or what's going to blow up in our faces in the next two seconds. That's a real comforting record for an intelligence service. Make sure Gefen knows to call us."

Orhlon was putting another butt to death when he felt Sharp's eyes. *Now what?*

"General, we've identified the truck. It was stolen from a tobacco farmer—"

"Yeah, between here and Kibbutz Tzuba, right?"

"Yessir. But, sir, we've also found two bodies. Arabs, each stabbed through the neck, their bodies were dumped in heavy undergrowth along the road down by the King's Garden."

Orhlon sat up straight, his chair turned toward Sharp. "Murderers, have our boys become murderers? Have they always been murderers?" Orhlon's mind tripped quickly into a more heightened state of alert. If he and Sharp had been facing a potential crisis before, now they were facing the real possibility of massive disaster. *These guys didn't shy away from taking two lives, so they won't shy away from taking thousands more.*

"General," said Sharp, snapping Orhlon out of his thoughts, "that's not all. We found the garden guide in the bus station in Tel Aviv."

———∿∿∿———

"The GPS is absolutely useless," said Johnson. "I don't have a clue where we are, but I believe we have been moving closer to the Mount."

Not much of a consolation, thought Bohannon. Just then, Rodriguez popped back out of the tunnel they had followed into this underground prison.

"It would take us hours to get back up that tunnel," he said matter-of-factly, "if we could make it at all. It would be very, very difficult with these packs. Besides, what would we be going back to? All the way to the cavern of the arches? No, gentlemen. If we decide to go back, we've got to ditch the packs here. We'll never get up the shaft with them. We ditch the packs, then we've got to keep walking right out of the tombs. This chase is all over, and we'll probably have some type of welcoming committee waiting for us once we emerge above ground."

Rodriguez's words were daggers, piercing hope, uncovering their fear. Lost? Stranded? Sentenced to death? Was this their tomb?

Bohannon broke the black spell.

"Okay, if we can't go back, we've got to get across. How can we do that?"

———∿∿∿———

Sammy Rizzo was exiting the men's room, having replaced his dripping bandages and having swallowed half-a-dozen aspirin to kill the pain, when his New York radar locked on the advancing soldiers. Rizzo, heart pounding, slipped behind a rotating magazine tower and watched from behind the pages of a Jewish "monster chopper" magazine.

Kallie was cool, he had to admit. As the four khaki-clad men converged on her, she managed to kick his pack deep under the bench. As they grasped her under the arms, she never cast a glance back toward the men's room. As they escorted her out the side door, carrying away only one pack, Rizzo replaced the magazine and slowly walked out the opposite door.

He found an unoccupied bench deep in the shadows out of the sun and gave himself ten minutes to think. He had his passport and his wallet on him, and not much else. The extra bandages were in his pack with his clothes, but the bus tickets were in her bag. When they searched her bag, they would know somebody was with her.

Calm down, Rizman, he coaxed himself. *This is a chess game. Play the game.*

Rizzo took a deep breath and resisted the demands of his body to lie down and rest. *What is the last move and what is the first move? You are no John Wayne, especially with this arm, so you are not going to rescue Kallie.* Now wasn't the time to dwell on that fantasy. *You are also unlikely to make it past the Israeli border patrol, unlikely to make it out of this bus station if you don't wise up. The guys are in Jerusalem. If they were to somehow escape from Israel, they would do it from Jerusalem. The soldiers will be taking Kallie to Jerusalem, where else? She'll probably get grilled by their toughest thugs, particularly if our guys got under the Mount. It's all going to happen from Jerusalem.*

You're not getting out of Israel, anyway, Rizzo told himself. *The spooks don't know you exist yet. When they do, the first places they'll look are the border crossings. No, you've got to make like a banana and split.*

Another deep breath, and Rizzo gingerly lowered himself from the bench. "Get back to Jerusalem," he murmured as he walked back into the station. "Maybe you can be of some help."

Rizzo beat a straight line to the benches where he and Kallie had been sitting not that long before. An elderly woman was sitting there now, a babushka wrapped tightly around her hair, framing her leather-cured wrinkles. Rizzo stopped directly in front of the old woman, put his fists on his hips and peppered her with a withering stare of accusation.

"Israeli mafia, is that it?"

Somebody's grandmother opened her eyes in alarm and her mouth in protest. *"Vos iz?"*

"No you don't," Rizzo short-circuited, increasing his volume. He didn't know what language she was speaking, but it wasn't going to stop him. "Did you really think you could steal my backpack? Is that the scam, use old widows as diversion while you rip off the handicapped, huh? Is that what you're up to?"

Grandmother shook her head, raised her hands, palms up, and looked around for help. "*Farshteyn?*" she said to Rizzo. "*Fregt mikh bekheyrem.*"

"What kind of country is this," Rizzo shouted, his left arm sweeping across the room, "where you prey on the maimed and the infirmed?"

Grandmother was aghast, all wide-open mouth, wide-open eyes. "*Idiot!*"

It didn't sound the same, but Rizzo understood that one. Time to vamoose. "Gimme back my bag!" Rizzo scuttled under the bench and emerged with his backpack on the other side. "This is a disgrace. I'm going to get some help."

He exited the same rear door, leaving only a memory and a shaken grandma in his wake.

—⁓⁓⁓—

Four well-armed soldiers led Kallie out of Central Command's conference room. She was weeping, headed to a waiting armored personnel carrier that would take her, under escort, to the military prison at Sha'ves Poser, six miles south of Jerusalem.

Orhlon watched her back retreat out the door.

"General, we've got to verify this; we've got to verify or discredit this story right away," said Sharp.

Orhlon watched the door close.

"General . . . ?"

Orhlon got out of his chair, stretched like a lion exiting its cave after a long sleep, and moved slowly to the coffeepot. He picked out a new mug, ignoring the half-filled one he had abandoned on the table, and absently began stirring sugar into the dark liquid. Seeing the spoon in the mug sent a signal to his brain, bypassing the roadblock that momentarily held his thoughts captive. Orhlon turned back to the table and, as he sat, put aside the new mug and retrieved the old.

"No, Levi, we are well beyond verification." He drew heavily on a newly lit cigarette. "Why would those men come here? Why would they have risked what they have risked, endured what they have endured, persisted the way they have persisted, if they didn't believe the scroll was authentic and the message was valid? And who is after them, besides the Northern Islamic Front? Who killed their partner in New York City? No, this is no prank, no attempt for cheap publicity. Trying to verify it would just bring too many other people into the loop."

Orhlon looked into his half-full mug of now-cold coffee, still very much in his own world.

Levi Sharp pushed his chair close to the general. They had known each other since officers' school.

"Moishe, if this scroll is true, if these men were to find a temple . . ." Sharp was at the general's left, his voice quiet, but strong, "the Arab nations will erupt. This could be the end, could lead to the ultimate conflict. We know how that will end, and there is no hope, not for Arab or Jew. We need to act while we still have the opportunity."

The general continued to study the liquid in the mug.

"Yes, Levi, yes, it could be the end." He began to swirl the liquid inside the cup, genuinely fascinated by the shape of its movement. "Not so bad for an old warhorse like me," he said quietly, almost to himself. "But the young. It's the young, Levi, the young whose lives weigh heavy on my heart."

With a whiplike snap of his arm, he hurled the half-full coffee mug at the far wall and watched it explode on impact.

"Please telephone Lukas and Chaim. I will call the prime minister myself. They must come here immediately. Nothing else is more important."

———∽∾∾∿———

Bohannon grabbed Rodriguez's belt. Holding a length of rope, a large rock tightly tied into one end, Rodriguez leaned over the water as far as he could reach, and slowly lowered the rock into the water. The rope was about twenty feet long. Rodriguez got to the end of the rope and the rock had yet to touch bottom.

"Well, we're not going to walk across," he said.

———∽∾∾∿———

When the cell phone rang, it wasn't Da'ud.

"All three of the men are Americans. The one who looked like an Israeli is

from someplace called the Bronx. His people are from an island in the Carib-
bean, thus the dark complexion. He got the clothing while they were at the
kibbutz."

The Imam waited, expecting more. Nothing stirred from the other end of
the connection. *I believe he enjoys these games*, the Imam thought.

"Where are these men, Leonidas?"

"No one knows. Probably under the Mount. But no one knows."

Again, silence.

"What do you know, Mr. Leonidas?"

"I know the Israeli soldiers found two bodies, stabbed to death, along the
roadside," said the bodiless voice.

Leonidas had lit the fuse. The Imam's blood began a slow raging boil.

"Tell me something I don't know," he seethed. "Earn your living, Mr.
Leonidas."

The Imam sensed a pause, pregnant with restrained malice. A momentary
shudder. "The Israelis found the garden guide, the one who led the Americans
to the King's Garden Tunnel two days ago. She was found in the Tel Aviv bus
depot and underwent a lengthy interrogation from Orhlon and Sharp, themselves. After that, she was taken, under heavy guard, to a military prison."

"That is quite unusual, isn't it?"

"Well, you are very insightful," said Leonidas, a note of sarcasm biting the
radio waves. "Yes, it is unusual for a civilian, who is not a terrorist, to be placed
under military arrest. And there is something else. After the interrogation,
Orhlon immediately summoned the prime minister, Painter, and Shomsky to
Central Command.

"Something important is unfolding, my friend," the informer said, his voice
reflecting a more sincere intimacy. "Perhaps these men are terrorists, after all.
I am certain you have already ensured the security of your shrines, especially
underground. Perhaps an even higher state of readiness would be appropriate.
The Israelis are concerned, very concerned."

The Imam's rage had been sedated by the more respectful tone. "Yes, I will
see to it."

"There is one more thing," said Leonidas. "Something is being withheld.
Normally, my sources share openly with me. Today, there is clearly something
they can't, or won't, divulge. There is a secret they are hiding. To be honest, I
would be more fearful of the secret than the Americans. Be well, my friend."

39

Orhlon felt for his heart. Unfortunately, it was still beating.

Three times I should be dead; why couldn't one work?

Nauseous, his head swimming, Orhlon's consciousness vainly scrambled for solid ground. *I should remain alive while my country and children are incinerated? I should die first.*

But he didn't.

—⁓⁓⁓—

With Orhlon still sprawled on the floor, the room was invaded by a frantic swarm of aides and medics, all determined to minister to the semiconscious general. Crowding the other three men against the back wall, they surrounded Orhlon and began the prodding, poking process that was apparently necessary to determine his viability. Others, obviously security, dispassionately established a stronghold around their three masters. In the current situation, no one was taking any chances.

"He just blacked out mid-sentence."

Levi Sharp, director of Shin Bet, stepped between his bodyguards and moved to the nervous knot hovering over General Orhlon. "He hasn't been out of this room in three days," said Sharp, "living on an endless supply of coffee and cigarettes. This same thing happened to Rabin in '67." Turning to the medical chief of staff, Sharp assumed his normal voice of authority. "Major Reitz, get some oxygen in here right away and a lot of cold water, with ice. He's probably poisoned himself with nicotine."

"Mr. Director, if the general has nicotine poisoning, we need to get him to the hospital immediately," said Dr. Reitz.

For the briefest moment, the now-crowded room was silent. Then a voice, soft in volume but powerfully commanding, reached out to the doctor.

"Do you value your career, Major Reitz?"

There was no answer, outside of the muffled groaning as Orhlon searched for the surface.

"Then I would suggest you fetch the oxygen immediately," said the prime minister, "before the general wakes up and decides to use your carcass for fish bait."

Not so fast as to make himself look ludicrous, but with significant zest, Dr. Reitz left the conference room in search of oxygen and water.

"Andrew, please get a cool, damp cloth and place it on the general's brow," said the prime minister, placing his hand on the shoulder of his most trusted protector, stepping away from the security detail and around the table in Orhlon's direction. "David," he said to the medic by Orhlon's side, "allow him to come around gently. When he fully regains consciousness, he'll likely try to get to his feet. Don't allow that to happen. Flush his system with the oxygen and the water, take very good care of him, but get him back to that table in ten minutes."

Eliazar Baruk was a unique version of the Israeli prime minister. Neither grizzled kibbutzim nor battle-scarred military veteran, Baruk was tall, thin as a rail, and fastidious in his grooming. Only the finest silk suits expertly covered his bony frame, only his private hairdresser ever touched his silver-streaked locks. Baruk was the first lawyer to serve as the Israeli prime minister, but he hadn't been in private practice for more than a decade, when he entered a more "respectable" career. For ten years, Baruk served as Dean of the School of Law at Tel Aviv University, a fact that apparently endeared him to the normally skeptical Israeli electorate.

Now, after two years in office, he was beginning to wonder why he had ever sought this position in the first place.

Two hours ago, Orhlon, Israel's Defense Minister, and Sharp, director of Shin Bet, had urgently requested the prime minister, the director of Mossad, and the prime minister's chief of staff to gather in the conference room of Central Command's Operations Complex for an emergency briefing. Only Sharp, who had been working closely with Orhlon, was prepared for the emergency that Orhlon had patiently explained in detail. But all of them immediately grasped the potential catastrophe they faced as a result of Orhlon's report. It was no overstatement to realize that Israel's future as a nation and the safety of its seven million men, women, and children would be forever determined by their decisions and actions in the next few hours.

Stretched to its limit, poisoned by the incessant intake of nicotine and caffeine, it was not surprising to Baruk that Orhlon's mind and body had just shut down. But Baruk, all of them, needed Orhlon fully functioning in order to deal with this impending disaster.

Baruk could see the color returning to Orhlon's face as he sucked in long gulps of the cleansing oxygen. With Dr. Reitz opting for the background, Dr. David Maier, one of the medics assigned to Baruk's constant entourage, had given Orhlon an injection to steady his heart and calm his racing pulse, while not clouding his discernment. He was also nearly force-feeding Orhlon ice water. Outside of some initial retching, the water irrigating Orhlon's body, blood, and organs was also having a salubrious effect.

"David," said the prime minister, "I would like you to remain with the general for a few more moments until he can get to his feet without feeling faint. The rest of you may leave. Major Reitz, please go to the commissary and bring back some soup, something light, and some bread for the general. Please return quickly; we have much we need to discuss."

Baruk stood impassively on the far side of the table that dominated the center of the conference room, watching as Reitz scrambled off for soup while the rest of the staff silently emptied the room. The only ones remaining were Dr. Maier; a slowly strengthening Orhlon; Lukas Painter, director of Mossad, Israel's legendary security and counterintelligence agency; Sharp of Shin Bet; and Chaim Shomsky, Baruk's chief of staff. Just as Dr. Maier guided Orhlon to his feet, then to a chair, Major Reitz returned with a hot, covered bowl of soup, something chicken by the aroma, and the bread. Thanking them, Baruk asked the doctors to leave, allowing the five most powerful men in Israel the privacy they needed to deal with the emerging crisis.

Orhlon's khaki uniform was soiled and disheveled, a condition none of them had ever witnessed before. While the general still looked a bit worn, Baruk was satisfied by the fierce alertness of Orhlon's eyes that the man had sufficiently recovered.

"Levi . . . Moishe," Baruk said, turning his gaze from Sharp to Orhlon, "are you certain? Not only of the claim, but are you certain of the findings?"

"Mr. Prime Minister," said Sharp, "since we cannot access the area without causing a riot, we cannot be absolutely certain. But we have been watching these men for days. The object of their intent has clearly been the Temple Mount. Now that we have the testimony of the garden guide, some of which we have already corroborated with our sources in New York, we are confident we know why they came here and what they are looking for.

"What we don't know, Mr. Prime Minister, is whether they have discovered what they were seeking."

All eyes were on Orhlon, but Baruk also cast a swift glance at his advisors. He wondered if they were having as much difficulty absorbing this possibility as he was.

"A temple, Moishe? Do you really believe this message they found could be leading them to a temple that was built one thousand years ago under the Mount?"

"It is certainly hard to believe such a thing is possible," said Orhlon, scratching his already tussled hair. "But, sir, consider this. Someone planted a bomb that killed one of the American team members in New York City. We have been in contact with their police department. Confidentially, we have been told there were attempts made on the lives of two others. Two nights ago, as we tried to detain them, they were nearly caught in a firefight between two rival Muslim factions. We now believe both of those factions were trying to stop the Americans.

"Whatever the truth from the other night, there have been several deadly attacks against these men to deter them from this pursuit. Why?

"Lastly, these men are neither treasure hunters nor political activists. One is a librarian, one an official with an organization that helps homeless people. The garden guide said it was these two who found the scroll. The third man is Dr. Richard Johnson, a respected archaeologist and scientist. For more than a decade he was a fellow of the British Museum. I doubt this man would allow himself to become seduced into an escapade such as this unless he believed the message of the scroll was genuine.

"Mr. Prime Minister, at this point, I believe we must proceed under the expectation that the scroll, and its message, are genuine, that there is a temple under the Temple Mount. And, sir, if the Temple is there, someone will find it. If not these men, then someone else. Perhaps the Muslims, perhaps the Northern Islamic Front, God forbid."

Baruk's unflinching gaze locked on Sharp. Then he shifted. "Moishe, what will this mean?"

For a moment, Orhlon was at a loss. Baruk wasn't sure if it was because of what he knew or how he felt. Baruk imagined Orhlon's brain was racing to review every possible strategy and unimaginable scenario.

"Mr. Prime Minister," said the raspy-voiced defense minister, his tone somber, "I agree with Levi. I am confident the reports he received were accurate. But grasping the consequences of these reports is something from which my mind has rebelled."

Suddenly, Orhlon looked older, more worn down, than at any time Baruk had known him.

"I am confident, sir, that if we should allow these men to proceed, if they discover the Temple . . . should they make public their discovery, we would rapidly find ourselves in an endgame scenario with the Arab nations."

"Moishe," Baruk said solemnly, "I need you to tell me precisely where this will lead us."

They all knew the answer that was coming, but someone had to speak it, to make it real.

"Mr. Prime Minister, if we don't stop these men from revealing their discovery," said the defense minister, "both Director Sharp and I are confident that Israel will find itself in the ultimate conflict with the Arab states that surround us." Orhlon hesitated slightly and took a deep breath. "The radical Muslim states are determined to eradicate Israel. The reality of a temple whose existence they have long denied would give historical legitimacy to the Israeli state, and they would be forced to act. They would try to wipe us off the face of the earth. Egypt and Syria will have their tanks rolling within the hour. Their missiles and bombers will be in the air, their divisions forming to swarm over our borders. Before the end of the day, we will face the ultimate decision, whether to use our nuclear weapons or to allow the Arabs to destroy us."

"Moishe, you have always been an alarmist," Chaim Shomsky, the overweight, overbearing chief of staff volunteered. "Nuclear war destroys everyone, kills everything. There is no Israel, there is no Middle East, there is no future for either Arab or Jew. No one is going to take that chance."

Baruk walked over to the chair at the head of the table and rested his hands on the top of the chair back. "And we're not going to take any chances, either," Baruk said decisively. "Lukas, I want the full resources of your organization dedicated to finding these men. You have complete authority to do anything that is necessary to prevent this information from becoming public."

The prime minister pulled out his chair and sat down. There was no other sound in the room. All eyes remained on Baruk.

"Have I made myself perfectly clear, Lukas?"

Lukas Painter was a lifelong professional of the intelligence community. There was neither an ounce of fat on his body nor an ounce of doubt in his allegiance. He had served four different prime ministers, and never before had he been given a blank check. He knew exactly what Baruk was instructing him to do.

"Yes sir, Mr. Prime Minister," Painter said in a verbal salute. "Absolutely clear."

Uninvited, Shomsky jumped in once more. "Really, Mr. Prime Minister, I believe General Orhlon is overstating the seriousness of—"

The prime minister's right hand came up quickly, his arm and palm extended toward his chief of staff. With his left hand, he reached for the red phone and put the receiver to his ear.

"Get me the president of the United States."

———◇———

There was plenty of time for thinking during the ride from Tel Aviv. Rizzo hitched a ride with a big-rig truck driver, who bought his story of being separated from his tour group and getting left behind. Wanting to be alone with his thoughts, Rizzo had feigned sleep during most of the trip while he sorted out his options.

Kallie is no female James Bond, he thought. *She'll give up the plan in no time. So the Israelis will be looking under the Temple Mount. They'll probably keep Kallie in custody until they figure out what is going on, so, no way of getting to her. But it's unlikely they would be watching her apartment. There would be no reason to keep that under surveillance. Makes it the best place of refuge, and I can take better care of my arm.*

It was well after dark when Rizzo exited the truck in Jerusalem, back in front of the Crowne Plaza Hotel and the central train station. Standing on a concrete planter, he waved down a taxi for the ride to Ammunition Hill and Kallie's apartment.

———◇———

In the blue light of a cyalume stick, Bohannon looked across the lake and felt the onslaught of despair. "What can we do?" he wondered aloud. "What can we do?"

Faced with the impossible, he did the only thing that, for him, was possible. He knelt down on the ledge, folded his hands over his chest, and closed his eyes.

"Father, I believe it is your will for me to be here. I know, when Annie and I prayed together, we felt a unity in our spirits that you had spoken to each of us, that I was to come to Jerusalem and search for this Temple. So, here I am, Father. I'm confident in you, but I'm not confident in me. Sometimes, I think all of this is nuts. It's crazy for me to be here, crazy for us to be risking our lives like this. Then I recall your words in my heart. So here we are. Are we nuts, or what? I don't know. All I know is that you've got to help us. If we're going to get across this lake, if we're ever going to find this Temple, you need to help us. And you need to help us now. Otherwise, we're probably going to die down here." Bohannon felt a hand on his right shoulder . . . a moment later, another hand on his left. "Father, lead us and guide us now. Give us your wisdom, your discernment, your strength. Put your hedge of protection around us and keep us safe. Help us get safely to the other side and, Lord, help us to get out of here, and home, in one piece. Amen."

His *amen* was echoed, once from his right and once from his left, and three times from across the lake. And the answer came to his heart.

"C'mon," he said. "We're going to try and float a raft across this lake."

40

In all of their planning, none of them foresaw the need for a boat.

So now they improvised, and their choice was not pleasant.

With light from one of the cyalume sticks, Bohannon and Rodriguez quickly reviewed all the gear in their Lost Creek packs while Johnson updated the written log of their exploration on the waterproof pages of a survey book. The decision was inescapable. Their packs were water-resistant, not waterproof, and there was little confidence the packs could support their weight. They had a watertight, airtight Pelican case to protect the satellite phone, but it was too small and there was just one. The only possible source of floatation would be their sleeping bags. And even those would be a risk. Larsen had wisely insisted they purchase the best possible bags they could find, so they were outfitted with North Face Nova "mummy" bags that not only had a zero-degree rating, but were also filled with goose down and constructed of a multilayered waterproof shell. The bag, when totally zipped shut, had only a very small opening over the face for breathing.

Bohannon and Rodriguez figured they had only one chance of getting across this underground lake. Seal all the zipper openings of the sleeping bags with duct tape, and duct tape the three face openings, sealing all but a very small corner of each. The plan was that each man would blow as much air into his sleeping bag as possible to inflate the bags, sealing the corner closed with a duct tape flap when they needed to catch their breath. When the bags were inflated as much as possible, they would be fastened together with more duct tape. They would put the raft in the lake, put their packs on top of the raft, and the three of them would kick-paddle the raft to the other side of the lake.

That was the plan. None of them thought it was foolproof. In the darkness, using their Maglites and helmet lamps, they thought they could see three openings on the other side of the lake. It was impossible to tell the lake's exact width. It was at least two or three hundred yards. So much could go wrong. The bags could deflate, either immediately, or slowly, as they crossed the lake. Without inflation, the bags would likely sink under the weight of their packs. Even if they remained inflated, the bags could still sink, they could buckle under the weight of the packs, allow water to get on top of the raft, and succumb to the growing weight. They could get to the other side and find that the openings either didn't go anywhere or were an optical illusion.

And no matter what the outcome, if they survived, they would all be soaked to the skin. If their sleeping bags took on water, it would be a disaster. They would have to find a way out, immediately, or risk death by hypothermia.

Or they could quit now, leave all of their equipment, and beat a hasty retreat to Zechariah's Tomb.

———∽∿∾———

"Yes, Jonathan, we know they are searching for the Temple. If a temple is found and these men report their findings, we are confident the Muslims will rise against us and precipitate an endgame conflict. We cannot allow that to happen."

Baruk and his advisors, clustered around the speakerphone, waited for the American president's response. Baruk knew that Jonathan Whitestone was now huddled with his own advisors.

"Eliazar, you said you don't know where these men are, currently. So there is nothing that can be done at this moment. Perhaps a temple does not exist under the Mount. Perhaps you will find them first. I believe we need to wait, see what transpires."

Baruk's back began to stiffen. Were they on their own?

"But, Mr. Prime Minister, this much I can tell you. We will never allow Israel to face a real threat of extinction. If these men do find a temple, the United States, and I, personally, will do all in our power to ensure the discovery will not lead to an ultimate conflict with the Arab states. Whatever steps that might require. Do you understand me, Eliazar? None of us could afford such a conflict."

Nodding his head in relief, Eliazar Baruk smiled at his assembled advisors. "Yes, Mr. President, I understand you perfectly. And we are deeply grateful. We will telephone you as soon as we have any additional information. Thank you, Jonathan, thank you very much."

The lights on the phone blinked off. Baruk surveyed his advisors.

"Levi. Lukas. Find them . . . and kill them."

———⊰∿∿⊱———

"The American president has given Baruk the freedom to execute these men, if necessary."

"War frightens all of them," said the Imam. "Has there been any clue as to their whereabouts?"

"No," said Leonidas. "It's as if the earth has swallowed them."

The phone clicked dead as a thought came to life in the Imam's mind.

———⊰∿∿⊱———

Grateful for the silk long johns he had decided to keep on, but wet and cold nonetheless, Rodriguez kept a steady, deliberate, but rapid cadence on the rope he was pulling. All of them wanted to get the raft across the lake as quickly as possible; none of them wanted to be reckless enough to capsize it.

Following Bohannon's prayer, they decided that the wisest course would be for Rodriguez to swim across the lake, the rope tied around his waist. It had taken longer than he expected, the water was colder than he expected, but he had gained the far side, where he found a wide platform standing before the three openings, much larger than they appeared from across the lake. There was no time to waste. He had to get Bohannon and Johnson across before the sleeping bags deflated.

"Okay, c'mon," he shouted, his voice reverberating off the cavern walls. "Go," he heard from the distance, and he began to pull in a rhythmic, constant motion. Rodriguez was concerned about the Doc. Johnson, remarkably, had joined in Bohannon's prayer but, afterward, appeared a bit wide-eyed and rattled. Before he got into the water for his swim, Rodriguez caught Bohannon's eye and nodded his head toward Johnson. Bohannon got the hint.

Now Rodriguez could see them both kicking with a fury. The raft had clearly lost much of its buoyancy. Desperately he pulled faster, and faster still. Water was on top of the raft as they pulled close. Rodriguez had already dropped the rope and, as soon as he could reach, began snagging the packs off the top of the raft. Bohannon and Johnson were still in the water, but first Rodriguez gave the rope a strong tug, settling the sleeping bags on the relatively drier platform. Next, he reached in with both arms, grabbed Johnson under the armpits, and hoisted him to the platform. Then it was Tom's turn, and all three lay on the platform, sucking in deep breaths, stunned that their stupid plan had worked.

They weren't dead, yet.

⸺⌇⌇⸺

Each man had stripped. Using Joe's wool sweater as a towel, they rubbed away the water. Then all three got into their still dry sleeping bags, zippered them tight, and fought off the bone-numbing cold that had invaded their bodies. A bottle of water, trail mix, and an energy bar joined each man in the comfort of his sleeping bag.

But Doc Johnson was far from comfortable. He knew that both water and food were running dangerously low. And he knew he was lost.

⸺⌇⌇⸺

"Da'ud, remain with your men, under the Mount," the Imam said into his cell phone. "But dispatch Famy back to the surface. He is to go into the Kidron Valley. I will be sending him more men, by ones and twos. I want them to search the tombs on the far side of the Kidron, the burial places on the Mount of Olives. Somehow, the Americans got underground, unnoticed. Perhaps they found an opening in one of the tombs. Tell Famy to scour the tombs, look for anything that may be out of the ordinary. There is a way in, and we must find it."

⸺⌇⌇⸺

Johnson looked like the old man he was, and Bohannon was alarmed. What if his body gave out, or his spirit? Then what?

All three were back in their sleeping bags, but they had moved away from the lake and were resting their backs against the wall. They had slept for hours as their bodies tried to recover from the strength-sapping cold. Joe looked okay, seemed to be snapping back. And Bohannon felt his strength coming back. But Doc . . . Doc looked like death. His silver hair was a wild mop, his face ashen, his eyes sunken and wild. He sat in his sleeping bag, body stooped over at the waist, his head lowered against his chest.

"I'm lost, we're lost." The voice came out of a fog. "I have no idea where we are, none of the gadgets are working, and I can find no symbols or clues on any of these tunnel entrances to guide us in the right direction. I am afraid I failed you. And," a long sigh flowed out of his soul, "I'm afraid that I am simply afraid."

No false bravado would mask the seriousness of their situation.

They had enough water for perhaps another day. Doc was close to cracking. The quiet, the darkness, the cold emasculated their determination. It was 4:11 AM, Thursday. Time was running out. They had to move.

"Okay, let's get going."

Bohannon peeled away his sleeping bag and dug into his backpack for dry clothes. "C'mon, let's go," he said, pulling on his pants.

"Where?" Johnson's voice was weak. "We don't know where to go."

Rodriguez was up and getting dressed.

"We're taking the middle tunnel," Bohannon said with authority. "That's it. We're moving. We can't stay here."

Bohannon looked at Johnson. He hadn't moved. He was still bent over at the waist, his gaze reaching out, over the lake. Bohannon took two steps, crouched in front of Johnson, and put a hand on his shoulder. "Doc, you are going to get up, and you are going to get up now. I can't carry you; Joe can't carry you. But we're moving out. If you want to stay with us, you better get yourself out of that bag and into some clothes. Otherwise, you're going to be here by yourself."

Johnson's vacant eyes searched Bohannon's face. Tom tried to put every ounce of resolve into his eyes and hide every one of his fears. Something worked. Johnson slowly unzipped and lifted himself to his feet. Rodriguez walked over with Doc's pack in his hand. "Here, you're going to need this."

Twenty minutes later, they entered the middle tunnel. They had no clue where they were going.

41

"Captain Levin, this is Gefen. Some of my men spotted some Muslims gathered around Absalom's Pillar on the far side of the Kidron. They couldn't see well enough because it's just getting light, and because of this lousy rain, but they thought the Arabs were going inside, so we went over to check it out. When they passed Zechariah's Tomb, there were more Muslims, or the same ones, going into the Tomb. So they followed them inside."

Levin was surprised by the sudden silence.

"Sergeant Gefen?"

"One of the Arabs pulled a knife, sir. Slashed one of my corporals across the forearm, cut his artery. My squad is carrying him to the ambulance right now. The Arab is dead, shot several times. My guys were a little upset. They took the other three into custody. But two things, sir.

"The Arabs said the Imam has hundreds of them out, searching for the Americans under the Temple Mount, to prevent the Americans from blowing up the Dome of the Rock."

Gefen was quiet again.

"How does the Imam know the Americans are under the Mount?" Levin asked both Gefen and himself.

"Yes, sir, I know. The second thing, Captain . . . I think we found how the Americans got inside. We've spotted some boot tracks on the floor. But more importantly, we found three old burlap sacks stuffed behind a crypt down inside one of the tunnels. They smell like tobacco."

Levin could feel his spine stiffen. "Stay there," he said, waving his arm at Stern to pick up the other phone. "I've got two squads in reserve at David's Tower. They are on their way now. Leave the rest of your men in place. When the squads get there, all of you move into the tunnels. Make sure you have clean communication. Track those men down, Gefen. Get them."

—⁓∾⁓—

In the front, Rodriguez saw it first. But the others were close behind. They saw the light.

"Where does the light come from?" Rodriguez asked the open space. No one answered. They were too busy looking around.

For three hours, they had been walking, nothing but tunnel, straight and true. No turns. No forks or junctions. And now this. They had entered a room. Not a cavern but a room, with a high, but flat, ceiling and straight, stone walls. And light—dim, dusty shards, diffused through minute chinks in the stone wall to the west.

After three days of wandering through an underworld, it was as if they had been resurrected.

"What is this, Doc?" asked Bohannon. "Where are we?"

The three men wandered about aimlessly. The room was about the size of a small house, perhaps sixty feet by thirty feet, with a ceiling that had to be twenty feet high. The walls were unadorned, but the stone of the walls had clearly been worked. They weren't hallucinating: this room was built by men. Scattered debris dotted the floor, a huge mound of debris nearly filled one corner, and everything was covered by a heavy, gray dust that stirred up into little clouds around their feet. The room did not smell of death or decay—a welcome respite. The insidious dampness of the caverns was left behind. In the dim light and swirling dust, Bohannon felt like he was walking through a dry fog.

Halfway down the long side of the room, on each side, was a low, stone bench. Bohannon wandered over to the bench and took off his pack. He kept on his helmet because, even though there was light, it wasn't strong enough to eliminate the need for the TAG lights affixed to their gear. Rodriguez crossed to the other side of the room and put down his pack, but Johnson still seemed to be wandering aimlessly, resting his hand on the stones, crouching down to sift the dust on the floor, peering intently at some of the debris.

"Doc," said Bohannon, "why don't you get rid of that weight? Here, let me help you."

Bohannon went over to Johnson, who had rested one knee on the dusty floor, his face just inches from a chunk of stone.

"Let me take your pack." As Bohannon started to lift the pack from his back, Johnson turned his head, a flicker of sudden recognition registering in his eyes.

"Thank you, Tom," he said absently. And he turned back to the stone.

"Hey," Rodriguez shouted, "the GPS is working again."

Without a word, Johnson was on his feet and beating a path to Rodriguez. *It's the same stride,* thought Bohannon. *Glad to see Doc back.*

"May I see that, please," said Johnson, reaching out his hand, forgetting that he had the same device in the padded, side pocket of his pack. Johnson sat down on the stone bench, pulled the folded map from his shirt pocket, and gazed at the GPS screen. Bohannon and Rodriguez simply watched in silence, not sure which was the more interesting sight, this totally unexpected room, or Doc, back to life, animatedly measuring and scribbling on his map, his eyes darting back and forth from the GPS screen. Abruptly, he was up, walking back across the room to the chunk of stone he had been inspecting before. This time, he sat himself on the floor, causing a minor dust storm, and began minutely inspecting the stone's face. Bohannon looked at Rodriguez. Both shrugged.

"*Av beit din,*" Johnson said to no one in particular. "This stone says, '*Av beit din.*' Isn't that marvelous?"

Perhaps his mind had been dulled by three days underground. Bohannon didn't know how to respond.

"Come, come here," said Johnson.

Bohannon and Rodriguez crossed to where Doc was in the dust and joined him on the floor. Johnson pointed to the stone, now more illuminated by his TAG light. "Do you see the inscription? It's ancient Hebrew. Only a portion of the entire, original inscription is visible, but this section is very clear. It's a list of priests who should perform the temple service at the direction of 'the Great Beit Din.' It also outlines the acceptable patterns of 'ritual acts for the Day of Atonement . . . the burning of the Red Heifer . . . the preparation of the water of purification.' Then, see here, it says all these things are, 'under the authority of the Nasi and the Av Beit Din.' Johnson turned at his waist to look at his two companions, a glow of triumph on his face. He bounced up to his feet, outstretched his arms, and twirled in the dust, nearly obscuring Bohannon and Rodriguez. "This, gentlemen, this is the Hall of Hewn Stone, in which the Great Sanhedrin met."

Johnson stopped his sweep of the room, turned to his friends, and looked them squarely in the eye.

"The Temple." Simple words spoken without a great deal of drama. "The Hall of Hewn Stone was part of the Temple," said Johnson. "I believe this may be the Hall of Hewn Stone."

42

Rodriguez was chewing on a granola bar, listening to Doc's history lesson, the three of them settled on the stone bench, trying to rebuild their energy and strength.

"The Great Sanhedrin sat in the Temple, in a room on the southern side of the inner court of the Temple. The room was called the 'Hall of Hewn Stone.' The larger part of the hall was on the site of the court of the laymen, and there were two entrances: one from the Outer Court, used by the priests, and one from the Water Gate, used by the laity. The Great Sanhedrin, the Beit Din, met every day except the Sabbath and feast days, between the morning and the evening services in the Temple. It was the highest religious authority in Israel and dated back to the days of Moses and the seventy elders who Moses invited to join him in the governing of Israel."

"So why couldn't this room be Abiathar's Temple?" asked Bohannon. "It looks like a temple, and it's hidden under the Temple Mount. Seems to meet the criteria."

Johnson reached out a hand and placed it on Bohannon's arm. "For a moment, I had the same thought," he said. "But it's not possible. By the time Abiathar's father started building the temple, the Sanhedrin was long gone. Nine hundred years before Elijah, the Romans destroyed every vestige of Jewish sovereignty. Every Jew who remained alive was banished from the city and the areas near the city. For nearly one thousand years, Jewish elders desperately tried to hold together a community that had lost the center of its universe. Without the temple, they created new forms of governance—the Academy in place of the Sanhedrin and new, hereditary leaders in place of the high priests. No, Tom, this room was part of the Temple complex before the Romans invaded."

Johnson's eyes kept scanning the room.

"The GPS has us positioned under the Temple Mount, near that space between the Dome of the Rock and the Al-Aqsa Mosque that we targeted."

"That is a miracle in itself, if you ask me," said Rodriguez.

"On that stone over there is a clear inscription of the duties of the Great Beit Din, the head of the Sanhedrin. This *must* be the Hall of Hewn Stone."

To Rodriguez, Johnson's words sounded like a desperate plea. Signs of stress were regularly manifesting in Johnson. And now, Rodriguez was going to burst what little hope the Doc had resurrected.

"Doc, you're the linguist, and I'm sure you translated the inscription correctly. But," he said, reaching his hand out to Johnson's shoulder, "I don't see how this could be the Hall of Hewn Stone. Like you said, there was nothing left of the Temple, not one stone left upon another, when the Romans destroyed the Temple. It's not possible for this room to be part of that Temple complex."

Rodriguez watched Johnson deflate just like the sleeping bags in the lake crossing. But just as quickly, he was blown back up again. "You're right, Joe. You're right. The hall is gone. But what is this room? And more importantly, where is this room? Why is there an inscription in here about the Great Beit Din? Look at the GPS. We've got to be close!"

"There is one thing the GPS doesn't show us." Bohannon got up off the bench, looking again at the ceiling. "It doesn't tell us how deep we are. It doesn't tell us how there can be light in here. Let's look around some more, take our time, see what we can find. Like a way out?"

Yeah, a way out, thought Rodriguez. They had all been so stunned by the appearance of this room that none of them had even thought to look for an exit. Each of them cracked a cyalume stick and headed in different directions.

"Hey, Doc, was that Ben Dit—"

"Beit Din, Mr. Rodriguez."

"Yeah, okay, Ben Dit . . . wasn't it the Sanhedrin that tried Jesus?" Rodriguez was scrambling over a larger pile of debris in what they had determined was the northwest corner of the room. *There must have been a massive collapse of material here at one time,* he thought, pulling himself to the top of a broken column.

"Well, no, actually." Johnson stopped. He had been searching carefully along the stone bench on the western side of the room. "Two bodies were labeled Sanhedrin. The *Great Sanhedrin,* which had dominion over all religious activities and met in the Temple, and the just-plain *Sanhedrin,* which had dominion over all legal and secular aspects of Jewish life. The secular Sanhedrin was chased out of the Temple courts by the Pharisees, who thought they profaned the Holy.

This secular Sanhedrin met, it is written, 'in the vicinity of the Temple Courts.' Some writers said the secular Sanhedrin, 'met below the Temple Courts.' It was the secular Sanhedrin, the legal court, which tried Jesus."

"Hey, Doc," chipped in Bohannon, "could this be the meeting place of the secular Sanhedrin, the lower place?"

"Tom!" A shout of triumph from Johnson's corner. "Yes, I think you're right. This can't be the Hall of Hewn Stone, but it could certainly be the meeting hall of the legal Sanhedrin. Joe, what do you think of that?"

The sweep of their TAG lights as they moved their heads, the blue-light brightness of the cyalume sticks, joined with the dim natural light and covered the room with an eerie dance of light and shadow. Added to the disjointed effects of the lights was the odd fact that there was no echo in the room, no reverberation of sound at all, as if sound was being absorbed by the stones themselves.

The room itself was silent, a silence they all heard.

Rodriguez scrambled over a large fall, a pile of both natural and man-worked stone debris, in the northwest corner. Gingerly, Rodriguez stepped over two polished columns, now lying in a heap. His foot slipped. Awkwardly, both his feet came out from under him, and he was headed for a hard crash in the midst of some very jagged stone. Instinctively, his hands shot out, looking for help. The left one grabbed air, but the right locked onto a solid piece of stone that wasn't moving.

"Hey, Joe, are you okay?"

He could hear Bohannon's voice, but his heart was in his throat as he clung to the stone and hung over a ten-foot drop. Close. Swinging his body slightly, Rodriguez reached up with his left hand to also grasp the stone that suspended him. He took a deep breath and was about to reply, when he looked up between his grasping hands. And saw some very familiar symbols. One looked like a mouse with an eye and a long tail.

"Joe, hey, Joe, where are you?" He could hear Bohannon's voice, responding to the crash and clatter of falling stones where Rodriguez had once been visible. "C'mon, Joe, are you okay?"

No, I'm not okay, thought Rodriguez. "Tom, Doc, you better come over to see this," he said, not removing his eyes from the Demotic symbols above him. "And you better come over to rescue me, too."

―∿∿∿―

Bohannon gladly sacrificed his toothbrush—he had no one down here to impress. Doc was frantically brushing away dust and dirt from every crevice and corner, while he and Joe stood looking over Doc's shoulder, their precious scroll held between them.

"It's Demotic, Joe. You're right, it's definitely Demotic. But"—Bohannon squinted—"what is that other language?"

"It's Aramaic," said Johnson, not breaking his rhythm. "And the third language is Greek."

"Then it's like the Rosetta Stone?" Bohannon asked.

"Yes," said Johnson, putting down the toothbrush. Before them, now resting on the room's stone bench, was a stone stellae similar to the Rosetta Stone, but much smaller. "Yes," said Johnson, a note of excitement rising in his voice. "But it's much more like our scroll. Look at the symbols. Look at how they are inscribed."

Like the Rosetta Stone, this stellae had three languages inscribed on its face. Unlike the Rosetta Stone, the languages were inscribed in vertical columns.

"Holy cow," said Rodriguez. He was pointing to a symbol at the far end of the inscription. "That's our guy, right . . . that's Abiathar?"

Johnson grabbed the survey book and his pencil. "Would you please bring the scroll over here, next to the stellae?"

Rodriguez watched intently as Doc, shifting his gaze back and forth from one list of symbols to the other, began furiously writing on the page. Ten minutes later, he stopped, but from the look on his face, Rodriguez knew he wasn't finished.

"What is it, Doc?" Bohannon asked. "You look as if someone just threw you a curveball."

Johnson ran his hand through his hair, turning his silver locks into a dusty gray, but cleaning his hand. "I'm confused," Johnson admitted. "I thought I had the message. I do have the message. I can check it against the Aramaic. But then, near the end, it changes . . . and just stops." He was shaking his head back and forth. "I don't understand."

Joe put his hand on Doc's shoulder. "What is it? What do you have so far?"

"Well, from what I can tell so far, the message on the stellae is a letter from Meborak of Egypt to Abiathar. Writing in 1093, Meborak is instructing Abiathar on how they are going to oppose the usurper David Ben Daniel. You remember how Kallie told us about him? Ben Daniel had swindled his way to the title of Exhillarch of Egypt. Meborak and Abiathar led the opposition and deposed him."

"And Meborak wrote this letter in Demotic?" asked Rodriguez.

Johnson had been very still since he had translated the letter. Now, sitting with his back to the bench, the survey book in his lap, Bohannon and Rodriguez propped on the bench on either side of him, his voice had none of the excitement that Bohannon expected.

"No, Joe, he wrote the letter in Aramaic. Very straightforward. Very simple," Johnson said, his voice barely a whisper.

"Then why have the other two languages? What are they for?"

"It's for making a code." A pause. "These two men were leading the opposition against the most powerful Jewish ruler of their time. If Ben Daniel discovered their conspiracy, he probably would have them executed. Any communication between them would be inherently dangerous, so Meborak gave Abiathar a master cipher, a way to translate any message into a secret code. Meborak used Demotic symbols, an ancient, extinct Egyptian language that Abiathar would never understand. To Abiathar, Demotic was just a list of symbols. All Abiathar had to do was take the Demotic symbols and convert them to Aramaic in order to understand the communication. He would do the same thing in reverse for any communication he sent to Meborak. Mix-'em-up; shake-'em-up; and you've got yourself a riddle for the ages."

"So that's how Abiathar wrote the scroll," Bohannon exclaimed, the revelation breaking through his weariness. "Meborak sent him the code from Egypt six years earlier, showed him how to take his Aramaic and convert it into Demotic symbols. Pretty slick. Meborak gave Abiathar the key for secret communication using a Demotic cipher."

Bohannon had his arm draped over the top of the stone stellae. He and Rodriguez had rerolled the scroll for the time being, trying to keep it clean in the dust-laden air. His finger traced the shape of one symbol, over and over.

"You know, Doc, there is an even more intriguing question raised by this stellae," said Bohannon, inspecting the face of the stone from above. "How do you mail a rock?"

"Yeah!" said Joe, punching Bohannon in the shoulder. "Why a rock? Why aren't we looking at another scroll?"

Bohannon looked to Johnson for an answer.

"The stellae is here for us. It was meant to be discovered," Johnson said with finality. "Although he could have sent the stellae, it's more likely Meborak would have originally sent the message on a scroll. It certainly would have been easier to transport. But a scroll, even in a mezuzah like the one we have, would be more fragile, more likely to be damaged or destroyed. No, I think it quite reasonable to assess that Abiathar, or one of his artisans, transcribed Meborak's message onto this stellae with the express intention that it would survive the test of time and serve as the final clue to the location of the hidden Temple."

Doc had a smile on his face that would light up Broadway.

"Then, what's the clue?" asked Bohannon.

The lights dimmed.

"Yes. That is my dilemma," Johnson muttered, turning away from Bohannon to look once again at the stone. "I can't find the clue. The last part of the message makes no sense. For some reason, it appears they changed the code. What is on the stellae does not match what is on our scroll. I don't know if I can decipher it."

A heavy weight began to settle on Bohannon's chest. He closed his eyes. No matter how he tried, a withering sense of dread and discouragement began to suck the life out of his bones. *God, no,* Bohannon pleaded in his mind, *not after we've come this far. What have I done to deserve this?*

His elbows were on his knees, his head in his hands. He felt as if he would fall flat on his face. He didn't know what to say; he didn't know what to pray. He didn't know what to do.

God, please, we need your help, Bohannon prayed silently. *The Bible says you will never leave us or forsake us. But I sure feel forsaken right now. How can you do this to us? Bring us to this point and just leave us here? Have I disappointed you that much?*

"I'm not disappointed with you at all. You have been faithful. Look at the scroll."

Bohannon looked up to see who had been speaking to him. Joe was in the middle of the room, pacing. Doc had his head down, working at something in the survey book.

"What did you say, Doc?" Bohannon asked.

Johnson looked up from his doodling. "I'm sorry?"

"Didn't you just say something?"

"I'm sorry, Tom," said Johnson, shaking his head. "I was looking again at this message, looking for some evidence of a clue. I didn't say anything."

Bohannon's eyes refused to leave Johnson's face. He was expecting a different response. Could Johnson be playing some sort of prank? Could he be that heartless?

"Tom," Johnson said with true concern, "what's wrong?"

As if shaking off the hand of judgment, Bohannon snapped to his feet. "Joe, let's look at that scroll again." Bohannon grabbed the mezuzah and brought it over in front of the stellae. "C'mon, the answer has got to be here somewhere, either in the scroll or in the stellae."

Bohannon held the mezuzah while Rodriguez gently unrolled the scroll in front of the stellae. Smaller than the scroll, holding three languages instead of just one, the stone tablet had only three vertical columns of Demotic instead of the twenty-one on the scroll. "Doc, how did you figure out the message so far, since there are only three columns of Demotic on this stone?" Bohannon asked.

Johnson picked himself off the floor and knelt in front of the bench.

"None of the three columns on the stone matched exactly to columns on the scroll. But it was easy to translate because I had the Aramaic to compare it with until I got here."

Johnson's eraser pointed to the last few symbols on the stone.

"Hey, that's the sled," said Joe. "I remember that symbol from the scroll. It looks like a sled all ready to go downhill on the snow."

"It's the letter *Q*," said Johnson. "But do you see that symbol just above it? Well, that's where the Aramaic and the Greek stop. There are no corresponding Aramaic or Greek letters for those last few Demotic symbols, nothing we can use to determine which of the possible thousands of meanings are intended here. I don't understand. Why did he get this far and not finish the message?"

The three of them sat staring at the dumb, stone tablet, trying to will the three inanimate symbols to release their hidden meaning. There was *Q*, the sled. Below, and just to the right, off center, was a symbol that looked like a lightning bolt, or an italic "s." Below that, again slightly offset to the right, was a symbol that looked like a small arch, or a lower case "n."

"Doc, what are the other two symbols?" asked Rodriguez.

"The second one, the one that looks a little bit like an 's,' that's the Demotic letter *C*. And the last one, the arch, is the Demotic letter *H*."

"Hey, Doc," said Bohannon, looking at the twenty-one columns of Demotic on the scroll. "We have the same letters on our scroll as the ones on the stellae, right? And we figured out what they meant against Elgar's cipher, right?

And back in New York, you told us about those two symbols that always went together, but didn't go together on our scroll, right? And all of us believed we would need the scroll one more time to find a final clue, right?"

Bohannon stopped and looked up.

"Right," both men echoed.

"Well, let's take the last three letters of the stellae and match them up against the same letters on the scroll, write down how those same letters were translated on the scroll, and see what we can figure out from the translations that we know. Hey, Abiathar brought us this far, he's not going to forsake us now."

Bohannon almost laughed at himself because of his curious use of words. But, like the others, he was almost immediately caught up in a fever of anticipation.

Johnson was back on the floor with the survey book in his lap and the translation of the scroll message tucked under the survey book's flyleaf, scribbling wildly with Rodriguez and Bohannon peeking over his shoulders.

"The arch, *H*," said Johnson, not looking up from the pages in front of him, "Abiathar uses it for representing the Temple. In Aramaic, I remember the same letter was often translated to mean 'heaven,' a room that entered into a holy place. That makes sense."

"There's the sled a couple of times," said Rodriguez. "What is that referring to, that first one?"

"The most excellent of rulers," said Johnson. "It was Abiathar's way of referring to Meborak in the scroll. But meanings change when you change the construction of Demotic. That's what makes it so infuriating. Look, that *C*, in the scroll it's translated as *great* when Abiathar was writing about the great cavern. But I know that this letter *C* is the most commonly used Demotic letter. The last time I looked, it had more than 160 pages of definitions in the Chicago dictionary."

Johnson started taking the possible definitions and began moving them around, substituting one, then another possible meaning. "This could take forever," he mumbled.

"No, Doc," said Bohannon, grabbing his shoulder. "Look, neither of these guys is going to be playing games with us at this point, not after all they went through. They're going to want the Temple to be found if anybody got this far. This has got to be straightforward. It has to be a simple meaning.

"These last few letters are telling us something about the Temple," he continued, picking up steam. "It's telling us about the holy place, right? You said it: that's why the stellae is here, to give us the final clue. Well, it's right there. Put the three letters together, the three translations we have from the scroll. *The great and exalted holy place of heaven.* The last three letters are describing the Temple. The Temple is here, it's got to be here, right around us."

"I know, Tom," said Johnson, "but where, here?"

The question startled Bohannon out of his euphoria.

"Excuse me, guys," interjected Rodriguez. "But why aren't those letters written straight up and down like all the rest? Why are they going off at an angle?"

Johnson jumped to his feet, turning to take in his two compatriots. He was beaming, grinning from ear to ear.

"You know, Joe, you are brilliant, absolutely brilliant. It's direction, Joe. Once again, you have given me direction. The letters are written off center because, amazingly, they are giving us a direction. Northwest."

Reflexively, Bohannon and Rodriguez swiveled their heads to the northwest corner. "Why is there so much rubble in the northwest corner, when there is relatively little in the rest of the room?" asked Johnson. "Unless . . .

"Unless someone collapsed the room on purpose," enthused Bohannon, "to seal off what's on the other side."

"And to hide the way," added Johnson. "Behind that wall. It's behind that wall."

43

Rodriguez was already asleep, curled up in his sleeping bag. They spent hours, like crazed men in gold lust, tearing a hole in the wall at the northwest corner of the room. First they shoveled out mounds of debris, trying to reach the floor, hoping for an easier way in than breaking through the huge blocks of solid limestone. Just above floor level, they found a place where two limestone blocks had been removed from the wall. But the resultant opening had ultimately been sealed with a form of plaster. Luckily, it was sealed more than one thousand years before and was beginning to crumble. An hour of determined digging in shifts, and the sealed portal yielded a small hole in its center. By the time they completely cleared the portal, they were physically and mentally exhausted. There was no more they could do. Whether it was day or night, they needed rest.

Bohannon dug into one of the backpacks, hoping to find one more pair of dry wool socks. *God was certainly watching over us. Who would have expected this much cold and this much water, under the Mount?* Bohannon had enough camping and hiking experience to know that the woolen clothes they carried in—sweaters, pants, socks—protected them from hypothermia. Unlike cotton, which wicked away body heat, wool retained the body's heat even when wet. They might get uncomfortable in wet wool, but at least they wouldn't be dead.

"Thank you, God!" Bohannon exclaimed aloud as he pulled out an unused pair of socks. He closed his eyes. "God, you have been so good to us, throughout this entire journey. You have blessed us with so much favor. Thank you, Lord."

Johnson was standing in front of Bohannon as he opened his eyes.

"How can you be so sure?"

"So sure of what, Doc?"

Johnson lowered himself and rested on his haunches. "So sure that this God of yours is listening, so sure that he will answer your prayers, or even cares about your prayers?"

The question was simple. Doc's tone of voice was calm, not accusing. His eyes asked questions of interest. Bohannon looked hard at Doc for a moment and nodded.

Standing up, Bohannon took Johnson by the arm, grabbed his sleeping bag, and led him to the other side of the room. "Let's not disrupt Joe's sleep," he said. "He needs it."

"We all need it," said Johnson. "I know I'm wearing out, may have already. I don't think I can recall a time when I was this tired. Everything hurts. My bones hurt; my brain hurts. I just want to stop and sleep for a month."

Bohannon spread his sleeping bag against the room's far wall, and turned to Johnson. "Doc, we don't have to do this now. It can be another—"

"No," Johnson interrupted. "No, I don't think there will be another time. That's why I asked you the question. I just feel . . . I feel that I need to ask that question now. That it was important to seek an answer, now. This is the right time."

Resting their backs against the limestone wall, Bohannon turned his head slightly to look at Johnson. "What is it, specifically, that you want to know?"

Johnson hesitated for a fraction. "Tom, how you can be so sure of something that is so unknowable? How do you know that God exists? And if God does exist, why would he be concerned about you, individually?"

Bohannon sighed, knowing his answer might not make sense. Might not be enough.

"Richard," he said quietly, "you can't. *You* can't. It's not possible for a man like you or me to know anything for certain about God. It doesn't make any logical sense. Us, the finite, there is no way for us to understand the infinite. It just can't happen. Not on our terms."

Bohannon turned to his right and folded his legs, so he could look directly at Doc.

"All of the religions of the world are about the same thing, man reaching up and trying to understand God. Christianity is different. Christianity is God reaching down and making himself understandable to man. And inviting man into fellowship with him.

"That's it, that's the whole program. It's about relationship. That's what the Bible is about, front to back, it's a story about relationship. God created man because he desired to have a relationship with man. And the story plays out from there. It's a very simple theme. Man can know God, because God wants to be known."

A scowl was forming on Johnson's face, deepening its furrows with every passing word, an image of disappointment and bitterness. "That's just like you Christians," Johnson said, rancor dripping from his lips. "Nothing concrete, no real knowledge or understanding, no empirical truth upon which to hang your faith. Just God's love. Believe in God's love. Well, to me it's just a shell game: 'here it is, there it goes, where it stops, nobody knows.' What good is that?" The last words he spat out, purging his tongue of the bile as he began to get to his feet.

Bohannon reached out, put a hand on his arm.

"Hey, give me a minute."

Johnson's features softened somewhat. Holding Bohannon's gaze, he sat back down on the floor.

"When our daughter, Caitlin, was five years old, she needed to have open-heart surgery. When she was a year old, a heart specialist told us she had a hole in her heart, a big one, too big to fix at her age. By the time she was five, we had been making regular trips to the hospital emergency room for one ailment after another. Her little brother, Connor, got used to celebrating birthdays in hospital rooms. Caitlin got double pneumonia when she was five, and we could see her failing. It was time to get her heart fixed. In preparation, she had a cardiac catheterization. They found no hole in her heart. We had been praying so long for the hole in her heart to be healed, we were overjoyed. But the surgeon showed us that her heart was still damaged, one side was really enlarged. One of the heart valves was leaking badly. She needed surgery. Or . . . well . . . "We prayed with her surgeon that morning, and he told us to be patient, it would be a long surgery, eight to ten hours. A few hours later, he walked out of the operating room, shaking his head. 'It was too easy,' he told us. Caitlin had a bad valve, like swinging doors that were out of alignment and never closed flush. But she also had a very small hole in the wall between the chambers of her heart. The surgeon used the small hole to get access to the valve, fixed the valve, then closed the hole on his way out. A couple of hours."

Bohannon could see he had Johnson's full attention. "The next morning, Caitlin was up on her feet, wires and tubes and monitors hanging all over her, wandering around, asking about her breakfast. Doc, one day after major heart surgery, she's walking around asking where her pancakes were. To me, that's a miracle. That is God reaching down.

"Doc, God made himself known to me that day. God made himself known to Annie, and Caitlin, and to all our friends and relatives who were praying with us outside those operating room doors. And God made himself known to that surgeon, too. God made himself known to me day after day after day, long before the surgery. Every time I cried, every time I asked him why, every time Annie and I put our daughter into his hands."

Bohannon felt that catch in his throat, that slight quiver in his chin, that moistness in his eyes that often came when he remembered God's faithfulness to him and his family. He had lowered his head, was looking at the sleeping bag.

"I could take up hours of your time, telling you one story after another. About how God picked me up out of the newspaper business and clearly planted us at the Bowery Mission in New York City and how it saved our marriage. I could tell you about times when Annie and I stepped out in obedience, did what we both confidently believed God was asking us to do and saw miracles, things that only God could orchestrate, work out before us. Our lives are one story after another of God's faithfulness to us. Of God manifesting his love for us, each of us individually, over and over and over again.

"You know, other people might sit here and talk to you about theology and try to convince you that God exists; somebody else might use creation, or archaeology, or the history of Jesus, or who knows what to try and convince you that God exists. I guess that would be okay.

"But, Doc, you asked me how *I* know. This is how I know." Bohannon picked up his chin, ignoring the tears in his eyes and his quivering lip, and laid his heart out in front of his friend. "I know because in the darkest places of me, where I hid all my secrets, he brought me light and rescued the scared little kid who lived there. In the worst moments of my life, when fear was stampeding through my brain, he brought me a peace that was impossible to comprehend. In those times when I was ready to quit, when life was just too hard and I was desperate to escape, to run away, he came, put his arm around me, and walked alongside me.

"God is real, Doc, because he walks with me every day. Without him, I can't breathe. I don't know how else to explain it to you. I don't know how to tell you, where to tell you to go, to find God. You can't. But I can tell you one thing I know is true."

Bohannon looked at his friend and prayed for him to understand.

"I know that if you truly, in your heart, ask God to come to you so that you can know him, personally, intimately, he will always answer that prayer. And he will answer it when you are most in need. That is his character. That is who he is, and he wants you to know him, too."

Bohannon was done. He looked across at Johnson, who shook himself, then threw back his shoulders and sat more upright.

"Thanks, Tom, thanks for taking the time to share all that with me."

Bohannon nodded, now a bit sheepish because of his vulnerability. "You're welcome."

"To be honest," said Johnson, staring at his fingertips, "at this moment, I'm not sure what I think, or believe, about what you've told me. But you have certainly given me a new perspective, a different perspective. I promise you I will give close consideration to what you have shared with me. Thank you. I mean it, thank you."

Johnson extended his arm and the two men shook hands, the firmness of their grip communicating the seriousness of their resolve. *Now,* Bohannon thought, *it's all in God's hands.*

"We better get some sleep," said Johnson, rising. "Whatever time we've got left, we've got to make it count."

44

Bohannon found himself on the floor, still in his sleeping bag. It was a strange dream. Everything was bouncing. A deafening roar filled his ears and filled him with a fear of being buried alive. He was somewhere in the dark, trying to find light. Then it stopped.

He looked around. In the half-light of the room, which was now filled with dust from floor to ceiling, he could see that Joe and Doc were also on the floor, also still in their sleeping bags.

"Was that an earthquake?" Johnson squeezed out of his throat, his body and mind rebelling against being awake.

"I went to grad school in California," answered Rodriguez, "and that was no earthquake. Earthquakes, everything moves in every direction. This, something crashed, or something exploded. Either something very big and heavy just fell, or somebody just set off one heck of an explosion and shook this entire mountain."

Bohannon pulled away his zippers, stirring up more dust storms, and slowly crawled out of his bag. "Ooww, oh, man, everything hurts." He tried to stretch out the kinks, but each move brought more pain, to different spots. He sat down on the stone bench. His watch said 3:06, but he didn't know if that was AM or PM. He reached over to his pack and pulled the handheld computer/GPS unit from its padded pocket.

"Hmm, it's three in the morning," Bohannon said, almost to himself, as Rodriguez and Johnson scrambled off the dust-laden floor. "Well, something moved this mountain, and we should be able to find out what it was." Bohannon fired up the unit. His first stop was Google Earth, where he quickly zeroed in on Jerusalem, then the Old City, then the Temple Mount. Dependent on satellite imaging, Google Earth is about as real-time a look at the earth as any average person is going to get. Still, the images are not instantaneous, they don't change until the next satellite pass. Bohannon didn't expect to find any great revelation, but he checked the Temple Mount area nonetheless. With nothing visible on

Google Earth, Bohannon logged into Yahoo's home page for news bulletins. Probably still premature for . . .

There it was, popped right up to the top of the list. "The southern wall holding up the Temple Mount just collapsed," Bohannon said out loud, speaking as he read along, "at least a large section of the southern wall. Nobody is sure yet how much damage, or if it was a natural disaster or terrorist-related. Seems it's been raining up there for the last three days, raining heavily. The last time a portion of a wall came down, the eastern wall, it had also been raining for days. That's all they—"

At the sound, Bohannon jumped to his feet, ready to run, internal alarms sounding. Rodriguez was also on his feet, crouched, apparently ready to ward off attack. Only Johnson appeared normal, walking briskly over to his pack. Again and again the noise demanded their attention, but Bohannon couldn't place it, until Johnson pulled out the metal-clad, heavily padded Pelican case. The satellite phone was ringing, and vibrating, with a Richter rating of its own. With a deft smoothness that belied the concern on his face, Johnson engaged the receiver.

"Dr. Johnson here. How may I assist you?"

In spite of his overall ache, Bohannon just started to chuckle. *Underground for three days, people trying to kill us, the mountain's falling down, and he sounds like the butler.*

"Yes, one moment." Johnson turned to his left with a quizzical look. "Mr. Bohannon, sir, this call is for you."

At first, he didn't want to put his hand on it. Who could be on the other end? Who would be calling them, here? This was getting too weird.

Johnson, holding out the phone, wordlessly urged it in Bohannon's direction, then firmly placed it in his hand.

Operating in a realm of unbelief, Bohannon barely squeezed out the "H" in hello, when a voice crackled from the other side of the world.

"Bohannon? This is Ethan Larsen, Winthrop's uncle. Listen, you boys are in quite a fix. The Israeli military has squads of men coming at you from the entryway in Zechariah's Tomb. Seems you left them a nice trail of fluorescent dots to follow. And the Northern Islamic Front has hundreds of men under the Temple Mount, prepared to protect their sacred shrines to the death. You would be in deep spit if those were your only problems. But now the southern wall of the Temple Mount has collapsed, a whole, big slab of the thing, at least a third

of it. And it's still raining, so the Israelis are havin' conniption fits that the rest
of it is going to give way.

"All of which means to tell you, son," said General Larsen, "that you and
your buddies better get out of there, pronto. Like now. Or you are going to be
having company, lots of company. And they're not coming to throw you a party.
You listening to me, Bohannon?"

"Yes, sir . . . I . . ."

"Stuff it, mister. Keep your ears open. You've got no friends over there, and
very few friends over here. Israeli media has been fed a tip that Shin Bet's been
chasing a pack of suspected terrorists who have disappeared underground into
the Temple Mount area. That's got the Jews going ape. They've also got a report
that Israeli military found two Muslims, stabbed to death, in an area just south
of the Mount. That's got the Muslims going ape. And now everybody thinks
you clowns have blown up the southern wall—you didn't do that, did you?"

"Ah, no sir, we . . ."

"Well, that's got everybody going ape. You listening to me, mister?"

"Yes si—"

"So you and your pals better get your sorry selves outta wherever you are, or
you're going to get squashed. You only got one problem, mister . . ."

Bohannon was as stunned by the silence as he had been by the verbal battering ram known affectionately as Uncle Ethan. There was a gap, and he didn't
know how to, or whether he should, fill it. Ethan Larsen answered the unasked
question.

"You've got nowhere to go."

"What?"

The tough-talking general suddenly became Winthrop's uncle again.
"Tom, you guys are virtually surrounded. Now that the wall's come down, both
the Muslims and the Israeli military are going to be pressing after you with a
renewed fervor. You can't come to the surface because, no matter where you pop
up, somebody is going to pounce on you. And we can't help you. Us, the good
old USofA, there's nothing we can do to help you. Otherwise, it would look as if
we've put you up to it. And it would just get us in the middle of a spittin' storm.

"I'm sorry to say it, but you boys are on your own. I wish it wasn't so, but it
is. Outside of this phone call, there is nothing I can do to help you."

Bohannon didn't know what to say. Uncle Ethan, he figured, had simply
run out of breath.

"Son, I've got to ask you one favor." The general's voice had lost all its hard edges, all its bravado. "Keep that sat phone with you but, before you get captured, *er*, if you're going to get captured, destroy the phone and the handheld GPS units, anything that could be traced. I promised to protect the guy I sent Winthrop to. What are you carrying this phone in?"

Bohannon had to pick his stomach up off the floor before he could answer. He had never allowed the idea of capture to really enter into his consciousness. Now, it covered him like wet concrete. "We've got a metal-sided Pelican Case, padded on the inside."

"Good, that's perfect," said General Larsen. "The satellite phone has a self-destruct mechanism. Turn it over and look just below where your palm rests. There's a metal plate with clock hands on it. Push down on both ends of the plate and turn it with your thumbs. Inside is a red knob that can point to three settings—thirty, sixty, or ninety seconds. Set the knob, put the phone and the GPS units inside the Pelican case, and tightly secure the case. There will be nothing but dust in that case if anybody takes a look. You got that, Tom?"

"Yes, sir . . . you can count on us, General." For a brief flash, Bohannon saw himself in uniform, camouflage, on a mission for his country, the military motto echoing in his brain. "There is no excuse, only responsibility." Covering Ethan Larsen's rear was now his responsibility. Bohannon welcomed it.

"I know I can count on you, Tom. Winthrop told me you were a man of integrity, a man he could count on. I appreciate that, it meant a lot to me then, means a lot to me now. You men take care of yourselves. I don't know where you're going, but I wouldn't stay long where you are. And, Tom, I'll be praying for you."

Bohannon was touched.

"Thank you, General. That means a lot to me, sir."

"I know. Now haul out of there, mister. You don't have much time. The Israelis are making rapid advance. Godspeed, son. Godspeed."

The voice was gone and the lights went out at the same time, leaving Bohannon staring dumbly at this space-age marvel in his hand. He was almost transported to a land of make-believe until he saw the look on the two faces opposite him.

"That's gotta be bad news," said Rodriguez, "that's gotta be real bad news."

⌐∿∿⌐

Deep inside the earth of southwestern Israel, beneath the cover of a small petroleum depot that helped hide their many satellite dishes (made to look like storage tanks) and antennas, the Israeli army's clandestine communications center constantly scanned all electronic communications wavelengths.

"I've got a hit," said the lieutenant. "Satellite phone . . . encrypted."

"Location?" asked the captain.

The lieutenant clicked and scrolled, closed in on the coordinates. He looked at the captain. "Temple Mount."

"Lock in the coordinates. I'll call the general."

45

"We've got to move, right now." That was all Bohannon said.

Within minutes, their gear was packed. Leaving dust squalls in their wake, they were up and over the debris field in the northwest corner, squeezing through the hole in the limestone wall. Bohannon was the last one through when Rodriguez suddenly shucked his pack. "Here, hold this, I'll be right back." And he was gone, back through the hole. One . . . two . . . three long, anxious minutes, before Rodriguez launched himself through the hole and scrambled to his feet. "Get back!"

It sounded and felt and tasted like the tremor that awoke them, perhaps on a smaller scale, but just as dramatic because of its proximity. A huge crash on the other side of the wall, the rumbling sounds of caving earth, billows of blinding dust shooting through the hole from the room on the other side. Pressed into the darkness, his helmet slammed onto his head at the last minute, Bohannon looked at his brother-in-law.

"So? I closed the door. That column over there was just rockin' on an edge, didn't take much to make it decide its fate. Now, even if the soldiers find that room, they'll have a tough time finding out how we left."

"Okay, but, next time, how about a little warning so we don't get clobbered." Bohannon reached over and gave the pack back to Rodriguez. "Doc, listen, we should . . ."

Bohannon had turned, the beam on his TAG lamp illuminating a portion of a hallway. The wall to the right, and a portion of the floor, were intact, but everything else looked like a mountain had caved in on it. And Johnson was nowhere to be seen.

~~~~~

Jonathan Whitestone was seated in an armchair, situated between and dominating the two facing sofas in the Oval Office. His hair was black, his suit was black, and his eyes were on fire. At that moment, his withering stare had fallen upon the FBI director.

"Well then, you *will* find out who they are, Bill, and you will find out, now!"

Whitestone's fury swept all those in the room. The election was five months away and the polls had him in a dead heat. Now, three Americans were burrowing under the Temple Mount and inciting a Middle Eastern crisis that could impact the entire world. And his advisors, some of the most powerful men in the world, knew nothing.

"This has disaster written all over it." Whitestone seethed. "Find out all you can about these men and give everything you find to the Israelis. They must be found, and they must be stopped. I don't care how. They must be stopped."

⸻⟨∿∿⟩⸻

Blue light was shimmering up ahead, to the right, the side that had not been destroyed. Bohannon and Rodriguez had been prepared to shout Doc down, find out where he went, until they realized they may no longer be alone . . . that sound could travel long distances in these underground caverns. So they chased his shadow.

Inside the portal opening, they found Doc in a small anteroom or closet, the blue cyalume stick in his hand held high to light the wall at which he was staring. He was talking to himself. In Aramaic. *Here we go*, thought Bohannon, *back to the surreal*.

Rodriguez got right in his face. "Doc, why did you take off? Don't you know the whole Israeli army is coming after us, along with a few thousand Muslims pledged to end our lives? Do you think that's a good time to take a stroll?"

Johnson looked blankly at Rodriguez.

"But the inscriptions," said Johnson, turning to point at the wall with his cyalume stick.

They were exhausted. None of them was thinking clearly. There was so much input competing for a place on their memory cards. Before Rodriguez could react, Bohannon put a hand on his shoulder and stepped between them. He turned his head to get his eyes in front of Johnson's. "Doc, I know, this is amazing . . . Doc . . . c'mon, we've got to figure out our next step."

With a start, a look of surprise, Johnson's focus switched from the wall. "But this *is* our next step."

—∿∽∿—

"Gefen, we got the coordinates from a satellite communication—31°47' north; 35°10' east. Get there."

—∿∽∿—

He had the cell phone open before the second ring. "Yes?"

"A satellite communication into the Temple Mount was intercepted," Leonidas said without preamble. "The coordinates are 31°47' north; 35°10' east. Israeli soldiers are on their way. Do what you will. But the Israelis are getting suspicious. This may be my last communication."

The Imam felt a twinge of regret and a stab of resistance. "You have been of great service, Leonidas. You will be rewarded handsomely . . . but only once these men are dead, or in our hands. Do you understand?"

His cell phone lost its signal, providing a simple answer.

—∿∽∿—

They were on the floor of the anteroom, Doc's maps spread out in front of them.

"You see, Winthrop and I agreed that Tuvia Sigva got it right, that his theory on the Temple placed it between the location of the Dome of the Rock and the Al-Aqsa Mosque. We thought that location also worked for Warren's Gate, that Warren's Gate was about as close as anyone could come to the original site of the Most Holy Place, the Holy of Holies, of the Temple. We also agreed that if Abiathar and his father, Elijah, were determined to construct a temple under the Temple Mount, they would try to do it in as close proximity as possible to the original Temple's location.

"We always thought the area around Warren's Gate would be the most likely location for Abiathar's Temple. Except, now we know the Western Wall Tunnel runs right past Warren's Gate. And there has been no secret Temple discovered.

"But if you accept Tuvia Sigva's location, then the Holy of Holies would have been much farther south than where Warren's Gate now sits."

Johnson turned to them, expectantly, but Bohannon was drawing a blank, he didn't know where this was going.

"Okay, let me make it easy," said Johnson, beginning to draw on his map.

"Down here are the Hulda Gates, in the south wall. The Triple Gate, the one to the east, had tunnels leading up to the Temple Mount. We believe we just came through the meeting hall of the Sanhedrin, that would have been above, higher than, the Hulda Gates, in the vicinity of the Temple. And that's where we found Meborak's stellae with the master code. So Abiathar had to have been in that Sanhedrin room. Here is Warren's Gate over here, on the Western Wall. Here's the Dome of the Rock and Al-Aqsa. If the Temple sat in the space between the Dome and Al-Aqsa, it would have been in here." Johnson drew an oval on his map, between the two buildings. "Here is where the Hulda Gate tunnels likely would have surfaced." Johnson made a mark, that touched his oval. "There was a Herodian street that ran along the western side of the Temple Mount, from the Damascus Gate to the Pool of Siloam." He drew in the street, touching the western side of the oval. "With the Dome of the Rock on the north and the Al-Aqsa Mosque on the south and the Western street on the west, there was only one way for Abiathar to gain access to the area around the Temple's location with the lowest level of risk, from the southeast. As we have done.

"So, looking at the likely location for the Temple, where should we look for Abiathar's secret cavern?" Johnson asked.

Bohannon looked down at the map and wondered, if it was so simple, why they hadn't figured it out before.

"Look at your GPS," said Johnson.

Rodriguez got to his quickly and held it up for all of them to see. A small, green star flashed on and off. "Throw on the Temple Mount coordinates," said Johnson. Rodriguez punched in a few numbers, and an outline formed on the screen.

"We're right here." Rodriguez tapped the map, right on the oval, in the middle of where the Hulda Gate tunnels should have risen to the surface of the Temple Mount.

Bohannon watched while a huge, cheek-to-cheek smile broke out all over Johnson's face.

"That's right, that's right. We are in what is left of one of the passages that rose from the Triple Gate, the eastern-most Hulda Gate, up to the Temple Mount. These passageways, like everything else, were filled with the massive debris that occurred when the Romans destroyed the Temple in 70 A.D. Remember, every stone was thrown down and Herod's Temple was enormous. That's why all of this stuff is underground. The Romans knocked it all down;

the Muslims smoothed it out and built again on top of the rubble. Two thousand years ago, we would have been in the middle of a busy passageway. Today, we are hundreds of feet below the surface of the Temple Mount.

"So, Mr. Rodriguez, since you appear to be more alert this morning than your near relative, where would you say we should look for Abiathar's cavern?"

"Holy Christmas, Doc," spurted Bohannon. "We got posses breathing down our necks from every direction, and you want to play twenty questions?"

Johnson looked deeply offended, wounded that Bohannon wouldn't indulge what was obviously a triumphant moment. "I'm sorry, Doc. My apologies, you're doing great. So, where do we look?"

With a nod of his head as absolution, Johnson swept up his map, grasped the still glowing cyalume stick, and stood to his feet. "Gentlemen, follow me."

Johnson turned on his heel and went back down the Hulda passage, hugging the wall to his right.

It was as if they had been moving through the middle of a landslide. A seemingly impassable wall of rubble rose to their left, filling most of the Huldah passage, the debris precariously stacked above their heads, wedged against the wall of the Huldah passage on their right. Johnson gingerly navigated the tight corridor and reached the space where they had broken through the wall. The limestone walls of the Sanhedrin meeting room facing him, Johnson barely broke stride.

He turned to his left and squeezed past the corner of the limestone block wall, into a crevice about four feet high, between some of the fallen stones and the finished block wall.

"Come along," said a muffled voice.

Bohannon stood in front of the narrow opening. If Johnson had not disappeared into this crack in the debris, Bohannon would never have looked at it twice. Rodriguez measured the thin crevice with his eyes, took off his backpack, and slid it through the opening in front of him. Then he lay down on his side, wriggled his body in several contortionist positions, and finally slipped from sight.

Johnson was much thinner than Rodriguez. Rodriguez, younger and more athletic than Bohannon, was also much thinner than Bohannon, particularly around the middle.

"I'm never getting through there," Bohannon groaned.

〜〜〜〜

He could hear the voice in front of him, chattering away, talking as much to the rocks as to anyone else. And he could see the blue cyalume light that left a trail of illumination bright enough for him to navigate without bashing his head. But that was all he knew of Johnson, or his progress. At each turn, the Doc had moved on, waiting for no man.

Rodriguez would have kicked himself if his foot could have reached his butt. He had forced himself through that tight space, wanted to show Tom he could do it, and now his back hurt like . . . well, it hurt. It was a pain he knew; and a pain he knew wasn't going away.

"It's hard to tell the difference in the debris."

Doc's voice drifted over the rocks from somewhere ahead.

"But there should be a difference. They were a thousand years apart."

Rodriguez had quickly given up on the idea of pushing his backpack in front of him. The space was too narrow—too irregular—it kept getting stuck. So now his backpack rested on his right hip as, on his left side, he pulled, pushed and twisted himself, foot by foot, along this narrow crevice. Where was Doc going?

"Oh . . . oh . . . excellent," came from the blue light in the distance.

⌒⌒⌒

Rodriguez was grateful for two things, the four ibuprofen tablets he had just washed down and the fact that he could sit, with his legs stretched out. He and Johnson were catching their breath, each glad to be out of that snaking little crevice.

"That was part of the debris that must have come down when Abiathar collapsed the entrance to the Temple cavern," said Johnson, who was taking deep breaths and gnawing on an energy bar. "He and his men could never have come through an obstacle like that. And the floor is relatively flat. This must have been a much more open space in his time."

"Where are we, Doc?"

As Johnson unfolded his map, they could hear Bohannon grunting, cussing, and squeezing. "It's a good thing that crevice slopes downhill. Otherwise, he might never get through.

"Here, I would say we are here." Johnson pointed to the Triple Gate. "But I believe we are behind the gate—inside the gate—and lower than the gate. I believe this is where Elijah, Abiathar's father, decided to dig out his cavern. I admit, we may have taken a wrong turn somewhere in our decisions. Perhaps they didn't deal with that lake of water, or maybe, at that time, there was no lake, or most likely, there was more than one way to gain access to the cavern. But I have no doubt that both Elijah and Abiathar used the meeting room of the Sanhedrin as the headquarters room for their work. And if their desire was to have their Third Temple as close to the site of the Second Temple as possible, without being discovered, this is where they would have looked."

Rodriguez wasn't sold. There could be thousands of arguments that would be just as valid, even if this Third Temple did exist. And he was beginning to have his doubts. This whole crazy chase had just been a bunch of ignorant guys bumbling their way from one fiasco to another. At least, that was one way to look at it.

⌇⌇⌇⌇

Bohannon pulled himself into the open space.

"Your brother-in-law is a dolt." Johnson projected the petulance of a child. His head was bowed, the silent GPS unit in his lap.

"You're just flat wrong, Doc," Rodriguez snapped. "There's no need to get your nose out of joint. I simply don't agree with your conclusions."

"It is truly sad to discover your reasoning is so fatally flawed," Johnson snarled.

Bohannon felt as if he had just been squashed by a steamroller. All he wanted to do was lie down and go to sleep. That was out of the question. If he didn't get between Doc and Joe right now, his brother-in-law was likely to make coleslaw out of Doc's brains.

"Lighten up, Doc," said Rodriguez, "I hear what you're saying about the Huldah entrance tunnel and the guy's theory on the Temple location. But we're hundreds of yards south of where most archaeologists believe Herod's Temple would have been located. I don't think we're going to find anything around here. And we've got to get moving. There's probably only enough time for us to probe one site, and we've still got to find a way to get out. We can't waste our time on a site that is so obviously not a possibility."

Bohannon slid between the two combatants, pulling himself to a sitting position.

"Look." He was stunned by the raspy, weak sound of his voice. But his words matched his physical state. "Joe's right. We have one shot at this, maybe not even one shot. If Ethan Larsen is right, our time is up. We've got one choice.

"But Doc could be right, too. Either we try to probe the area on the other side of this wall, or we all agree that there's another location that is more promising, we get there as quickly as possible, and hope that we have enough time to send in the cameras. So, what's it going to be? Do we sit here arguing with each other, or do we take advantage of the one chance we have?"

Bohannon rested his head against the wall and closed his eyes. "Personally, I think we've come a long way and sacrificed too much to blow the one chance we have."

"But that's the challenge, isn't it?" said Johnson. "How do we decide where to look?"

Bohannon opened his eyes. They were both looking to him for guidance.

"I don't know. I don't know." Bohannon felt desperation rising in his chest, bringing fear as a companion. "We need a miracle."

And he knew.

"Listen, I don't know how to decide what to do, but I believe we can discover what to do."

The other two men looked in his direction. Understanding and agreement rose like an underground sun. "We could pray. Will you pray with me?"

Johnson began to stammer his uncertainty, but Rodriguez was immediately at Bohannon's side.

"Let's go. I'm willing to believe you'll get the answer. I'll join with you, but you're the guy who's connected."

They both looked at Doc.

"All right, I guess we don't have much choice." Johnson slid the short distance to their sides.

God, this is weird, Bohannon thought. Praying with an audience, a relatively unbelieving audience, but an audience who, nevertheless, expect a miracle. No pressure there.

He closed his eyes.

He thought about the other times, the times he had called out to God in need, in pain, in fear, in doubt, and how often God had given him answers in the past. And he was confident, they had no other choice.

He set his heart.

He slowed his mind. He felt hands reach out for his.

"Father, I praise you for who you are, the God of heaven. And I thank you for your faithfulness, to me and my family, over so many years. Father, I believe you are the reason we are here. That it was your purpose and plan for us to be here. But we're lost right now. We don't know what to do; we don't know where to go; we don't know where to look to try and find this Temple, and we don't know how to get out of here without going to jail or losing our lives. We are at the end of ourselves, at the end of this chase unless you show us the way. I don't know what else to ask you, how else to ask you, except that we are desperate for your help. We need an answer. We need it now. Please, Lord, tell us what to do."

There was silence in the small, open space they shared.

Bohannon lifted his face toward where he believed the sky would be. *Please, Father,* he breathed.

—⁓⁓⁓—

Bohannon got up off the floor and turned to Joe's pack. While the others watched, he opened the lower compartment and withdrew the camera mounted on tiny tank tracks. "Bring the catheters and the video."

The crevice was higher on this end, high enough that Bohannon could rest the mounted camera on his hip. Bohannon pressed himself back into the crack from which he had just come. He inched along, penetrating a few yards. He could hear Doc and Joe pushing in behind him. Suddenly, he stopped, and looked up.

The shelf was there, just as he knew it would be, just as he had "seen" it during his prayer. Bohannon poised the mounted camera on the shelf and, despite the close quarters, quickly pulled himself up alongside it. His body wedged back against the far wall, Bohannon looked up and saw the second shelf, and the opening above it, just as he expected. Bohannon reached up, stretched, and tipped the camera mount onto the second shelf. Climbing was relatively easy, the space so narrow he could lean back against the far wall if necessary. Standing on the second shelf, he looked up, into the opening. The camera mount went in first, he followed quickly. But before disappearing, he peeked down into the crevice. Joe and Doc were watching from the bottom.

"Use the shelf, there's two of them. There are plenty of handholds. And you can lean against the far wall if needed. Follow me when you get up here."

Bohannon turned on his hip. The opening was fairly regular, about a four-foot square, rough enough to be natural but also having the look of being purposeful. Getting into a crouch, he pulled the controller from his pocket, flicked on the power, and began guiding the motorized platform ahead of him, crab-walking behind it. Amazed at the little device's effectiveness, Bohannon watched as the treads independently overcame each obstacle, like twin snakes undulating across the floor, each at its own pace.

He turned on the small Maglite on the front edge of the camera assembly, helping to break the growing darkness, and began following the camera's progress more through the small LCD screen on the controller than through his own limited eyesight. The assembly moved forward rapidly, as if by its own volition, as if being called.

"Tom?" Joe's question was reverential.

"Come on in," he called softly over his shoulder. "Bring the equipment."

One hand braced against a sidewall, the other holding the controller, his eyes now glued to the screen, Bohannon inched ahead, stumbling at times, bumping against outcroppings, but never taking his eyes off the screen. So, he saw the end of the tunnel in time to slow and stop the mounted camera before it cracked into the rock face.

Look to your left. He knew it would be there.

A slab of rock protruded from the left, about halfway up the wall. Under the overhang was a hole, about a foot-and-a-half round. Not smooth and finished, but also not simply a jagged, natural formation. The mounted camera fit into the hole, with little room to spare. Enough, he knew. Then he waited.

To his left, Joe and Doc crawled along the shaft. Joe had the equipment bag with the video catheters, hanging down his back from around his neck. Doc followed, the Pelican Box strapped to his chest. Tom waited.

"What have you found?" Doc was breathless, but excited.

"Let me have the catheter tubes." There was no time for conversation.

Rodriguez pulled three coils of tubing from the equipment bag.

Bohannon took the first. "Start connecting them together. We're going to need all three." Turning to the camera assembly, Bohannon connected the front edge of the catheter tube to a prepared clip, just below the lens of the mounted camera. The tubes were really tubes within tubes, the probing camera at the front edge of the catheter able to snake out from its housing.

Controller in hand, Bohannon inched the mounted camera along, inside the hole, which almost immediately began sloping downward. *I wonder how reverse works,* he thought. "Get the video set up." Momentarily glancing over his shoulder, he spotted Doc unhooking the Pelican case. "You brought the satellite phone?"

Johnson, clearly consumed by what Bohannon was doing at the entrance to the hole, looked down at the metal case as if seeing it for the first time. "I didn't know what we would need. General Larsen said not to let this out of our sight. I grabbed the first thing . . . what are you doing there?"

"Wait, you'll see." Bohannon turned back to the controller screen. The mounted camera was still slowly descending through the hole, apparently swinging in a gentle curve toward the south. Joe had connected the first, and then the second catheter extension and the last one was getting alarmingly short. Bohannon pressed his gaze into the LCD screen. *Where is it? Where is it? Stop.*

The word was so clear he turned to see who had spoken.

Only quizzical glances answered his questioning look. He lifted his thumb. He rotated the joystick to the left. Smooth and dark, a small hole rested right at lens level. Bohannon could feel Doc and Joe at his shoulders.

"What is that?" asked Johnson.

Bohannon changed his grip on the controller and began propelling the catheter's camera end out of the tube attached under the lens. Like a docking spaceship, Bohannon guided the miniscule camera into the waiting hole. "Feels like an operation," he said. More and more of the slim tubing disappeared into the hole.

There was some rustling behind him. "The GPS has us located alongside the Huldah Gate entry tunnel," said Johnson. "The probe must be deeper, and farther south. Right where . . ."

The eyes of all three men were glued to the LCD screen, drinking in the same image. The catheter had just cleared the end of the hole, and Bohannon had quickly stopped its progress. The image was faint. Bohannon turned up the illumination on the camera tip, pushing it all the way to maximum. As the image emerged and cleared, none of them breathed.

Beyond the end of the hole, a room opened up, a large, cavernous space. Inside the space was a towering, ornate structure on a massive scale. Larger than anything Bohannon had imagined, the Third Temple of God came to life in the glare of the amazingly bright light emanating from the miniscule tip of the catheter tube. The light burst into the cavern, and blasted back, reflecting gloriously off the golden columns that seemed to fill the space.

"You see what I'm seeing, right?" Bohannon flipped a glance over his left shoulder.

Rodriguez slowly nodded his head. "I didn't believe it. All this time, I didn't really believe it. I didn't really think we would find it. But it's here, wow, it's really here. And God, it's beautiful."

"It's amazing," said Johnson. "Look at the richness. I never expected it to be so big . . . and so much gold. I'm amazed. How could they have done this? But there it is, the Temple of God, right in front of our eyes. Can you move the camera any? Is there any way to get a different view?"

"Limited," said Bohannon. "The camera tip can rotate slightly, but it's not independent of the tube holding it. I can extend it about another inch, then run it through a three-sixty arc after that, but I don't know how much more we're going to see. Joe, you got the video running?"

"Yeah, it's been on since you entered the hole."

"Okay, I'm going to bring it out . . . "

"What, what do you mean?" Johnson was blustering in Bohannon's ear.

Bohannon stopped, turned away from the LCD screen, frustrated with Johnson's interruptions.

"Doc, you, more than any of us, should know what we've got to do. Right now, what we've got is an isolated image. With today's technology able to create just about anything, we'd be mocked and ignored. We've got to validate what we've found. We're going to start over, set the stage and start over. We need to make sure this proof is unassailable. Get the satellite phone powered up and both GPS units operating while I pull the unit out."

Bohannon went back to the LCD screen and the controller. Only the rustling behind him confirmed that Johnson and Rodriguez had heeded his instructions. With the camera now pointed to the rear, bringing the unit out seemed easier, and faster, than the inbound trip. Grasping the tank tracks, Bohannon extricated the unit and turned it to face Johnson and Rodriguez.

"Turn on the audio, Joe. Doc, call Sam Reynolds at the State Department. Let me know when you have him on the line. We should all sit against the far wall."

Bohannon set the mounted platform on top of the stone shelf above the entry shaft, then inched himself to the far wall, beside his two partners. With the controller, he swiveled the camera so he had a good, clear picture of the three of them. Johnson was to his left, Rodriguez to his right.

"Mr. Reynolds, this is Dr. Johnson. I know . . . I know. Can you just hang on for a moment?" Doc looked at Bohannon. "Now what?"

"Everything rolling?" Bohannon asked.

"All set to go," said Joe.

"This is Tom Bohannon. Sitting next to me are Dr. Richard Johnson Sr. and Joseph Rodriguez. We are under the Temple Mount in Jerusalem. Outside of the Hall of the Sanhedrin, we've found a shaft that led us to this point. The mobile camera that is filming us sits on a stone shelf on the far wall of the shaft, only a few feet from where we sit. Doc, hold up one of the GPS units that shows our location. I'm going to turn down the illumination just a bit."

Bohannon turned to Doc.

"You can see from the GPS screen two important pieces of information. First is the date and time, set automatically by a link to Greenwich Mean—June nineteenth, 6:43 AM local time. The second piece of information is our GPS location. Doc, begin to decrease the zoom, take us farther out." The image on the screen blurred, then cleared. "There, you can see the Temple Mount." Blurred again, and then cleared again. "There, you can see the Old City of Jerusalem.

"Okay, Doc, get the other GPS, but start with an entire view of Israel. Okay, good. So, there you see the same time and date as the first GPS. Okay, Doc, begin zooming in closer, bring it in on Jerusalem. Have the GPS home in on its own location, do it automatically."

There was silence as Johnson fiddled with the controls.

"There, it's marked its own location . . . 31°47' north; 35°10' east. Doc, hold up the other GPS. What are the coordinates?"

Johnson held the two units up, side-by-side, so the camera had a clear view. "They are identical."

"Okay," said Bohannon. "On a secure satellite phone, we are talking with Sam Reynolds, an official from the United States State Department. Sam, are you still there?"

"I'm here, but you guys better listen to me. The entire—"

"Yeah, I know," said Bohannon, "but that's not what we need right now, Sam. Tell me, what is today's date? What is today's time, there, in Washington?"

"Tom, you men are crazy. Get out of there."

"Date and time, please, Mr. Reynolds. We need to make sure there is no question about what we're about to record."

"Tom, don't be a fool." There was no answer. "Ahhh . . . it's Thursday, June 18. It's 11:46 PM here in Washington. And I can verify the coordinates of the satellite phone. We can track that kind of stuff from here. They are where they claim to be, either on top of, or underneath, the Temple Mount in Jerusalem."

"Great, Sam, thanks. That really helps. Can you hold on for a few more moments?"

"Sure, I'll be here. You at least deserve a warning, if you'll ever listen to it."

"Okay, Sam, okay, but in a minute." Bohannon turned back to the camera. "I'm going to get up now and grab hold of the assembly on which this camera is mounted. I'm going to pick it off the rock shelf, turn it around 180 degrees, and insert it into a smaller shaft that appears to be naturally occurring. It looks like it's been formed over years by the passage of water. There . . . there is the opening of the shaft. I am going to place the mounted platform into the shaft.

"About one hundred fifty yards into the shaft, I will stop the camera and rotate it ninety degrees to the left, where it will face a small hole. I will move the camera toward the hole and then insert a small, medical catheter, with a camera on its tip, into the hole. Here is a view of the catheter. The catheter will move through the hole for approximately seventy-five feet. It will then enter a large cavern, where we will turn the illumination to full power.

"We did this same exercise some fifteen minutes ago. Inside the cavern we found the Third Temple of God, erected in the eleventh century by the leaders of the Jewish community in Jerusalem, Elijah and his son, Abiathar, Gaons of Jerusalem. With the conquest of the crusaders, the cavern where this Temple was built was sealed. It has remained hidden until today."

Bohannon stopped his lecture and cast a glace at his two companions. Both nodded silently.

"We're going to leave the audio on," said Bohannon. "Here we go."

Bohannon continued his narration as first the camera assembly, then the catheter, retraced their progress to the cavern of the Temple. Turning up the illumination, this time Bohannon extended the camera tip as far as it would go, then began the three-sixty rotation. Although the difference in the camera's distance from the catheter was not great from their first visit to the second, the rotation still gave the three explorers a significantly expanded view of the Temple. The hole in the limestone emerged opposite what appeared to be the front, right corner, or the southeast corner of the Temple, fairly high along the cavern wall. Rotating the camera angle showed not only more of the front and the side of the Temple's construction, but the top of its arc revealed a remarkable view of the Temple's roof area and what appeared to be an opening in the roof.

"That opening," said Johnson, once again hanging over Bohannon's shoulder, "is likely situated over the Holy of Holies. I've seen renderings that had the Holy of Holies open to the sky above."

"The Temple construction appears to be cut limestone," said Bohannon. "The columns in the front also appear to be limestone, but the capitals are covered with gold, as is the decorative detail at the roofline." Bohannon rotated the camera as far to the left as he could. He could clearly see the large courtyard, the Outer Courts, at the front of the Temple. But from their vantage point, the actual front of the building was obscured for the most part by the front columns. Still, there appeared to be a wall and a great entrance doorway behind the columns. "We apparently can't get a clear look at the front of the Temple, but there appears to be a doorway, a huge doorway extending more than two-thirds of the way up the front wall. From this angle, it looks like the building is not built square, but more as a trapezoid, wider at the base and more narrow at the roof. The doorway also, though it's hard to tell, seems to be angled to be more narrow at the top."

A quiet, but insistent beeping accompanied a vibration in Bohannon's hand and a blinking battery signal in the LCD screen.

"We're running out of power. Looks like time to bring the baby home," said Bohannon. "I'd leave it where it is and just let the power run out, but I want to bring all the equipment home, if we can, just in case there are any questions. Sam Reynolds, for verification, can you tell us again the date and the time?"

"Sure, it's time to call your lawyer." Bohannon could hear the frustration and rising anger in Reynolds's voice. "Are you telling me you actually found a Jewish temple built under the Temple Mount, hidden for a thousand years? You're telling me you've actually got that on videotape?"

"Mr. Reynolds," said Johnson, "I can understand you might have some skepticism when an investigative journalist claims to have made some historic discovery that's been hidden for generations. But I assure you, if I have any reputation left, I wouldn't squander it by foisting what would be a monumentally stupid attempt at deceit. Yes, sir, the Temple is there. I haven't touched it, but I've seen it twice. It's there, Mr. Reynolds. There is no doubt, it's there."

"God help us," Reynolds whispered. "It's now Friday, June nineteenth, and it is 12:18 AM in Washington, DC. And I can verify that not only have I heard everything that Tom has been saying, but I have also been recording it and will be able to verify any recording he has made. What you've been seeing, well, that will be for someone else to corroborate."

"Thanks, Sam. One thing? Is there any way you can keep this to yourself? At least for the next several hours? We're going to need every break we can get to get out of here in one piece."

"Tom, I can't do that. You don't have any idea what you're asking. The president knows you're in there, and the cabinet. And we've all been ordered to share with the Israelis any information we discover. I don't have a choice, Tom. And even if I did have a choice, I would never be able to keep this information to myself because I'm not the only one who has this information."

The three men in the cave looked at each other.

"What do you mean, Sam?" said Bohannon.

"Tom, the Israelis have the same technology that we have. If I could locate you guys, they can locate you guys. And, if they intercept the signal and if they can crack the code . . ."

"Can they do that?"

"Yeah, oh, yeah, they can do that," said Reynolds. "I'd have to put my money on the Israelis. They probably already have you located and have soldiers trying to get to you right now. Even on the off chance the Israelis haven't intercepted this communication, when I hang up with you, I will immediately call the secretary of state and fill him in on everything I've said and everything I've heard. And he will call the Israeli prime minister and hand them the GPS coordinates. I don't know how you figure to get out of there but, whatever your plan, you'd better move on it right now. You are out of options. Good luck."

The satellite phone went dead. They had found the Temple. They had gotten it on video. They had gotten the evidence. Now, would anyone ever see it?

"What do we do now?" asked Johnson.

"Just what we did before," said Rodriguez. "Tom, your faith and your willingness to listen to God got us here. I believe they can also get us out of here. Ask him to show you the way." And he grabbed a hand in each of his.

46

Orhlon was proud of his team. It had taken much less time than he would have expected for them to break the encrypted communications, primarily because they were U.S. military codes the Israelis had stolen a year ago. Understanding how these men got U.S. military codes, that was tomorrow's problem. Now, he waited for the screen to clear. "There, quick, mark that location." He picked up the radio. "Gefen?"

"Yes, sir?"

"North of you about three hundred fifty meters, west about seventy-five meters. They appear to be above you, higher than your location. They said something about the Hall of the Sanhedrin and the entrance tunnel of the Huldah Gates. Then we lost the transmission. I've had the Office of Antiquities on the phone. They believe there must be some way for you to move northwest, some tunnel or opening. The entrance tunnel to the Huldah Gates would be to your northwest, in the vicinity of their last location. See if you can find a way for your men to move northwest. Try to reach the entrance tunnel. There would have to be stairs. After that, you'll just have to search wherever you can. They are in there somewhere. Whatever they are trying to do, they've got to be close to getting it done. Move, Gefen, move quickly. Or I fear the Temple Mount may come crashing down upon all our heads."

Orhlon replaced the radio.

"General, we cannot trace the recipient of the satellite transmission," said Major Mordechai. "We don't know who they were calling."

"It doesn't matter who they were calling," said Orhlon. "They were transmitting coordinates. They've got a specific location. If they've found it, we cannot allow them to escape. I don't care how ballistic the Arabs get, call in the reserve units. Surround the Temple Mount from every direction. I want that entire area buttoned down, enough men to have a soldier stationed every ten meters."

"Even on the southern side?" asked the major. "Our engineers are worried that even more of the southern wall may break loose, especially with this accursed rain."

"I don't care about the rain, I don't care about the wall, I don't care about anything except preventing those men from leaving Jerusalem. Whatever the cost. If necessary, their discovery will die with them. Get it done, Major. Get it done, now."

━◇◇◇━

Bohannon was beginning to feel like a lottery winner who knew he didn't have all the answers but suddenly was perceived as some savant. He wanted to pray, he believed God wanted to answer his prayers. But now, Doc and Joe looked at him as if he were like some kind of fortune-teller, a trickster who could pull a rabbit out of his hat at his whim. What if God didn't answer his prayer? What if God didn't show him how to get out? What if he didn't have another of those "visions" in his brain like the one that told him to make a raft or look again at the scroll, or the last one that told him to climb up in that crevice, that showed him the shaft, the stone shelf, the hole for the catheter?

How could they get out of the tunnel, and out of Jerusalem, without being captured or killed by the Shin Bet, the Arabs, or some Jewish soldier who might stumble over their attempted exit?

With workmen inspecting the foundations of the Temple Mount after the collapse of the southern wall, with Israeli army units in possession of their location and scouring the maze of tunnels under the Temple Mount, the team knew they had to get out quickly. But it was now a sure bet, with the sun up and the Mount the focus of attention, that they couldn't get out the way they had come in. They were trapped, holding the greatest secret of the last thousand years, unless they could find another way out. So they prayed.

Almost immediately, stunning the other two, Bohannon released their hands, grabbed the satellite phone and dialed the States, connecting with a journalism buddy now heading up PR for a massive, multinational firm. *If he has the access I think he has . . .*

As soon as Bohannon hung up, he immediately began praying again. Within minutes, the phone beeped a return call. On the other end of the call was Alexander Krupp, CEO of Krupp Industries, the European industrial giant, and

Bohannon's Sigma Pi "little brother" when both attended Penn State University. Krupp Industries, manufacturer of steel, arms, oil refineries, and a laundry list of other government essentials, exercised incredible clout in the Middle East. Because it helped bring home the oil on which the prosperity of the Arab states depended, and because it manufactured some of the finest and most dependable armaments in the world upon which the safety of Israel depended, officers of the conglomerate were on friendly terms with every government and every significant organization outside of government in the Middle East.

Bohannon quickly summarized the situation for Krupp, who didn't ask any questions as the story unfolded. "Alex, I'm sorry to get you involved in this. The whole thing seems to be blowing up. But I didn't know anyone else to call. You know this area. You know these people. I'm hoping you can help us get out of here in one piece."

A momentary silence on the other end filled the line, and Bohannon feared he had misjudged his relationship with Krupp, whom he hadn't seen in several years.

"This situation sure has changed, Tom. In the past, it was always you rescuing me. I'm glad you called. I believe I can help."

Bohannon's heart leaped with hope, and his eyes lit up with promise.

"Listen, Tom, the southern wall of the Temple Mount has collapsed, probably because of all the rain."

"Yeah, we know that," said Bohannon. "We picked it up on the GPS we have."

"Well, as soon as we heard about the wall coming down, I called the Israeli Interior Minister directly and offered the help of our engineers and crews. We've been building a chemical refinery outside Jericho, and we've had to do a lot of work shoring up hillsides. We just airlifted in additional crews of men and engineers for this job, along with a load of equipment, and they were sitting at the airport, waiting to be transported to the work site. The minister was grateful for the help, and our crews are on their way. They should be there any moment. Listen, this is what I want you to do."

〜〜〜〜

The light, more than the dark, tripped the alarms in Sergeant Gefen's brain. He was nearly motionless as he began to scan the large hall he and his men had reached. Embracing the shadows, Gefen trained his night-vision on the large mound of rubble at the northwest corner of the room and the six Arab men who were carefully inspecting the debris. He flashed six fingers to his squad leader, who passed the info down the line. Gefen then signaled for silence, and was out, into the hall, without a sound. Eight Israeli soldiers followed, each without a sound. In the half-light of the large room, nine shadows fanned out unobserved. The Arabs were stirring up so much dust it was as if the Israelis were moving in a cloud. Gefen was only two feet from his mark when a rock broke loose, the Arab stumbled and looked back into the dust cloud. Before any sound could escape his open mouth, Gefen had a blade to his throat and had fired two shots into the ceiling. Each of the other Arabs were stunned when they turned and found the point of an Israeli muzzle.

————〰〰————

Minutes later, three large, industrial trucks pulled up on the Ha'ofel Road and quickly disgorged more than two-dozen workmen. The trucks were covered in canvas, and the workers covered in overalls, each a pale blue with the giant, orange "KI," for Krupp Industries emblazoned as a signature. With few words and even less wasted motion, the workers rapidly split into pairs: six pairs grabbing steel bracing beams, and the other six pairs gathering up various tools, implements, and coils of wound, steel cable. All twelve teams broke into a trot, hustling to the southern wall as quickly as they could.

With a precision that was remarkable to observe, the Krupp crews swiftly had the six bracing beams positioned against the remaining upright sections of the southern wall. While six teams jogged back to the trucks for more steel beams, the remaining workers began drilling holes for the anchors and unraveling steel cable. A growing crowd of both soldiers and civilians anxiously watched the efforts of the Krupp crews as they scrambled all around the southern wall—the parts that remained standing and those that had collapsed in wildly strewn, massive stones. Engrossed by the flurry of activity unfolding in front of them, none of the bystanders paid any attention to the two workers with the large tool bags who appeared to be inspecting the wall farther to the south. Moments later, if anyone had bothered to look, the two workmen slipped out of sight as if by magic.

————〰〰————

Rodriguez, Johnson, and Bohannon rapidly stowed all of their gear following the conversation with Krupp, paying special attention to ensuring the video equipment was adequately padded. Urgency marked their movements. Bohannon, as he began climbing down the wall face, tried earnestly to keep that urgency from turning to panic.

They heard shots fired somewhere in the distance as Bohannon completed the call. Now they were running for their lives, for their only possible means of escape. But they were only running in their minds. Physically, they were inching along the narrow crevice, pushing themselves through this crushingly small space, striving to reach the tunnel they had entered outside the Hall of the Sanhedrin, the one they believed—hoped—would take them down to the Huldah Gates, to the escape route, before they were cut off by Israeli soldiers or Arab zealots.

Krupp had warned them. They must get to the base of the Huldah Gates tunnel within the next thirty minutes, before his engineers and workmen completed their emergency repairs to the southern wall. "Get to the base of the tunnel," Krupp had said, "and I will get you out safely. But you must move quickly."

Bohannon's brain was about to burst. *How can I move quickly, when I can barely move at all?* He heard Joe and Doc behind him, scratching along the surface of the crevice. They agreed that silence would be necessary, so Bohannon wrestled mightily with the urge to call back over his shoulder, to encourage Joe and Doc to a pace he couldn't keep himself. Then he saw the light, and he pushed ahead with even more vigor to the edge of the tunnel. Searching carefully from his concealed location, Bohannon could neither see any movement, nor hear any sounds in the tunnel that led to the Huldah Gates. He looked at his watch. *Only ten minutes,* he groaned inwardly.

Bohannon squeezed himself out of the crevice, pulled out his backpack, and then began pulling against the rope that Rodriguez had connected to all three men. Straining against the rope, Bohannon could feel Doc Johnson moving, but not moving fast enough. *C'mon . . . c'mon!* Eight minutes left.

⁓⌇⌇⁓

Sergeant Gefen procrastinated for a few, long minutes. There was no explanation. Yet, there had to be an explanation.

Just as the Arabs were doing when they arrived, Gefen and his squad scoured this huge hall, looking for an escape route. The Americans had been here. He was sure of it. The coordinates matched what he was given. The dust of centuries was noticeably disturbed, not just by Arab sandals, but also by men in hiking boots. The Americans had been here. But Gefen had no idea where they had gone.

〜〜〜

They were an unsightly and comical trio, trying to perfect an impossible balancing act. Bohannon and Rodriguez each grasped one of Johnson's arms. They were trying to guide him around the endless, wildly strewn, massive stones that littered the tunnel's descent to the Huldah Gates. The well-intentioned support only made Johnson's task that much more difficult, because it was near impossible to keep control of his backpack, now bouncing wildly side-to-side since he had no control of his outstretched arms. Each time one of his rescuers tugged at one of his arms, his balance would be abruptly destroyed and the backpack would go flying in the opposite direction as Johnson was shunted around another obstacle.

In the midst of this game of human Ping-Pong, flinging the flailing body of Doc Johnson down the tunnel ahead of them, Johnson nearly crushed a man in pale blue overalls.

〜〜〜

Less than forty minutes after they disappeared from view, the missing Krupp workers appeared again at the far southern edge of the southern wall. But this time, there were five workers, all of them in pale blue Krupp overalls, all of them carrying bulging tool bags. All five men had their heads down, straining against the weight in their bags. But all five were also listening for any shout of alarm. No warning shout came. No one noticed that two men had gone in, and five had come out.

Quickly, silently, the five melted into the rest of the Krupp team, which was now tightening the tension on the steel cables that kept the crisscrossed steel bracing in place while others gathered up the tools and leftover material and began returning them to the trucks.

In less than an hour, Krupp's engineers and crews stabilized the remaining sections of the southern wall, gathered up their tools and materials, and were on their way . . . this time with three extra workers on the trucks. The convoy returned to the airport where a Krupp A-70 cargo jet was still unloading steel to be used in the chemical refinery, the team's original mission. While most of the overall-clad workers commenced loading the steel beams onto the trucks, three walked up the ramp into the gaping maw of the super-hauler, the jet's only cargo on its return trip to Germany.

Strapped into a rudimentary jump seat, Bohannon looked out a small window at the rapidly receding countryside of Israel. He should be happy to be out of those caves alive. He should be ecstatic with the discovery they had made and the evidence he carried. He should feel vindicated that there would be many perplexed looks and frustrated conversations in the offices of Shin Bet and the Northern Islamic Front, demanding to know what happened to the three Americans who were so recently trapped under the Temple Mount and the tunnels that snaked under its surface.

But those were not the thoughts that filled Bohannon's mind as the plane disappeared into a cloud bank. He thought of Sammy and Kallie Nolan and wondered if they were safe. He thought of Winthrop Larsen and his critically important help. He thought gratefully of Uncle Ethan and Sam Reynolds at the State Department, and wondered if they would be caught in the middle of what the general expected would be "a spittin' storm." Not for the first time, he thought of Annie and their children, of Deirdre, and wondered if Rory O'Neill had been able to keep them safe. And he attached a prayer to each of his thoughts.

He was still thinking of others when his body finally shut down, and in spite of the incredibly uncomfortable chair and the spiderweb of straps holding him in place, he collapsed into a fitful, manic sleep.

PART THREE

PROPHECY
FULFILLED

47

Bohannon could see the sunshine, feel its warmth, before he opened his eyes. Its power penetrated through his eyelids, calling him to wakefulness. He was wrapped in a soft, safe cocoon and was unwilling to leave its embrace. Slowly, his consciousness was coaxed to meet the morning. Or was it morning? It could be any time during the day. Bohannon had lost all conception of time over the previous five days. It was a bed. Crisp, clean, white sheets and comforter, soft down pillow. *I think I'll just roll over for a moment.*

The sun was setting when his eyes opened once again. This time, the growling in his stomach and the inevitable "call of the wild" required Bohannon to reluctantly get back on his feet. His room was really a suite in a castle, with every modern amenity. He used the most basic. Clean clothes were waiting for him when he came out of the shower in his private bathroom. Piles of food were waiting for him when he finally ventured down the great stairs and was directed into the conservatory by the respectful and attentive staff. Krupp and his wife, Maria, were sitting in wicker chairs in a corner, reading, waiting for their guests to appear.

—∿∿—

The stars were out, the team reunited, and their bellies were full. Now, with the equipment assembled, Alex and Maria Krupp were the only audience for their world premier. Using their maps, supported by their GPS units, the three men unraveled their tale from the first discovery at the Bowery Mission, their adventures in trying to discern the scroll's message, the threats against their lives and Winthrop's murder, through to the harrowing two days racing around Jerusalem and the sometimes frightening three days under the Temple Mount. As the story unfolded, Bohannon was stunned to realize that he had been gone from New York City for a week. It felt like seven years, not seven days. Bohannon was drawn from his reverie when Rodriguez, who talked the Krupps through the Hall of the Sanhedrin and the crushing crevice, looked his way, expecting his brother-in-law to pick up the story.

The utter unreality of the situation nearly caused Bohannon to laugh out loud. Here he was, a guy who managed a homeless ministry in Manhattan, in what was essentially an ancient castle in the depths of Bavaria, sitting across from one of the richest and most powerful men in the world, asking him to believe that what he was about to see was a one-thousand-year-old secret that could change the course of history.

If Bohannon watched this on television, he never would believe it possible. How could he expect anyone as savvy as Krupp to believe this unbelievable story?

"Go on, Tom," Krupp said, apparently guessing what Bohannon was thinking. "Don't leave us breathlessly on the cliff."

Dressed in somebody else's clothes, Bohannon felt like a disembodied voice-over providing the commentary for a documentary, for a story that wasn't even his.

"We didn't know what to do . . ."

"So we prayed," Joe said suddenly, then looked sheepishly at his brother-in-law.

"Yeah, so we prayed," said Tom, running his hand through his hair. "And I got this sense that we needed to climb up. I could see, in my mind, a shaft, above us, and we needed to get to that shaft. Then there was a hole in the wall of the shaft. I don't know, it was as if I had a road map in my mind. Anyway, this is what we saw when we sent the camera through the hole."

Bohannon pushed the Play button on the recorder. All five of them were sitting on the edges of their seats, Krupp and his wife holding hands. Bohannon held his breath as the picture brightened. His chest constricted with sudden fear. *Was it really there?*

"Oh!" Maria Krupp's hand was covering her mouth, her eyes wide and staring, transfixed to the image pulsating on their plasma. Bohannon turned from Maria's shock. Krupp had risen from his chair, hands on his hips, concentrating on every line and shape in the pictures. He had the presence of a predator, the pointed focused concentration of an eagle preparing to pierce its victim. Krupp kept leaning in from his waist, closer and closer each moment, until it appeared he was going to launch himself through the screen.

"How do I know," Krupp started, pointing to the television. He turned to Bohannon, the elegance of his casual clothes trumped by the wild uncertainty on his face. "How do I know . . ."

"That it's real?" Bohannon finished. "Watch, listen."

They watched the second series of video, the one with the GPS coordinates and time recorded by the camera, the one with Sam Reynolds verifying date and time, the one that forced Krupp into an unusual position, sitting cross-legged on the floor, transfixed by this most unorthodox of shows.

The image on the screen faded from an underground Temple to gray fuzz, a rude intruder into the somber silence of Krupp's study. No one was interested in the Black Forest oak that lined the walls, or with the sealed, softly lit, glass-encased resting place of the Guttenberg Bible. All eyes remained on the empty screen as if they were expecting something magical to materialize.

Krupp broke the spell, turning while still sitting on the floor. "I'm sorry, Tom."

He got up and stepped over to his wife, held her hands, got down on one knee, and whispered in her ear, leaving Bohannon to wonder what Krupp was apologizing for. When Maria got up and, without a word, left the room, Bohannon had more to wonder about. He didn't have long to wait.

"I believed everything you told me," said Krupp, pulling his chair closer to theirs, "but I didn't believe that you actually found a hidden temple. I kept thinking"—he clasped his hands behind his head and stretched his neck—"that you found something, but once I got you back here to reality and out of that insane situation under the Temple Mount, we would discover that it was per-haps some other, ancient, forgotten building, or some strange illusion. Any-thing. But the Temple of God? No, that would be impossible."

His eyes closed, Krupp continued to stretch his neck, first to one side, then the other. "No, I didn't believe you found the Temple. I'm sorry, Tom. I shouldn't have doubted you."

Bohannon put his hand on Krupp's right arm. "That's okay, Alex. I was there, and I don't believe it, either."

Hidden away in the luxurious family estate of Alexander Krupp, located deep in the Ruhr Valley in southern Germany, near the medieval town of Fussen, Bohannon felt safe for the first time in months. It was a well-protected enclave with a sophisticated level of security, befitting a billionaire industrialist, putting them all at ease. So it was with a growing sense of dread that Bohannon registered the fear in his friend's eyes.

"Alex, what's wrong? Why did you ask Maria to leave?" said Bohannon.

"I didn't ask her to leave," said Krupp, rising again from his chair and crossing to the wall of windows that separated them from the outdoors. "I asked her to contact our security chief. We're going to need more men."

48

The next morning, Rodriguez and Johnson were out on the terrace, consuming vast amounts of delicious wurst and fried eggs, washing it down with vast amounts of freshly brewed Bavarian coffee, celebrating their deliverance from granola bars and trail mix. But Krupp steered Bohannon to his private study, overwhelmed with what he had seen the night before, and alarmed at its meaning.

"Here, Tom . . . please, have a seat." Krupp had lived here all his life and was quite comfortable in his home. It was only others who would gasp, gape, and fawn over tapestries from the ninth century; ancestral portraits by Holbein, Rembrandt, and Sir Thomas Lawrence; and a fifteen-thousand-volume library. To Krupp, it was a place of quiet retreat.

Now, with Bohannon sitting beside him, Krupp had a difficult time not flashing back to his years at Penn State, years of freedom, adventure, academic exploration, and a camaraderie that Krupp experienced neither before nor after his undergraduate days. Initially, the transition from feudal lord to foreign geek had been embarrassing, disheartening, and painful. Then Bohannon came along, threw a mantle of protection around Krupp's carrottop, and escorted him into the best time of his life. Through their years in University Park, Bohannon was the only true friend Krupp encountered. Bohannon wasn't interested in his money, his power, or his family. They liked each other from the first moment, and soon became nearly inseparable. In this moment, Krupp realized how much he missed Bohannon, how much he missed their youth, and just how much he truly loved his friend.

"Tom," he said, resting his hand on Bohannon's arm, "what you men discovered under the Temple Mount is incredible, absolutely astonishing. I've seen it, and I am still having difficulty believing that it is true. But," said Krupp, "this discovery is also incredibly dangerous, not just for you and the others, but for the rest of the world. Do you know what might happen when this discovery is revealed?"

"We've played out many different scenarios over the past few months, but"— Bohannon scratched the back of his head—"I don't think we really know what to expect. All of us, including Sammy Rizzo and Winthrop Larsen, were simply driven to find out if the message of the scroll was true. If the Temple was there, we believed it would change the past, the present, and the future. How, or how much, we didn't have a clue. Except, we figured it would be significant."

"Significant? Classic understatement. Yes, it will be significant." Krupp arose from the tufted leather armchair and crossed to a long, dark wooden table with huge legs, each one ending in an enormous lion's paw. It was the table that King Leopold of Austria used to play host to Richard the Lion-heart, upon his return from the Crusades.

"Tom, discovery of the Third Temple could propel all of us into a world-wide conflict, possibly a global nuclear war. I'm serious," Krupp said, seeing the look of skepticism in his friend's eyes. "This discovery changes everything."

Krupp came back to his chair and looked Bohannon straight in the eye.

"Tom, did you know that there are Israeli groups who have been preparing for generations for the creation of the Third Temple, and that religious Jews are already prepared to hold ritual sacrifice in the Temple as soon as it is restored? We do so much of our business in the Middle East, for both sides, that we have come to know any group that could be a destabilizing threat to our commerce.

"There is a group called the Temple Institute who have already manufac-tured all of the implements and created all of the clothing that would be neces-sary for the Jewish priesthood to hold ritual sacrifice, including the bronze altar, the great basin, even the high priest's breastplate. While the institute believes the Temple will emerge in God's time and Jews should not force the issue, they have completed all of the implements needed for an immediate activation of Temple rights.

"There is another group, Atteret Cohanim Yeshiva, that is located in the Old City, close to the northwest corner of the Temple Mount. This is a school that identifies Jewish men who qualify for the priesthood and then trains them to carry out duties according to the Scriptures and the Talmud. Many of the Atteret Cohanim are quite radical, and some believe that Jerusalem should be free of all non-Jews. One of their rabbis is the brother of Meir Kahane, the assas-sinated radical whose organization, "Kahane Chai," is classified by Shin Bet as an illegal terrorist organization.

"Then, you've got the Temple Mount Faithful, a loosely affiliated group of

Jews and Christians who march on Jerusalem several times a year and attempt to bring their so-called 'Cornerstone' of the Third Temple with them. Of course, the police refuse them entry, but the Faithful believe we cannot wait for the Messiah and must immediately build the Third Temple. Worst of all is the Jewish Underground, an illegal group that may have disbanded, or may simply be inactive, who tried in the past to blow up Muslim structures on the Temple Mount. Many of their members were arrested and imprisoned, but their vow is to rebuild the Temple and destroy the Muslim presence on the Mount.

"And those," said Krupp, pointing emphatically at his listener, "are only the groups we know about. There are likely others, splinter groups or hidden cells who hold views just as radical and just as radically opposed to each other. You know of the Northern Islamic Front, which wants to obliterate any evidence that the Jewish Temple ever existed atop the Temple Mount.

"Tom, Jerusalem is the most hate-filled, six-square miles on earth. A false rumor sparks ferocious riots. What do you think revelation of an existing Third Temple would do?"

Bohannon slumped. "So, this is a disaster? All we've done is to discover a disaster?"

Krupp smiled. He wanted his friend to understand the full measure, not only of his discovery, but also its implications. But now, he needed to give him another picture of the future, a picture that would give Krupp an opportunity to repay an old debt. Here was a reality he never expected to see, a chance, at last, for his family to wash away the guilt they still felt for the war crimes committed by his grandfather, who was convicted of using slave labor and terrible brutality in his factories while supporting the Third Reich in World War II.

Krupp swung his chair around so he could face Bohannon directly.

"Tom, yes, this discovery could have grave consequences. It could blow up the world. But"—and the smile filled his face again—"I have a different plan. Tom, I think your discovery could bring about ultimate, world peace. Let's go join your friends. I have a proposition to make."

⌇⌇⌇

"The lightning rod for war between Israelis and Arabs has always been the fate of the Temple Mount and Jerusalem," Krupp said with an earnestness that soon had each of them transfixed. "Each side has demanded the same thing because each side needed the same thing to fulfill the exercise of its religion—control of the Temple Mount. Now, with this secret, but existing, Temple, you have created a bargaining chip that just may bring about peace in the Middle East."

The three Americans sat looking at Krupp with furrowed brows.

"I know, I know. On the surface, the existence of the Third Temple seems to guarantee an explosion in the ongoing conflict between Arab and Israeli," said Krupp. "But don't let yourselves get caught up in stereotypes.

"If the Jewish Temple was already established, and it did not threaten the Dome of the Rock or the Al-Aqsa Mosque and—a big *and*, I may add—if the Israelis could convince the Muslims that they would, jointly, ensure the safety of the entire Mount and the freedom of all to worship in their appointed shrines, then each side would be presented with a way out of the current, endless fighting and death. Or at least, a first step that Israelis and Muslims could take together.

"Muslims could worship on the top of the Mount; Jews could worship under the Mount; and Jerusalem could be opened, once more, as an international city where Christian, Jew, and Arab could coexist."

Krupp got up from his chair and walked over to a small table deep in the shade of the terrace. He poured himself some tea, over ice, and added a slice of lemon.

"You may not be aware of this," he said, returning to his cushioned chair, "but a majority of the Israelis could care less about the Temple, whether it exists or doesn't exist. But they do care about peace, about an end to this endless season of fear, bloodshed, and hate.

"Israelis are essentially divided into three basic positions, and about ten million smaller ones," Krupp explained. "The religious, the nominal, and the secular Jew.

"Religious Jews—whether orthodox, ultraorthodox, national religious, or Sephardic orthodox—are a minority in the entire Jewish population of Israel, yet a slim but growing majority in Jerusalem. The basic ideology of the religious Jews is that the culmination of the Zionist dream is a Torah-abiding nation of Jews, a people who are as religious as they are. Religious Jews believe that one day there will again be a temple in Jerusalem, but this will come about at the time of the Messiah. Truthfully, rabbinic Judaism is not wholly prepared to face the idea of a renewed ritual sacrifice, and the Temple is, at present, only a sentimental hope for the future. But if the Temple actually existed, it would be enthusiastically accepted and embraced by the religious Jews.

"Now," said Krupp, warming to his explanation, "if only nonreligious citizens were counted, nominal Jews would make up slightly less than half of Israel's total population. Nominal Jews do not oppose the idea of a temple, on the grounds that it probably shouldn't be opposed by Jews, but neither do they hope for one. The Temple is considered a historical thing that will probably never be rebuilt, but whose restoration should be prayed for during Passover and the High Holy Days . . . if one ever decides to go to a synagogue. If the Temple were to be rebuilt, it would simply introduce yet another difficult burden into their lives."

With a pinched, thoughtful look on his face, Krupp reached for a small portion of wurst on the tray between them, dipped it in mustard, and chewed on it absently for a moment. In the shade, there was still a nip of chill to the air, and he wished he had thought to throw a sweater over his shoulders. But that was really the least of his concerns.

"Now, the secular Jews, the secular Jews are a problem." He looked at his now-yellow fingers and reached for a napkin. "Secular Jews are the majority in Israel. And for them, the idea of a temple is simply a no-go. If a temple were to be rebuilt, this group would actively oppose it and possibly even call for a separate state. Secular Jews would consider animal sacrifices a strange, ancient form of religious barbarism and would argue vociferously that sacrifice can hardly be tolerated in a modern and progressive society. They would quite likely march on the Knesset and demand legislation preventing religious coercion while, at the same time—and, yes, this is a bit schizophrenic—demanding their right for open access to the Temple and Western Wall for cultural and historical reasons. We could reasonably expect large groups of vegetarians and animal rights activists demanding protection for sheep and other possible ritual victims."

"Man, I thought Americans were nuts," said Rodriguez, stretching himself and rising to a seated position on the lounge chair.

"True," said Krupp pensively, appearing to agree with Rodriguez's assessment. "But the animal activists will not be the greatest threat to gaining agreement between the Jews and the Arabs. In the middle of any turmoil caused by the secular Jews, the question of a high priest will come up. The Atteret Cohanim Yeshiva in the Old City will undoubtedly claim exclusive rights to choose the high priest for the Temple, Maimonides' rules for the priesthood will reemerge, and a million rabbis will probably spout two million opinions about what should be done with the Temple, who should do it, and when it should happen.

"In short," Krupp said wistfully, "uncovering a temple will probably result in a period of chaos among the Israelis, not to mention the possibility of being on the brink of a world war with the Muslim world. So presenting the possibility for a peace treaty might not only be a welcome diversion, but could also settle on fertile soil."

Krupp shifted on his chair, leaned forward, and settled his elbows on his knees.

"I know, personally, all of the major players in the Middle East. And they, personally, are all indebted to me. Our firm has bailed out each and every one of them at one time or another. I've bailed them out myself. If anybody can get these hardheaded, prideful, determined leaders to even consider sitting down and talking about peace, I believe I have the influence to see that accomplished. All of them need Krupp Industries; none of them can afford to be on our bad side. So they will listen. Whether they commit or not, well, that is in God's hands. But they will listen.

"My question," he said, searching each of their faces, "is whether you will give me permission to make those calls."

He paused for a moment. Krupp knew that even he didn't understand all the possible ramifications of this discovery.

"Once I make these calls, the genie is out of the lamp. There will be no going back. This discovery of yours will take on a life of its own. None of us," Krupp said emphatically, "can predict where that life will lead. It may lead to peace. It may lead to a nuclear conflict that would annihilate the nations of the Middle East. It may lead to a consequence that we have not even considered. As you've said, there is already more than one group that has attempted to stop you. So we will be at risk, each of us and millions of other innocents in and around Israel."

Krupp could feel the knot in his stomach tightening. "So the question is, do we really want to do this? Do we have any idea what we are getting ourselves into? Are we okay with the possible consequences?" he asked staring each man in the eyes.

Johnson turned in his chair to the right of Krupp and looked at Bohannon for a long moment. Krupp watched as Johnson then turned to Rodriguez, caught his gaze, and held it silently. Then, he turned back to Krupp. "Herr Krupp, we left one of our friends in a coffin back in the United States because he believed this quest was worth the risk. Another, Sammy Rizzo, was severely wounded a few nights ago in an ambush aimed to take our lives. We still don't know what happened to Sammy and Kallie Nolan. Kallie may be forced to leave her home, her job, and her dreams because she helped us. Frankly, I don't believe it will be possible for the existence of a temple to be kept secret. But even if it was, what other choice do we have at this point except to make public our findings? Too great a price has been paid to find the Temple, to keep it a secret now. Besides, what other chance is there for peace in the Middle East? The Israeli-Arab confrontation will inevitably explode, and when it does, it will take millions of lives with it. At least now, with the Temple, there is a chance for peace. A chance that everything we know about life in the Levant could change in an instant, hopefully for the better." Johnson again swept his gaze across the faces of his friends. In all of them, Krupp saw both undeniable grief and incredible hope. His heart stalled, mourned, and hoped with them.

"We have all agreed to see this through to the end," said Johnson. "We're not there yet, so there are more steps to be taken. Please, make the calls. And then we can all hope in Tom's faith that God is in control. Because, now, we will need that divine intervention you told me about, Tom."

Krupp set his jaw and nodded his head. This was the moment.

"Guys," Bohannon said softly, "would you mind if I said a prayer?"

In the silence and the shade of the terrace, Krupp joined the others. He bowed his head, opened his heart, and waited to see if God would show up.

49

Using all of his billion-dollar clout, Krupp was immediately on the telephone across the secure lines he used for his most sensitive communications, speaking with the prime minister of Israel. Krupp proposed a secret meeting in Switzerland, to convene in no less than seven days, bringing the key Arab and Israeli decision-makers together in one room. His enticement was that they could, possibly, walk out of the meeting with a secure and lasting peace for the Middle East.

"Mr. Prime Minister, I know there is an inherent danger in this," said Krupp. "I admit I could be wrong. But at the same time, I am also convinced that this may be our best hope, our last hope, to discover what has been impossible to discover for generations. A road not only to peace, but also to peaceful coexistence for Jew and Arab in Jerusalem, in Israel, in Palestine. Eliazar, this could be your moment to change history. For your children, Eliazar, for all our children, come to Switzerland."

Krupp could nearly touch the tension and fear on the other end of the line.

"You may be asking for the impossible, Mr. Krupp. I'm sure you understand the dangerous implications of what you are proposing. If you gave them a choice, half of Israel would vote against a temple. And you really think there is a possibility the Arabs won't respond even more emphatically? This is foolishness. Alexander, you cannot ask me to make this decision."

"Mr. Prime Minister, with all due respect, this is a decision you cannot avoid," Krupp pleaded. "These men told me the Arabs were also pursuing them. Why would that be, except to keep this discovery from becoming public? They know. At least two Arab groups out there know what these men were seeking and that it's possible they found. How can any of us keep the existence of the Temple a secret? In today's world? Where everyone appears to have their own blog up and running on the Internet? No, my friend, this is not a time to dwell on our concerns; it's a time for practical politics and unprecedented diplomacy. We have the chance for peace. Something none of us ever expected. Eliazar, you and I have admitted that we both feared the endgame with the Arabs was inevitable. Well, perhaps we will face it sooner than we expected. But, Mr. Prime Minister, we must allow ourselves to take a step for peace, when peace is possible. Peace is worth a risk, is it not?"

As Krupp gauged the responding silence, he felt the eyes, and the hopes, of Bohannon, Rodriguez, and Johnson on the back of his neck, but he dared not turn to meet their fear.

"Alexander, you must do two things before I can give you an answer. First, you must provide me evidence that what you say is true. Forgive me, my friend. It's not that I doubt your honesty or your sincerity. But I would be a fool to move forward with this request of yours unless I had conclusive proof in my hands that this Temple exists. How you get that proof to me, I don't know. But nothing will happen without it. Secondly, if we receive such proof, I must require you to keep this conversation confidential for the time being. I imagine you were prepared to make additional calls to our neighbors to enlist their participation, correct?"

"Yes," said Krupp, "I already prepared lines to contact King Parvez in Jordan and President Ghasaan in Egypt."

"You must not, you must promise me that, Alexander," said Baruk. "I must consult my cabinet and my military leaders. I can't take this step alone. That would be political suicide. You know that. We must have at least twelve hours of silence once we receive your evidence. I have no other choice. These two things I must demand."

Krupp was faced with an impasse. Refuse the prime minister's demands and this whole thing would blow up. He would not only alienate the Israelis, but he could also give them an excuse for considering a preemptive, first strike against the Arab states—get in the first punch if it was going to come to a nuclear punching match. In spite of the warm sunshine flooding into the room, he shuddered.

"Yes, Mr. Prime Minister, I agree," said Krupp. "We will transmit to you, electronically, as much of the existing evidence as we possibly can. Once we've received confirmation that you received the evidence, we'll just hunker down until we hear from you. And, Eliazar . . ."

"Yes?"

"Thank you. Thank you, Eliazar."

"Farewell, Alexander."

It took an hour to decide what they needed to send to the prime minister and how they were going to transmit it. With technological skill and dexterity,

Rodriguez took point on the assembly and transmission of the material, just enough to conclusively prove the accuracy and validity of their discovery—photos, sections of the video with the GPS units, the voice transmission from Sam Reynolds.

Then they waited.

—⌁⌁⌁—

Baruk pushed the button, ending the conference call, and looked around the table at his closest advisors.

No one blinked.

"Lukas, now you know where they are," said the prime minister, endorsing the blank check he had presented to the Mossad chief not that long ago. "How long before you can have mission planning complete and a force in the air?"

"Our teams have been ready to go since your first orders," replied Painter. "All we need to know is where and when you would like us to intercept them."

"Intercept?" Baruk physically recoiled in his chair. "No, let me be more precise, Mr. Director. How long before you have wheels up for an operation into Germany? You have eleven hours and fifty-seven minutes to silence these men, however that may be necessary, and to recover all of their evidence. How soon will you be airborne?"

Baruk liked Lukas Painter, very much. Lukas was a no-nonsense man who got things done. A man in whom Baruk could put his trust.

"We'll be off the ground within the hour," Painter said. "Mission planning will be completed while we're in the air. We will send two Gulfstreams, private, no markings, across the Mediterranean and come in from the west to Calvi, in Corsica. Businessmen, en route to Munich. We will refuel in Calvi and do a HALO drop along the border of Austria and Germany, somewhere in the vicinity of Fussen." Painter pursed his lip, glanced at the ceiling, then looked at his watch. "We will be on the ground, and on the move, in Germany by eighteen hundred hours, seven hours from now. By twenty hundred hours, the information should be in our possession."

Baruk cast a withering look at Painter. "By twenty hundred hours the information *must* be in your hands. There is no alternative."

"Yes, sir," said Lukas Painter, who was out of his seat and out the door before his voice faded from the room.

"Chaim," Baruk said to his chief of staff, "I know it is very early in Washington, but please see if you can reach Jonathan Whitestone. I would very much like to speak to the American president."

—∿∿∿—

Krupp led Bohannon down the steps from the terrace, along the outskirts of the swimming pool compound, and out into the gardens, a carefully sculpted riot of color stretching for hundreds of yards. They turned a corner at the end of a hedge more than six feet tall. Behind the hedge was a hothouse—half glass-domed nursery, half gardener's workplace. Krupp entered the potter's shed, Bohannon in tow, and pointed to a rack of work clothes and overalls. "Better to make yourself comfortable. We're going to get dirty."

Shouldering a bag of tools, hefting a wheelbarrow that held a spade and stacked racks of ruby red geraniums, Krupp wordlessly rolled into the depths of the garden. Unlike the searing heat of Jerusalem, summer was just breaking on Bavaria. The tulips and daffodils remained colorful, but were in their final moments of life. Mountain laurel had long lost its blooms. So the beds were being filled with yellow marigolds, purple salvia, mixed impatiens in the shade, and, Krupp's favorite, thousands of red geraniums. Most of them he had planted himself.

"This is my therapy," he said over his shoulder, pointing Bohannon to an open space in the flower bed. "This is where I can think, where I can put everything else out of my head except dirt, sun, rain, and weeds." Following the call to Baruk, Krupp needed something to take his mind off the twelve-hour wait. He believed that time was of the essence, that any delay now only invited calamity. But here in Bavaria, for Krupp and his guests, all they could do was wait, hope, and pray. And try to keep themselves busy. "It's simple, straightforward, and has the benefit of immediate gratification. Dig the dirt, plant the flowers, bring the water, and you have beauty all summer. I wish all things in life were this simple. Here, let me give you a hand."

Smiling at Bohannon's awkwardness around plants, Krupp lifted one of the flats of geranium plants and carried it to a large bed of soft, loamy soil. "Bring the spade, will you?"

Setting the flat of geraniums at the side of the bed, Krupp took the spade. Quickly, effortlessly, he carved a furrow in the soft earth. "You can do this one of two ways," he said, turning to Bohannon, "the industrial way or the personal way. Using the spade is the industrial way." A more-than-willing instructor, Krupp displayed his technique. "Carve out a furrow; pop the geraniums out of their small pots and into the furrow; slide the spade along the top of the furrow to refill it and cover the root ball.

"We can be careful with life, Tom, savoring it, protecting it, luxuriating in its richness, or, we can rush through life, exchanging quality for quantity, mistaking a completed task for a completed life. Each day is a choice."

Krupp pulled a small hand trowel from the back pocket of his overalls, sat down among the planted geraniums, and waved the trowel in Bohannon's direction. "You have made some interesting choices lately, my friend. What will you choose today? The industrial way," he said, waving his hand at the dozen geranium plants where the furrow once was, "or the personal way?" Turning on his hip, Krupp leaned over to smell the very faint aroma of the geranium. When he turned back, Bohannon had also grabbed a rack of geraniums and was making his way to another spot in the bed. He had no spade.

"Where do I start?" Bohannon asked.

Two hours, and several hundred geraniums later, they were back in the potter's shed, filthy, perspiring, and fully alive. Krupp reached into a corner refrigerator and pulled out two large, very cold bottles of Evian water. He pointed to an open space on the floor, and the two college friends again sat in the dirt, only now they had the potter's bench upon which to rest their backs. The first few minutes belonged to the Evian, which they poured down their throats and over their heads.

Silence. The smell of decomposing loam . . . chatter of birds . . . buzz of insects.

"Thank you." Bohannon turned his head, and Krupp saw profound gratitude returning his gaze. "I feel cleansed. Exhausted, but cleansed. As if the weight of the world has just been lifted off my shoulders. Thank you."

For a moment, Krupp was "Alex K" again, and his heart ached in gratitude for this man who had been so kind, so crucial to him in a very critical time. "There is nothing that you could ever thank me for," said Krupp. "When you became my big brother, it was as if you had placed a wall of protection around me. As if you stamped me with a seal of legitimacy. You helped me gain the confidence to just be myself. I'm serious, Tom. I owe you my life. My wife, my children, all of us are indebted to you. And I will do anything you ask of me to honor that gift."

Bohannon wore an embarrassed, self-conscious look on his face. *Perhaps,* Krupp thought, *I've gone too far. After all, we've only just* . . .

An intercom phone, tucked into a corner of the potting bench, rattled its demand. Pulling himself from his friend's gaze, Krupp reluctantly answered it.

"Yes?" Krupp was quiet, listening, a frown forming at his temples. "Yes, we will be there immediately."

Suddenly, all the peaceful karma of the afternoon dissipated. Krupp's neck stiffened, his heart raced, his breathing shallowed. *What had they done? O, God, what had they done?* It was Krupp, the international billionaire business baron, who turned to face Bohannon. "There is a telephone call in the house," he said sharply. "It is your president." He paused, watching the alarm register in Bohannon's eyes. "He wants to speak to you."

50

Lukas Painter stepped from the plane dressed in an impeccable, black Italian silk suit, tailored in Naples, and a vivid pale green tie designed in Venice. His silver flattop had been slicked into submission with a fistful of mousse. Painter looked like a typical Italian business tycoon, emerging from one of his two private jets. While the planes were being rapidly refueled, Painter approached the French customs official waiting on the tarmac.

"Good afternoon, Gerard," said Painter. "It is a pleasure to see you once more."

"The pleasure is mine," said the official, accepting the envelope containing ten thousand American dollars. *"Bon voyage."*

With that brief exchange, Gerard returned to his office, and Painter returned to the Gulfstream and the eight commandos dressed in an entirely different kind of black suit.

∽∿∾

He had been awake all of the night and most of the day, following the pursuit of the Americans and positioning his men under the Temple Mount. It was time to pray. The Imam took his prayer carpet and climbed the stairs once again to the roof. He never got there.

Twisting past the landing on the upper floor, his foot on the last flight of stairs, the Imam's immaculate white kaftan began sprouting rosettes of red down his chest. *Quite unusual*, he thought as he looked down. It took a moment more, as the red stains began to spread, for the Imam to realize his throat had been slashed. A thought that registered as his body crumpled to the steps, as his eyes locked on a short man, dressed in dusty and tattered clothes, emerging from the shadow of a corner. The Imam noticed the stained, razor-thin blade in his hand, an amulet around his neck and a new, round, brown leather cap on his head. Then his brain stopped, and the Imam's eyes closed forever.

Rasaf was retreating back into the shadows when he heard a gentle cell-phone buzz. Quickly, avoiding the spreading blood, he reached into the kaftan and found the phone. Without hesitation, he pushed Talk.

"Yes?"

A pause. Then an accented voice on the other end made his heart leap. "They are in Germany, in Bavaria, staying at the home of Alexander Krupp, the industrialist. The Israelis have sent a commando strike team to make an incursion, a HALO jump, with the intention of killing these men and seizing all their evidence. They will be on the ground in four hours. Do what you want with the information. It is the last you will receive from me. It is no longer safe. Goodbye."

Rasaf pushed the End button, his mind racing with the new information. *Perhaps all is not lost,* he thought.

Soon, the cell phone was in use again.

When he assumed the office of president of the United States, the voice of Jonathan Whitestone was immediately familiar around the world. Bohannon had no doubt who was on the other end of this phone call.

"Mr. Bohannon, you will not divulge any of the information you have discovered in Israel." No preamble, no pleasantries, no introduction. Bohannon felt as if he had been punched.

"As the commander in chief of the United States of America, I am ordering you to maintain full and complete silence on your claimed discovery. You are to share this information with no one, do you understand me?"

Bohannon was stunned, in body and mind. "Yes, sir," was all he could muster.

"Good," said the president, his voice sounding more relaxed. "Do you have any idea what your discovery could precipitate? You could ignite the complete annihilation of Israel and most of the Middle East. Do you understand that? A nuclear war, that's what we're facing if the Arabs and Israelis get into the ultimate conflict. A war that would not only wipe out all of the Jews and many of the Arab populations, but a war that would also make that region uninhabitable for generations. God knows what a calamity like that might trigger.

"No, sir. You do not have the authority nor the power to make a decision like that," said Whitestone, his voice recovering its menace. "Who has elected you to make a decision that could cost millions of lives? No one, Mr. Bohannon. No one. You will keep this information to yourself, and you will return to the United States immediately. Or you, and your partners, could spend the rest of your lives in prison. Do you understand, Mr. Bohannon?"

When he had been a journalist, there had been a few foolish souls who tried to bully Bohannon off a story. He grew weary of threats, especially when they came from self-important politicians who were trying to save their hides and their reputations. Threats only made Bohannon dig deeper, look further, turn over more rocks. Threats always meant there was more to the story than he was seeing at the time, that he was close to something really big. Threaten him, and Bohannon became a task-oriented predator, preparing for battle with an adversary.

That same Tom Bohannon came to the surface as the president of the United States tried to fill him with fear. Clarity filled his mind while caution seasoned his thoughts, his instincts pencil-point sharp.

"Mr. President, I understand you fully . . ."

"Good," said the president.

"However, Mr. President," Bohannon said, carefully choosing his words, "I am compelled to remind you, sir, that neither I nor my friends are members of the military. So we are not subject to your authority as commander in chief. In addition, Mr. President, what we do with our private property is our concern—"

"Listen, mister—"

"Mr. President," Bohannon interrupted, "what will you do when a request under the Freedom of Information Act releases the tapes you have just made, threatening American citizens with unwarranted imprisonment?"

With that shot across the bow, Bohannon softened, trying to negotiate for time.

"Mr. President, don't you think we understand the gravity of the situation? Mr. Krupp is intimately aware of the powers and pressures on both sides of the Mideast conflict. And all of us understand the risk of revealing the existence of the Third Temple. But, sir, this could also be an unprecedented opportunity to forge a lasting peace that would benefit generations to come. I understand your concerns, sir. But, respectfully, this is not your decision to make. And trying to pressure us is not going to help. I'm sure your advisors, who are listening in, will agree with me on that."

Bohannon took a breath. Whitestone stepped into it.

"Don't underestimate the power of this office, Mr. Bohannon. You would be surprised how much power I have at my disposal."

"Mr. President, I want you to use your power. But use it for bringing the two sides together in Switzerland. Use it," urged Bohannon, getting out of his chair and beginning to pace, "to help bring about peace."

Bohannon looked at the others as he waited for the president's response, wondering if he had pushed too hard, too far.

"Bohannon, listen to me. There is no time for debate. You're a Christian, you know the clock you will be starting," said Whitestone, purportedly an evangelical Christian and demonstrably an ardent supporter of Israel. "But that's not my concern right now. Right now, I'm concerned about the radical Islamists, the ones who are primed to ignite a holy war and precipitate the slaughter of millions, Jew and Arab alike. You or Mr. Krupp may convince the leaders of Jordan and Egypt to attend your intended summit in Switzerland. You may even convince them there is a solution to the Jerusalem dilemma. But what you will not be able to accomplish is the eradication of Al Qaeda or the dozens of splinter groups who are committed to jihad. Revealing this information is tantamount to lighting a fuse. We don't know how long it will take, but eventually, the flame will reach the explosive. And then, God help us all.

"You can't do this, Tom," said Whitestone, now adding intimacy to the weight of his office. "In all good conscience, Tom, you can't do this. Millions will die if you do. That's all I can say to you. Except, if you go through with this folly, you and your family will feel the displeasure of this government. That's not a threat. It's not a bully tactic. It's just what will happen. Think carefully about what you do next. Please, consider this carefully. Tom . . .

"Sir?"

"Take it to prayer, Tom. Please. That may be our only hope."

"Yes, Mr. President, yes, I will. Thank you, Mr. President."

⚮

Drained, chagrined by his combative attitude toward the president of the United States, Bohannon placed the handset in the cradle and turned to the others. Rodriguez was standing right next to him. "Man, I can't believe how you gave it right back to the president," said Rodriguez, giving Bohannon a chuck on the shoulder. "Hey, you could be from the Bronx."

Bohannon put his hand on Rodriguez's shoulder. "Thanks, Joe. I don't know where that came from."

"He was bullying you, bullying us," said Johnson, joining the other two. "Good for you for standing up to his strong-arm tactics. I was proud of you." Bohannon took Johnson's offered hand, but his eyes sought out Krupp, still seated, hands clasped on top of his head, a wounded grimace on his face.

"Alex, what is it?"

Bohannon led the way to Krupp's side. "What's wrong, Alex? You look like all the air just went out of you."

Krupp ran his hands through his red hair, shaking his head from side-to-side. "I don't like this, I don't like the way it feels. Something is way out of order here."

"What do you suspect, Herr Krupp?" asked Johnson, sitting in the chair next to the industrialist.

"I suspect," said Krupp, "that the Arab groups are not the only ones who are determined to keep this information from becoming public. Two hours ago I call the Israeli prime minister, give him the information, and invite him to Switzerland. Then we get a call from your president, here. How did your president know you were here, in my home?"

"Eliazar Baruk called Mr. Whitestone," said Johnson, stating the obvious.

"Yes, but when?" Krupp asked. "Did he call the president when he and I hung up? Then why did it take the president two hours to contact us here? If Baruk waited for two hours before calling the president, what was he doing with the time? No, both of these men were emphatic, you will not divulge this information; it is of the most dangerous nature. If we don't fall at their feet and promise obedience, what will they do next? Hope for our good faith?"

Krupp's eyes darted to each in turn. "I doubt it. Here is the most powerful man on earth ordering us to back off and that you must return home . . . or what?" He got up and began pacing in front of them. "The highest official in the state of Israel, after Switzerland the most buttoned-up country in the world, tells us he needs twelve hours to make a decision, then calls the president of the United States for muscle? Israel, which sent raiding parties into Uganda, bombed a nuclear energy plant in Syria, and invaded Lebanon for abducting one of its soldiers. Can you believe *that* Israel would just sit back and allow the American government to bail them out?

"Since when did the Israelis ever rely on someone else to take care of their problems? Never. And the Israelis are not going to wait and see what happens, now. The Israelis are on their way here," said Krupp, smacking his left hand with his right fist. "They are coming after you, after all of us. And you can be absolutely certain they are not coming to politely request our evidence. They are coming to wipe all evidence from the face of the earth, including us."

Krupp stopped in mid stride, put his hands on the top of a winged-back armchair, and gathered them all in his icy stare. "They're coming to kill us, and we will get no help from your government. The Israelis could be here in twenty minutes, or in several hours. Whatever we do, we had better do it quickly."

——

Once they entered European airspace, there would be no radio contact, either with the other plane or with Orhlon in Israel. Painter, standing in the doorway between the two pilots, patiently watched as the radar tracked their progress. The blip crossed a white line on the dark screen.

Painter pulled a cell phone out of his pocket. *So simple,* he thought. *With all of our high-tech equipment, this is so simple.*

Painter pushed a button and sent his text message: "Final leg. All well. Down soon." That was it. *Simple. I wish all in life was that simple.*

——

"What are we doing here?" Bohannon asked no one in particular. "How did I ever allow any of us to get into such a mess?"

These men had left their families and risked their lives to pursue something they believed was vitally important. Bohannon was angry with himself and with everyone who tried to stop them. And now this—abandon the pursuit that already cost so much, or face the wrath of both the Israeli and American governments. They had found the Temple. But now, they couldn't tell anybody about it? Heads and spirits were bowed. No one spoke. What could they do against insurmountable opposition? Either their discovery would die, or they would put themselves, their families, who knew what else at significant risk by trying to reveal it. What a waste! Why did they ever get involved in something this crazy to begin with?

Krupp reached out and put his hand on Bohannon's arm. He looked into

Rodriguez's eyes. "No matter what we do," Krupp said quietly, "we are all still at risk. And will always remain at risk simply because of what we know. And that risk will include our families . . . our wives and our children."

"So, gents, this is it," said Rodriguez. "What are we going to do?"

Krupp turned toward Bohannon, rested his other hand on Bohannon's shoulder, and drew him closer. He wanted eyeball-to-eyeball contact.

"Tom, ever since I've known you, there are a couple things I could rely on," said Krupp, embracing Bohannon's mind with his eyes. "One of them was that you would always do the right thing. It didn't matter if it was difficult, didn't matter if it was unpopular. You took the time to find out what the right thing was, and then you went out and did the right thing. Always. Consistently. It was something we could hang our hopes and expectations on."

Krupp reached out with his right hand and gently touched Bohannon's left shoulder.

"Tom, go ahead, do the right thing," said Krupp. "Ask God to tell you the right thing. I know he will. And then, all of us, we'll follow you. All of us, we all want to do the right thing. We just don't know what it is. Will you do it, Tom? Will you ask God for the right thing?"

With a light spirit, but a heavy heart, Bohannon opened his arms. What resulted was a football huddle; four men, their arms resting on each other's shoulders. Three silently supportive, one mumbling for help and guidance, all of them determined to follow.

Moments later, Bohannon opened his squished eyes and saw the other three staring at him. "I just kept thinking of one thing. We have got to go public. Right now, it looks like us against the world. To tell you the truth, I don't see how we'll ever be able to get this information out. We have to go public, but it looks pretty hopeless."

Rodriguez, silent for some time, stepped away from the huddle and crossed to the windows, looking at the faint outline of mountains in the darkening distance. "I know a way."

51

For the next hour and a half, the four men worked feverishly, though separately. Krupp increased security around his estate and, against her wishes, dispatched his wife and children to the farm of his security chief, not too far distant. Bohannon wrote a detailed account of the search for the Temple, from start to finish, and Rodriguez reviewed, edited, and compiled the video evidence of their investigation and discovery, arranging it all in proper order with the help of Johnson.

When all was ready, Krupp opened his direct, secure landline. Within seconds, Rodriguez plugged in his laptop and connected to the Internet, to the worldwide library exchange system that keeps every library in the world updated with cutting-edge technology and the latest information in the world of books.

For a moment, Rodriguez looked up at the faces around him. He took a deep breath. And pushed Send. Instantly, all of the information concerning their discovery of the Third Temple of God, hidden under Jerusalem's Temple Mount, was electronically communicated to every library in the world.

—∿∿—

Less than ten minutes from the jump zone, Painter and his captain reviewed the terrain maps once again, questioning each of the men on their particular assignment and what each would do if everything that could go wrong, went wrong. His men, like those in the other plane, were fully geared-up: high-altitude diving suit, helmet and night-vision goggles, bat-wing mini-chute, and a wide array of ammunition and weapons including, ironically, a nasty little submachine gun manufactured in Bavaria by Krupp Armaments.

—∿∿—

Painter was so focused on studying the map that he was totally unaware of the pilot by his shoulder until he was startled by his touch.

"We've been recalled," said the pilot, handing Painter a piece of paper, returning immediately to his cockpit to calculate fuel and flying time.

Painter looked at the sheet in his hand in disbelief. "The cat is out. Too late. Come home." The message had been sent over regular radio. Obviously, there was no longer any need for secrecy, or any need for their lethal skills.

⸺∿∾⸺

The cell phone in Rasaf's pocket began its incessant rattle. *This one, I will not answer,* he thought, pulling into the parking garage at the airport.

⸺∿∾⸺

Lieutenant Daniel Stern was getting more worried with each passing moment. The Hawk had been apoplectic since the telephone call, screaming at the top of his lungs, smashing his balled fists against anything that entered his orbit.

⸺∿∾⸺

True sleep was impossible, but Kallie was lying on the stainless steel slab that was mockingly called a bed when she heard the click and the faint hiss, and the door to her cell slid silently open. Her breath caught in her throat when the guard called for her to step through the opening.

He was big, not an ounce of fat on his chiseled muscles.

"You are free to go."

It was like a slap in the face, unseen, startling in its speed, stinging in its wake.

"What . . . what . . . what do you mean?" she stammered.

"You are free to go," said Mr. Muscles. "Your clothes and all your belongings are in the dressing room." He pointed down the cell block with his truncheon.

This is a trap. This is a setup, Kallie thought.

"Please, ma'am, this way, please. Your clothes are down here. Then you can go. Please."

With that, Mr. Muscles turned down the cell-block corridor, leaving a dazed and confused Kallie in his wake.

Twenty minutes later when she stumbled out the door and into the bright sun, Kallie still didn't know what was going on. What she did know was the guy standing on the sidewalk across the street, propped against a tree.

"Man," said Rizzo, moving in her direction, "I've had other women keep me waiting, but this was ridiculous."

Rizzo reached up with his hand to steady Kallie as she cleared the last step. "How did you find me?"

"It's amazing what you can dig up on the Internet." Rizzo led Kallie to the rental car. "You've forgotten what a cyber-wizard I am. The Israeli military operates only one prison that can house civilians. From there, it wasn't hard."

Blinking against the sun, Kallie stopped at the passenger-side door. "How long have you been here?"

"Oh, not long," Rizzo waved, "not long at all. Two days, I think. But I was all set to leave. I was only going to wait a little bit longer, maybe just another day . . . or two. If you weren't out by then I was—"

"Shut up," said Kallie, kneeling on the ground and giving Rizzo a bone-rattling hug that lasted and lasted and lasted, matching the tears that flowed from her eyes.

———ᴧᴧᴧ———

Eliazar Baruk was in the one place he could be alone, a stall in the men's room outside the situation room. He took a deep, cleansing breath. Then another. He grabbed a handful of tissue and wiped the tears from his eyes. Took another deep breath, sighed, and left to return to the emergency meeting.

"Chaim, call up the reserves," Baruk said simply, as he cleared the threshold and walked to his chair at the head of the table. "Bring all of our forces up to full alert. Have half of the air force in the air at all times. Warm up the missile batteries, but keep the hatches closed. No need for unnecessary provocation. Have the navy put to sea. Every ship. I don't care what kind of shape it's in. Get everything away from the docks."

The prime minister got to his chair but declined to sit down. He looked around at his colleagues of so many years, so many crises. He wondered how many of them would survive. "Well, at least we will not be caught napping."

———ᴧᴧᴧ———

Secretary of State Jennings was a compassionate man, a wonderful guy to work for. That made it even more difficult for both of them.

Sam Reynolds closed the door to the secretary's office and immediately he began to wonder if there were any openings with his old law firm.

≈≈≈

Annie saw him first, and her heart jumped into her throat. Sitting on the porch Saturday morning, reading the *Times*, she immediately saw the unmarked, black SUV pull up in front of the house with an escort. The two uniforms in the leading squad car got out and stood at attention.

Please, God, let it be good news.

52

Thirty days later, every head of state in the Middle East attended a Mideast Summit hosted by Krupp and the European Union at Krupp's sprawling, but easily defended, estate in Bavaria. There, at 7:00 AM local time on Tuesday, July 21, Israel signed a peace treaty with leaders from every Arab nation in the region. Jerusalem was declared an "international city," open to all. Muslims controlled the top of Temple Mount, the Jews controlled everything below the Mount "platform," and a European Union multinational police force was empowered to maintain order and access on and around the Temple Mount.

"I wonder how all of this is going to play out?" said Bohannon. "There are so many ways for this peace plan to unravel."

They sat on the terrace of Richard Johnson's apartment in the brittle darkness, collectively swimming in the backwash of anxiety stirred up by the delayed reaction to unimaginable trauma and fear. It was just past midnight in New York City, and the seven of them had wandered out onto the terrace after watching the treaty-signing ceremony broadcast live by CNN from Germany. Central Park spread out before them like a green bandage on a concrete body, the night sounds of Manhattan far below.

Convened at Doc's apartment to witness both the treaty ceremony from Germany and, in a couple hours, the live broadcast from Jerusalem of the first Temple sacrifice, it was a reunion of sorts, the first time they had all gathered together since the team returned home. Kallie, banished by the Israeli government, was living with the Bohannons for the time being, piecing her life back together. Tonight, she couldn't seem to avoid, nor looked like she wanted to, the constant attention of Sammy Rizzo, her self-proclaimed rescuer.

"I hope the Palestinians don't blow up the process," said Annie.

It seemed to Bohannon that he'd barely let go of Annie's hand since he returned from Germany. Even now, she sat by his side, wrapped around his left arm, her head on his shoulder.

"Each day I think something is going to go wrong," said Joe, sitting side-by-side with Dierdre on a made-for-two, cushioned patio swing. "I mean, we got home okay, we didn't get arrested, the world didn't blow up . . . and we still have our jobs."

"I told my boss I wanted a raise," said Rizzo. "Combat pay."

"Maybe Tom can arrange for the Bowery Mission to provide you with a bonus," Johnson generously offered. "How much did the organization realize from the auction of those books?"

"Six million dollars," said Bohannon. "But don't get any ideas. It's all allocated to doubling the size of the women's home."

"Well . . . there you have it, my diminutive friend." Johnson was draped along the length of a lounge chair, one hand airily waving in the soft breeze. "Wounded in the line of duty and nothing to show for it."

"Maybe we can hock the mezuzah," suggested Rizzo, "and all take a trip to the Virgin Islands. You still got it locked up in the vault at the Collector's Club?"

"Don't worry about it, Sammy," said Rodriguez. "The scroll and the mezuzah are safe and secure. I wish I felt the same way about this peace treaty."

"Well, Mr. Rodriguez, in my opinion one of the thorniest moments will come in a few hours," said Johnson, who was finally beginning to regain some of his lost weight, "when the resurrected priesthood of the Aaronites is going to offer ritual sacrifice in the Temple. After so many years of violence, I find it difficult to believe what I'm seeing, that Arab and Jew could so easily put aside generations of hatred."

"But, Doc, they just signed the treaty," said Rizzo.

"Yes . . . yes, I know. But the pace has been so rapid . . ."

"That's what I'm concerned about," Kallie interrupted. "Everything is just moving so fast. I was astonished when the Waqf relinquished control of the Huldah Gates, allowed the Israelis under the Mount, and granted them permission to clear away an entrance to the discovered Temple—even before the treaty was signed. Now, everything is in place for the sacrifice. Don't the Arabs get it?"

Perhaps it was the late hour, but Bohannon was getting confused. "Get what?"

"The significance," Johnson mumbled. "The Temple has been consecrated, all the furniture and elements are in place. All that remains is for the priests to lead a procession into the Temple chamber, bringing the sacrifices with them. It's astonishing . . . historical . . . the first time in nearly two thousand years that the Jews will be able to worship in the Temple with ritual sacrifice."

Johnson stretched, then abruptly sat up straight and turned to his friends. "But first, how about a midnight snack? Who wants Chinese?"

—⁓⁓—

Doc Johnson's media room smelled like soy sauce and onions. White cardboard containers with swirly red designs littered nearly every flat surface. A potted plant was skewered with a pair of chopsticks, courtesy of Sammy Rizzo, who found his hands full as the boxed cuisine was passed from person to person. They were sipping tea and cracking open fortune cookies as they watched the Temple ritual played out on Johnson's plasma TV. While the take-out was excellent, it was no match for the drama unfolding before their eyes.

It was the third hour in Jerusalem, 9:00 AM local time, and the Levites were about to open the Temple. Like fireflies to a yard light, Bohannon, Johnson, Rodriguez, and Rizzo—pulling Kallie with him—were drawn from their seats and gathered close around the television screen. Annie and Deirdre sat just behind them.

"We were right there," said Rodriguez, jumping in his seat with excitement. "Remember that fallen column on the left? That's where Doc dropped his last cyalume stick."

"Thank you, Mr. Rodriguez, for reminding me of my bumbling, and in front of such nice people, too."

"Ease up, Doc," Rodriguez said with a poke. "Tom and I would still be wandering around in those caves like Hansel and Gretel if it hadn't been for you. You saved our backsides more times than I'd like to remember."

"Duly noted," Johnson said with a nod of his head.

Bohannon was enjoying the moment on many levels. He was blessed to hear the bantering between his fellow adventurers. Bohannon knew how many times they had come close to losing everything: their search, their hope, and their lives. He knew how many times God had answered their prayers, his prayers. But what warmed his heart the most was a new, just sprouting, conviction that seemed to be coming alive in Richard Johnson. Earlier that night, Doc had pulled Bohannon into a side room.

"You know, Tom, I'm thinking that you may be right. God really does love each one of us." Bohannon nearly choked. "I don't understand it, but I know I've just lived it. I think I've been searching for God all my life. It's going to take some time to sink in, but the empirical evidence is that I think he's found me."

Remembering that moment, reflexively, Bohannon put his hand on Doc's shoulder.

"They are about to cleanse the altar with the blood of the sacrifice," said Johnson. "This is the key moment. It is the blood offering that washes away the sins of the Jews."

"Eeewww . . . gross!" Rizzo shuddered from his perch in front of the TV. "Holy transfusion, that is a lot of blood from one ram, don't you think? Oh-oh, here comes another."

The sacrifice ritual came to an end, and the priests began to line up for the procession out of the Temple and back to the surface. CNN brought in some "expert commentators" for the event, and the one who was getting the most face time was Ben Heath, the evangelical pastor of a megachurch just outside Dallas. Heath continually emphasized the significance of the just-completed Temple sacrifice to the course of history. "This is not just a Christian thing or a Bible thing," Heath responded to a question. "This event is going to dramatically impact the lives of every human being currently living on the face of this planet. The prophecy in the Bible has been unerring in its predictions for the future. We have seen the fruit of prophecy fulfillment in every generation since the books were first written down."

"Why is that so important to us?" asked the commentator.

"Because the Bible is full of predictions about what will happen when the Third Temple of God is consecrated, as is being done this very moment."

"And what are some of those predictions?"

Heath hesitated.

"He sees the trap." Bohannon pushed up to the edge of his chair and wiped the palms of his perspiring hands against his thighs, just as he had done during the Giants' final scoring drive in the 2008 Super Bowl. "He knows what CNN is looking for. The question is, can he avoid it?"

"There's truth here," said Heath, "but it's truth that needs to be revealed gradually. Temple prophecy is abundant, it's powerful, and it's easily misunderstood. The return of ritual sacrifice to the Temple of Jerusalem will have great historical significance. Judaism believes it will herald the long-awaited arrival of the Messiah. But for those who believe the entire Bible is true, both Old and New Testament, one thing is indisputable. Consecration of the Third Temple of God brings us into the last days of this world."

Eyes blinking rapidly, the announcer leaned toward the pastor. He looked bewildered. "Are you saying this is going to lead to the *end* of the world?"

"No," said Heath, his voice soft and calm. "What I'm saying is that the con-secration of the Third Temple brings us into a time, an era, at the end of which biblical prophecy predicts that the world as we know it will end. No one knows when that time will be. But if you are someone who believes that the Bible tells the truth—and in two thousand years, the Bible has never been proven to be inac-curate—the Bible tells us that the consecration of the Third Temple begins the march of time toward the last days of the world. We are now, all of us, all around the world, in the last days. The thought of that is enough to sober any man."

The CNN announcer continued to stare at Heath, his mouth agape. After an awkward moment of dead air, CNN went quickly to commercial.

"Wow, what do you think that means?" asked Rodriguez.

"What that clock means," said Johnson, pointing to the mantle, "is that it's time to get to bed if I ever hope to get to work tomorrow."

A loud yawn sounded as Rizzo stretched from his corner of the sofa. "Say, Doc, can't we just have a sleepover? I'll cook breakfast."

"Great idea, Sammy . . . if we were teenagers," said Rodriguez. "Sorry to burst your bubble, but Deidre and I have to get home."

Kallie and Annie were gathering up the mangled food boxes, and CNN was still replaying clips from the morning's events in Jerusalem when Tom pulled Doc into a corner.

"Thanks for sharing your heart with me earlier," Bohannon said. He pulled away and held Doc at arm's length, their gazes locked on each other. "This will likely be a challenging search you're on. Lots of bumps and disappointments along the way." Bohannon struggled to keep his emotions in check. "If you ever need me—"

They were silenced by a CNN breaking-news report from the still oper-ating television.

"This is CNN. We are having difficulty reacquiring the video feed, but reports are coming in of a violent earthquake in Jerusalem, just minutes after the completion of the first sacrifice in the new Jewish Temple. Reporters on the scene, who have been able to contact their desks, report that, among other extensive damage throughout the city, the Temple Mount has essentially been split in half by the strong earthquake, destroying all of the structures on the Mount. So much water has been released from the massive, natural cisterns under the Temple Mount that it appears, for now, there is a new river flowing through Jerusalem. We will have more on this breaking story as it unfolds."

AUTHOR'S NOTE

While *The Sacred Cipher* is a work of fiction, several plot elements are based on fact.

The Bowery Mission (http://bowery.org) has served the lost, the least, and the lonely of New York City since 1878. It is the third-oldest rescue mission in the United States, and one of its most effective. Besides serving over 250,000 meals yearly to the homeless and poor, the Bowery Mission's nine-month, faith-based, residential recovery program has guided thousands of men in transforming themselves from addiction and hopelessness to productive and healthy lives. There are over three hundred rescue missions in the United States helping the poor and homeless with a combined one million donors and over four hundred thousand volunteers. Most of them belong to the American Gospel Rescue Mission organization (http://agrm.org).

Charles Haddon Spurgeon (1834–1892) was England's best-known preacher for most of the second half of the nineteenth century and pastor of London's famed New Park Street Church. Spurgeon's *All of Grace* was the first book published by Moody Press and is still its all-time best seller. Three of his works have sold more than one million copies, and there is more of Spurgeon's work in print than any other Christian author (http://www.pilgrimpublications.com).

While Spurgeon's trip to Alexandria, Egypt, depicted in this book, is a creation of the author's imagination, Spurgeon traveled widely in the Near East and Europe and was an avid student of history. The Spurgeon Archive (http://www.spurgeon.org) is a voluminous collection of Spurgeon history.

Spurgeon's London publication, *The Sword and the Trowel*, was replicated in New York City in 1878 by his cousin Joseph Spurgeon as *The Christian Herald and Signs of Our Times*. Dr. Louis Klopsch purchased the magazine in 1890 and was instrumental in preventing the Bowery Mission from closing its doors, purchasing the rescue mission from the Reverend A. G. Ruliffson in 1895 after its original superintendent passed away.

The history of the Rosetta Stone, displayed in London's British Museum (http:// britishmuseum.org) since 1802, is true.

The inscription on the Rosetta Stone is a decree (circa 196 B.C.) passed by a council of priests, one of a series that affirm the royal cult of the thirteen-year-old Ptolemy V on the first anniversary of his coronation. The decree is inscribed on the stone three times, in hieroglyphics (suitable for a priestly decree), Demotic (the native script used for daily purposes), and Greek (the language of the administration).

The Demotic language was first a spoken language, then a written language, which was extensively used in Egypt for over one thousand years, from 660 B.C. to 425 A.D. Chicago University's Oriental Institute embarked on a Demotic Dictionary Project (http://oi.uchicago.edu/research/projects/dem) thirty years ago and has cataloged twenty-seven Demotic letters, only fifteen of which have been deciphered. For those fifteen letters, which were the equivalent of words in the spoken Egyptian language, the Demotic dictionary currently contains over eleven hundred pages of possible meanings for words associated with those letters or combinations of those letters.

The Collector's Club, founded in 1896 (http://www.collectorsclub.org), is one of the nation's most influential stamp-collecting societies. Its permanent home at 22 East 35th Street in New York City, a baroque-style townhouse designed by Stanford White, houses the vast Collector's Club Library; its 150,000 volumes comprise one of the world's largest and most comprehensive collections of phila-telic literature. The building and its library are open by appointment.

—∿∿—

Sir Edward Elgar (1857–1934) was an English romantic composer most notable for his many compositions of *Pomp and Circumstance* and his orchestral work *The Enigma Variations.* Elgar was also a devotee of codes, puzzles, and ciphers. On July 14, 1897, Elgar sent a letter to a young friend, Miss Dora Penny, the twenty-two-year-old daughter of the Reverend Alfred Penny, Rector of St. Peter's, Wolverhampton—the now famous Dorabella Cipher.

The cipher consists of eighty-seven characters, apparently constructed from an alphabet of twenty-four symbols. The symbols are arranged in three lines; contain one, two, or three semicircles; and are oriented in one of eight directions. A small dot appears after the fifth character on the third line. No one has yet deciphered its meaning. Dora Penny died in 1964.

The Elgar Society (http://www.elgar.org) holds an annual competition for those code-breakers who are attempting to crack the Dorabella Cipher. In 2008, seven entries were submitted, but the cipher remains a mystery and the £1,500 prize has yet to be awarded.

⸻

Abiathar was the leader, or Gaon, of the Jewish community in Jerusalem, and Meborak was the leader, or Exhillarc, of the Jewish community in Egypt, when the crusaders captured Jerusalem in 1099. The Temple Mount in Jerusalem is a platform, supported by a series of arches built by Herod the Great. The Mount is a formation of karstic limestone that has eroded over time by water, creating a honeycomb of cisterns, tunnels, and caverns. Other than the unofficial diggings of Charles Warren in the nineteenth century, there has been virtually no archaeological study of the space under the Temple Mount platform.

⸻

Other than the basic facts and associated research listed above, the rest of *The Sacred Cipher* is a result of the author's imagination. Any "errors of fact" are a result of that imagination.

ABOUT THE AUTHOR

Terry Brennan was born and raised in Philadelphia, where he grew into a life-long Phillies and Eagles fan, and is a graduate of Penn State University.

Brennan launched his twenty-two-year journalism career as an award-winning writer and sports editor for a suburban Philadelphia chain of newspapers. He spent seven years covering the Philadelphia Flyers hockey team, auto racing, and other sports for the *Philadelphia Bulletin*. He continued to win writing awards during a ten-year career with Ingersoll Publications, a multi-national newspaper firm with papers in the U.S., England, and Ireland. He was an editor and publisher for Ingersoll newspapers in Pennsylvania, Illinois, and New York, and in 1989 joined the Ingersoll corporate staff as executive editor of all U.S. newspaper titles. Brennan led the *Pottstown* (PA) *Mercury* to a Pulitzer Prize for Editorial Writing during his tenure as editor.

Brennan transferred his successful management career to the nonprofit sector in 1996 as vice president of operations for the Christian Herald Association, Inc., the parent organization of four New York City ministries, including the Bowery Mission. In his eleven years with Christian Herald, the organization helped more than 3,700 adults and 11,000 children experience the power of a transformed life through its faith-based programs.

Currently a management consultant, Terry, his wife Andrea, and their two adult children, live in New York City. He also has two married sons who live with their families in Pennsylvania.